"Fiction is a vehicle for growing in empathy for and understanding of this world. The magic of fiction is its ability to draw in the reader, to coax him or her to put on the shoes of the characters and go for a walk in those shoes. In *Like a River from Its Course*, Kelli Stuart worked this magic. The terror of the novel is its glimpse into the potential for human evil. The beauty is the way in which people can be instruments of grace and mercy in the darkest of circumstances. Raw, vulnerable, horrifying, beautiful, and true, this novel is a mirror for us to gaze into, to see our potential for good or ill. It nudges us to choose the path of love for those in need, regardless of what it may cost. This is a novel I will not soon forget."

—SUSIE FINKBEINER, author of *A Cup of Dust: A Novel of the Dust Bowl*

"A carefully researched, compassionately written journey into Ukraine at the height of World War II. Stuart brings her story vividly to life with warm, believable characters and vivid writing."

—ANNE BOGEL, modernmrsdarcy.com

"A chilling and lyrical treatise to faith in a time of tragedy, *Like a River from Its Course* is brimming with luscious imagery and characters who entrench themselves in your heart. Stuart weaves the travails of Kiev with the unfailing hope of Luda, Ivan, and Maria. Deft research, expert prose, and heart-clenching moments combine in a resplendent historical reading experience. This isn't just a historical fiction debut—this is a well-crafted piece of art."

—RACHEL MCMILLAN, author of *The Bachelor Girl's Guide to Murder*

LIKE
A RIVER
FROM
ITS
COURSE

KELLI STUART

Kregel
Publications

*To the brave men and women of Ukraine
who fought for freedom in the
Great Patriotic War of 1941–45.
This book is for you.*

This cruel age has deflected me,
like a river from its course.
Strayed from its familiar shores,
my changeling life has flowed
into a sister channel.

ANNA AKHMATOVA
LENINGRAD, 1941

On August 23, 1939, Nazi Germany and the Soviet Union surprised the world by signing the German-Soviet Nonaggression Pact, in which the two countries agreed to take no military action against one another for the next ten years.

On June 22, 1941, Adolf Hitler violated that pact, launching Operation Barbarossa, a well-coordinated invasion of the Soviet Union.

This is where our story begins.

PART ONE

THE BEGINNING

MARIA "MASHA" IVANOVNA

June 22, 1941
Kiev, Ukraine

"Papa! *Papa!*"

The screams lift from my chest, but I don't feel them escape. As the flat flashes and shakes, I turn circles. I know I'm home, but I don't know just where I am. I can't cry, can't walk, can't find my family. I can only scream, and again I cry out, the sound pulled involuntarily from my soul.

"Maria!"

I gasp as strong arms wrap around me, pulling me to the floor.

"We're here, *Dochka*," my father cries. "Follow me."

He flips to his hands and knees, and I grab on to one of his ankles behind him, shuffling along the floor to the hallway where my mother, sister Anna, and brother Sergei huddle close. They are three who look like one, intertwined in such a way that I can't tell where one begins and the other ends. I join the heap, my father lying over all of us.

For the first hour, I'm sure that we're moments from meeting the saints. I pray to Saint Maria to bring me quickly to her with little pain. I fear pain.

As I pray for an easy transition into the afterlife, my father speaks soothingly in my ear. "You're fine, my daughter," he whispers, a balm to my terror. "We're going to be fine."

I don't believe him. I want to, but I can't. So as the sky flashes, I continue to whisper my litany mostly because I can't stop. Truthfully, I know very little about this act of prayer. I know some saints are useful to the protection of our souls. Outside of this basic fact, however, I know nothing of the spirit world.

But tonight as the earth spins and booms, I allow my soul to reach out to the unknown with hope that protection waits in my faithfulness.

As the rumbling fades into the distance, we remain piled on the floor, terror and fatigue anchoring us tight. Sergei is the first to extract himself, and he sits up slowly, rubbing his hands through his short, coarse hair. Anna and Mama remain hugged together, their cheeks streaked with tears, both sleeping soundly. I envy their slumber.

When Anna sleeps she looks like a younger, more delicate version of our mother. At sixteen, Anna is two years older than me, but in maturity I believe she's a lifetime ahead. She's kind and thoughtful, brave and helpful. I am none of those things. I can be, of course, and I do want to be. But I have to work very hard at being that kind of girl, whereas Anna was born with the ability to love. Grace runs through her veins, spite through mine.

Mama, like Anna, is small and gentle. Her light brown hair is long and soft, though she rarely wears it down. Every day Mama twists it into an elegant bun at the nape of her neck. It seems a shame to hide such glorious hair, but with it pulled back, her perfect features are much more visible. Mama's eyes are a warm brown and reveal the depths of her very being. Mama can never hide how she feels. Her eyes dance with laughter and swim with sorrow, and when she's angry, I'm certain I've seen lightning flash straight through them.

"Masha," Father whispers. I look up to see Sergei standing and stretching alongside him. "We're going to have chai, would you like some?"

I nod and stand up slowly, my legs and back stiff. Sergei grabs my elbow and pulls me into the crook of his arm. He smiles at me, then kisses my forehead. Looking up at my older brother, I get the frightening sense that I'm telling him good-bye. He'll be eighteen in two weeks, and we're at war. A fresh lump develops in my throat and tears prick the corners of my eyes.

"Shh, Masha," Sergei whispers. He knows my thoughts.

Together we walk into the small kitchen where Papa already has the kettle on the stove. He lights a match and puts it inside the firebox, then leans back against the wall. The kitchen in our flat is very small. The three of us can barely fit in it together. In fact, we rarely ever enter this room since Mama long ago declared it her domain and ordered us out under threat of starvation.

Papa sits quietly, his arms crossed over his narrow chest. He's a thin man, my papa, but very tall. Sergei and I stand side by side as we wait for the kettle to sing. We don't speak. I don't know why Papa and Sergei remain mute, but I simply don't have words. Every time I open my mouth, the words disappear on my tongue like the puffs of smoke from Papa's pipes. So I sit, my shoulder pressed to Sergei, my eyes shifting nervously across Papa's worn face.

"We'll wait a few hours to make sure the bombing has stopped," he finally says. His voice bubbles with the heat of one who's been falsely accused. "Then you and I will go out and survey the damage," he says to Sergei. The kettle shakes slightly and lets out its mournful whistle. I don't remember ever hearing it wail like that. It brings a fresh batch of tears to my eyes, and I wonder if I'll even be able to swallow over the lump in my throat.

"Is it safe to go out, Papa?" I ask.

Papa pauses and looks at me softly. The tenderness in his bright green eyes dissolves the lump and warms me from the inside. My papa, whom I favor much more than Mama, has always been my confidant, his strength carrying me through the pain of youth. For years I endured the dreadful taunts of my schoolmates. They laughed at my broad, stocky appearance, and I laughed with them because I refused to cry.

I can be strong like Papa.

"I don't know if it's safe, Masha," Papa says softly. "But we'll go carefully."

I nod and take the steaming mug he hands me, wrapping my fingers around the searing metal. "Can I go with you?" I ask. I already know his answer, but I ask anyway. Papa's lips spread out thin, and his thick brows gather over his eyes. "No, *dorogaya*," he says firmly. "It may not be safe for Sergei and me. It's definitely not safe for you."

And that's it. I know not to ask again. My papa is a patient man, unless you ask twice. Nobody asks twice.

Two hours later, Mama, Anna, and I stand in the doorway as Papa and Sergei walk out into the dimly lit hallway of our flat. It's damp, and the air smells of gunpowder and fear. It's oddly quiet as they shuffle down the narrow staircase. I can hear their shoes scrape against the ground, but nothing else. No happy laughter. No morning greetings. The streets bear no sounds of normalcy. The quiet of the morning screams, and I want to clamp my hands over my ears just to block it out.

Mama closes the door and leans against it. Her eyes close, and her beautiful hair lies in cascades over her small frame. Anna and I watch, not daring to move.

After a moment, Mama opens her eyes and forces a smile. "It's time to clean up, girls," she says quietly. She sounds calm, but I still see terror swimming in the black center of her eyes. She pulls her fingers through her hair and reaches in her pocket for a band to secure it in a knot.

"Maria, I want you to make the beds and dust the furniture. Anna, you come with me to the kitchen to help prepare tonight's soup."

Anna quickly mumbles, "Yes, Mama," and heads to the kitchen. I, however, look at my mother in surprise. We're cleaning? Today? For a moment I forget the attack and the bombs. All I can think is that today is our first day of summer break and we're cleaning.

Mama returns my gaze evenly. I see her willing me to challenge. I won't win a challenge with Mama, and I know there's little benefit in trying. The grief that she wears on her face swiftly brings back our new reality.

We're at war. Nothing will be the same again.

IVAN KYRILOVICH

June 23, 1941

The memory of last night will forever haunt me. The whistle of Nazi bombs and the thunder as they found their targets move through my head, my heart, my soul. Intertwined with the noise is the screaming. Masha, turning and crying, confused and afraid. Tanya and Anna gripped in the corner, their cries mingling to form a low wail. In the midst of it all, I saw Sergei, my son. I watched him through the flashes and tremors. Between dark and light, he became a man.

As the terror of night slipped into a balmy, dusty morning, I observed them all closely. Tanya and Anna wrapped in one another's arms, their faces worn and strained. Masha tucked beneath Sergei's arm, her head nodding and falling, stubbornness alone keeping her from succumbing to the sleep that so clearly longed to take her away.

And the man Sergei, who sat with his back straight against the wall, his arm wrapped protectively around his sister. I saw him wrestling, an inward battle beating through his gray eyes. I knew the decision he made in those long, quiet hours.

As we leave to survey our battered city, I notice that Sergei's back is straighter and he stands a little taller. Cautiously striding into the still street, I turn and grab his broad shoulders. I feel the muscles round over the tops of his arms and for the first time notice the sinewy nature of his frame. My son has developed the taut muscles of a man without me even noticing. Surely this didn't happen overnight.

Looking straight into his eyes, I speak to him father to son, comrade to comrade. "You'll wait until your birthday. When you're eighteen, you may enlist."

My voice comes out gruff, almost harsh, and tears sting the corners of my eyes. Sergei's chin lifts slightly, and he nods calmly. "Yes, Papa."

Not caring who might see us, I pull him into my arms and grip him with the passion that only a father can feel for his son. Sergei's arms engulf me in return, and for a long while we hold one another. In that embrace I bid farewell to the boy I rocked, fed, played with, and taught for nearly eighteen years.

We finally pull away and wipe our eyes, turning without words to walk up the narrow alley that leads to Shamrila Street, the road on which we've lived since Sergei was born. I glance back at the tiny window into our kitchen, the green frame dusty and worn. I remember the echoing sounds of my infant son's cries so many years ago when I rounded the corner and stood beneath the window. I spent countless moments listening to Tanya sing softly into her firstborn's ear, lulling him to sleep.

Where has the time gone?

Taking a deep breath, I turn away from the memories. "We'll walk toward the Dnieper River," I say. "Then we'll make our way to Kreshadik Street." It's a long walk, and I'm not sure what kind of trouble we might run into, but I know that our best observations on the state of Kiev will come from these two vantage points.

"Will we see Nazis?" Sergei asks. He says *Nazi* as though spitting out bitter seeds.

"I don't know, *Sinok*," I say, burying my hands in my pockets. The morning is warm and wet, but I still feel chilled. As we round the corner, I look around cautiously.

"I thought there would be more damage," Sergei murmurs. "The bombs were so close." I don't respond, but I agree with him. The walls of our small flat rattled with such ferocity, I was certain they would crumble on top of us.

"None of the bombs hit here," I say after a pause. "But they hit close. We'll see damage today, Seryosha." I use his pet name to reassure him, and myself, that for now everything is okay.

We walk quickly after that, and it isn't long before we come upon the effects of last night's surprise bombing. "Papa, look," Sergei says, and the shock in his voice stops me in my tracks. I follow his pointing finger to the hill in the distance where the Pechersk Lavra stands proudly. But today, the golden domes of the ancient monastery don't sparkle in the morning sun. Instead, black smoke unfurls from the hillside in mournful tendrils, and my heart sinks. I look away from the carnage on the hill and observe the wounded section of my city, known as Podil. People wander the streets, shocked eyes moving slowly over blackened holes in buildings. Once the trading and crafting center of Kiev, Podil has in recent decades deteriorated with many now living in poor, wretched conditions.

"The Jewish live here," I murmur. I feel Sergei's eyes on me, but I don't look at him. Instead, I simply take it all in—the damage, the shock, the sinking feeling that this is the beginning of something terrible.

Streets lie in ruin, flats fallen to the ground. At the sound of an infant crying, Sergei and I run to help sift through the rubble. We hear the child but cannot see him, and after an hour of digging, the cries turn to whimpers. After two hours, the cries stop altogether.

We continue to dig, Sergei and myself with two older women and a young boy. It's useless, though, and at some point we all just quit. The child is gone, and with no hysterical parents around desperately searching for him, we know he was probably better off passing from this world with his parents than being left without them. Buried by hatred is better than orphaned by it. I know this too well.

Sergei and I slowly walk away, not even saying good-bye to the babushkas who had so desperately worked alongside us. There's nothing to say— no words to soothe the shock. We walk for a long time, hands stuffed deep into pockets, hearts weighted down with all we've seen and all that's changed.

"Papa," Sergei says as we approach Kreshadik Street, the center of our city.

"*Da, Sinok.*"

"I'm ready to fight for my country." Sergei pauses, his breath halting with emotion. I stop walking and wait. "I'm ready to fight for my country," he repeats after a moment, his eyes facing forward in a distant gaze. "And I know that it won't be easy. But Papa . . ."

I observe him closely, my throat closed tight, and take in the sight of the late afternoon sun highlighting his wiry hair and square jaw.

"I don't know if I'm ready for death," he whispers.

I look down the street to try to mask the intense pain that engulfs me from the inside. Was it really only a day ago that we dreamed of going to the dacha for our summer break, escaping to a country home of peace?

"It's not that I'm scared of . . . my own death," Sergei continues. "But Papa, how do I handle watching others die? We just listened to a baby take his last breath. How do I keep moving forward when I have the sound of that child rolling through my head?"

I don't have an answer.

FREDERICK HERRMANN
June 24, 1941

I always knew I would be a great man. I look no further than my father to see greatness. The face of a hero is framed by the accomplishments he realizes in front of all who watch. As a child, I watched everything my father did, copying every movement, every inflection, every swell and fall of his voice.

I'm not tall like Father. I bear the unfortunate stature of my mother and have small, delicate features that fail to give me the formidableness of the great Tomas Herrmann. My father is tall and broad, his thick blond hair giving him a youthful appearance. Father never hides his feelings; every pleasure or disappointment reflects openly in his blue eyes.

My sister inherited the strong figure of our father—my rebellious sister who I once wished to be. Remembering her bold words against our fatherland brings a surge of disappointment, and my hands tighten around the barrel of my gun. When Talia left home, I vowed that I would make Father proud enough for both of us.

It never occurred to me that I might be anything but a soldier. I am the son of a proud German. My father stands in the presence of the Great Führer.

As a boy, I often listened to Father speak with his fellow countrymen about the growing need to create a pure Aryan race. My earliest memories reside in the dusty garden of our home, my mother moving about the house at the bidding of her powerful husband. I moved the dirt in circles not because I enjoyed it, but because it gave the appearance of youthful ignorance. My play made me invisible to the men of stature and allowed me to listen and glean.

As I dragged my fingers through Munich's hallowed earth, I learned the ways of manhood. I listened closely as, eyes steely blue, the great men spoke, their thin lips organizing the mobilization of the masses. As a boy of only four, I knew of the shameful death at Feldherrenhalle that left true German nationalists martyred at the hands of a misguided Bavarian government. I learned of a man who was greater than all others. I heard of his courage as he ignited a putsch against his own government there in the beer hall.

One night long ago, after listening to my father retell the story, I stood before the mirror in my small bedroom. My hands and feet were covered in dirt, my cloak of invisibility. I imagined what this man they called Hitler must look like. Grabbing the stick I'd brought in from the garden, I marched back and forth, steps of power masked in the body of a child. I was the great, brave Hitler . . . until Mother came in and ordered me to bed.

"You must never pretend to be that man again," my mother hissed, tucking the covers around me so tight I struggled to breathe. "This game your father is playing is dangerous," she said, her breath hot on my cheek. "Don't become like him."

The last words were a vapor. They wafted from her lips to my ears and locked inside my memory.

That was the night I realized her weakness and I decided to hate my mother.

Two days later, I saw him for the first time. When Herr Hitler entered the room, I stopped short. We were inside the house, which left me without the protection of the dusty earth. The floorboards creaked, and the hollow walls reverberated with my heartbeat like a warrior's drum.

After greeting my father formally, Hitler turned and locked eyes with me. I couldn't hide, so I stood still, awed by his presence. He was not a tall man. My father, in his great stature, dwarfed the mighty Hitler. But the confidence that the future Führer possessed made him a giant.

"Hello, boy," he said. His voice was stiff. It wasn't warm or friendly. I made him uncomfortable. I knew it, and so did Father.

"Leave us, Frederick," Father barked, and I immediately obeyed. As I hurried from the room, I heard our future leader speak again. "Train him right, Tomas," Hitler said evenly. "Train him right and he'll do great things. Someday he will be a part of history."

He was right.

It's been fourteen years since that first meeting. Hitler visited our sitting room many times after that, but I was always ordered to bed before his arrival. I spent nights sitting at the top of the polished staircase, listening to the passionate conversation from the men gathered around the hearth. So many words, all of them moving and swirling together like the dust of the ground, and as I listened, I imagined what it would be like to be part of the future that they spoke of so highly.

I haven't spoken to Father since I left to wage this war, but I know he hears of me. He hears of my failures, and today he will hear of my success. My father is a man of great wealth and power within the SS. He commands respect when entering a room, and anyone who wants his approval must work hard for it. As I have done.

I've been promoted to Einsatzgruppen C. My colonel, Standartenführer Paul Blobel, is a personal friend of Father's, as is Major General Eberhard. They served together in the first war and quickly became partners and confidants.

I grew up with Blobel nearby, as he and father worked together in architecture after the first war. But, dissatisfied with the direction our country headed, Father and Blobel joined the SA and then the SS, where they quickly worked their way up the ranks into the highest levels of responsibility. Blobel was later moved into a high-ranking position with the Nazi army while Father, a brilliant architect and creator, has remained in the mother country working in close quarters with Hitler's top officials.

My father is a hero. My hero.

For my part, I worked my way through training, always at the top of my class, always ready and willing to go further and push harder. I've earned this position—I am sure of it. Father would have no part in my undeserved promotion, and I want no handouts. I don't mention my connection to Father, or to Blobel or Eberhard. I don't tell anyone I've shaken hands with the Führer. If I'm promoted to a position of privilege, I want it to be of my own accord. And now, under the great Standartenführer Blobel, I have the distinct privilege of carrying out the Final Solution.

Today, as I march through the dust of another man's land, I hear the Führer's voice once again in the recesses of my memory. Looking down, I take note of the rich soil caking my boots, and I feel the same sense of power I got as a child when the dust of the land covered me. This dirt belongs to my people now. My heart swells as the dust fills in the crevices of my boots.

"He will be a part of history."

We move steadily forward, two days into the journey toward our destination. The dust rises and falls in puffs, our steps echoing the mission. We're not just a *part* of history. We *are* history. I taste it, gritty and rough. My father's passion, Hitler's vision, my destiny—it's all within reach.

Kiev, Ukraine, is to be our final destination. As we now pass the center of another village, a man steps timidly out into the road, his arms stretched out toward us, offering a large loaf of fresh bread. We stop and stare for a brief moment. Finally I step forward and take the loaf from his hands. He bows slightly, mumbling something in the language I've come to destroy.

They welcome us here. They think we've come to liberate them, to end their oppression and set them free. My eyes shift from the man to the villagers who surround him. Women cling to the hands of small, thin children whose eyes are big and round. The young ladies curtsy, and I nod my head politely in return. They're afraid of us. I see it.

I relish their fear.

LUDMILLA "LUDA" MICHAELEVNA

Vinnitsya, Ukraine
June 30, 1941

"Luda!"

I stand in the small bedroom and glance into my mother's hand mirror. It's the only piece of her I have left. My father got rid of everything else when she died. I don't remember her, how she looked or spoke or even how she smelled. I don't know if her laugh sounded like a thousand bells or a babbling brook. I have imagined her so many times, but I have no photographs to tell me what she looked like. There are no grandparents to tell me stories. So I'm left to my imagination.

I see her tall and pretty. Her eyes dance when she talks, and her delicate hands feel like silk when she holds me. In my mind, she is the very picture of love. In my mind, she sings softly to me each night as I drift to sleep. In my mind, her voice is a melody and her movements a beat.

But it's only in my mind.

I was two when she died. I don't even know what happened. Father won't tell me. The only time he mentions her is when the vodka bottle is half empty. My father at half empty is pleasant, relaxed, almost happy. When the bottle is empty he's sad, mournful, and wants only to be alone. Most of my nights are spent wrapping a blanket around the shaking shoulders of my empty-bottled father.

My father with a full bottle of vodka is frightening. This means he's sober. My full-bottled father is filled with dashed dreams and self-loathing. He is the father I fear most. The full-bottled papa is why I keep pouring.

"Luda!"

I jump and look in the mirror again. Is this the same reflection she saw when she looked in it? Large brown eyes, thick brown hair, and a small red mouth? Today I don't have time to wonder. I quickly hide my precious mirror, protecting it from the potential rage of a full-bottled father. Rushing out the door, I smooth my tattered skirt. My father stands by the front door of our flat, his hand wrapped around a nearly empty bottle of cheap vodka.

I haven't eaten for two days so he could have his poison.

"Go out and get us some bread," he says, pushing open the door and gesturing into the dark hallway.

"I . . . But . . . Papa," I stammer. "It's late. The market isn't open."

"Stop being stupid," he snarls. "Go get me bread. I'm hungry."

With a sigh, I reach down and pull on my tattered shoes. I pull the pouch of money off the hook on the wall and hear the pitiful tinkling of two lonely coins knocking together. Even if the markets were open, I wouldn't have enough money.

Stepping out into the hallway, I turn to try to speak reason to Papa once more, but he shuts the door in my face. With a sigh, I slowly make my way down the stairs and out into the street.

Looking up at the dim sky, I wonder what the future holds. I know that the country has been invaded, and based on Papa's drunken rants, it seems that impending doom awaits. I wonder how long it will be before the Germans find their way to my town and if their arrival could possibly make things better for me.

I walk quickly to the only place I can think of for bread. Within ten minutes I've arrived, and I knock on the door timidly.

"*Kto tam?*"

"Katya, it's me," I answer. "Luda."

The door flings open, and my friend Katya pulls me inside. "What are you doing here?" she asks. I look up to see her father walk into the room.

"Excuse me, Alexei Yurevich," I say with a small nod of the head. "I'm sorry to come so late, but—"

"What is it, Luda?" Alexei Yurevich takes a step toward me, his brow furrowed.

"My father told me to get him some bread," I reply.

Katya and her family are the only ones who know of my troubles with Papa. They know that I quit school last year to work. They know of Papa's drinking and his cruelty, and whenever possible they allow me inside their home. Katya's brother, Oleg, joins his father and Katya inside the small foyer.

"Mama!" Alexei Yurevich calls out. Katya's grandmother appears in the doorway, and I shift in embarrassment to now have the entire family looking at me in pity.

"Mama, Luda needs a loaf of bread. Please give her what we have," Alexei says. She disappears quickly into the kitchen and returns minutes later with two small loaves of bread.

"Take this, child," she says softly. "You eat one of these before you return. Give the other to that pig you call Papa."

"Mama." Alexei Yurevich's voice is sharp behind her. She turns with a huff and leaves the room.

"Oleg will walk you home, Luda," Alexei Yurevich says. Oleg leans down and begins pulling on his boots.

"Oh, no. Please," I respond. "It's not necessary. I can make it."

"Luda." Alexei Yurevich takes another step toward me. "You shouldn't be out walking at night. Not anymore. It isn't safe."

I nod slowly, not really understanding but warmed by the concern in his voice. Oleg joins me, and with a wave to Katya, I turn and follow him out the door. We walk slowly down the sidewalk so that I can eat the second loaf of bread in my hand. I didn't realize how hungry I was until I took the first bite. I instantly feel my energy return, and as we turn the corner toward my flat, I brush my hands and mouth clean of all crumbs.

"Take care of yourself, Luda," Oleg says. Shy and soft spoken, Oleg doesn't speak often, but I always sense that he's standing at the ready to protect me.

"Thank you," I reply. With a small nod, I push open the door and make my way up the stairs. I put my key in the door and push it open.

"Papa?" I call. "I'm back."

I step into the room to find Papa slumped over on the couch, the empty bottle still clutched in his hand. With a sigh, I pull a small blanket over his shoulders, then lay the loaf of bread on the floor beside him and retreat to my room . . . alone.

IVAN KYRILOVICH
July 28, 1941

Pain is an interesting sensation. It's more than physical, though it certainly manifests itself in physical ways. I said good-bye to my son today. I watched him kiss his mother's tear-stained cheek and hold tight the sisters he adores as they soaked his shirt with bitter tears, and I felt the pain well up from somewhere deep inside.

Hugging my son for the last time, my arms physically ached as though the muscles tore from bone, and when I pulled back and looked into his brave, tear-filled eyes, I felt my heart rip.

I think I even heard it.

I won't get that piece of my heart back, and that's the interesting thing about pain. It never leaves you. Sometimes it's dull. Other times you feel healed, but pain always leaves a mark, a scar as a reminder that life and love aren't free.

Pain changes everything.

I have to walk slowly this morning, stopping frequently to make sure I'm going the right way. When a man surrenders his firstborn to wolves, it's not without repercussion. Mine is a feeling of loss and of being lost.

I've spent most of my life in hard labor. I worked the collective farms as a boy, my back bent over rows of vegetables and my hands caked with the dirt of another man's supper. My father didn't love me—he used me. I was his mule, and this made me strong. It also made me rebellious. I left my home the day I turned eighteen, as well. I left for different reasons, less noble than my son's.

I wanted to be on my own. The first war was over, and my older brother, my father's pride, was dead. He was the boy, the *man*, my father wished I could be: loyal, dedicated, hardworking, with a love for the land.

I was the lover. I wanted to live life, and I wanted to give it. Tanya and I met when we were sixteen, and we both longed for the cosmopolitan life of the city. This was unheard of in our small country community. Boys didn't leave home unless they went to war.

But I did leave home, and I took the love of my life with me. With no money and enough food to last us one week, Tanya and I snuck aboard trains and walked the two hundred kilometers to Kiev, where I quickly began my work in construction. I loved the sweat and risk of building. I knew I was on a pioneer team to bring progress to my great country. Our work was slow, but I felt satisfied each day as I walked home, covered in dirt and grime.

Tanya threw herself into developing our lives with equal fervor and heaps of grace. We quickly found a judge who agreed to marry us, and by the time we were twenty years old, we were the proud parents of a son. I held my child tightly through those long night hours and stared into his delicate face. I vowed then to never be as my father had been. My children would understand love and would be free to develop in their strengths.

As I stop and study my surroundings once more, I wonder for the first time how my father felt when he woke up that morning and discovered my note. Did he experience a shred of the pain that I now feel? Was there any regret?

I tried to contact my mother twice after leaving. The first time was a month after we settled in Kiev. I sent a letter explaining why I chose to leave and asked if she could ever forgive me. I didn't receive a reply. I sent one more letter years later, after Maria was born. I thought my mother should know she had grandchildren. That time I received a reply, not from Mother but from Father.

"*Ivan. Your mother is dead. You killed her. Does this finally make you happy?*"

That was the final communication I ever received from home. I don't even know if he still lives . . . and I don't care.

I finally reach Shamrila and turn up the narrow alley toward our flat. My girls wait for me, wounded and scared. I wonder if I can be the man they need me to be right now. I pause and take a deep breath, my chest tight, hands shaking. My arms ache for my son, leaving me weak and fatigued.

Pushing open the heavy door, I breathe deeply. It's damp and wet, and the smell heightens my heartache. Taking one slow step at a time, I suddenly feel much older than my thirty-eight years. As I step onto the third landing, I pause to catch my breath, and the door in front of me opens a crack.

"Who's there?" comes a gruff voice.

"Ivan Kyrilovich," I answer with a jolt. "I live in the flat above you."

The door opens wider, and my neighbor steps out just beyond the door. I've seen him before once or twice, but only in passing. I take a moment to study him closely and realize he is doing the same.

He's a short man with small eyes framed by round glasses. His hair is a mop on top of his head, curly and wild, giving him a crazed appearance. His clothes are wrinkled, and the bags under his eyes tell me he hasn't slept well.

His eyes dart left to right as he ducks his head. "Would you join me inside, please?" he whispers, jittery and spooked.

I step inside his dim flat, and he locks the door behind us.

"I am Josef Michaelovich," he says in a nasal voice. "Can I ask for your help as a neighbor and countryman?" He wrings his hands. "My wife and I are Jewish."

I suck in my breath sharply. Suddenly his raw nerves make sense.

"We have a daughter, Polina. She's close in age to your daughter, I believe." I nod. I've seen her walking to and from school with my girls.

"What do you need?" I ask.

"Food," he says, finally stilling his hands. "I'm afraid to leave the building, and we have run out of food. In fact, we have not eaten in three days."

For the first time I look past him and notice his wife and daughter huddled on the couch. Polina is gaunt, her small frame thin, eyes circled in dark. Her hair hangs limply over her shoulders, and my heart cracks.

That's the other thing about pain. Just when you think you're incapable of enduring any more, you're split wide open again. There is no threshold.

"I will bring you down some bread and borscht. You're right to stay inside."

Josef's eyes fill with tears, and he grabs my hand, his palms cold and clammy. "Thank you," he whispers. I nod, then turn to leave, walking upstairs briskly.

Pain can also lead to action, and the feeling of purpose is like a balm to the wound. It doesn't close the hole, but for a moment the pain is silenced.

FREDERICK HERRMANN
September 24, 1941

Stepping out into the cool morning mist, I take in the sight of the city. After months of pushing our way farther into this wretched country, we finally reached our destination. Kiev was always to be the place that we stopped, but getting here hasn't been without a struggle. Closing my eyes, I fight nausea at the memory of coming upon my own countrymen hung from trees, charred and grotesque. Their socks had been dipped in gasoline and lit, burning them alive from the feet up. "Stalin's socks," my comrades whispered late at night, and I pretended that it didn't bother me. But it does.

And now this. Bombs went off three days ago just after we set up our command posts. How those stupid Soviets managed to coordinate the explosions is something I can't understand, and anger mounts as I think of their defiance.

"Frederick!" I turn and fight a snarl as Alfonse approaches. I offer him a curt nod. "Do you know what the meeting's about today?" he asks.

"Retaliation," I reply. I hear the impatience in my voice, and I make no effort to disguise it. I find Alfonse annoying. I want him to know it.

"They killed two hundred of our men in those explosions," I continue. "They'll regret it."

Alfonse nods. He pulls out a cigarette and lights it, then offers me one. I decline.

"Soviet tobacco is good," he says, smoke unfurling from his lips. I choose not to respond. We walk in silence toward the building that's been set up as the new command quarters.

"What do you think command has in mind?" Alfonse asks.

"I don't know," I respond. "But they will pay."

MARIA "MASHA" IVANOVNA
September 28, 1941

The Germans are here. Papa came home ten days ago and asked Mama to put a little more water in the soup for he had invited Josef Michaelovich and his family to dinner. Papa told us the news that night as we slowly swallowed the broth in an effort to stave off hunger and mask fear. Polina grabbed my hand under the table and clung tight, her thin nails digging into my skin. I can still feel the terror in her grip.

My stomach is empty, and stress has made me anxious. Somehow my papa still manages to get food and even share a portion with Polina and her family, despite the fact that we rarely leave the flat at all. In fact, since we've been invaded, I haven't left at all except to walk downstairs to Polina's, where she and I tuck into a quiet corner and dream of all the meals we will someday eat. There is simply not enough food for all of us. I long for a steaming bowl of Mama's borscht: the beet-red broth, the meat and vegetables, the sour cream, and a slice of warm bread to dip into the bowl until it's mushy. My mouth waters, and I often wake up feeling crazed with emptiness.

Mama still makes borscht, but it's weak. There's no meat, and the vegetables are sparse. We receive bread sparingly and always share a portion of what we receive. So I live in hunger.

Today is no different. I wander around the house, looking for ways to occupy my time without thinking of food. Anna has begun unraveling old sweaters and blankets and using the thread to sew new clothing for all of us. I find myself jealous of her. I'm envious of her ability to find something to do.

I spend a lot of time thinking of Sergei. Daily I retreat to the corner of our flat that has always been my escape. It's dark and musty and befits my mood. I used to sit in this corner to read and draw. When we were young, Sergei joined me, filling my head with fantastic stories of talking animals, magical forests, princesses, and kings. He described every detail of his creatures: the green frogs with purple spots; glittered owls with tufts of blue springing from their bodies; majestic eagles that walked regally and wore crowns. Sergei took me to far-off places.

He's been gone two months now. We received one letter two weeks ago. It arrived folded in a tiny triangle, Sergei's neat block letters formed perfectly on the front. The letter was so heavily censored that we were unable to make out much of what he wanted to communicate. Entire lines of my brother's voice were darkened with a thick black marker, edited out by someone for reasons I can't understand.

But that small piece of paper is evidence of him, evidence that he's alive, and for a brief moment I saw the old light return to Papa's face. His beloved son lives.

Bombs went off again this week. They weren't near our home, but we could still feel the rumble and knew that something happened. Papa quickly left to investigate. Every time he leaves, I worry. We all worry. But the war has only just begun, and I wonder how long we can all live in worry before we physically break.

Mama pushed open the windows this morning to let in the sun. We're experiencing *Baba Leta*, the time of year when warmth makes one last effort to stave off the waiting winter. The end of September tempts us to enjoy her beauty before October swoops in and darkens the sky. From my seat in the corner, I see the trees outside. As I gaze at the brilliant leaves, I wish for a moment that I were the blackbird sitting peacefully on the branch.

What must it be like to be a bird with all the freedom to fly? I imagine spreading my wings and letting the balmy breeze of autumn lift me high above the ground. What does the world look like from that vantage point?

Does the bird float lightly on the wings of freedom? Does he feel sorry for those of us who are chained to the ground?

I should like to be a bird.

My daydreams are cut short by four staccato taps on the front door. No one has knocked on our door since the war began, and immediately my heart drops. Is it the Germans? What do they want with us?

I step outside my bedroom only to see Papa wave me back in. I obediently shrink just past the threshold so that I can hear. Papa approaches the door.

"Kto tam?" he says firmly. "Who's there?"

"Ivan Kyrilovich, it is I, Josef Michaelovich." Papa quickly opens the door, and Josef enters. Knowing it's safe, Mama, Anna, and I step out of hiding and nod politely at the perpetually nervous man. His bespectacled face is always filled with a sense of dread. I don't believe I've ever seen him without a thin line of sweat on his upper lip.

He clutches a paper in his hand. "Have you seen this?" he asks, his voice trembling and weak.

Papa takes the paper and reads quickly. He sucks in a deep breath and lets it out slowly. "Where did you get this?" he asks.

"Someone slipped it under my door this morning. I know it couldn't have been you because you would have knocked and given it to me personally. You know what this means."

Papa nods gravely. "It means someone else knows you're Jewish." Papa looks somberly at Mama and hands her the paper. I look over her shoulder to read the notice:

ATTENTION

All the Zhids of Kiev and the suburbs are to appear on Monday, September 29, 1941, at 8:00 a.m. on the corner of Melnikovskaya and Decktiarovska streets [near the cemeteries]. They are to bring their documents, money, other valuables and warm clothes, linen, etc. Any Zhid found disobeying these orders will be shot. Citizens breaking into flats left by the Jews and taking possession of their belongings will be shot.

"What are you going to do?" Papa asks Josef, who flits from side to side nervously.

"We're going to go," he answers without pause.

My heart drops at his words. Polina is the only friend I have. What will I do if she leaves?

"I don't think it's a good idea, Josef," Papa replies.

"I think it is necessary," Josef answers back. His tone is mournful. He stops moving, and looks Papa in the eye.

"Someone else knows we're here, Ivan. Someone knows we're Jewish. If we go, maybe we'll be spared. The notice says to bring our possessions. Perhaps they'll send us away, and we'll escape this horror."

"Or perhaps the horror you're sent to will be worse," Papa responds, his voice soft but firm. Josef says nothing. His face reads defeat, and the stillness of his often-fluttering hands unnerves me. He has given up.

"I will take my wife and daughter tomorrow morning as the notice commands," Josef says finally. "I don't have a choice. If I don't, I take the chance of being reported and killed."

"No," I cry. I wince as Papa turns and gives me a sharp look. "I'm sorry," I say, softer this time. "Please don't go, Josef Michaelovich."

Josef walks slowly to me. Grabbing my hands he squeezes them tight. "Thank you, *dorogaya*, for your concern. You've been a good friend to my daughter." He looks up at Mama and Anna standing silent in the middle of the room. "Thank you all," he says, "for taking care of my family these months."

Looking at me again, Josef smiles, thin lips stretched tight under his sharp nose. "We'll go tomorrow and escape the uncertainty of this isolation."

Josef steps past me, kisses Mama on the cheek, then reaches out and places his hand on Anna's shoulder with affection. Taking the notice, he turns to leave, stopping to shake Papa's hand.

"Good-bye, friend," Josef said. "*Spaseeba Bolshoya*. Thank you for everything."

Then he is gone.

IVAN KYRILOVICH

September 28, 1941

The images floating through my head are too horrific for me to fully succumb to the slumber my body needs. Each time I close my eyes, the visions grow darker and heavier. I see Josef and Klara, with Polina standing in front of them. Their mouths are open, but they make no sound. As I watch, the worms crawl out—hundreds of worms wriggling out of the open crevices of their bodies. I want to scream but can't will my voice into action. Then the sky turns red and I shake, trying to pull myself from the horror.

When the image fades, a new one pounces. There's a person in a field. The grass is tall, and as I slowly zoom in from above, I notice the sharp angle of this body. I move closer and make out the form of a man in uniform. I see the crimson ground surrounding him, and I try to pull back, to shudder away from the vision that looms nearer.

Finally I hover above him. My body doesn't touch the ground. Like a bird floating on the breeze, I study close the profile of the man beneath me. *It's my son.*

I want to touch him, to call his name and reach for him, but I can't make a sound. I will him to open his eyes . . . to breathe. I want to hear the timbre of his voice. And then slowly, his head moves. For a brief moment my heart soars, but then I see it: a hole in the middle of his forehead, the blood streaming, a river of life flowing out. His eyes are hollow, devoid of spark. I scramble, willing myself to retreat from this terrible dream. Just before I pull myself out, I hear his deathlike whisper.

"Papa . . ."

I awake with a start and jump out of bed. I'm covered in sweat, and I run my fingers through my coarse hair.

Standing, I quickly pull on my thick wool trousers and step into the dimly lit hallway where our shoes sit in a neat line. Four pairs of shoes where there used to lie five. I know what to do.

"Papa?"

With a start, I whirl around to find Maria standing behind me in her nightdress. She looks so young and innocent, her wide eyes full of question. Her thick brown hair cascades over her shoulders in long waves.

"What are you doing?" she asks.

"It's okay, *dorogaya*," I answer softly. "I'll be right back." My voice catches in my throat, and I try to stop it. But she hears and she knows.

"But where are you going? It's dangerous to go out at night." Her voice rises slightly in panic.

"I'm not going out," I assure her, reaching over to smooth out her hair. "I'm going downstairs to check on Josef Michaelovich." My daughter, ever perceptive, studies me closely. Her eyes search mine, full of questions. She nods and steps back as I quickly, silently, slip out the front door.

"I'll soon return," I whisper just before closing it behind me.

I swiftly descend the steps and knock gently on my neighbor's door. I know he'll be awake. A man as nervous as Josef Michaelovich doesn't sleep easily or often. I hear shuffling and a soft voice.

"Kto tam?" he asks.

"It is I, Josef," I answer. The door swings open.

"What's wrong?" he asks, looking around me, then closing the door behind.

"I'm going to follow you tomorrow to the meeting point," I answer, looking at my friend evenly. He stares back in surprise.

"Nyet," he says, shaking his head.

"Josef, you're walking into a trap, I can feel it. I went downtown last week after the explosions. I saw what happened. The Soviets bombed German buildings. Retaliation will come."

"I understand, Ivan," Josef says, still shaking his head from side to side. "But I will not have you in danger on behalf of my family. What do you hope to do by following us? You put yourself at risk of deportation or . . ." His thin voice trails off.

I look past Josef into his darkened flat. "I want to be available to protect Polina," I say quietly. "I'll follow you at a distance where you'll be able to see me. If for any reason you sense danger, I'll take Polina and bring her home."

The room is silent. Josef studies my face with tear-filled eyes. "Why would you do that?" he asks.

"Because she's a child. Please, friend," I beg, imploring him to understand the gravity of his situation. "Please let me protect her."

Taking my hand, Josef bows his head low and kisses it. He doesn't say a word, but I know his answer. "I'll meet you here in the morning at six thirty," I say, turning to leave. Something catches my eye, and I look back to see Polina standing in the doorway. She looks lost and terrified.

I open the door and walk out. I don't know what I will say to my girls.

The next morning I leave promptly at 6:30. The girls don't walk me to the door or say tearful good-byes. The tears have all dried.

Josef, Klara, and Polina say nothing as they exit their home. They each carry a small satchel, and they're wrapped in their warmest clothing. Despite the fact that it's unseasonably warm for the end of September, they are dressed for winter. They're dressed for the unknown.

Once outside, I fall behind them and stay twenty paces back. We make the long hike toward Syrets, and along the way hundreds of other men, women, and children join the group. I am swept up in the tide of Jews, all of whom seem hopeful. They murmur of a better life, of being shipped to another country where they'll be allowed to live in peace.

Some seem to believe they will be sent to concentration camps. "It's better than living in constant fear of being caught," I hear one mumble.

For a brief moment as I walk along the side of the road, the sun peeking up over the tops of the trees and kissing our steps, I feel as though I'm not truly here. Everything slows, and I see all things in full detail: The child with the dark brown ringlets, her red mouth a perfect heart against her full cheeks. The elegant woman wrapped in a fur coat that stretches to her ankles. On her head sits a full fur hat, and she walks with the determination of one who is accustomed to getting what she desires. The old man walking slowly beside his frail wife. I observe the deep-set wrinkles on their faces, evidence of a lifetime of hardship, and the overwhelming tenderness in their eyes.

Half a mile from the meeting site, Ukrainian police officers begin walking alongside the mass of people, herding them into a line. I am stunned by this betrayal. I know it's time to extract myself from the crowd, so I stop walking and step to the side, outside of the group. I cannot continue to walk alongside these men who call themselves my countrymen but who seem so quick to do the bidding of the enemy.

The street has narrowed onto a dirt road. Up ahead I see the line leading toward the old cemetery. My heart plummets. There is not to be a deportation. I see no buses, and we're miles from the train station. Hundreds of German soldiers stand in wait, watching as the line of Jews stretches as far as the eye can see. I feel a wave of nausea overwhelm me as my worst fear is confirmed: they're walking in willingly.

Jogging up a few paces, I search the crowd for Josef and Klara, having lost sight of them when the thick crowd narrowed. There's still time for me to escape with Polina, but not much.

Finally I spot them and stride forward briskly. Josef looks up at me and shakes his head. I look over my shoulder to see a young Nazi walking toward me, his gun trained at my head. I freeze.

"Get in line," the young man snarls. The other soldiers laugh, as if on a picnic, but the soldier before me holds no such cheerfulness. His Russian is thickly accented, and his eyes reflect the heat of hell.

"I'm not a Jew," I answer haltingly.

The young man laughs. "I don't care," he replies. "Get back in line, *Untermensch.*"

I raise my hands in surrender and step back into the line. The women and children now cry softly, though panic has yet to set in. For the first time, I consider the foolishness of my actions.

"I told you not to come, Ivan," Josef whispers next to me. Klara and Polina clutch hands, tears streaming down their faces.

"I'm sorry," is all I manage. But I can't surrender just yet. I look desperately for a way out, though I still don't know what I'm trying to escape.

As we walk, much more slowly now, I notice the images around me. The sun shines brightly today. It's the kind of beautiful day that would have been filled with the delighted sounds of children laughing in the streets—a day Tanya and I would have enjoyed. I think of all the walks we took together, her hand firmly pressed inside mine. It wasn't enough time with my love. I've failed her. I promised I would return, but my foolishness now leaves her abandoned. What have I done?

Up ahead, the sounds of panic rise. Screams, cries, shots. I look up to see the Germans swarming the crowd now. They dare someone to try to run, but no one does. The front of the line is far ahead, but I can make out a crowd of people throwing their possessions into a pile. The cries course down the line, sweeping over and above me—a tidal wave of grief and despair.

Polina looks up, and her eyes hollow before me. There is nothing left to do but wait for the worms.

"Schnell!" The German soldiers bark their orders, finishing every order with a sharp command to hurry.

The boy who ushered me into line stays close as we slowly pace forward. "I don't trust you, *Untermensch*," he hisses. Eyes trained forward and chin up, my heart races with the knowledge that I'm headed toward my fate.

Josef, Klara, and Polina walk in a tight huddle in front of me. "I'm sorry, my darlings," Josef says, his words staccato bursts of grief. Klara stands at his side, clutching his hand, her knuckles white and the thin blue line of her vein running up her wrist and disappearing beneath her thick coat.

Polina walks on the other side of her mother, her eyes dim. The light faded from her face several weeks ago, leaving her nothing more than a shell. She turns her head slowly, looks up at me, and I shudder. It's the same look I saw in Sergei's eyes in my dream.

Death.

I jump as a scream pierces the air. "What are they doing, Josef?" Klara breathes softly. Her voice, like a glass bell, rises just above the throng.

"They're going to kill us, my darling," Josef answers bluntly. I glance sideways at the German standing next to me. His gun lowers slightly as he looks intently toward the front of the line. He sees me look and gives a formal nod.

"See you soon, *Untermensch*," he says.

He leaves us and walks swiftly to the front of the line while I'm left, heart torn. Tanya, Anna, and Maria wait at home. They wait for me. The tea in their cups is cooled, and their shoulders stiff. They're watching the door that I won't open.

As the line moves slowly forward, we pass through wired gates that funnel us into pairs, like the cattle farmed across the road from my childhood home. My father's voice rings loud and sharp in my head.

"Don't trust anyone and don't be a fool. You make your living and you keep your mouth shut. Don't worry about someone else's suffering—it will only bring suffering upon you."

On and on my father ranted every evening while the rest of us quietly pretended to listen. Mama knit scarf after scarf amid father's rants. She never questioned his thinking, never doubted or disrespected him verbally. But her silence spoke volumes, especially to me—the boy most like her. I once asked her, when I was very small, why she let Papa yell foolishness every night.

"You're father isn't a fool, Ivanchik," she answered gently. "He's prideful and longs for nothing more than to feel that he's in control. I just give him the space he needs to explore his heart."

To this day, I struggle to understand my mother's allegiance to my father. Hard and cold, he revealed tenderness only to my brother, Misha. There are few regrets that haunt me as I approach these final moments, but without warning I am seized by one great sorrow: I abandoned my mother with a hateful, bitter man. Without the courtesy of a good-bye, I left her behind.

"Are you okay, Ivan Kyrilovich?" a timid voice asks. Polina's voice cuts through my heartache. Taking a deep breath, I nod.

"I'm not ready to give up just yet," I respond. Grabbing Polina's hand, I feel a sudden urge to flee.

"Listen to me, *dorogaya*," I say, my eyes darting up toward the Germans

laughing on either side of us. "Stay close to me and do not, under any cir-
cumstance, leave my side, understand?" Polina nods her head, eyes wide.

"Josef, Klara," I say quietly. "If the opportunity presents itself, I will
take Polina and we'll flee. Do I have your permission?" We all step forward as the line moves. It's then that I hear the staccato bursts that drown
out the beating of my heart. Soft cries turn to wails as we all finally know,
without doubt, what fate awaits us.

We *are* the cattle, and our slaughter is imminent.

"You won't succeed, but thank you for trying," Josef answers. I yearn to
look at his face, to read the thoughts etched into the lines around his eyes
and mouth. Klara's shoulders shake, and with her free hand, she reaches
back to her daughter and clasps tight.

"There's still time, Josef," I say, but my words are swallowed by a
scream. We're twenty paces back now, and the shots are louder. A woman
at the front of the line is thrashing and pulling, her thick auburn hair
moving back and forth in horrified rhythm. It is the elegant woman with
the fur coat.

The Germans on either side of me strain to see the altercation between
the beauty and their comrade. I, too, stand high on my toes to watch. I
need to see the weakness of my enemy—to study his response to challenge.

A single shot pierces the air. I jump as she falls to the ground in a heap.
The German who pulled the trigger thrusts his gun behind his back and
kicks her twice, then pulls the coat out of her clenched hands and tosses
it on a growing pile of clothing and suitcases. He nods at the other men,
who each grab one of her arms and drag her lifeless body around a second
gate that blocks the slaughter zone.

As the Nazi who shot her strides back toward me, I see that it is the
same boy who forced me into the line. He catches my eye, and I return his
gaze evenly. I fight a shudder as I catch the heat.

FREDERICK HERRMANN
September 29, 1941

I am not a killer.

My mother and sister believe me to be such, but the truth is I am not. Killing isn't sport, nor is it a game. My job in this country is clear and noble: to cleanse. The art and act of doing so take many forms, and ending one life to preserve another is not killing.

It is saving.

She wasn't the first person I killed, but it was the first time I pulled the trigger at point-blank range. I wasn't prepared for the shock of watching life leave a person's face. In the split second before she fell, I saw it drain: pink to white, warm to cold, life to death.

With her blood still on my cheek, I walk toward the back of the line, my knees shaking, and for the first time I feel fear. If I show any sign of weakness, my father will find out, and that alone is enough to bring on a sense of fear so strong I'm briefly stunned. A warrior groomed by the man who calls Hitler a friend cannot show weakness in the face of death.

As I march toward the back, I meet his gaze, and I see it there in his eyes. Defiance. Courage.

Marching swiftly to Blobel, I salute and stand at attention.

"What is it?" he asks gruffly.

"Permission to join the shooting squad," I reply, never looking him directly in the eye. My father taught me that when you look directly at one who is greater than you, it automatically reveals rebellion. This is how I know the *Untermensch* plans to escape. He looked me in the eye.

Blobel waves blithely and nods, releasing me to join the ranks of those who methodically shoot each Jew standing in line. For them this is sport. The man who has the greatest number of accurate shots between the eyes at the end of the day receives a pack of cigarettes from each member of the line.

I have no interest in the triviality of these games. I'm here to do my job. As I pass the rebel, I stop and face him. He has a tight grasp on the hand of the young girl next to him, who holds the woman's hand in front of her. They don't look at me, but they feel me. That's all I need. Walking briskly to the front of the line, I cross through the gates and hurry to the line of men waiting for the next crop of crying, shaking Jews to stand opposite the ditch.

Taking stance at the end of the line, I shout to the gatekeeper. "Send one more through this time!"

The gatekeeper nods his head apathetically and gestures outside the gate. Moments later, a group walks through, their stripped bodies shivering despite the unseasonably warm weather. They stand across the ditch, some wailing, others praying, many of their faces registering disbelief.

I raise my gun and train it at the woman in front of me. Just before I pull the trigger, her face floats across my mind—the woman with the coat. The light of life turning dark before my eyes.

Fire!

Taking a deep breath, I remember the Führor's words: *"He'll do great things."*

Then I shoot.

IVAN KYRILOVICH
September 29, 1941

"I can't do it. I can't. I can't do it." Polina shakes now, her body quaking, electric shocks moving through her hand to mine. We're paces from the front, and the time has come to remove our clothing and add all possessions to the pile.

"Shh, *Dochinka*, shh." Klara turns and pulls her daughter close, her thin hand smoothing Polina's straight dark hair over her gaunt shoulders.

"Klara, you need to say good-bye," Josef murmurs. Mother and daughter cling to one another with such ferocity that my throat melts in heated spasms as I imagine my own wife parting this life with her children.

I squint in the mid-morning sunshine, my chest heavy with memory and doubt. I long for the safety of my family.

"Schnell!"

We stand before the second gate, unable to see what's on the other side but understanding that our imagination is likely not enough to prepare us. It's time to make a move. I slowly pull off my shirt and try to block out Polina's sobs next to me. She's a fourteen-year-old girl being asked to strip in public. The shame of that act alone sends her into a fit of panic, and I speak without turning my eyes in her direction. I will spare her every bit of dignity possible.

"Polina, this isn't over yet," I say as I remove my pants. "I have a plan. Keep your eyes forward and calm down."

"Listen closely," I whisper. A German voice rises above the throng as he prepares the firing squad.

46

"He's going to give three consecutive commands in rhythm. Listen. There's one, two, three, and *fire*." Polina and I both wince as shots ring out in chorus just beyond the gate.

"After the third command, wait one moment and then fall. Don't wait for the *fire*. Fall into the ditch a split second before the guns go off." Polina refuses to look in my direction. I wonder if she's heard me at all.

"Polina, if you understand, squeeze my hand one time, please."

Reaching over slowly, Polina grasps my hand and gives one firm squeeze. The plan is set. "Josef, Klara, you do the same. Fall into the ditch before they shoot," I hiss just as the gate opens, a terrifying metal-on-metal screech sending a wave of nausea through me.

"Nyet," Josef whispers in return. Klara's shoulders slump. "If we all fall at once, they'll get suspicious."

"Papa," Polina whimpers.

"I love you, *Dochinka*," Josef says, turning his head toward his daughter. I see the tears coursing down his cheeks.

"Take care of my girl," Josef says just before stepping through the gate.

Entering the killing zone is more horrifying than I imagined. Marching in a single-file line, our dignity stripped bare, we slowly wind our way up the small incline to the top of the death ditch.

I try not to look at them, the men and women below, their limbs all tangled in a mass of grief and horror. But the image is too great, so my eyes slowly lower, and when I finally see, my lungs constrict.

The bodies—all intertwined and twisted, thin arms and legs woven in and out in a pattern of heartache—they are the worms I see in my dream.

The sounds around me separate from one another. I hear every movement: the crunch of dying grass beneath trembling feet; the quiet sobs of those resigned to fate; my own hollow breathing as I fight suffocation; Klara whispering her daughter's name over and over like a lifeline.

"Polina. Polina. Polina."

I hear the click of German guns as many of them reload, the clanking sound of metal entering chambers. The easygoing banter of the soldiers across the ditch, as if today were just another day at a menial job. All of the sounds reverberate through my mind.

It isn't just the sounds that magnify. I'm keenly aware of everything. The way the sunlight dapples through the trees, casting brilliant shapes and shadows across the open fields. The warmth of this *Baba Leta* day on my exposed flesh, fighting against the inner chill that leaves me raw.

I watch a black bird drift through the sky, his wings spread in freedom, gliding through the air without fear. He doesn't flap his wings, nor does he fight the current of the breeze. He catches it and rises suddenly, suspended for a brief moment before leaning to the side and riding the wind to a nearby branch.

All of these things pass through me in an instant, and then it's over. A German command brings the soldiers forward, their dusty caps set high on their foreheads. It is then that I see him.

He walks briskly down the line to the man stationed across from me. It's the steely eyed killer who pushed me into line, the same boy who killed the woman in the fur coat. Leaning forward, he whispers in his comrade's ear. The soldier glances in my direction, shrugs his shoulders, and steps back, letting the boy with fire in his eyes take his place. I feel the heat, and in my final moments grow emblazoned.

Looking back at him from across the killing ditch, I stare straight into his eyes, feeling a surge of hatred that surprises me.

Ready!

The first command rings out, bursting through the air with a measure of indifference.

Set!

"Get ready, Polina," I whisper as the Germans raise their guns. Though we're separated by a ditch, I look directly into the barrel before me. It's black and cavernous and threatens to swallow me whole. I taste metal, and my ears ring as I await the final command.

Aim!

I wait a beat, then yelp, "Now!" I grab Polina's hand and crumple just as the shots burst through the air. We tumble forward onto the heap, and I throw my arm over the trembling girl protectively.

"Don't cry. Don't move," I whisper. Polina bites her lip, willing herself to go limp, and together we lie still among the dead.

I glance at Polina and see her eyes wide and glassy. She doesn't blink, her mouth fixed in horror, and my heart sinks.

"Polina?" I breathe as quietly as I can, not allowing myself to move.

Her eyes flick my direction quickly, then close as hot tears pour off her nose. Lying on top of me is her father, a river of life flowing out of the wound between his eyes.

I, too, close my eyes and wait, the open-mouthed corpses burying my sorrow, swallowed by the worms.

PART TWO

THE DARKNESS

LUDA MICHAELEVNA

September 29, 1941
Vinnitsya, Ukraine

"Get up!"

I awake with a jolt, Papa's booted foot pressed hard into my rib cage. Pushing myself to a sitting position, I squint in the early morning light.

"What?"

"Get up and get dressed. We're going to pray."

He spins on his heel and marches out of the room, a nearly consumed bottle of vodka clutched tightly in his hands. I dress quickly, then rush to the front door where Papa waits impatiently.

"Should we be going out, Papa?" I ask, stepping quickly past him. I've seen them walking below my window. Germans. Boys with cropped blond hair and crisp uniforms marching the cobbled walkways of my childhood. They're here, and my father wants to go to the church and pray. Despite his ever-present anger at God, my father still feels it necessary to pray in the church at least once a week—if it could be called a church.

The Soviets took possession of the building some time ago and turned it into a public recreational facility. They painted the walls white, and pictures of Lenin and Stalin hang proudly. Rather than praying to the saints and to Mary, young people were trained in this building in the order of the Red Army through the Komsomol and Pioneers. Each day, children in their Soviet uniforms lined the large room, once a place of prayer and reflection, and learned instead the ways of Lenin. With the Germans in control, I don't know who we will encounter inside the building, but I fear it will not be the friendly faces of local children.

As we approach the sterile building, I blink hard against the memory that haunts me. I close my eyes briefly and see His face peering from beneath the cracked, white paint. It was years ago, a day when I begrudgingly followed Katya and Oleg to the building after school. They played ball in the cavernous hall while I looked on shyly. When the wayward ball was kicked a little too hard, it slammed into the wall, chipping off a large, circular piece of paint and revealing the face of the Christ child, a mural that had long ago been covered. The eyes looked straight into my soul, and I felt the heat of being known. We were quickly ushered from the building that day, and the next time we returned, the missing paint had been refreshed.

But I cannot forget the image, and my heart quickens at the thought of once again standing beneath those eyes.

Everyone I know respects the changes to this old building and treats it as nothing more than another Soviet facility, but not my father. He goes early, when the building is stale and quiet, and he prays. He prays for solace, he prays for death, he prays to be free—free from me.

I don't pray simply because I don't know how. I imagine my mother would have taught me the proper way to approach the saints, but she isn't here and somehow father's prayers seem so futile and wasted. So I sit quietly on my knees with my eyes closed and dream of freedom—freedom from him.

We step out into the still street, and I feel a chill run up my spine. The morning bustle is cut off today. No students file down the cobbled walkway, eager to get to school before the straggling crowd. Not that that means anything to me. But it's unnerving to see the town so quiet. Walking out into these empty streets feels foolish and dangerous.

As we step out of our flat onto the sidewalk, I look around slowly, waiting for the Nazi soldiers to come dashing out. Will they order us back inside? Will they harm us? Standing next to my father, I feel vulnerable. I know if danger arises he'll save himself. I also know that he will do nothing for me out of a lifelong habit of simply not caring.

We turn and quickly make our way down the road. When we reach the building that was once the church, I look up and shudder. The white walls frighten me. I don't want to go in. It feels dangerous and ominous. I take a risk.

"Papa, I'd like to stay out here and wait for you, please." My voice is small, my words equal parts hope and terror.

"No," comes his gruff reply. "You'll come in with me, and you'll pray."

And that's it. Arguing will do me no good, so I follow, shoulders slumped and heart beating quickly. We push open the heavy door and walk inside the dim room. It's a large hall with expansive ceilings and narrow windows fitted down the sides, seven on each wall. The sunlight from outside looks gray and shadowed due to the dust and dirt that settled on the windows overnight. The walls are stark white, burying beneath them the paintings of the Mother Mary holding the infant Jesus. But I feel His mournful eyes, and I shiver.

Suddenly, my father grabs my hand and pulls hard, bringing me to my knees. "Pray," he growls. I close my eyes. Within minutes, empty-bottled Father is beseeching his patron saint, his body racked with the sobs of a man who doesn't know the meaning of hope.

As my father prays and sobs, I sit quietly. I want to pray, but to whom? And what can I pray? Perhaps I too have lost hope. I no longer see any possibility for a relationship with my father. At sixteen I've long outgrown the desire to see him changed. Too much time has passed. Too many bruises from his hands have faded.

I jump when they come in—three of them, all with strong, icy blue eyes. They're young, perhaps only a few years older than myself, but they look terrifying.

Father stops praying and looks up. His sagging cheeks are wet and his small eyes hollow. He still clutches his empty bottle in his left hand, his right hand balled up under his chin. This is his prayer pose. Looking at him, I feel pity and loathing. He's a small, balding man, and his life is built upon shame. In that moment, as the German soldiers approach, I know that my father is finished.

One of the Nazis barks an order that sends me scrambling to my feet. Father stays on his knees looking warily at the three men. The oldest of the three approaches me. He reaches up and runs his fingers through my thick hair, a smile spreading across his face. I shiver, and this sends him into a fit of laughter.

When he finally composes himself, the German gazes at me with such intensity that I'm momentarily hypnotized, his eyes so deep and blue I feel as if I am looking into the ocean that I've heard so much about. When he speaks, I snap back into the horror of this present reality. His words send his comrades into peals of laughter as his hand runs down my shoulder. One of the other men walks to my father and jerks him to his feet, knocking the vodka bottle to the floor. He laughs as it shatters. My breathing comes in short bursts as the Nazi before me runs the back of his hand across my lips. He's talking to me, his honeyed words bitter to my ears.

I glance at Papa who is now being held steady by the other two German soldiers. They're taunting him, the sound of their language harsh and guttural. My father looks at the ground, and I know he has no fight. Empty-bottled Papa, steeped in self-pity, wouldn't know how to fight. One of the men punches the side of his face, and I wince as his head snaps to the left.

"You won't fight them?" he hisses. I shake my head no. I don't see any reason to fight the inevitable. Besides, what my father doesn't understand is that he killed the fight in me long ago. I have nothing left.

Laughing, they turn him around and drag him out of the building while I remain frozen. Looking back at me over his shoulder, my father utters the last words I will ever hear him say before the world goes dark and cold.

"You are a whore. Just like *your mother*," my father growls, spitting out the words like poison. The Germans roar with laughter. They kick open the front door and push him out into the street.

My heart turns to stone as the door shuts with a loud click and the three men quickly surround me. For the first time my father has directly spoken to me of my mother. His words bounce through my head, spinning and tumbling like the icy winds of winter.

"Whore. Like your mother."

This is the only description of my mother I have ever been given. I'm so absorbed in digesting what I heard that for a moment I don't feel their hands on me. I snap to attention as the tallest of the three rips my shirt, pulling it from my now trembling body. I know what will happen next. I don't know if I will survive.

As they push me down and take their turns, I try to conjure up the picture I had created of my mother. I try to hear the song in her voice and see the rhythm of her movements. I try to remember her as I've seen her in my mind for so many years. But all I can see is black, and inside the swirling darkness I see His eyes. They bore through the walls and slowly change and morph into the eyes of my father. I feel the judgment like hot coals poured over my head.

"Whore. Like your mother."

The verdict echoes and reverberates, bouncing back and forth through my frozen soul. I don't feel the pain, don't feel my nakedness or the cold. I don't hear the strange men grunting in my ear, and I cannot taste their greedy mouths. But most of all, I can't see my mother.

She is gone.

FREDERICK HERRMANN
September 30, 1941

He isn't dead.

As the sun sinks low over the trees, I watch. Every once in a while, a shadow dances across the scene before me, and I jump to my feet, my gun trained toward the pile.

Looking up, I notice for the first time the colors that surround me. The leaves are changing, fading from vivid reds and yellows into a brown that signifies imminent winter.

Death.

When I pulled the trigger, my target was no longer there. It happened so quickly that it took me a minute to realize. My first instinct was to jump into the ditch, but the sight was so repulsive that I couldn't bring myself to do it. I am a weak man, indeed.

So now I wait. Many more were killed after him, and the mound piles high. I will keep watch for as long as it takes. He will crawl out, and I intend to meet him.

At the sound of footsteps I whirl around, pulling my gun up sharply.

"Lower your weapon, boy!" he barks.

Quickly snapping to attention, I salute Standartenführer Blobel.

"Heil Hitler!" I say, raising my arm rigidly. Blobel nods and returns the salute. I remain straight backed in front of the man who masterminded this day—the man who calls my father comrade.

"Why are you still here?" he asks. His voice is thin, and the words rake through his lips with sharp precision. I don't look directly at him but rather just above the brim of his hat.

"I'm waiting, sir," I answer evenly.

"Waiting?"

"Yes, sir." I don't know why I don't say more, and neither does Blobel. I hear his annoyance.

"What are you waiting for?" he asks, his teeth clenched. Blobel has little patience for anything but a straight and complete answer.

"There's someone down there who is going to try to escape," I reply. I realize how I sound: obsessive, impulsive, foolish. But for some reason I can't stop myself. To do so feels like an unacceptable defeat.

Blobel chuckles softly and pulls a cigarette out of his pocket. Striking a match, he draws in deeply from the thick Russian *makhorka*. The tobacco is strong, and the smoke drifts through the air, creating a fuzzy mirage before me.

"Don't be a fool," Blobel says turning back to me, smoke flowing out of his nose in a long, steady stream. "There is no one alive down there." I hear the satisfaction in his voice.

"Go back to the bunkers, boy," he says after drawing in another deep breath. "No one can survive this ditch." He looks at me. I lower my eyes slowly to meet his for the first time. The serpent slowly flickers beneath the steel gray. It is momentarily mesmerizing.

"No man escapes my ditch."

His words are marked with confidant finality. I watch Blobel stare into the mound. He's like an artist studying his own painting. His eyes move slowly from left to right and then back again.

"This is my work," he says softly.

"Sir," I begin. My voice falters. I clear my throat. No weakness. "Sir, I know there's a man still alive inside that pile. He fell before I shot."

Blobel stands silent for a moment, then turns his serpent eyes my way.

"He can't escape," he says. "If he tries, the guards will shoot him." Then he lets out a laugh—a low, rasping hiss of a laugh that moves up from his throat and across his lips, sending a chill down my back. The sun has now set, and the trees around us feel thick and tall and ominous.

"This is my life's work," he says, his arm extended over the twisted bodies. "What do you think of *my* ditch? Isn't it grand!"

In that moment, my respect for Standartenführer Paul Blobel plummets. This is all a game to him, too. Disappointed, my shoulders slump. Blobel notices and stops laughing. He narrows his eyes.

"Go back to the bunkers, boy," he says, his laughter now tangled in the air around us. "No one can escape my ditch alive."

Sickened at his ridiculous and prideful repetition, I raise my arm in salute, then grab my gun and march toward the gate.

"Herrmann!"

I turn toward Blobel, who quickly fades into the blackness, the cool autumn air engulfing his small, thin frame.

"This is my ditch."

I nod in his direction. He knows he's lost me. He knows that he can't measure up to or compete with the two men I esteem above all others. He knows that, no matter how hard he tries, he will never be as grand in my eyes as my father and the Great Führer.

Glancing once more into the ditch, I think I see movement, and I stop.

"Leave, boy," he hisses behind me.

Willing myself to turn, I slowly walk away more determined than ever to complete the task before me with excellence. My mission is not to defeat the Jews.

My mission is to make my father proud, to be a part of history.

LUDA MICHAELEVNA
October 5, 1941

I'm spinning and tumbling, the black night pressing down on me from all sides. I feel the weight of the darkness heavy on my chest, and I gasp for breath. As I suck the air in, it turns to smoke in my lungs, and that's when I hear them.

They're laughing, the sounds floating up and around the black and covering me. I smell the sardines on their breath, and I realize that the weight I feel pressing me down is the weight of their bodies. They're on top of me, breathing heavy, and I cannot move. I can't breathe or see or escape as their hands move steadily, painfully. I open my mouth in a silent and terrified scream. Then I hear the whisper. It starts low, a haunting rasp that plays in a loop and steadily grows louder over the maniacal laughter.

"Whore. Like your mother. Whore. Like your mother. Whore."

I sit up with a gasp and throw the thin blanket from me. Leaping to my feet, I flail at the still air in the room and turn around, disoriented. It takes a moment for me to remember that I'm no longer there. I'm with Katya. I look down at the floor where she sleeps and draw in a ragged breath.

With trembling arms, I lower myself back to my bed and squeeze my eyes tight in an effort to forget the smells and sounds of that terrible day.

I haven't returned home since the incident. The moment my father walked out, leaving me to be devoured by the hungry beasts, I knew I would never again see him. My entire life had been spent trying to care for and preserve the only connection I had to my mother. Though I had little hope of knowing who she really was, I always had my dream. But with just four little words, my father destroyed the dream. And I can't seem to bring her back.

After the Nazi soldiers finished with me, I waited for death. It only seemed like the natural next step after having endured such horrific abuse. Instead, they threw my clothes at me and pulled me to my feet. As they stood back and watched, I slowly dressed myself, my back bruised and bleeding from the repeated movement on the rough wooden floor. Having them watch and laugh as I dressed was more humiliating than what had already occurred.

The Nazis did not kill me as I expected but simply pointed to the door and ordered me to go. I saw how they looked at me. Their stares hardened from callous laughter to disdain, hatred, and utter contempt. I don't remember much after I left the building of horror. I remember sunshine and warmth, complete contrasts to how I felt inside. I slowly made my way down the sidewalk, staying as close to the buildings as I could. I felt exposed, bare, and terribly guilty in the bright sunlight.

I managed to stumble to Katya's flat. When her grandmother opened the door, she yelped and called out for Alexei Yurevich, who came running and caught me just as I passed out.

They told me later that I slept for two days, frequently waking up in screaming fits before settling back into fitful, feverish slumber. When I finally awoke, it was Oleg who sat by my side.

"*Privyet*, Luda," he said softly, as my eyes focused. He smiled and placed a cool cloth on my forehead. "It's nice to see your eyes."

Even now, as I think of the tenderness in his voice and the genuine concern in his eyes, I find myself filled with gratitude. In the five days since I woke, Katya's family has given me the blessed gift of space. They've asked very few questions, and I am grateful. They haven't asked me to explain what happened, nor have they tried to contact my father. And I've said little in return.

How do I tell someone what happened that day? How do I explain the sounds I heard and the pain I felt? How do I communicate the shame and the despair that has settled upon my soul? I wish I could describe the darkness. I wish I could release the pressure that constricts my heart and keeps me enslaved to the floor of that drafty building.

I wish.

I get up from my cot in the corner of the flat and numbly make my way to the kitchen. I haven't eaten in days, and suddenly I feel famished. Entering the small eating room, I find Katya's grandmother and Alexei sitting at the table, silently drinking their chai.

"Sit, Luda," Baba Mysa says. I'm not sure why Katya calls her grandmother Baba Mysa, but somehow it fits her. *Mysa*, meaning "little fly," is endearing and sweet when paired with the tender lady who sits before me. She's a small woman with a stout frame, but her face doesn't bear the hardened marks of many Soviet grandmothers. Her eyes are still soft, and the lines around her mouth reveal years of laughter. I'm drawn to her, pulled in by the peace that seems to ebb and flow freely about her spirit.

"Would you like some chai?" Alexei asks. For the first time I notice how much he resembles his mother.

"Yes, please," I answer. My voice no longer sounds like my own. It's hollow. The Nazi's robbed every piece of me.

Baba Mysa hands me a steaming tin cup, and I wrap my hands around it. She sits down beside me, staring intently into my face. Feeling my cheeks flush, I break her gaze, shifting my eyes to the steaming tea.

"Look at me, Luda," Baba Mysa says. I look up and immediately feel hot tears prick the corners of my eyes. I have yet to cry, but as Baba Mysa penetrates my soul with her stare, I fear the time is coming when I'll begin and be unable to stop.

"Are you ready to talk?" she asks.

"Mama," Alexei says, his voice laced with concern. "Don't push her."

Baba Mysa dismisses her son with a wave of her hand and looks deeper into my eyes. This time I look back, and it's then that I realize she knows. She knows what they did to me. She understands my pain.

"Whore. Like your mother."

"Are you ready to talk?" she asks again, gentler this time.

I take a sip of my chai, the hot liquid burning my tongue and throat and bringing a welcome relief. Knowing that Baba Mysa waits for an answer, I take a halting breath and nod slowly.

"Good," she says. "You tell me as much as you want. When you're ready to stop, we will stop talking."

"Luda, you don't have to tell us anything if you don't really want to," Alexei says, leaning close. I smile gratefully at the man whom I have often wished was my father instead of the pathetic waste of a man I was cursed with.

"Thank you, Alexei Yurevich," I whisper.

"Please. Just call me Alexei," he says with a smile. "Do you want me to leave while you talk with Mama?"

I think for a moment before answering. The humiliation of what I'm about to admit would be no less so if he left the room, and having him near makes me feel safe. "No," I answer. "Please stay."

Both Alexei and Baba Mysa sit back and wait for me to begin. I suck in a deep breath and haltingly relive the moments of a day that I will never escape. At some point—I don't know when—Oleg and Katya slip into the room, drawn by the sound of my heartache. When I reach the part of the story where my father leaves me, Alexei shoves his chair back with such force that it tips backward and hits the concrete wall. His faced is rigid, and his eyes flash with fury.

"Sit down, Alexei," Baba Mysa commands as I falter. Perhaps I've said too much.

"It's okay," I mumble. "You can stand. It's a terrible story. I'm a terrible person." Hot tears gather inside my heavy eyes.

Alexei's face softens, and he kneels down in front of me. He grabs my hands in his, engulfing me with strength. "It is a terrible story, Luda," he says. "But you're wrong. You are *not* the terrible person."

And in that moment, I break. The pain, the fear, the hurt, and the anger dissolve under the kindness of his stare. He's concerned, and his concern is centered upon me. No one has ever been concerned for me before.

Through racking sobs and heavy tears, I finish the story. I look up to see Katya wrapped up in her brother's arms, sobbing. Oleg's face is wet, and even the unbreakable Baba Mysa looks wounded.

"I'm sorry," I say. "I'm so sorry to burden you with this."

Baba Mysa jumps out of her chair and lunges toward me, pulling me up so quickly that the remaining chai in my mug splashes to the floor. I'm stunned by her reaction and flinch out of habit, my hands covering my head in defense.

But I'm not prepared for what happens next.

Grabbing my chin, Baba Mysa forces my face downward so that I am eye to eye with her. "Open your eyes, Luda," she commands. I do and look straight into the slate blue depths before me. I see lightning flash there, a jagged line of anger mixed with fierce love.

"You are safe now, do you understand?"

I nod, her hand still firmly on my chin.

"You're safe, and you will be loved here. In this house we fight for each other, and we're going to fight for you."

With that she drops my chin and brushes her hands together as if finalizing a deal. The room has grown quiet. I suspect that even Alexei, Katya, and Oleg have never seen Baba Mysa react with such passion.

"Everybody go," Baba Mysa barks, grabbing a small rag to clean up the tea on the floor. "Go and rest. I'll call you when dinner is ready."

As I slowly walk out of the small room, Oleg grabs my hand and squeezes. "It's not your fault, Luda. It is *not* your fault."

I look into his eyes, shocked by the emotion laced through his words, and I see it.

Devotion.

I nod, then slowly walk away, numb.

MARIA IVANOVNA

October 7, 1941

My father is gone.

We heard of the slaughter outside of town at Babi Yar. It's impossible not to know what's happening just outside our beloved city. Screams have filled the streets these horrible days, and they have yet to be silenced. I hear them even in my sleep.

In the three nights since Papa left, my mama has wailed, her hot tears burning through the blankets that Anna and I pile on top of her in an effort to keep the violent tremors at bay. Mama with the deep-set eyes. She's drowning in her sorrow, and I fear we'll lose her, too.

But tonight is the fourth night, and for the first time, the flat is silent. I sit on my cot, staring out the window, trying to wrap my mind around all that has changed. I don't hear her approach, but I sense her presence, and when I look up, Mama stands over me. Her face, always so young and beautiful, is now pinched and drawn. Wrinkles have set in—deep lines etched in sorrow that pull the corners of her delicate mouth into a harsh arch. Her eyes are dim and gray.

"Get up, *Dochinka*," she commands. "It's time to get to work."

I pull myself off the floor and let the book in my hand fall with a thud. I've held it for hours, hoping to read and escape the horrible feeling of despair that seems so willing to destroy us all, but I could never focus on the words. Quickly stuffing my thick, frizzy hair into a bun at the nape of my neck, I follow Mama into the kitchen. Anna stands at the stove, slowly stirring a simmering pot of broth. We have no vegetables or salt, and the soup is weak. It's mainly hot water meant to fill our shriveled stomachs.

"Your papa won't return," Mama says, her tone flat. Anna puts down her spoon and turns, eyes wide; Anna with the pretty face, always good and kind, now horrified and angry.

"If we are going to survive a winter under occupation, girls, there are things we must do now. There's no more time to be children." Mama says this while looking straight into my eyes. "The time has come for both of you to work and to work hard. We'll need to be smart with the rations we're given, and we must get rid of everything we possibly can right away. Money is the most important thing now if we're to eat at all this winter."

Mama turns and runs her hand over the woodstove that Papa bought her for the New Year holiday two years ago. He was so proud of his purchase, dancing as he installed it for her. *"Your mama is a woman who deserves her own oven, girls. She's a princess, and I am her prince."*

I think wistfully of the joy we all felt that day as Mama lit up at the prospect of no longer having to cook her food over a communal fire in the building. My eyes snap back as Mama speaks again.

"It's a good thing your Papa bought us this oven when he did. We're going to need it to stay warm now that he's gone—"

"No!"

I jump at the sound of Anna's voice and stare at my sister, stunned by her flashing eyes and bitter stare.

"No. Papa is still alive," she says, this time in a near whisper. Her quiet words wash over me and out of the room.

"Anna," Mama says, reaching for her older daughter's hand, but Anna recoils. For a moment, the two lock eyes. I stand motionless, a spectator to the silent showdown. Normally, I would have automatically assumed Mama the winner, but something about Anna's look stops me.

It is belief. A true, deep, and wholehearted belief that bubbles from inside and radiates from her pores, and the longer I look at my sister's face, the more I share her conviction.

"No, Mama," Anna says again, this time more gently.

Mama draws herself up, smoothing her hair back behind her ears. She nods her head, a solitary tear spilling on her cheek.

I turn away and fix my gaze at the small window set high on the wall above the kitchen stove, the one Mama used to keep open while she cooked. Papa felt it too dangerous to have windows open since the Germans invaded, so for months it has remained latched tight. Tonight, as I gaze at the black sky, I allow my mind to wander.

Could Papa be out there somewhere?

The last few days have turned cold, the final strains of *Baba Leta* fading into that awful stretch of winter that seems never ending. Night comes quicker and lasts longer, and it's just a matter of time before the colors of spring can only be seen in vivid daydreams.

As I lose myself in the black sky, I hear a hollow thud outside our flat. Anna and I freeze as Mama holds up her hand. We listen intently. A light knock skips across the wooden frame of the door and down into my chest.

"Stay here," Mama whispers. She slowly moves out of the kitchen to the front door.

Standing with her mouth pressed to the crack, she asks quietly, *"Kto tam?"*

I don't hear the reply, but Mama screams and bats at the lock, pulling the door open wide. Anna and I rush out just as Papa falls into a heap at Mama's feet.

"Bozhe Moi. Ah, Bozhe Moi." Over and over, Mama cries out to the God we rarely discuss. She pulls Papa's head into her lap, her delicate hands running up and down his hollowed cheeks. I stare in horror at the man I know to be my father but hardly recognize. He is naked and covered in blood and dirt. I have never felt more frightened.

Mama leans down and puts her cheek on his face, crying and wailing hysterically.

"Help me, Masha!" Anna calls, but I'm frozen, paralyzed by the vision of my father so helpless and weak—my papa who always has the answers and the strength.

Anna drags Papa inside and slams the door, locking it again quickly.

"Masha! Help me. *Now!*" Anna's voice jolts me out of my trance. I quickly race to the bedroom and grab the blankets off the bed, then return to my father's side. Covering him, I lean forward and touch his face. It's cold and dry. His eyes are sunken, and his cheekbones protrude from his face at an ugly angle. He opens his eyes and looks at me for a brief moment.

"Mashinka," he whispers. His head falls to the side as he loses consciousness. I look up, first at Anna, then Mama. Their faces register the same thing I feel: shock, joy, bewilderment, and complete and utter terror. What has happened in the days since he left?

IVAN KYRILOVICH
October 8, 1941

The memory haunts me. It moves from my head to my heart, and it leaves me cold. I cannot escape the sounds. I'm home now, but in my mind I'm still stuck in that ditch, in the forest of nightmares. How many times did I tell my children the stories of Baba Yaga, the witch of the forest who walks about waiting to capture lost children and eat them for lunch? How many times did I leave them tucked in their beds, eyes wide with terror at the shadows of the night? Perhaps Baba Yaga isn't a myth after all. It seems she may be real, and I met her at the Babi Yar, the death ditch that I somehow survived.

Closing my eyes, I replay it all again. The moment I fell, the sound of the gun, and the bodies. All of the bodies. I sink into the memory, back into the ditch.

I felt them. The dead and the dying all pressed in a ditch, writhing and moaning. Not everyone died immediately. Some lingered in the pile of worms.

One by one they fell on top of me, burying me from the sight of my enemy. The first to land was Josef, and soon after him a dark-haired child tumbled down the embankment. She landed with her nose inches from mine, and I watched as the life slowly drained from her face until her gaze was fixed and steady. I cradled her into death, ushering her from this life as her auburn hair grazed my cheek. And still the bodies fell.

Next to me, Polina whimpered. Her body was fine—no bullet pierced her skin. But her spirit wallowed in the darkest place imaginable. "Mama," she cried over and over. For hours on end, she clutched the hand of her dead mother and wept for her, and I wondered if I made the right choice in forcing her to survive.

If the spirit is dead, can the body live on?

When night finally fell and the sound of shots became only an echo in our minds, I slowly began to shift beneath the bodies. I felt heavy and weighted down, suffocated.

"Polina," I whispered. "Polya?" I waited for her to answer.

"*Da.*" Her voice was flat, devoid of life.

"It's time to go."

"*Da,*" she answered.

I moved again, slowly setting the child in my arms to the side. I kissed her soft cheek, this girl of no more than six. It was cold and smooth like a fine stone.

"Good-bye, small angel," I whispered. I moved from side to side, pushing the bodies away until I could finally see out from beneath them. For a brief moment I marveled at the sky above, the deep black dotted with a million stars. How big and giant is this world?

"I'm ready," Polina whispered. Very slowly we both shifted and moved until we'd broken from the prison of death.

"We'll have to find our way out of here," I whispered. "They have a wide section of the forest fenced off. The gate is guarded, I'm sure."

Just then we heard the crack of a boot walking on the ridge above.

"Lie down," I hissed. Polina and I collapsed on top of the open mouthed corpses just before the solider strolled by. Frozen, we both waited until he passed out of sight.

"We need to use extreme caution," I whispered, and Polina nodded. There was no life to her movements. She merely complied with all I said.

"Let's go now before he comes back."

Slowly standing up I felt my muscles scream as they stretched and moved for the first time in many hours. I pointed to the opposite side of the ravine, and Polina and I moved over the bodies, pulling ourselves up the side of the death ditch. Polina glanced back once more at the place where her parents lie buried. She lifted her hand to her mouth then blew a soft kiss before turning and grabbing hold of a small root, pulling herself up over the edge.

Once on the other side, Polina and I moved as quickly as we could without making a sound. The ground beneath our feet was cold and hard, evidence of the nearing winter. I looked to the right and saw several campfires lit about four hundred meters away.

"This way," I breathed, pointing in the opposite direction.

We moved deeper into the wooded land, the trees closing in above us, blotting out the stars. I kept Polina directly in front of me so I could see her shadow.

The fallen leaves and branches required us to slow our pace so that we walked more delicately. Periodically I checked back over my shoulder, the orange glow of the Nazi fires growing smaller—embers in the distance.

I didn't know where we were, and without benefit of light, it felt odd and unnerving to keep walking. I placed my hand on Polina's bare shoulder. She stopped. Her body trembled, and I felt her shame and horror. We were naked and covered in the dried blood of our countrymen.

"Polya," I said, my voice low and soft. "Let's walk a bit farther, then find a place to lie down for the night. We need to rest and stay warm. Tomorrow we'll continue."

I knew that if we pushed back into the forest deep enough we were likely to run into a small village or dacha. I just needed to get my bearings in the light of day.

What I didn't know was what the next day would bring.

"Papa?"

I jump, my eyes snapping open. It takes me a moment to register the girl standing in front of me. I know her.

"Are you alright?" Her eyes are concerned, but I also see fear. It's my daughter. I remember now. I'm not in the woods anymore. I'm at home.

I nod my head once, a very slight acknowledgment of her question, but not really an answer. Am I okay? I don't know.

I think I'm trapped.

MARIA IVANOVNA
October 12, 1941

It's been five days since Papa came home, and still the questions linger over us like a cloud. Though he's physically in our presence, he's not fully here, and I long to have him back. He's vacant and silent, his eyes glassy. I sit by him all day long, just holding his hand. He won't look at me and mumbles only short, staccato answers when a question is asked of him. Mostly though, he stares long and hard at the wall. He is locked somewhere that I cannot go.

I have so many questions, so many things I want to know. What happened? Where are Josef and Klara and Polina? But I don't say anything. Instead, I become Papa's companion. For hours we sit, hand in hand. I fight the urge to speak, and he doesn't offer any answers. The old papa would have been able to read my thoughts and would have known what to say, but this papa doesn't seem to know I'm here.

Anna walks in with a tray of bouillon and a steaming cup of chai. Mama's chief mission in the days since Papa's return has been to bring his health back through food using the sparse rations that we have. Anna sets the tray down and gives me an inquisitive look. She wants to know if Papa has spoken. I give a slight shake of my head, and she straightens up again.

"Mama is making *Vereniki*, Papa. We know it's your favorite."

Papa looks up at his oldest daughter and forces a slight smile. "Tell your mama I said thank you," he whispers. Anna tosses me a wide-eyed glance. That's the longest sentence Papa has spoken since his return.

Anna hustles to the kitchen, and Papa picks up his spoon. I don't think he's hungry, but he eats anyway. For Mama. We sit in silence for a moment while he sips from his bowl.

"It's good," he says finally. I look up, and my eyes fill with tears. My father has always been the rock, but today he looks small and sad and terrified.

"Papa," I say, then hesitate.

"Yes, *Dorogaya*?"

"Papa . . . are . . . are you okay?"

It's not what I want to ask, but I don't have the courage yet to ask the other questions. Papa sighs and looks at the wall again. I worry that I've upset him.

For a long time we sit.

"No," he finally says.

I nod with disappointment. I already knew the answer to that, and I kick myself for not asking a better question when I had the chance. He's retreating again—I feel it.

"She's still alive," he breathes. My eyes snap to his face. The color has drained away, and his mouth hangs open slightly. He looks so very old. It's as if all youth left him overnight. His hair is gray around the temples, his eyes dull, and his entire body sags under the weight of a memory that he'll never escape.

"Who, Papa?" I whisper.

"Polina," he answers, shifting his gaze to my face. "Polina is still alive. And I . . ." Papa's eyes fill with tears, and his chin trembles violently.

"I left her there. Polina is alive, and I left her in the open for the wolves."

With that, Papa's eyes close, and he faints. I catch him just before he hits the floor.

LUDA MICHAELEVNA
December 9, 1941

I've known for several weeks now, and I know the time is coming when I won't be able to hide it any longer. In the darkness I'm free to caress my abdomen, the pouch hardening and swelling just slightly. Though I've never had a woman to help explain life to me, I instinctively know when it's growing inside. I wonder how much longer I can keep my secret before they know. And I wonder if at last they will be ashamed.

When you grow up without love, accepting it becomes almost burdensome. I wait for the glass to shatter, like the vision of my mother. I anticipate the hot stares of judgment from Alexei and the fear in Katya's eyes. I prepare for Baba Mysa's reprimands, and I long for Oleg to quit looking at me with such tenderness. It could all crumble at any moment, and as I sense the life that moves inside, I fear that the time may soon come when their pity and love turn to condemnation.

"Psst . . . Luda! Are you awake?"

I quickly pull my hand away from my stomach as though I've been caught. I turn to look down at Katya who has insisted on sleeping on the floor next to me since I arrived two months ago.

"*Da,*" I reply.

"Papa and Oleg said today that they might have an assignment that I can be a part of!" Despite the fact that smiles don't come easily these days, I feel a small grin take hold of my mouth. Katya's glee is contagious.

Alexei and a group of local men have begun what they're calling the

Night Wolves. It's an underground partisan group determined to thwart the Germans' efforts. Their operations are dangerous, risky, and designed for the brave of heart.

Every night for the past several weeks, Katya has begged her father to let her join one of the operations, but he remained firm in his refusal. I know it's because of me. He watches me closely, his eyes trained on my every movement, and I see that he cares about me. I find this unnerving.

Now, it seems, Alexei has found a project that Katya can join, and I'm happy for her. But I'm also frightened. I don't want her near the vultures, either.

"What is it?" I ask.

"I don't know," she answers. "He has a meeting tomorrow with the Night Wolves about ways to shake up the Germans. They were able to stop the supply train coming in to town last week with explosives, Papa said. It's not going to stop the Nazis, but Papa says that's not the point."

"What's the purpose for their resistance, then?" I ask. I roll over on my side to look more closely at my animated friend.

"Oleg told me that we just want the Nazis to know they aren't going to get our city without a fight."

I bend my arm and rest my head on my hand. I admire Alexei and Oleg and their bravery. It's so unlike the cowardice that I knew in my own father.

"Speaking of Oleg," Katya says, turning to face me now. "You know he's in love with you, right?"

For a moment I feel my heart drop and a familiar wave of nausea sweeps over me. Yes, I do know this and it terrifies me. Why does he love me? Why would he want me? Sometimes he looks at me with such a deep longing in his eyes that I feel physically sick. I avoid his gaze and work to keep my time with him limited to short conversations when others are in the room. It's not that I don't want to love him, because I wish that I could. But it doesn't feel right or real with him. At this moment, I don't know how to return the loving gaze of a man when I've only ever felt the contempt of one. I don't think there's anything left inside of me. Not for Oleg. He is too good and too pure. I'm not worthy of him. But I can't say any of this to Katya. So I merely nod.

"How do you feel about him?" she asks, her voice spirited and happy. She doesn't understand. To her, love is still fun and innocent and magical. But to me, love is pain. Love is sweat and groaning and awful. Love isn't innocent. Though we're the same age, I feel old lying next to Katya.

Instinctively I reach for my abdomen. "I think your brother is a good man," I say to Katya, and I can practically hear her eyes roll. She flops back down and stares up at the ceiling, quiet for a moment.

"He could make you happy again, Luda," she murmurs. I don't answer because the truth is, I don't know what happiness is.

The night is long and sleep difficult. The images that spin in my head these days are muddied. I see the church and my father, all warped and twisted. The vision of my mother, once so strong and bright, is now misty, clouded. Her melody is both sad and sinister.

In my dreams, I hear the sounds from that awful day, and I can see my fear. It's a black fog that moves in and out of the pictures in my mind. But every time I hold my hand on my stomach, the fog dissipates. It's only then that I see a glimmer of light.

When I enter the kitchen the next morning, I see Katya and Alexei sitting at the narrow table with Oleg standing behind his father. I avoid his gaze and look to Baba Mysa who is standing over the counter, slicing bread and cheese for our breakfast.

"So please tell me how I get to be a part in an operation, Papa! Tell me now, please!" Katya begs. She sounds like a child asking for a gift. Alexei takes a deep breath and leans closer to his daughter. She narrows her eyes and looks back at him over her delicate nose dotted with fine freckles.

"We want to begin a little psychological warfare with the boys," Alexei says. He always refers to the Nazis as boys. It's his way of showing his disdain and disrespect for them.

"How do we do that?" Katya asks.

Baba Mysa tuts softly over her loaf of bread, clearly unhappy with her son's decision to let Katya in on the action.

"We'll play a bit of a joke on them," he replies with a grin. "We will make them look and feel foolish because that is what they are—fools."

Katya grins and slaps her hand on the table, clearly relishing the thought of her role in this. "So tell me what to do. I'm ready!" she cries.

I listen closely as Alexei lays out the plan. "You'll go to the outdoor market tomorrow afternoon to buy vegetables. Wear your nicest dress, and make sure you look your finest. The plan is to lure some of the German boys back to the safe house."

The safe house is a small, abandoned flat where the Night Wolves meet to strategize and plan their movements against the Germans. Alexei continues. "When you get the boys alone—and I want you to bring no more than two of them—prepare and offer tea. You want them to think they're going to get something from you, and your job is to make sure they let down their guard."

Katya flushes at the frank nature of what her father is asking of her. I do too. I turn once again to Baba Mysa, who lays our feast out on a long platter. I can hear her muttering under her breath and have the distinct impression that very few people have ever truly crossed her in life.

"When the boys are relaxed, you will excuse yourself for a moment and go to the door where they will have left their jackets and shoes. If all goes according to plan, they will also leave their guns. I want you to take their things and run as fast as you can to the library, where we will meet you."

Baba Mysa slams the tray on the table. *"Durak,"* she barks. *Fool.*

"Mama," Alexei says sharply. Baba Mysa narrows her eyes at her son, and I hold my breath for the showdown. I'm not sure why anyone would willingly defy Baba Mysa.

"This is a foolish plan," she huffs. "You put your daughter in danger for a joke. Foolish!" She throws her small hands up in the air in disgust. She stares at her son long and hard as the rest of us wait.

It's Katya who breaks the silence. "I can do this, Baba," she says confidently.

Without thinking, I speak. "I can do it, too," I say. "I'll join Katya."

They all turn in surprise, and Alexei clears his throat. "Luda," he begins, "this requires close contact with Germans. I can't promise safety."

Though my heart twists, I stand my ground. I don't know why I feel a burst of courage or a desire to take part, but I don't want to back out.

"I can do it," I say, stronger this time. I look at Katya, who has plastered on a forced smile. It dawns on me that she may have wanted to do this on her own. This was her way to gain her father's approval. What I don't understand is why she doesn't see that she already has his approval.

Oleg turns to his father and speaks softly. "I don't think it's a good idea, Papa."

"Why?" I challenge, for the first time looking him in the eye.

Taking a step toward me, Oleg's words drip with tenderness. "Because you're not ready, Luda."

"I'm not incapable," I snap, feeling my face flush. "I can do this, and I will."

Alexei nods. "Okay, Luda. You can do this with Katya. Oleg will be following close behind, staying in the shadows. If at any moment you need to retreat, you do so. Am I understood?" I nod my head. Alexei motions to the breakfast plate, signaling the end of the conversation. Baba Mysa turns with a huff and points at me. "You," she barks. "Come with me."

I follow her out of the kitchen and into the tiny bedroom, where she closes the door behind us. I turn and wait for her to unleash her fury. Instead, I find she is looking at me intently. Not knowing what she wants of me, I wait.

"You're pregnant," she says. I gasp. My hands clutch my abdomen self-consciously, and I wonder how she knew. Is it that obvious?

"No one else knows," she says a little more gently. "But I know these things."

"Please don't tell anyone," I beg, tears pricking the corners of my eyes. "Please."

She studies me harder, her eyes searching mine, then drifting to my midsection where my skirt grows tighter. She crosses her arms with a sigh and turns toward the chest of drawers against the wall.

"Nobody listens to the old lady around here," she grumbles. "Everyone just runs after foolishness and wants the old lady to sit around with her head in the sand and let it all happen . . ." Baba Mysa continues to mumble as she pulls out a small sewing kit and motions me to take off my skirt. I hesitate, and she bristles. Tossing me a blanket to wrap around myself, she turns around as I quickly undress and give her my skirt.

In minutes Baba Mysa has let out the buttons of my skirt so I have more room for my expanding waist.

"This will last for a little while," she says after I'm redressed, "but you won't be able to hide this much longer. I won't tell, but soon you will have to."

I nod and leave the room. As I turn to close the door, I have an impulse I've never had before. I rush back in and wrap Baba Mysa in a hug. It's the first time in my life I have willingly hugged someone.

"Thank you," I whisper. Baba Mysa hugs me back.

The next morning, Katya wakes me up full of energy and excitement. I, however, am filled with dread. As I stare at my reflection in the small mirror over the bathroom sink, I briefly consider backing out, but something urges me to press forward. Some inner desire that I can't point to compels me to join. I want Alexei to be proud of me. I want to conquer fear. I want to exact some kind of revenge.

I want to feel alive.

The plan is to wait until late afternoon to go to the marketplace. By then the German commanders are more likely to have retired for the day, and all that should be left are the young, foolish revelers who wander the parks and the streets jovially, as if this war were reason for party and celebration.

Alexei leaves after breakfast for work. He still has employment at a local grain supply store where he sorts and stacks sacks of grain and wheat. "Supplies are getting smaller and smaller each day," I heard him whisper to Baba Mysa a few days ago. "My job will soon be eliminated. We're going to have to figure out a way to earn more funds."

Baba Mysa is a beautiful seamstress. Before the war, she made quite a sum sewing dresses for women all over the Soviet Union. Parcels of fabric arrived for her with notes on measurements and desired style. But since the bombings began, no parcels have arrived. I see how this affects Baba Mysa, and I wish there were a way I could contribute to this family rather than simply becoming one more mouth for them to feed.

I know, of course, what affects Alexei most is the fact the Oleg, at sixteen, could be taken at any moment. For now, Oleg is employed at the local bread warehouse, but his age leaves him vulnerable to leaving for war or, worse, to attacks by the Germans. The situation is tenuous, and we all feel the pressure of the years that loom ahead, shrouded in a veil of doubt and danger.

At four o'clock, Katya and I walk out onto the street. Oleg follows behind us at a distance, and despite my resistance to his affections, I'm relieved to know he's close.

"You ready?" Katya says, her eyes glassy and bright. She is wearing her best dress and has her hair pulled up in such an elaborate braid I wonder how she will possibly undo it later. I also wonder how Katya learned to be so feminine when she, too, lost her mother as a baby. Katya knows how her mother died. There are pictures and stories of her mother told almost daily. Is the simple knowledge of a mother all it takes to become a true woman? Next to Katya, I feel plain and unsure of my actions.

We walk in silence the short distance to the market where only a handful of stands remain open. Despite the Germans' strict restrictions on our freedoms, they insist that the farmers and sellers keep their food stands open during the day. They need food, and my people must provide it for them. Most don't pay for what they take, though I have heard rumors that some do. I often wonder who they are and why they do that.

I've heard stories of food being rationed throughout much of our country. Alexei told us last night that the time is soon upon us when we'll have to wait in lines with meager ration cards to be given a parcel of food. But for now it seems our town is still able to sell goods to whoever has the funds to purchase them. With Alexei and Oleg both currently employed, the family has not yet run into a serious problem with money.

When we reach the first fruit stand, an older woman looks at us suspiciously. "Why are you girls here?" she asks roughly. "It isn't safe. Go home."

"We need bananas," Katya answers defiantly. "And apples and three kiwi." The woman glares as she gathers the requested items. While she waits, Katya goes to work. Looking over her shoulder she immediately catches the eye of two German soldiers standing close by. Nudging me in the ribs, she nods her head, and I turn to look as well. I'm relieved to find that neither of them looks familiar, though I'm not sure I could identify my attackers from months ago.

"Smile at them, Luda," Katya says without moving her lips. She grins and waves, then giggles when one of the boys waves back. I marvel at her confidence and try to force a smile, which I'm certain doesn't succeed.

The other man stares back at me intently, so much so that I quickly lower my eyes. He's handsome—tall and blond, with a square jaw and sharp features. I suddenly feel very sick and the ground begins to spin underneath me.

"Luda, if you can't handle this, leave," Katya hisses. She turns and takes the fruit from the seller, who now looks at us with severity. "You girls get out of here," she snarls. "Those boys aren't here to play."

If only she knew . . .

Katya tosses her head with a sniff, turning toward the Germans. "I'm going to talk to them," she says. I hear a hint of fear in her voice, and all reason inside me screams to stop, but I'm compelled to follow if for no other reason than that I cannot abandon my friend.

We reach the boys, the tall handsome one still staring at me. The other boy grins at Katya. I recognize immediately the look in his eyes. I've seen that look before.

Katya holds up an apple and offers it to the German standing next to her. She raises her eyebrow seductively as he takes it.

"*Spaseeba.*" He thanks her with a smirk. Katya takes a few steps away, with me hurrying to stay by her side. She then turns and gestures at the soldiers to follow, and like two lost puppies, they do. The one with the apple quickly falls into step next to Katya, and I can see she has played her part well. His entire countenance screams desire.

I, however, walk awkwardly behind the two with the second German close on my heels. I don't look at him, and he doesn't attempt to engage me. But I know he's studying me closely. I can feel it.

When we reach the safe house, Katya quickly unlocks the door and gestures to the boys to leave their shoes and coats. "I'll make chai," she murmurs. They both nod. Katya looks at me with raised eyebrows. She wants me to make sure they leave behind their guns and get seated comfortably away from the door. A brief moment of panic sets in, and I hope that Oleg is still standing close by.

I turn awkwardly to the men, apple boy looking hungrily after Katya's retreating figure. I point to the hooks on the wall and then to their jackets, drawing my breath in sharply as they remove their thick black belts and lay them on the bench, their guns glinting in the orange light. The tall, handsome man looks over at me and nods his head politely. I find myself momentarily stunned by the kindness that's evident on his face. His eyes are soft, and his mouth relaxed. I don't feel scrutinized or judged or . . . wanted. He quickly removes his coat and lays it on top of his gun, hiding the weapon that clearly frightens me. He then turns to me with a slight smile. I feel my head cock to the side in wonderment. This man is different.

I lead the two men into the sitting room and excuse myself to the kitchen to help Katya lay the cookies on the tray and fill the samovar with bubbling hot black tea. Our hands shake as we set out the cups. We don't speak but simply work as swiftly as possible. Moments later, we return to the room, where the men are in the middle of what seems to be a heated discussion. They stop when we come in and watch as we set the small table before them. Katya continues to flirt mercilessly, and were I not so terrified, I would find it comical.

It's quickly apparent that real discussion is impossible with the language barrier, though I get the impression that the tall man with the deep eyes knows more than he lets on. After five minutes of giggling and grazing hands with apple boy, Katya leaps up from the table.

"Sugar!" she cries out. "I forgot sugar."

She looks at me intently, signaling the time to move. She crosses through the foyer to the kitchen. I know I need to distract the men so that she can move back across the hallway to the front door and grab the necessary items without them seeing her. Dropping my spoon, I knock over my cup of tea causing both men to react and reach to mop up my mess. Hoping that was enough, I jump up and tell the men I'll go look for more napkins. They return blank stares as I rush from the table.

My heart racing, I run into the kitchen and find it empty. Katya has succeeded. She accomplished her mission. I peek out into the foyer and see the tall soldier's jacket, belt and shoes. I need to cross the threshold of the door without the men seeing me. Suddenly I feel sick with fear as I realize I'm trapped alone with two Nazi soldiers.

Leaning over and looking in the sitting room, I see both men still on the floor cleaning up the tea I spilled. In one swift move, I dash to the soldier's clothing and scoop it up. In my panic, I fling open the door with such force that it bangs against the wall. Both men freeze. I have seconds to react.

Dashing into the hallway, I make a split second decision to head to the roof since I'm closer to it. Taking the steps three at a time, I burst out the door and look over the edge at the street below. Not a minute later, I see the entrance door fly open and the first boy, still gripping his apple, tears out into the street. He looks left to right and lets out a growl of frustration, flinging the apple hard against the ground. He's without his shoes, his uniform jacket, and his gun.

Katya won.

Apple boy turns and huffs down the sidewalk, clearly livid and looking for a fight, and I hope that Katya has made it safely to the library. I watch and wait for the other man to come out. Then I hear the step behind me.

I whip around with a gasp. Grabbing the gun, I pull it up in front of me. He's ten feet away, his cropped blond hair glimmering in the setting sun. My hand trembles violently as I feel a surge of terror. I prepare myself to jump over the side of the building. I determine that it would be better to take my own life than let a Nazi have another piece of my soul.

Taking very slow steps toward me, he holds up his hands. "Shh," he whispers. My hand trembles harder, and my throat burns.

"It's okay," he says. I stare at him, stunned and confused. He's speaking my language.

"It's okay. I'm not going to hurt you." He takes another step.

"My name is Hans," he says. His voice is honey. He steps closer.

"I am from Northern Germany, from a town not much different from this one." *Step.*

"I promise I won't hurt you." *Step.*

He's now within arm's reach of me, and he slowly reaches forward. He doesn't grab the gun, as I expect him to. Instead, he touches my hand and electricity courses through my body. I yelp and yank back, the gun dropping to the ground with a thud.

"What is your name?" he asks without reaching for his weapon or for me.

"Luda." My voice sounds distant and small.

"Luda." A thin smile spreads across his lips. "Luda, you're a brave girl," he says. I don't reply. There are so many questions.

"I'm going to leave. You may keep my things," he says, taking a step back. "I'll tell my commander that you tricked me as you also tricked my foolish friend."

I wait in baffled silence. I still feel the warmth of his hand on mine. I watch him continue backing up, his gaze locked on me until he reaches the door to the staircase.

"Wait!" I cry, and I move toward him. I am completely out of control of both my mind and my heart. I simply need to be touched by him one more time. I need to feel the heat of his hand and the power of his goodness. Confusion and fear mix with something I've never known: passion and bravery.

I stop in front of him, my chest heaving, heart pounding. I feel the tightness in my abdomen, and I remember the horror that caused it. But somehow in the presence of this man, I feel different. I'm not afraid of him. I want to know why. I grab his hand and squeeze it tight. He reaches up with the other hand and runs it over the back of my head. Again I feel the electricity of his touch. It's as if the dead parts of my soul awake.

"You are a brave girl," he murmurs. He pulls back and disappears into the dark stairwell, leaving me alive for the first time.

FREDERICK HERRMANN
December 20, 1941

"Herrmann!"

Blobel's raspy voice bursts through the break room where I sit with two of the men from my unit. The smoke from the Russian *makhorka* floats around us like a cloud. I've long since developed a tolerance for the strong tobacco. No longer does it leave me dizzy. Instead, I feel the tension in my lower back release when I draw deeply of the thick smoke.

Nikolaus and Alfonse jump to their feet at the sound of Blobel's voice, dropping their hand-rolled cigarettes on the floor and snuffing out the lit paper quickly. I do the same, but I move at a slower pace. No longer do I feel obligated to please Blobel, and this infuriates him.

Blobel marches forward and stands in front of me. I straighten my shoulders and lift my chin. He is a small man and has to look up to meet my eyes. I stare straight ahead. I know better than to return his gaze.

"I have a special assignment for you, Herrmann," Blobel says with enough glee in his voice to pique my interest. I nod, still looking at the wall above his head.

"You boys can join him," Blobel says to Alfonse and Nikolaus, and my annoyance swells. While I have developed a tolerance for these two men, I don't really desire to spend any more time with them than is absolutely necessary.

Blobel turns to me again, eyes narrowed. "There's a nightclub in the center of town where many of our men gather to relax in the evenings."

I fight to roll my eyes. While I'm intent on the mission of our grand German culture, my fellow soldiers spend their nights drinking and dancing with *Untermensch* in dark, dirty nightclubs.

"The club's only real attractions are the girls who dance there. Those girls are a distraction. I want to shut the club down," Blobel continues. His voice echoes as his words sink in. Alfonse and Nikolaus tense next to me.

Breaking my stance for a fleeting moment, I glance at my commander, curious as to why he feels the need to take this particular course of action. Why are we wasting our time on dancers in a club when there are so many bigger things with which to be concerned?

"I want you to take the van and take care of this little problem for me," Blobel says, his thin lips stretched taut over yellowed teeth.

This method is madness, and I know it. Going to a nightclub to remove a handful of girls is a waste of precious time and resources in our overall mission. Blobel is a coward who finds satisfaction in the kill, but he cannot bring himself to turn on the gas. I know this, but say nothing. I've been taught well.

Blobel narrows his eyes, the smile fading slowly. "You leave immediately."

Snapping his heels together, Blobel raises his arm in a rigid salute. *"Heil Hitler!"* he barks. We return the salute, then watch him leave, his short thin legs carrying him swiftly from the room.

"Why are we doing this?" Alfonse asks when the door closes.

"He's angry that so many spend time in the club," Nikolaus answers, his face flushed with shame. He's spent time at the club.

I let out a frustrated sigh and reach down to pick up my hat. "No, Blobel doesn't care what we do on our free time. All he wants is to make a statement. This is a game to him, and the prize is a pile of bodies."

Alfonse raises his eyebrows as he absorbs the disdain dripping from my tongue. "And what is this to you?" he asks.

Looking him straight in the eye, I answer. "This is the mission of my life."

"Killing dancers?" Nikolaus asks.

I shake my head hard, furious at his ignorance. "No. Making Germany all powerful and great. This is my mission, and I'll follow orders, no matter how pointless, because that's what I was trained to do. Greatness begins with the ability to obey a command."

"Interesting," Alfonse answers. "I thought greatness began with the ability to have an original idea and the courage to mobilize others to join you in accomplishing your vision."

"Greatness," I spit back, "is the ability to do both. Greatness is the willingness to be both a leader *and* a follower. Greatness is knowing your place and taking it seriously." I glare at Alfonse and wait for his reply.

"Let's go." Turning on my heel, I march toward the door. My hands shake with anger at Alfonse's obvious jab. He questions my potential, and this cannot be so. I need him to believe me destined for greatness because if I can't convince him, how will I ever convince my father?

We arrive at the nightclub forty-five minutes later. I pull the van up behind the large stone building and cut the engine. Alfonse and Nikolaus sit quietly next to me. I sense their discomfort. It's easy to detach yourself from the killing when it's from afar, but we're preparing to look into the eyes of our victims. Even I swallow a growing sense of dread.

"What's the plan?" Nikolaus asks.

"We go in the back entrance and find the club owner," I answer. "We'll tell him to round the girls up and bring them to the dressing room."

"What then?" Alfonse asks.

"We finish the job," I answer.

"That's it?" Alfonse asks. He laughs mockingly. "We tell a group of girls to come to the dressing room and then ask them to quietly and calmly follow us to a van where we'll gas them? That's going to work?"

I sigh impatiently the way my father used to do to me when he found my stupidity annoying and ignorant.

"No, stupid," I answer. "I have more of a plan than that."

"Then tell us, Frederick!" Nikolaus throws his hands up in the air, clearly fed up with the whole process.

"We're going to tell the girls they're being transported to a local spa as thanks for entertaining our soldiers. We'll ask them to remove their clothing and leave it behind so that we don't have to deal with that task when it's all over. We'll put them in the van and start the engine. Then I will turn on the gas."

I glare at Alfonse. "Is that enough information for you?"

He nods. The little respect that I had built up for these two men over the last month has vanished. I want to finish the job and be rid of their company. It's clear to me that no one has been groomed for this war as I have.

I push open the van door and slide to the ground. The evening air is cold, and a tuft of frozen air floats from my mouth. I watch my breath momentarily cloud the building in front of me. I am calm and steady. Though I don't understand or agree with Blobel's order, I prepare to follow it wholeheartedly. It's what Father would do.

It's what I will do.

We enter the dimly lit hallway of the back building and make our way toward the pulsating music out front. Just before we reach the club doors, we pass the nightclub manager's office. A small, thin, sniveling man sits behind a desk, his head down in his arms, sound asleep.

I stride swiftly into the room. "Wake up," I bark, kicking the table. He jumps and throws his head back, cracking it on his rickety wooden chair.

I wait a moment for his eyes to focus and the shock of seeing three armed Nazis standing in his office to wear off.

"Where are the girls?" I ask. My Russian is still thickly accented, but I'm gleaning the nuances of this vile language a bit more each day.

"G–Gir–" He stammers nervously. Reaching to his right, he grabs a small pair of spectacles and puts them on with shaking hands. I'm momentarily amused at this greasy little man. I wonder how he managed to acquire the job of manager.

"Where. Are. The. Girls," I repeat.

"They're finishing the show," he says, his voice high and whiny.

"When will they be done?"

Pulling a small watch out of his pocket, he glances at it, then at me. "They're set to finish this show at eight thirty. The next one begins at ten thirty."

I sneer in disgust. "When this show is finished, gather all the girls and bring them to the dressing room." I nod toward Alfonse and Nikolaus. "We'll be waiting."

He nods, eyes large and round behind the glasses on his face. His nose is thin and pointed, and his dark black hair sticks to his forehead. A small bead of sweat appears on his temple. I feel powerful when I look at him.

Forty-five minutes later, Alfonse, Nikolaus, and I stand at attention as the waitresses and dancers file into the nightclub dressing room. They are young, these girls. Most look to be between the ages of sixteen and twenty-one.

Huddling together, the girls grip hands and look at me, their doe eyes filled with terror. I open my mouth to speak and am rendered momentarily mute when I notice a taller girl standing in the back toward the wall. Her bright red hair is wavy and hangs soft over her shoulders. Her eyes are bright and her skin a delicate porcelain.

She looks exactly like my sister.

I pull my eyes away from her and focus on the rest. They're dressed in thin, short gowns that leave little to the imagination and much to delight desirous young men. They look innocent and frightened, but instead of feeling powerful, I find that my bravado has waned.

"We're here," I begin, and my voice cracks. I clear my throat as my face grows hot. I can see the girls shift, some with amused looks on their faces. I straighten my shoulders and envision the face of my father staring at me with disapproval. I start again.

"We are here to reward you for taking good care of our comrades in this difficult time," I say, my voice strong and disconnected. I won't look at the redhead again.

"You'll be transported tonight to a local spa, where you are to be treated to a relaxing sauna."

Nervous whispers break out among the girls, and a few begin to cry softly. I continue.

"I need all of you to remove your clothing and leave it here. You won't need it at the sauna. We'll leave shortly, so please hurry." My words are sharp and clipped. The girls immediately fall into hysterics.

The redhead grabs the door handle and yanks it open, her eyes wild with fear.

"Close the door!" I yell. Instinctively, I raise my gun. The girls scream, ducking their heads. The redhead freezes and looks directly at me. She slowly closes the door, two large tears escaping her bright blue eyes and rolling down her cheeks.

With my gun held high, I look at the rest of the group. "Remove your clothing now!" I command. As if weighted down, the girls undress, humiliated and terrified. I don't look at Alfonse or Nikolaus to see their reactions. I don't want to see the look of hunger on their faces. Refusing to be taken in by the beauty of this group, I see nothing but a mission before me.

I falter when the redhead stands up, and for a brief moment I cannot breathe. She has tied her hair up in a delicate yellow scarf. She stands tall and regal, her shoulders back. She is beautiful. She, like the others, has left on her undergarments in what appears to be a vain attempt at maintaining some dignity. I decide to allow it as my mind is cloudy and sluggish at the sight of her.

Alfonse leans over and breaks my momentary lapse in judgment. "They're all undressed, Frederick," he whispers.

I nod, and pull my eyes away from her. Taking another deep breath, I push forward.

"Follow us outside where a van waits to take you to the spa," I say with firm authority. "My comrades will gather your clothing for you, and we'll have it ready when you're finished in the sauna."

As I push through the group, I feel their thin, shivering bodies brush against me and I fight a tremble that runs up my spine. I'm in charge. I have the power. I can't become distracted. I reach the door quickly and pull it open, then step into the dark, seedy hall. The manager waits, wringing his thin hands nervously. He looks past me at his group of employees and his eyes grow wide.

"Wh–Wh–Wh–" he stammers. I roll my eyes, pushing past him. The girls follow me, muted cries filling the narrow hallway.

"Where are you taking them?" His voice pierces the darkness, and I stop short. The manager has grabbed the hand of one of the girls, a young one with dark hair, dark eyes, and bright red lips. She shakes violently next to him, her small frame racked with fear.

"To the spa," I answer as calmly as I can.

"Why are they undressed?" he asks in astonishment.

"To avoid the hassle," I answer back. I have no patience for this man, and I turn on my heel. "Follow me now!" I bark. *"Schnell!"*

"Nyet!"

I halt at the sound of his rebellion. Turning slowly, I'm met with silence and nothing but his determined stare.

"What did you say?" I ask. My voice is thin, my words clipped.

"I . . . I . . ." His voice falters. He looks at the girl to his right, then turns back to me. "I said no," he answers, this time with less force behind his words.

It happens fast, and in the split second that I raise my gun and pull the trigger, I know I've gone from soldier to cold-hearted killer.

Would that make Father proud?

He falls to the floor, a pool of blood immediately forming under his head. His arm juts up at an awkward angle as the young girl, now screaming, still grips it tightly. The noise in the hall is deafening, and we need to act fast.

"Get them to the van," I yell to Alfonse and Nikolaus. Like two sheep dogs, they begin to herd the girls forward. I push out into the cold and run to the waiting van, opening the heavy door. The girls spill out into the dark alley sobbing and screaming. In the wide, open spaces, they begin to spread, and I fear they'll try to escape so I fire one single warning shot into the stars.

The group jumps and quiets. They all look at me now. I see the red-head, her eyes dry and staring up at me with such hatred and venom that I'm stunned. That's the same look my sister gave our father the day she left home. She hated him the way this girl hates me, and my heart twists at the memory.

"Get in the van," I rasp. It's time to end this. I want to be done with this mission. I want to be done.

One by one, the girls climb into the van, and I count as they do. There are twenty-eight girls, all beautiful, all young, all about to die.

Once crammed inside the small space, they huddle close, gripping one another with racking sobs. Many of them have their hair tied up in color-ful headscarves, customary for visiting a spa. But their growing hysteria tells me they know that I'm not taking them to the sauna.

I swing the door shut with a clang and hear muffled screams inside as everything goes black in the truck. A wave of nausea hits me, and I feel my knees buckle. Taking long, deep breaths I let the cold night pierce my lungs. I drink the air as though it will make me free.

"Frederick . . ." Alfonse pierces my anxiety, stepping up next to me. I didn't realize I had bent over, my head now parallel to the ground. I still hear them screaming. I cannot tell if it's real or perhaps their screams are trapped inside me, reverberating off the walls of my conscience.

Standing up and shaking off the dizziness, I suck in one more deep breath, then turn to face Alfonse and Nikolaus, who stare at me in wonder. They don't know who I am.

I don't know who I am.

Striding to the front of the van, I turn the key and listen to the engine sputter briefly before roaring to life. Without allowing myself to think about the ramifications of my next step, I reach for the dials to my right and I hear the hiss of gas as it pours into the back of the airtight compartment.

Then I close my eyes and try to block out the sounds. Knocking. Screaming. The van rocks side to side as panic ensues. Twenty-eight bodies try to flee, but not for long. Oxygen grows sparse. Slowly the movement subsides.

Then the screams stop altogether.

I leave the gas on and step out of the van to find Alfonse and Nikolaus smoking next to a tree several meters away. The cowards escaped the worst of this awful moment. They won't be haunted by the sounds like I will. Looking up at the sky I'm struck by the contrast. It's a clear, beautiful night, and stars blanket the blue-black canvas above. The moon hangs high, full and round, casting a perfect white glow on the earth below.

Yet somehow I feel that the moon sends a stream of light down upon me alone. I'm exposed under the spotlight of the orb, and my heart quickens to think of all that's changed.

I am not the man I thought I would be. This isn't the mission I thought I would accomplish. In this still moment, I miss my sister. I shake my head, trying to shake the memory free.

Stepping into the van, I turn the dial, cutting off the gas that has snuffed out life. I turn the valve that opens up the back vents, releasing the poison into the night air. Would it also snuff out the watchful eye of the moon?

When it's all done, I climb slowly out of the van and look in the direction of my comrades. "Alfonse! Nikolaus!" I bark, marveling at the strength in my voice. It belies the fear in my heart.

"Come empty the van. Quickly." Turning, I look at the road that leads us away from the horror of this dark alley. "I want to leave this place," I whisper.

Alfonse and Nikolaus act fast. Covering their noses and mouths with cloth, they pull open the door, coughing and sputtering as bodies tumble out. They pull each body out until the girls lie in a heap, their faces contorted and grotesque. I walk slowly around to face the consequence of my orders.

Alfonse pulls out the last body and lays her on top of the pile. Her red hair has escaped the scarf on her head in long, curly tendrils. She's the only one who looks peaceful. Her mouth is turned up and her eyes closed. Her porcelain skin looks soft and still bears the pink of a life that once was. She looks as though she's sleeping.

She had a name. They all did. But now they are no more. I followed my orders. I exerted my power.

Power.

LUDA MICHAELEVNA
January 10, 1942

It has been weeks since he touched me, weeks since the electricity of his hand crashed through my exterior and left me seeing color for the first time.

It has been too many weeks since I've seen him.

Every time I go out, I look. I scan each German who passes. I do this discreetly, because when a Nazi soldier sees a young girl looking at him, his first reaction is to return the stare with a look that terrifies me.

I grab my abdomen, which now swells noticeably. I think that Alexei, Katya, and Oleg know. They must, yet no one's said anything. Not even Baba Mysa speaks of the life I carry, though every once in a while I notice that she's once again moved the buttons of my skirts out just a bit further. They'll no longer stretch and the time is growing near when I won't be able to hide it at all.

It's an odd thing to be harboring life, particularly a life that began with such darkness. But no matter how hard I try, I cannot muster hatred for the child inside me. I want to hate this baby, but I can't.

"I need you," I whisper, my lips not even moving. I breathe the words out and then pull them back in. I need something to love. I need to be a mother so that, somehow, I can find my own mother again.

I cannot forget the last words my father said to me that dark day. I hear them echo day and night like a drum. *"Whore. Like your mother. Whore. Like your mother. Whore."*

What did he mean? There's no one who can explain to me anything about my mother, and no matter how hard I try, I cannot conjure up the one serene image I held of her. This scares me.

"Luda?"

I jump at the sound of my name. The dark of this night has wrapped me in a familiar solitude, and the interruption shatters my thoughts. Sleep is still difficult. If I fall too deep into my slumber, the haunting whispers chase me until I awake in shrieking terror. So I fight the darkness as long as I possibly can.

Katya sits up on her pad on the floor, her legs tucked up underneath her long nightgown and her golden hair spilling over her shoulders. She's a picture of youthful beauty—so different from me, a girl aged by the cruelties and heartache of life.

"Da?" I answer.

"Are you . . ." Katya hesitates, and my heart stops. I push up on my elbow and turn to face her, the moonlight streaming in through the window casting a soft glow on the room. We stare into each other's eyes, and I feel her question. I don't say a word as I nod my head slowly.

Katya's eyes widen. She knew, but she hoped she was wrong. I sense it, and I have the distinct feeling that the space between us in the room will expand and separate even more as time moves forward.

Katya.

My only friend and the closest thing to a sister I know. *The tragedy of that awful day in the church continues to destroy.*

"Are you scared?" she whispers, her eyes resting on my stomach.

I nod again, unable to speak over the lump that has grown in my throat.

"Are you going to . . . uh . . . let the baby . . . live?" Katya drops her eyes to the floor as she asks this last question.

Finding my voice, I sift through the shock to answer. "Yes. Of course."

"I'm sorry. I didn't mean to say—"

Katya sighs and picks at the fraying lace on the bottom of her gown. "It's just that . . . Luda, you're carrying a *Nazi*. Doesn't that scare you? Don't you want to flee as far away as possible from that awful day and what they did to you?"

"No, Katya," I answer with surprising firmness. Lying back down, I stare at the ceiling, tears pricking the corners of my eyes. "This child is all I have."

I hear Katya lie down, and for a long while, we're both quiet. Finally she speaks. "You have me, Luda. And . . . you have Oleg. He could make you happy." Katya turns to face the wall, and in a few short moments, I hear her even breathing as sleep overtakes her.

I sigh and close my eyes. "I would destroy Oleg," I whisper. A few minutes later I feel my body relax and drift. Sleep comes, but rest—I don't even know if it's possible.

When the early morning sunlight pierces through the room, I open my eyes and stretch wholly and fully. The skin around my abdomen pulls and tightens in a way that is becoming increasingly uncomfortable. I pull my arms down and rub my hands slowly over the swell. Turning to look at Katya, I find her bed empty, the small blanket pulled back neatly and her nightgown folded delicately at the end.

I sit up and dress quickly, the chill of the winter air causing a shiver to run from the top of my spine down to my toes. I can see my breath in small tufts as I move through the motions of dressing in the cold. The house is quiet and hushed, the lack of movement leaving me uneasy. Once dressed, I step softly into the main room and wait for a brief moment. Muted talking drifts from the kitchen. I tiptoe forward.

". . . Carrying a Nazi."

Katya's hiss floats through the air and settles in my heart. I push her words around, trying to make sense of what I'm hearing.

"Katya, that's enough," Baba Mysa commands.

"But Baba—" Katya protests.

"*Nyet*. I won't have any more mention of Luda carrying a Nazi. Luda is carrying a child—*her* child. You need to understand that."

Silence follows. I want to return to my room, to crawl back beneath the safety of the wool blanket, but my feet are frozen. I'm compelled to listen to the only family I know decide whether or not to accept or shun me.

I hear Alexei clear his throat. "Katya, you must remember that Luda didn't ask to be placed in this situation. She's frightened, and she needs to know that she is safe here."

Katya sniffs. She's crying now, soft sobs echoing out into the narrow hallway.

"But Papa," she whispers. "It's just so terrible. I don't know how she can want this baby. I *don't* understand. I know you say I should, but why would I understand something like this?"

A chair scrapes across the floor. Katya runs around the corner and straight into me. She pulls back and looks into my eyes, her cheeks streaked with tears. We don't speak, but I hear her anyway.

Shame. Anger. Confusion.

Katya shakes her head and pushes past me, rushing to the room and slamming the door. I'm left alone, my hand subconsciously gripping my midsection, a longing to protect already strong and necessary.

Oleg steps around the corner, and I face him. Looking into his eyes is terrifying. I cannot face the love there—the ocean of concern that surges for me. The truth is when I look at Oleg I can see only a glimmer of *him*; the German man who electrified my soul and made me believe in goodness once again.

"Luda," Oleg begins. His faces flushes. I knew this would happen. I knew when they found out everything would change. I look down at the ground, and my eyes fill with tears. Oleg loves me. I know that he does. And I love him, too. But I love him as I imagine one must love a brother. I feel devoted to him and grateful for his protection. But I'm not in love with him.

"Luda, it's going to be okay. Katya will come around. She'll learn to accept and understand what's happening."

He reaches forward and grabs my hands, his warm palms engulfing mine. "Luda," he says again. His voice is sweet and gentle. "Please look at me." Slowly I pull my eyes up to his.

"I'll take care of you," he says quietly. "I'll keep you safe, and I will love you, and—"

"Oleg, no," I interrupt, but he shakes his head.

"Please let me finish," he pleads. I close my mouth and swallow hard against the bile building in my throat. This declaration could be the thing that destroys us all. I know it, but I cannot stop it.

"Luda, I love you," Oleg says, this time looking at me with such earnest desire that I feel momentarily swayed. "And I will learn to love this child. I'll help you, Luda. I will."

I try to pull my hands away, but he grasps tight. "Oleg, please," I beg. "Please don't." I can't give him a reason why I won't be able to return his love. I can't tell him that I'm enamored with another man—someone who wears the enemy's uniform. I can't reveal that I'm terrified of the prospect of love because it's only ever been painful. I can't tell him any of this, but I see the hurt, and I feel his pain.

Oleg drops my hands, his brow furrowed. He nods his head.

"I'm sorry," I say, my whispered words quavering. I'm trembling, and I want nothing more than to be held . . . but I don't want to be held by him.

"I'm sorry, too," Oleg says. He moves past me—a defeated shadow.

I take a few deeps breaths and wipe my eyes. Stepping forward, I round into the kitchen where Baba Mysa and Alexei sit, quietly drinking their morning chai. I sit down and look directly at Alexei.

"I'm sorry," I begin. My voice cracks again, my emotions betraying me. "I'll leave soon."

Alexei leans forward and looks back at me, a slight smile pushing his mouth upward. "You'll leave?" he asks. "Where will you go?"

I shrug. "I don't know. Perhaps I should go back to my father. I managed to survive for sixteen years with him. I can do it again." But in my heart I know I'm wrong. If I go back to my father, I will die.

"And *why* would you leave?" Alexei asks, still looking more amused than concerned.

"I'm ruining everything," I answer. "I'm ruining your relationship with Katya. I've disappointed Oleg. I'm pregnant with a German child that I love and want to keep." My voice breaks, and I lean forward, burying my face in my hands. Sobs rack my shoulders. Every pent-up emotion is released, and I cry harder than I've ever cried.

"I'm sorry," I sob as warm arms pull me in tight and strong. Baba Mysa has wrapped herself around me, and she whispers in my ear. "*Oh dorogaya. Maya dorogaya. Ya tebya lyublyu. Oh tak ya tebya lyublyu. Maya dorogaya.*"

With each whisper of love, each declaration of darling and stroke of the hair, my tears subside until I am spent. I rest on her shoulder and stare at the cracked table. I cannot look at Alexei.

"I wish I had known her," I whisper, calm now. "I just wish I had known her."

"Who, my dear?" Alexei asks gently.

"My mother."

The words skip through the kitchen. I feel Alexei shift in his seat. "Do you know anything about her?" he asks.

"No. I don't know what she looked like. I don't know if her voice was deep or high, if her words were spoken like a smile, or if she sang to me. I know nothing. My father never spoke of her until—"

I stop. Can I share it? Can I reveal the terrible secret I've held since that day, the words that shattered the only image I had of her?

"Until when?" Baba Mysa asks gently.

I look first at her, then at Alexei. I sigh and pull myself up straight. "Until that day in the church. As he left, my father looked back and told me I'm a whore. Like my mother."

My eyes burn fresh again, and my shoulders slump. "I don't know what he meant because I don't know who she was."

I lean forward and place my forehead on the cool table. "I hate my father," I whisper. "I hate him. I hate what he did to me. I hate that he abandoned me. I hate that he destroyed my image of her." My voice raises as all the anger and hatred bubble out. "I hate him. I hate . . . I hate . . . I *hate* . . ."

"Luda, stop." I freeze, heart beating wildly, and look at Alexei, surprised by the sharp tone of his voice. "Be still," he commands, softer this time.

I pull myself up straight and look first at him, then at Baba Mysa, who stares at her son intently. He glances at his mother as she gives a slight nod. Alexei sighs and pinches the bridge of his nose.

"I think it's time you learned the truth."

"Th–the truth?" I ask. "The truth about what?"

Alexei drops his hands and runs his finger slowly across the crack in the table. His eyes fill with tears, and I feel the vein in my forehead pound with each beat of my heart.

"Do you know something about my mother?" I whisper.

Alexei looks at me, his eyes deep and dark and filled with pain. "Yes," he says softly. "I knew your mother. I knew her well."

Baba Mysa tightens her grasp on my shoulders and pulls me closer. It takes a moment for this information to sink into my heart. He knew my mother. *Alexei knew my mother.* He knew her well?

"What do you mean?" I ask.

Taking a deep breath, Alexei continues. "I loved your mother." As he says this, his voice cracks, and I feel the air in the room shift. I draw in a sharp breath.

"You-you loved her? When? How? I don't understand."

I can't comprehend the information just given to me, and I find myself impatient with Alexei. I need him to share more quickly, and I pull away from Baba Mysa in frustration. "What do you mean, Alexei Yurevich?" I demand. "How did you know my mother?"

"Your mother and I were schoolmates in college. We both attended the Polytechnical Institute. Your mother was beautiful, Luda. You look so much like she did. She was kind and gentle, and her laugh was magical, like a thousand bells. I fell in love with her the moment I saw her."

A thousand bells.

Alexei looks out the window, and for a moment I see him leave us. He's in another time with a different memory. He's with my mother, and I feel a surge of anger overtake me. I should be with my mother.

"Please, Alexei," I say, my voice sharp. "Please tell me more. Tell me everything. I need to know."

Baba Mysa reaches across the table and touches her son's hand. "*Sinok,* you need to keep going," she says. "You can't stop."

Looking at Baba Mysa, my eyes grow wide. "You knew her, too," I say breathlessly. "You knew my mother, and you never said anything to me." Baba Mysa meets my gaze, her eyes swimming with sorrow.

"The time wasn't right, *dorogaya,*" she says gently. "And it wasn't my story to tell." She shifts her gaze back to Alexei, who now looks at me with deep sorrow.

"Your mother and I had an instant and deep connection and quickly became inseparable," Alexei says, his eyes looking deep into mine. "You have her eyes. Deep and inquisitive, brown flecked with green. Every time I look at you, I see her."

My eyes well with tears as I wait for him to share more. Like a drink on a hot day, I soak in each word.

"Our second year at the institute, your mother and I began to talk of marriage. We spent every waking moment together, so much so that she began to struggle with her studies and her father grew angry. He forbade her to see me, insisting that he wouldn't raise a daughter who was ignorant and stupid. For a while, we tried to meet secretly at night, but when her father caught her sneaking out he grew so angry that he hit her. I vowed to never put her in harm's way like that again."

Alexei stops and takes a breath. He glances at his mother, and she smiles gently. "Alexei was very much in love with your mother, Luda," she says, her eyes locked on Alexei's. Then she shifts her gaze to me. "We loved her, too. She was good and beautiful and sweet. But we urged our son away from the relationship, believing it to be dangerous for her and for him."

I sit back slowly in my chair, my head spinning with these new details. "What happened next?" I ask. I feel like I've tapped into the vault of my past, and I need more.

"Time passed, and I didn't see your mother except in passing at school. She wouldn't look at me, and she never initiated contact. I didn't want to make life more difficult, so I quit pursuing her. But I could not stop looking. Every time she passed me in the halls or on the street, I had to stare. She was magnetic.

"After about eight months, I noticed your mama walking on the arm of another man, and my heart was broken. I didn't think I could possibly continue my own schooling when I realized that she had moved on from our relationship. Your mother had met your father."

Alexei pauses before continuing. "Just before we graduated school, the two of them were married."

"But why?" I ask. "Why him?"

"I spent a year mourning the relationship, sure I would never love again," Alexei says, continuing to talk as though he hadn't heard me. "Then one day I ran into her in the market, and I just needed to speak to her. I needed to hear the sound of her voice once more. I needed closure.

"Your mother motioned slowly for me to follow her into the alley behind the store, and for the first time in two years we spoke again."

"What did she say?" I interrupt, my heart racing.

"She told me she still loved me and that she always would. Her father had forced her to marry Boris as a means to keep her from me. If you can believe me, your father was once a good man. He was misguided and pompous, but he did love your mother. She just didn't love him in return." Alexei drops his eyes. "She loved me," he says quietly. He looks up, his eyes full of tears, and gives a gentle smile. "She kissed me good-bye that day, and we wouldn't speak again for a long time."

"So, what happened next?" I ask.

"I met my Ekaterina several months later. I never thought I'd love again after your mother, but I did love my wife. Soon after, she and I were expecting our first child. I heard news of your mother every once in a while. She taught in the local school, and on occasion I'd see her walking along the street, beautiful and serene. I still loved her, but I was content and happy with my wife."

"What happened to your wife, Alexei?" I ask, for the first time realizing that I don't know anything about Katya's mother.

"She died the day after Katya was born," Alexei answers softly. "There were complications. You and Katya are similar in many ways, you know," he says with a soft smile. "I hope, for your sakes, you can repair your relationship because you will need one another."

"Did you know my mother had a child at the same time as Katya?" I ask. Alexei nods.

"I had heard that she had a baby girl a couple of months before our daughter was born. I was happy for her. I knew she would be an excellent mother. Your mother had so much love to give."

"But . . ." The room spins as I try to process all this information. "What about my father? How did he treat her?" I can't fathom that Alexei, the man I had spent so much time wishing was my father, had once been in love with my mother.

Alexei sighs and pinches the top of his nose again. "Luda, I wish I could tell you more about their relationship, but I simply don't know. From what I heard at the time and noticed, your father treated her well, but I think he knew. Your father knew her heart belonged to me long before he came along."

"How did she die?" I ask. This is the question I dread. I fear knowing details of my mother's passing, yet I feel I must learn what happened in order to ever be able to function as a mother myself.

"She got sick," Alexei answered, his eyes welling up with tears. "She came to see me one day when you were about eighteen months old. You were a beautiful baby with big brown eyes and thin, wispy brown hair. Your mother clung to you that day." He stopped, voice breaking. "It was like she thought she could live longer off of your youth and innocence."

Tears prick the corners of my eyes as I imagine my mother trying to draw life from me to her.

"Your mama told me that she had just visited the doctor and the prognosis wasn't good. There was something inside her stomach that was killing her."

I let the hot tears drip onto my cheeks. The image of my mother clinging to me rips through my heart white hot.

"She asked me to make sure you were taken care of," Alexei says softly, turning to look out the window.

"Why you? What was wrong with my father?"

Alexei sighs again. "She told me your father had grown bitter and jealous. He knew of her love for me and—Luda, your father had already been drinking for some time. Your mama told me he started drinking shortly after you were born."

Sitting back, I stare down at the bulge in my abdomen. I was the demon my father had been trying to escape. I was the one who sent him into the hell of his vodka.

"Your mother died six months later." Alexei bends his head forward, a soft sob escaping from his throat. I sit numbly for a moment before asking the other question pressing on my heart.

"Where were my grandparents?" I ask. "Why was no one there to fill in the holes for me? Why weren't you there?" I look at the top of Alexei's head, imploring him to answer the questions that have plagued me my entire life.

"Your mother's parents died before you were born. It was very difficult for her. I think that's why she finally felt the freedom to visit me again," Alexei answers, sitting up and wiping his eyes slowly. "She was free from the fear of shaming her father."

"And my father's parents?"

"I don't know much of them," Alexei says. "I don't know that they were ever very involved. I think when your mother died, Boris pushed everyone away."

"And you?" I ask. "Why didn't you look after me? Why didn't you protect me from him?"

Alexei looks deep into my eyes, an ocean of grief and sorrow swimming in the abyss between us. "Your father hated me, Luda. In your mother's final days, as she slipped in and out of consciousness, she asked for me, and it infuriated your father. He came to me the night she died and told me that if I ever came near you he would kill you. I couldn't take the risk, so I stayed far away."

"But you made sure Katya and I became friends," I say softly, and Alexei nods.

"Yes. She was my connection to you."

Leaning back, I turn my face up to the ceiling and take in a long, deep breath. The pieces all begin to fall into place. "So my mother wasn't a whore," I say, less to him and more to myself. Every single image of my mother that I'd conjured up as a youth comes flooding back. Her laugh that sounded like a thousand bells. The sound of her voice singing softly over me. The way her hair swung loosely over her shoulders. Could these be real memories? Could it be that the very few moments I had with my mother had been stored inside of me all along?

"I'm sorry, Luda," Alexei says quietly, breaking the silence. "I'm so sorry I wasn't there. I'm sorry that I failed you—and your mother."

I nod, then ask one last question that has been pressing against my heart like a vice. "What is my mother's name?"

Alexei's eyes widen. "He never even spoke her name?" he whispers.

I shake my head no. "He only spoke of her when he was drunk, and he always referred to her as 'My darling.' I've never heard my mother's name."

"Marianna," Alexei said, and a gentle smile spreads across his face. "Your mother's name is Marianna."

I nod, my eyes filling up with tears. "Thank you," I whisper. "Thank you for giving my mother back to me."

Alexei reaches across the table and grasps my hand. "You're just like your mother, Luda."

I nod slowly and allow a smile to form. The first genuine smile I've given in months. I look at my stomach and breathe in deep.

For the first time in all my life, I feel peace.

Like your mother.

FREDERICK HERRMANN
January 18, 1942

I can't get her face out of my head. Every time I close my eyes, I see her red hair and wide, blue eyes. She tumbles out of the gas van over and over in my dreams, a loop of guilt and terror. And each time I look down at her grotesque death-face it morphs and changes into that of my sister.

This morning, like every morning, I dress slowly, my muscles stiff and aching from a long night. I sit down hard on my cot and think of Talia, my wayward sister who left home long ago in protest of Father's dealings. As a child, she had been my dearest friend and most faithful protector. As an adult, she betrayed our father and our country and became a hated enemy. The brazen redhead awakened the memories, and I'm stuck here now, weak, wishing my sister were near.

I long to be a boy once more with my fingers in the dark earth, Talia standing nearby humming and dancing to the beat inside her heart. When we were young, my sister was full of whimsy and laughter. She could look once at Father and the rough exterior of his eyes would ripple and fade, leaving twinkles and grins meant only for her. With me he was always firm, always strong. But with Talia he spoke gently and tenderly. At any moment of the day, Talia could climb into his lap and command his full attention, where I had to stay clear of him to remain in his favor.

Father reserved all of his gentleness and love for Talia. This is how I know he broke when she left.

Leaning back, I replay the last moment I saw her. It was nearly four

years ago, just as the plans and secret whispers were beginning to inten-
sify. Talia, then nineteen years old, had been a student at the local university for several months, and with each passing day, she seemed to grow
more independent and brazen in her thinking. She and Father began to
argue about everything, most of all politics. Talia was an idealist, entirely
shocked by our father's concrete and steady beliefs. She had lived most of
her life under the assumption that Father was a progressive, when in fact
he was always quite conservative in his nationalism.

I close my eyes and remember that terrible day when everything
changed. I hear Talia's voice, shrill and frantic as she stormed into the
house, a crumpled piece of paper clutched tight in her fist. *"Papa!"* she
yelled, and my heart goes cold even now.

"Papa!" she cried out again, slamming the door shut behind her. I
stepped out of my room, where I had been reading, to see her standing
at the bottom of the stairs. Her chest heaved with fury, and she turned
toward me, eyes flashing beneath her long, wavy red hair.

"Did you know about this?" she asked, shaking her fist at me.

"What?" I replied, blinking. I had never seen my sister express such
passionate emotion.

"This!" She threw the paper at my chest. I caught it, straightening it
between my hands to read the words. It was a torn-out notice with bold
words at the top:

TOP-SECRET PLANS REVEALED OF GERMAN INVASION

"What is this?" I whispered, handing it back to her with shaking
hands.

"These were being passed around the university today," Talia responded
with gritted teeth. "The article explains how Adolf Hitler, our father's
friend, is mobilizing a plan to attack Poland and the Soviet Union. Papa
has to be a part of this, and I want to know why."

I was shocked at Talia's anger. I couldn't believe she found this so surprising. I had known of these plans and talks for many years. But then, I
had always been good at making myself invisible. I knew much more than
most people realized.

"Papa!" Talia yelled again, her eyes wild. Moments later our father stepped out of his study, smelling of tobacco and bourbon.

"My Talia," he slurred, stumbling toward her. Talia shrunk back from his touch and held out the notice.

"You knew, didn't you?" she asked, her voice dripping with scorn and anger. "You're part of this plan."

Father narrowed his eyes. "These are not things you need to be concerned with, Talia," he said. As he spoke, Mother appeared in the doorway behind him. I could see her silent plea with Talia to not push him. I suspect I had the same look in my own eyes.

"It does concern me, Papa. It concerns all of us. What kind of country do we live in that allows these actions to be taken? What kind of people are we that we're willing to lie, sign false treaties and pacts, place our entire future in the hands of an insane man who cheated his way into power—"

"*Stop right there!*" I jumped at my father's roar and took a few steps back into the shadow of the doorway. It was always safer in the shadows.

"You don't know anything, Talia," Father said, his words clipped. "You don't need to speak about things you don't understand."

"I *do* understand, Papa," Talia yelled. "I understand that my father has paired himself with a lunatic who wants to invade other countries for no reason at all. It's selfish and arrogant and it's wrong, and I can't believe you would be a part of it. I'm so disappointed, Papa."

That's when he hit her. Talia stumbled back and landed in a heap on the floor. Mama gasped and took a step forward.

"Stay out of it, Hilda!" Father bellowed. He grabbed Talia under the arm, jerking her to her feet. I heard Mama crying and begging Father to let her go. I peeked around the corner to see Father lean in close to Talia, who stood shaking, her nose bleeding profusely from the force of his blow.

"If you don't want to have anything to do with our country becoming the greatest nation in the world, then you can leave. Take nothing with you, and don't plan on returning. Ever."

Talia looked at our father with a mixture of malice and betrayal. She threw her head back, then flung it forward again, spitting into Father's eyes. Stunned, he let go of her, and she fell back. Steadying herself, Talia straightened up and looked him in the eye.

"Good-bye," she said softly. She turned and slowly walked out. Mama reached out to her as she passed only to have her hand slapped away by Father.

"She's a traitor," he hissed, and I saw Talia's shoulders slump. She opened the door and shut it calmly behind her.

That was the last time I saw Talia. She didn't look back as she left, and in that moment I felt abandoned. She was supposed to be on my side— on the right side. She left and never looked back. I want to hate her for it, but today I simply feel sad and alone. I miss my sister. I wonder what's become of her.

Pulling myself from the window of the past, I sit up and rub my eyes, taking in a long, deep breath. I have spent most of my life alone with my thoughts. Growing up as the only son of Tomas Herrmann meant that I had to be perfect. Especially after Talia left, Father poured more energy than ever into making sure that I didn't become a disappointment. Now here I am, alone and still under his watchful eye though we are hundreds of miles apart. I'm certain that Blobel gives Father frequent reports of how I manage myself, and despite the distance, I know that I cannot escape my father's disapproving glare.

If Blobel gets any sense that I feel guilt or shame for my actions in the nightclub, he will go straight to Father. I cannot show fear. Following orders is the only path to greatness.

But since that night at the club, when the memory of Talia was opened wide, her words nag against my conscience. I can't escape the accusations of her final day. *"Selfish. Arrogant. Wrong."* Her voice echoes inside me, and I find that, each time I pull the trigger, the sound of her words grows stronger and harder to ignore.

Shaking my head, I stand up and button my uniform. "She was a traitor," I mutter as I slip my arms into my thin wool coat. I need to convince myself of my sister's wrongdoing. "There's only one path to victory, and that is to conquer." I continue mumbling as I make my way to the exit. As I walk, I jump at the shadows. There's a growing certainty that I'm being watched, reports of my every move being sent home to my father.

I pull on my cap and step out of the barracks into the crisp winter air. Taking a deep breath, I try to clear my head of all doubts.

I will be the man he created me to be. No matter the cost. I repeat the mantra Father drilled into me all my life: "Germany is the greatest nation on earth. And I am a son of Germany."

MARIA IVANOVNA
January 25, 1942

We're well into the new year. It's 1942. For seven months, we've lived under the uncertainty of Nazi rule. For seven months, my brave and resilient mama has sold off every possession we do not absolutely need in order to put food in our bellies. For seven months, Sergei has been gone. We've had two letters from him in all that time, and Papa has read them so often that the words fade and smudge from his desperate fingers.

He tries to feel Sergei through the page.

Papa hasn't spoken any more to us about what happened to Polina, but in his sleep, the memory betrays him. He moans and cries fitfully, and we've pieced together enough to know that Polina was caught, but what could have happened to her we just don't know.

I don't think my papa will ever recover from this one event, and the cloud that hangs above our small flat is oppressive and dark. I long for laughter.

Without Sergei here to break the tension, the air in the house feels almost too heavy to breathe, much less have any kind of conversation. So we all simply move around one another in silence, speaking when necessary and never more.

This morning, I follow Anna into the kitchen for our morning chai and find both Mama and Papa sitting silently at the table. Their mugs sit before them, the hot water sending a tendril of steam upward in a silent dance. Between them, lying on the table, is a piece of paper with a picture on the front.

"What is that?" I ask, somewhat hesitantly. I never know when my words are going to break the surface of Papa's emotions.

Mama looks up at us in surprise, as if our presence here is something new and strange. Anna and I stepped forward to read.

The picture shows a young man standing tall, his arm gesturing proudly to a large field of workers. In front of him are many other young boys, all smiling and eager, their hands grasping farmer's tools.

> Let's do agricultural work in Germany. Report immediately to your nearest station. On January 28, the first special train will leave for Germany with hot meals in Kiev, Zdolbunov, and Przemysi. Come all young men and women ages 14–16. Live in beautiful Germany and enjoy your youth.

"What is this?" I ask.

"The Germans have hung these all over town." Mama stares at the wall behind me. "They're looking for workers to go to Germany."

"And we must go?" Anna asks. Silence grips us all as the question hangs in the air.

"No."

Papa's voice cuts through the kitchen with more force than I've heard from him in the months since his soul was taken at Babi Yar.

"You won't go," Papa says looking first at Anna, and then at me. "I won't lose my girls, too."

I see a spark of life ignite behind the dark black of Papa's eyes. Anna and I both nod, and Mama reaches over to grab his hand. For that brief moment, we're united again. We are a team, a family.

Papa holds tight to Mama, and then, as we all watch, the spark dies down. His jaw goes slack, and he drops Mama's hand. Papa retreats once again to the darkness that just won't let him go.

IVAN KYRILOVICH
February 2, 1942

The memory of Babi Yar is chasing me down. It used to only haunt at night, when the fading light pulled out the dark moments of those days so many months ago. But now I'm remembering in the light, and this scares me even more. If the memory catches me in the day, it may never let go.

I've left the flat a few times since that horrible night, going with Tanya to stand in the ration lines, but otherwise my days are spent inside—often alone as Tanya still works, and the girls join her frequently to help. It is they who keep this household afloat, adding to my shame. Today, as most days, I sit once again in the quiet corner of our home, Sergei's letters in my hands. I feel the nightmare coming upon me, and I don't even try to fight it. I just slip in, and let it take over.

For two days after that dreadful day of death, Polina and I walked through the woods looking for shelter, but we came upon nothing. We were still naked, and the frosty September air brought a chill unlike any I'd ever known. I worried constantly about Polina, who walked stoically beside me, her arms crossed over her chest in an attempt to maintain some dignity.

At night I gathered up piles of leaves and had Polina lie beneath them. I lay next to her, as close as I could without touching her, and covered myself. In this way, we survived. We weren't warm, but we didn't freeze.

I heard her wheezing, and knew if I didn't find shelter, food, and clothing soon, she would die. That final night, we reached desperation.

I woke up shivering, and in the pitch black, I instantly felt something wrong. Polina was gone.

Standing up, I waited for my head to stop spinning and willed my eyes to adjust to the total darkness. The gnawing ache in my empty stomach made me light-headed and sluggish. Nothing felt real or concrete—just cold, dark, and hollow.

"Polina?" I whispered to the shadows. *"Polya!"* My voice was urgent, and my heart beat rapidly. I heard the rustle of leaves and prepared to call out her name but never got the chance. Her scream pierced the air, the sound forever burying itself inside my head. It reverberates and echoes even now. When the piercing screech stopped and the terror floated from the ground to the sky, I heard them; boots on the cold, hard ground, shouting in a language that sounds like hate. The Nazis were there.

They'd found her.

Ducking beneath my pile of leaves I tried to gauge their distance. Her scream felt so close, but the sound of their shouting seemed much farther away. I waited, trying to focus. A shadowed forest is a playground for ghosts. The sounds moved before me, then behind, but the source of the fear was elusive and unseen.

She screamed again, the sound bouncing off the trees. I could see her fear, taste and feel it to my core. But I couldn't see *her*. Crouching low, I remained silent as I tried to discern how to rescue the child.

To my right, I heard the scuffling of boots again and Polina's fatigued whimpers. They had her, and they were near. Taking slow, steady steps in the direction of the sound, I forced myself to remain calm. I had the element of surprise, but little else. I just needed to get near. I needed to see.

I heard laughing, and Polina screamed again. She didn't utter words. I don't think she had them. Sometimes horrors are too great to be put into words.

Moving quicker, I came upon three shadows in the dark. Two of them stood over the third, one who looked to be low to the ground. I heard them laugh, watched as one raised a fist and brought it down on her face, and I felt a depth of hatred I've never known. If love gives flight to the soul, hate kills it completely. My soul felt the fire, deep and hot, the flames shooting through my heart straight to the top of my head.

The moonlight burst through the trees in that moment and cast upon Polina, sitting on her knees, her eyes looking straight up into the beam. Her skin was porcelain, the deep, dark circles under her eyes an eerie black. Her dark hair hung in long strands over sharp shoulders. Crouching in the ready position, I prepared to move in when it happened. It was so fast.

The German to her left raised his hand, the butt of his gun bared bright in the white sliver of moonlight. With a crack, his gun met the corner of her temple and the whimpering stopped. Polina crumbled to the ground.

I didn't realize I'd cried out until I saw the Germans whip their heads around. The taller of the two held his finger to his lips and waved the other forward. They slowly made their way straight toward me. Crouching low into the brambles, I bit hard on my knuckle, suppressing the cries and stilling my trembling arms. I bit until I tasted blood, and the urge to race to her side waned. It wouldn't do for me to be caught. I had to live. For my family, I had to live.

I watched through the strands of branches as the soldiers walked slowly past. For an hour, the two men walked circles around me, and in that time, Polina never moved.

Finally, the Nazis grew weary of their search. I watched as they high stepped over the drying leaves toward Polina's crumpled body. The darkness of night had morphed into the pale gray of early morning. Each grabbing one of her arms, they hoisted her upper body up. I winced at the dried stream of blood that ran down her cheek and neck. My eyes burn at the memory, and I feel a pit of regret settle in my stomach. My final promise to Josef had been to take care of his daughter. I failed.

As they pulled her thin body away, Polina's head lulled to the side and for a brief moment her eyes opened.

"Ivan," she gasped, her words a breath. The Germans looked down in surprise, then laughed as her head fell back once more.

After they left, I sat for a long time in stunned silence. Polina was alive.

Alive.

LUDA MICHAELEVNA
February 24, 1942

Everything changed the morning Alexei gave me back my mother. I feel more alive, and I'm more eager than I thought possible to meet my child. Every time I feel the baby move, my heart sings. I've lived my entire life feeling as though I had no purpose, and now my purpose swells more with each passing day. And with each kick, I sense her—my mother. It's as though I've been given a gift.

The conception of this child is no longer a nightmare. In fact, I find it to be a miracle. Were it not for that terrible day in the church, I never would have known my mother. I wouldn't know her name or see her face so clearly in my mind.

It's been weeks since Alexei told me his secret, and in that time Katya and Oleg have barely spoken to me. I wake up early this morning to find Katya sitting on her cot, her knees pulled up to her chest, her face turned toward the window. The early morning light casts a golden glow on her perfectly shaped face. She senses my stare and turns. Her eyes are bright beneath her long, wavy blond hair.

"Good morning," I say softly. Katya nods in return. Her chin trembles, and her eyes well up.

"Papa told me," she whispers. "He told me about your mother." Her voice breaks, and she lowers her face into her knees. Sliding off my cot, I crawl to her and wrap my arms around her trembling shoulders. My protruding stomach presses against her legs. She pulls away from me.

"I'm sorry," Katya mumbles. I sit back awkwardly, and drop my hands into my lap.

"I'm sorry, too," I say. And I am. I'm sorry that my joy is her heartache. We're connected to one another in a way that is glorious for one and painful for the other. I wish it didn't have to be so.

For a long time we sit quietly. Though every bit of me aches to stroke the child moving inside me, I refrain, keeping my hands still in my lap. Katya cries quietly, her head still pressed to her knees. Finally, she raises her head.

"I don't hate you," she whispers. I nod because I can't speak. "And I'm not angry at my papa," she says, her voice trembling. She stares deep into my eyes. I see the pain. It moves in circles like the rough spring winds that storm across the river.

"Has your papa told you much about your mother?" I ask Katya. She nods and gives a faint smile.

"He's always spoken of her to us," she says.

"Tell me about her."

Katya shifts her gaze back to the window. The morning sun is higher now and brighter. Her face lights as she speaks.

"My mother's name was Elena," she starts, her voice buttery as she tugs at the words she's heard all her life. "She was small, like me, and her hair was darker than mine. Papa says he doesn't know how I got such light hair." Katya pauses for a moment.

"Papa told us that Mama was very serious. She didn't laugh often, but when she did, he says her laugh could light up a room. Mama saved her laughter and praise for when she really meant it. I imagine that Oleg is very much like her in a lot of ways." She looks at me intently. "He doesn't say anything unless he really means it."

My hand instinctively moves to my abdomen and I rub it slowly, my heart racing. I break Katya's gaze and stare hard at the bulge. She clears her throat. "Do you want to hear more?" she asks.

"*Da.*"

"When I was born, things went wrong. It was a terrible winter night and the doctor couldn't come. Papa won't tell me much about that night except that there was a lot of blood and he laid me in her arms when he knew she was going to die." Another long, emotional pause and I wait, barely breathing, feeling every ounce of pain.

"My mother took her last breath with her lips pressed to the top of my head," Katya says. She smiles as tears stream down her face, pooling at her chin and dripping onto her white gown. "Sometimes I still feel her kiss," she whispers.

"I'm sorry," I cry, and I pull her into my arms. This time she doesn't pull away when my stomach presses against her. She clings to me, both of us weeping for that which we never knew. We find rest on the common ground of sorrow.

"I wish I had known her," Katya cries.

"Me too." I mean it. I wish Katya had known her mother, and I wish I'd known my own. How different would we both be today if only we had known?

"I'm so sorry I've been awful to you, Luda," Katya says, pushing herself up off my lap. "It scares me, what you're going through."

I grab Katya's hand and place it on my stomach, pressing it into the side where the baby moves. "Do you feel that?" I ask, hushed. Katya's eyes grow wide, and she sits still, feeling the child slide across her palm.

"Are you scared?" she asks.

"I was," I answer. "But now, I'm . . . less scared."

"I still don't understand why you want to have this baby," she confesses. She pulls her hand away as if ashamed to admit something so raw while touching the life.

"I know you don't." I look down, silent and contemplating. How much do I tell her? "Katya, I can't explain what I'm feeling because I don't understand it all," I begin. "But I know without fail that this child is giving me a second chance at life."

Katya looks intently at me. She's listening, and I'm grateful. Hers is the relationship I can't bear to lose.

"What did your papa tell you about my mother?" I ask gently. Katya's eyes darken. She sighs and wraps her arms around her knees again.

"He told me that he loved her before he met Mama, and that he promised he would always look after you," she answers.

I nod. "Do you know that he told me more about my mother in ten minutes than anyone has ever said?" I ask. "I knew nothing about my mother, but Alexei gave her back to me." I stop and wait for her eyes to meet mine.

"I wanted this baby before because he was the only thing I had left. I *needed* him. But now . . . this child is my connection to my mother. He's how I'll know her."

Katya is silent for a moment before speaking. Her words aren't kind, but neither are they harsh. They're gentle and understanding. "You called the baby a 'he,'" she says. I smile.

"I guess I think it's a boy."

Reaching out slowly, Katya touches my stomach once again. "This is going to be hard, Luda," she whispers. "But I won't leave."

Covering her hand with my own, I stare hard. "Thank you," I whisper, and together we sit for a long time, our faces to the sun. Two wounded souls waiting to heal.

Later that day, I make my way down the stairs to head to the market. Baba Mysa needs onions and beets for her borscht, and I have volunteered to buy them. I leave Katya sitting close to her father as he reads the paper. She needs him to herself right now.

"Are you sure you can handle going out alone?" Baba Mysa asked before I left, the wrinkles around her eyes scrunched with concern. "I should go with you. We will go together."

I stopped her as she reached for her scarf. It was cold outside, and walking the icy streets and waiting in line at the market is difficult on her swollen joints. "I'll be fine, Baba," I assured her, and finally, after a bit of arguing, she agreed to let me go.

"Straight there and straight back," she said, wagging her finger in my face as she closed the door behind me. I giggle as I reach the bottom of the stairs and pull my coat up around my chin. The fabric pulls at my stomach, each button straining against the pressure. It's nice to have someone care when I come and go.

Just as I reach to push open the door, it flings wide. I jump. Oleg steps inside, his head covered in a thick, wool hat. He stops and stares at me awkwardly.

"Where are you going?" he asks.

"To the market," I answer, and we wait, each wishing we could fill the silence—each wishing to escape.

"It's cold outside," Oleg says. I nod. He sighs and pulls his hat down further over his ears. "I'll come with you," he says with a hint of annoyance in his voice. My own frustration flares.

"No, it's not necessary," I say, clipping each word off coolly. "I can handle it. I just need to pick up a few things for Baba Mysa."

Oleg shakes his head. "You shouldn't go alone," he retorts as he pushes open the door, gesturing me ahead of him.

"Oleg, thank you but I'm fine. I don't need you to come with me."

"That's it, isn't it?" Oleg barks, and he leans in close. I feel the chill of the air sweep over us, and I'm not sure if it's a result of the outdoors or Oleg's icy stare.

"What?" I ask, my voice raising.

"You don't need me. Or maybe it's just that you don't want me." He lets go of the door and it slams shut. Breathing hard, each puff of air floats anger and pain into the space between us.

"Oleg, I'm sorry," I say, quietly this time.

"Forget it," Oleg mutters, and he turns on his heel. I listen to each heated step as he stomps up the dark, narrow flight of stairs. I listen until I hear the click of the door closing up above. I listen until my heart stops calling me a fool.

Stepping onto the quiet street behind our flat, I make my way to the main sidewalk. The market is just around the corner, but I purposely take my time getting there. The cold air is refreshing and crisp. I breathe in deep as I turn the corner, and there *he* is. I stop and stare.

The tall, handsome German leans against the wall, his left hand shoved deep into his pocket. It's him. The man from the flat.

"Hans," I whisper, noticing the way his name fits so nicely on my tongue.

His jacket is thin, and I'm sure that he's cold, but he seems relaxed and comfortable. He raises his right arm and puts a short, thin cigarette into his mouth. I watch closely as he inhales deeply, his strong, deep-set eyes squinting as the smoke unfurls in his face.

He hasn't seen me. I'm not even sure he would recognize me so I begin to move slowly forward. I must pass directly in front of him to reach the market. I lower my head and try to keep my eyes from studying his smooth, handsome face.

Just as I step past him, he speaks.

"Privyet," he says quietly. I freeze. I don't turn to look at him, but I feel him step near. The hair on the back of my neck stands up, and I feel a shiver move down my spine. He steps beside me keeping his eyes straight ahead.

"I know you," he says. "You're the girl who stole my gun. Luda."

My heart skips when he says my name. It flows off his tongue with a tenderness that leaves my cheeks hot. I don't speak. I wait.

"I've been looking for you," he continues, still not turning toward me. He knows I'm shocked and nervous. I'm also struck by his kindness. "I've been hoping to see you again."

I swallow and take a deep breath, the cold air catching in my lungs. "I . . . I . . ." I blush as I try to stammer out the few words stuck on my tongue.

"How do you speak my language so well?" I manage to squeak out.

I hear him chuckle. "I was trained to speak your language," he answers. He looks around the street, then finally turns toward me. "We shouldn't talk here," he says quietly. "But I would like to talk with you more. Will you come with me?"

I hesitate for a brief moment before turning to meet his gaze. I'm met with the same honesty that I noticed the first time I saw him, and I nod. I've thought of him every day since we last met. I need to figure out why.

Walking a few steps behind, I follow him to a dark ally. Hans slips inside and, looking around to see if anyone is watching, I quickly follow. We walk all the way to the end, where the shadows of the two buildings provide a veil of protection. Hans leans against the wall and props one foot up, looking at me intently. I stand against the opposite wall and look nervously back. His gaze drifts down to my protruding stomach, and I see his eyes darken.

"It's not what you think," I say with embarrassment.

"And what do I think?" he asks.

I blush and grab my stomach protectively. "I—I don't know," I say.

"But this baby is . . . it's . . ." I don't know how to finish, so I simply look into his eyes. I can tell that he knows. He lets out a long, sorrowful sigh and shakes his head.

"I'm sorry they did that to you." His voice is deep and pure. His Russian is accented, but the accent is beautiful. I want to hear him speak more. He looks at me tenderly. "We're not all like that," he says.

I tilt my head to the side and study him. I'm feeling more courageous in his presence, and I suddenly have a hundred questions I want to ask.

"Why are you so kind to me?" I begin. "And why were you looking for me? What are you doing in my country and in that uniform?" I stop and put my hand over my mouth. "I'm sorry," I stammer. "I shouldn't have asked that."

"It's okay," he answers solemnly. "You have the right to ask." He puts his foot down and takes a step closer to me. "I'm kind to you because the first time I laid eyes on you I was captivated. I have been looking for you because I haven't been able to stop thinking about you since that night on the roof. I'm here and in this uniform because my country dictated that this is where I should be. But I do *not* agree with everything my country does."

I look up at his chiseled features and see the truth in his face. He means every word.

"I've thought of you every day since that night, too," I whisper. I'm trembling from head to toe. "I haven't been able to—"

I stop short as Hans lifts his hand and turns his head sharply toward the end of the alley. Someone's coming our way.

"Lean back quickly," he hisses. I press against the building behind me, the shadows covering my frame. To my surprise, Hans leans in on top of me, his hands on either side of my head and his face inches from mine.

"I'm not going to hurt you," he whispers. "Don't be scared, and don't pull away."

Before I have time to respond, he leans in farther, and his lips graze my cheek. It's soft and warm, the way he lingers gently over me. I let my hands drift to his waist and rest on his sides, and my whole body lights up. I draw in a deep breath at the nearness of him, my heart pounding.

Footsteps shuffle against the snow and dirt. I hear the drunken laughter of two Nazis. They stop short when they come upon Hans and me seemingly locked in an embrace. One of them laughs and says something. Hans turns toward them, his large frame still covering me. I turn my head to the side, away from their hungry stares and greedy laughter. He replies in his native tongue, and they all laugh together. He's playing a part—and playing it well.

My hands drop from his waist and the two men laugh again. One of them leans in, giving Hans a good-natured punch on the shoulder. Moments later, they turn to make their way back out. We're alone again; Hans still leans in over me.

He turns to look at me, and I keep my face turned away, ashamed and embarrassed. "Luda," he says gently. He reaches down and grabs my chin with his hand, pulling my eyes to his. He searches me, a look of concern and sorrow furrowing his brow and tainting his handsome features. Reaching up, he gently brushes the hair back from my forehead. "I'm sorry," he says, his voice sad and aching. "I'm sorry that my own people have taken so much of you."

Leaning in, he kisses my forehead gently. I close my eyes, paralyzed by this moment.

"I was looking for you," Hans breathes, "because you are the most beautiful, fragile girl I have ever seen, and I want to protect you."

My eyes fill with hot tears as I look up at him again. He smiles, though his eyes are still laced with sadness.

"You don't even know me," I whisper, my voice cracking. The tears hit my cheeks in hot streams, and he wipes them away. "I'm quite broken, and when you see this you won't want me anymore." The words tumble out heavy and thick as I hand him the shattered piece of my soul.

Hans runs the back of his hand down my cheek and shakes his head. "I know this is strange, Luda," he says. His voice is like a gentle melody, so soft and warm and smooth. "But I don't think you're broken at all. In fact, I'm certain you're stronger than you think." He leans all the way in until his mouth grazes my ear. "You captured me from the very first moment I saw you," he breathes. I close the small space between us and lay my head on his chest. He wraps his arms around me, his hand pressed tight and warm against the back of my head.

"I've never done this before," I say quietly, and he chuckles.

"What?" he asks.

"Met a strange boy in a dark alley," I respond. Both of us smile. Hans pushes me back, his blue eyes dancing with mischief and amusement. He raises one eyebrow slightly, then leans forward and he kisses me, soft and quick. I look at him, my eyes still brimming.

Hans smiles. "I've never done *that* before," he says.

"Kissed a girl?" I ask in surprise. "I don't believe you."

Hans chuckles and pushes back. "I have never kissed a girl I barely knew before," he clarifies.

"I've never kissed anyone," I reply. Hans looks down at me again, his eyes twinkling. He begins to lean toward me when I gasp, realizing all at once how much time has passed. "I'm going to the market," I say quickly. "If I don't hurry back they'll be worried about me."

"Who will be worried? Your family?" he asks. I shake my head.

"No. I don't have a family," I reply, then press on past the look of shock on his face. "The family I live with is very protective, though. They'll come after me if I don't return soon."

The thought of Oleg and Alexei searching for me and finding me in the arms of a Nazi makes me shiver, and I pull out of Hans's grasp. "I have to go," I say. "I'm sorry."

"I understand," he replies. "Go. I'll wait here while you leave."

I nod and step away, then turn and rise up on my toes, kissing him quickly on the cheek. It's a foreign act of emotion for me, and I blush as I step back. "Can I see you again?" he asks. I grin in reply.

"I'll wait here every afternoon between two and four," he says. "Come when you can."

I smile shyly, then turn and hurry toward the exit. Leaning out, I look both ways to make sure no one is coming before I step into the street and hurry to the market. I buy the needed items in such haste that I forget to take my change from the seller, and she chases me into the street, shaking her fist and yelling at me to slow down.

I race back up the street and round the corner, bumping hard into Alexei.

"Oh! Alexei, I'm so sorry." I stumble, looking down at my feet. "Where are you going?" I ask.

"I was coming to find you, Luda," Alexei says, his voice revealing annoyance and fear. "My mother is upstairs pacing the flat, certain that she made a mistake by letting you go alone. What took you so long?"

I look into Alexei's concerned eyes and swallow hard. It hurts to lie, but I know it's better than telling the truth.

"I ran into my father," I blurt out, and my eyes instantly fill with tears at my ability to lie so effortlessly to this man who has cared for me. Alexei sighs and pulls me to his chest, which only makes the tears fall. I choke back a sob.

"I'm sorry, Luda," Alexei murmurs. I fight back the tears as guilt wraps itself around me. I'm completely baffled by my ability to fluctuate between such polar emotions in such a short amount of time.

"Did your father say anything to you?" Alexei asks. I shake my head no. I can't embellish on the lie.

"Come, Luda," Alexei says, reaching down to take the small sack of vegetables from my hand. "Let's go home." I nod, wiping my cheeks. Alexei puts his arm around my shoulders, and together we walk toward the stairs.

"I'm sorry, Alexei," I say again and I mean it, but not for the reason that he thinks. Just before we step inside the building, I turn and see Hans standing at the end of the sidewalk. He leans against the building, his right hand on his lips, drawing in deep one last puff of a cigarette.

I offer a small smile, and I know—as much as it pains me to lie to Alexei—*I know I will do it again.*

"Masha! Masha, wake up!"

I bolt up, panting, my hair matted to my forehead and hand clutching my chest. "What? What is it?" I cry. Anna sits next to me. Her hand rubs slowly up and down my back as she whispers softly in my ear.

"It's okay. It's alright. It's all okay." Slowly, quietly, back and forth, her hand moves and my heartbeat slows. Somehow, though, I can't seem to swallow the lump inside my throat.

"I was dreaming again," I say, my voice flat.

"*Da,*" Anna replies. Fingers back. Fingers forth. Slowly, gently. It's been six weeks since Papa showed us the poster calling for volunteers to leave for Germany, and in that time Anna has slept as near to me as possible, trying to quell the nightmares that force their way into my slumber. When the screaming starts, she's always there, her fingers playing a melody of peace on my shaking frame.

"I'm sorry I woke you," I murmur. Anna doesn't speak in reply. She doesn't need to because I know she doesn't mind. Somehow my sister has become my protector.

"Do you want to talk about it?" she finally asks, and I shake my head. I can't yet. There's nothing to tell. The nightmares aren't concrete, but the terror they produce is very real. When I close my eyes, I'm chased by shadows. Everything gets hot, and clouds of black circle and swim. But the real terror begins when yellow creeps in. Slowly and methodically, the yellow pushes the black clouds out, and I'm left in its heat. I don't know what it is, but I feel the terror. It's beyond what I can comprehend, and as the yellow intensifies and builds, a scream escapes my throat.

This is when Anna wakes me up.

Slowly, as her nails work over my tight shoulders, I feel my muscles grow limp, and as she has done every night, Anna pulls me down until my head lies in the crook of her arm. For a long time, we lie silent, both exhausted yet unable to sleep. Finally I speak.

"Anna, what's going to happen to us?"

"I don't know, Masha. I just don't know," she answers with a sigh.

The first wave of recruits left for Germany a month ago. Mama and Papa continue to insist that we will not leave. Every day Papa sits and holds my hand in his own. "I won't lose you," he whispers over and over. I, however, can't help but feel that our time is limited in this place. Nothing is stable or secure.

"Happy birthday," I whisper. Today, March 2, 1942, when the daylight finally chases away the shadows of night, she will be seventeen. It feels odd to celebrate, and I imagine we won't, because somehow I feel as though the world stopped moving the day the Germans dropped their bombs. I think of this day, just one year ago, and I smile.

Sergei crept into our room in the early hours of that morning and tossed a red carnation across Anna's bed. When she woke up, he sat on the floor staring at her with a devilish grin. "Happy birthday, *rebyonka*," he said with a laugh.

"I'm not a child," she huffed, grabbing her small pillow and tossing it at him, which caused me to fall over in a fit of laughter. Anna had always been too serious to enjoy life, but Sergei—he could get her to smile.

Now as I lie so close to her, I find myself thankful for the serious nature of her protection. For the first time, I feel a bond with my sister. I'm grateful to have her by my side.

"Do you really think we'll be able to stay home with Mama and Papa and not go to Germany?" I ask.

"Masha, I don't know what to think. All I know is that Papa won't let either of us go voluntarily."

Sitting up, I turn and lean on my elbow looking deep into my sister's eyes. "Would you go if he let you?" I ask.

Anna looks back at me, and I'm stunned at what I see moving in her eyes: surrender. "It's got to be better than slowly starving to death here, Masha. Better than watching Papa fade away until there's nothing left but a shell."

Food has been scarce the last few weeks. Mama is still employed, which allows her a few extra ration cards per week. Bread is scarce, and meat even more so. Last week Mama managed to secure a large jar of lard, which we're adding every night to the warm water and onions giving our broth a little more weight, but it isn't enough. I'm hungry, and so is Anna, and we live in fear every moment of every day. Nothing is secure, and the weight of insecurity makes it difficult to breathe. And now my sister appears to be ready to give up—ready to leave forever.

"But . . ." I search for the right words. "But Anna, you have to know that's not true. You've heard Papa murmuring and muttering throughout the day. He knows what they're capable of, and telling the truth isn't it."

"Yes, I've heard him, Masha," Anna replies with a sigh. "But I've also watched him. He's not the same. The papa we knew before Babi Yar doesn't exist anymore. I hear him and feel for him, but I don't trust him."

Pulling away, I look at my sister in horror. "How can you say that?" I ask, my voice laced with betrayal and hurt.

Sighing, Anna pushes herself up and pulls her knees to her chest. "Masha," she says, her voice once again melting into that arrogant matronly tone that drips with annoyance.

"No, forget it. I understand," I say, and I turn my back to her.

"Masha, I just don't know who to trust anymore," Anna continues. "Papa isn't in his right mind, and the Germans promise food and comfort. Doesn't that at least sound a little bit freeing?"

I don't answer, and after a moment, Anna sighs again and lies back down.

"If we leave, it will kill him," I whisper, and a hot tear escapes my eye, running down my cheek and dripping from my chin. I squeeze my eyes shut and wait for the yellow to overtake again.

When I finally wake, Anna is gone, and I'm relieved. I replay our conversation and try to wrap my mind around the fact that my sister is willing to leave—that she believes life would be better in Germany. I feel betrayed by her confession.

Walking slowly out of the room, I enter the kitchen to find Mama and Papa wrapped in conversation. They look up at me, and for a moment, Papa's eyes twinkle. The spark quickly fades, however, and he turns back to his mug. But that brief moment is all I need to know that Anna is wrong.

"Come sit down, Masha," Mama says, gesturing to the chair across from them. "I have chai prepared, and there's a little bread left for both you and Anna. I get my ration cards for the week today and will hopefully be able to get us a little more food." She looks at Papa and offers a smile that belies the confidence in her voice. "Would you like to sit down and eat with your Papa? I must get ready for work." I nod and sit back in my chair.

"Where's Anna?" I ask Mama and Papa.

Papa looks up in surprise. "She's not in your room?" he asks.

I shake my head. "No. She was gone when I woke up. I thought she was out here helping Mama."

Papa turns and looks at Mama with concern and fear. "Where would she have gone?" he asks and I hear it: fear.

I jump from the table and run to where we hang our coats and leave our shoes. Anna's coat, her hat, and her worn, black boots are missing. Anger bubbles up as I remember our conversation, but then I hear the familiar scrape of shoes against the stairwell outside our door. I wait for a moment and listen to the key slide into the lock. The door opens and in steps my sister, her face flushed red.

"Where were you?" I ask, my voice high pitched and frustrated. Anna looks at me in surprise.

"I went for a walk," she answers. "I needed some fresh air to clear my head."

"Anna?" Papa steps around the corner and takes two long steps toward her, pulling her into his chest. "Where did you go, darling? Where did you go?" he asks, pulling her hat from her head and letting the light blond hair spill loose over her shoulders. He pushes her back and looks into her wide eyes. "Please don't do that again," he says. "Don't leave me, do you understand?"

Papa grabs me and pulls me in with him and Anna, and together the three of us stand still for a long time, Papa whispering, "Don't leave me. Don't ever leave me."

We finally pull apart and head to the kitchen, where Mama has set out three mugs of steaming chai and half a small loaf of bread. She doesn't speak to Anna, her lips pressed tight together. Anna tosses me a wary glance from which I quickly turn away, too angry to sympathize.

Papa sits down with us, visibly shaken, as he tries to will away the demons. For several minutes we're quiet, slowly eating our bread and sipping the chai. Mama buzzes from the room and returns quickly, her hair brushed and tied back at the nape of her neck. Her face is still pinched as she takes one last swallow. She stands tall, pushing her thin shoulders back.

"Happy birthday, Annichka," she says. Her voice is soft despite the accusation that still flows through her eyes. Anna scared her—we can all feel it.

Finally Anna speaks. "I'm sorry I didn't tell you I was going out. I just needed to take a walk," she says quietly.

"It's not safe for you to be out there alone," Mama replies quickly, her eyes blazing as she looks at her oldest daughter. "Have you not heard what's happening on the streets? The Germans are rounding young people up and taking them right from the market, from the square." Mama looks at all of us as her words sink in. "I even heard that they gathered up a group of young people at the soccer match last week."

Anna puts her head down, her long, thin finger circling the rim of her mug.

"Anna," Papa says gently. "What's wrong, *Dochinka*?"

Anna sighs and looks at me, then at Mama and Papa. "I—" she begins, and I quickly interrupt.

"Anna and I had a fight last night," I blurt out, a little too loudly. "It's my fault, really. I wore her only pair of good stockings and got a hole in them. I think Anna just wanted to get away from me."

Turning to my sister, I try to stifle my glare as I continue. "I'm sorry, Anna. I won't wear your stockings again without asking, okay?"

Anna narrows her eyes and nods slowly. Mama sighs and pinches the bridge of her nose. "Girls, the whole world is collapsing and you two are arguing about a pair of stockings? Really, Masha, you have to be more careful," Mama says, looking at me, and I nod in assent. "And Anna, darling, just because your sister upsets you doesn't mean you run out into the streets and pout. Honestly, you two. This is all ridiculous."

Anna stares at me, and I ignore her as I focus on the swirling tea leaves at the bottom of my cup. My head snaps up only when I hear Papa laugh. It's the happiest sound I've heard since the war began.

Papa sees our astonishment, and his laughter fades. He looks as surprised as we feel by his burst of emotion. Picking up his mug, Papa's mouth curves again into a soft smile, his eyes crinkling in the corners.

"You fight over stockings," he murmurs. I feel a grin spread across my face as well, and within moments we're all laughing. It is a cacophony of joyous sound. After a few moments, Papa leans in and pulls Anna close, kissing the top of her head.

"Happy birthday, *Dochinka*. I love you," he says, his voice soft.

Anna blushes and smiles at Papa.

"I love you, too," she whispers.

"Alright girls, I'm leaving," Mama says. "Please go take care of your morning chores and prepare for the day."

I push my chair back slowly and move to the bedroom, where the blankets and sheets are strewn about. Anna follows me and closes the door. Walking to the cupboard where we keep our clothes, she reaches in and pulls out her stockings with a sigh.

"What are you doing?" I ask as she pulls at her stocking until a small hole appears.

Anna looks up at me with a slight smile and holds up her stocking, and I giggle. "Sorry," I say and Anna snorts, then throws her head back and laughs. I watch her for a moment before interrupting.

"Papa's coming back, Anna. For the first time since Babi Yar, he's smiling and laughing. I'm not going to let you ruin it by telling him you want to go to Germany."

Anna stares at me for a moment before answering. "Masha, I don't *want* to go to Germany," she says.

"You said you wanted to last night!"

"No, I didn't," she answers. "I said it didn't sound as bad as sitting here and starving to death, but that doesn't mean I want to go."

Anna stops and takes a deep breath. "I went for a walk this morning to just think through a few things," she says quietly. "I'm tired, Masha. I'm tired of being sad all the time. I'm tired of working so hard for so little. I'm just really, really tired."

Anna looks up at me, and I see the resignation in her eyes. She has always been the strong one. She and Mama have kept us all operating as smoothly as possible in the nine months since the Germans first sent their bombs.

I reach out and grab my sister's hand and squeeze tight. "We are all tired," I answer. "But at least we're together."

Anna pulls me into her arms and together we stand, sisters united in a bond that neither of us has ever known, equally annoyed and exasperated with one another but overwhelmed with love. My face is pressed in her neck where I feel warm and safe. A giggle escapes me as we embrace.

"What's so funny?" Anna asks, pushing me back.

"Sergei would make fun of us cruelly if he saw this," I say. Anna's face breaks into a grin. Lips stretched tight over perfect white teeth. Together we giggle until the giggles turn into howls of laughter. Clutching our sides, we collapse in a heap on the floor, months of emotional strain falling from our shoulders.

"Ahem."

We look up to see Papa standing in the doorway, staring at us. He has one eyebrow raised, and for the second time this morning, he smiles.

"What's going on in here, girls?" Papa asks.

Anna and I look at each other and start laughing again, unable to stop the flow of emotional release because it feels too good. Before long, Papa joins us, and for some time we all laugh until our sides hurt and our cheeks are sore.

I've never felt more alive.

IVAN KYRILOVICH
March 3, 1942

I forgot what it felt like to laugh. I forgot the melody that joy could make, like a summer song on a rainy day, exhilarating and fresh.

For the first time in months, I feel capable of living again. Though my heart still aches with a wretched heaviness, in this moment I feel the one thing that I thought I'd never feel again: joy.

The sound of my girls laughing yesterday nearly took my breath away. To see my Tanya smile again was like magic. It's as though all the strain and fear and pent-up doubts came bubbling to the surface and escaped through our laughter.

It is Tuesday morning, the one day when Tanya doesn't have to go to work. I'm grateful for her willingness to work so hard at the library every day. Work, I'm finding, is scarce for men right now in Kiev.

Most Tuesdays, Tanya goes to the salt piles near the Dnieper River and gathers sacks full of the precious ingredient. It's now tainted and dirty, so my Tanya works late into the night, sifting and pouring the salt through cloth, carefully removing all the dirt, and wrapping it tight into small parcels, which she then sells to local markets and vendors. I marvel at her industry and yet feel so humbled by my lack of provision.

This morning, as we sit together at the breakfast table, I look around at my three girls, and I take in the sight of each of them: Anna with her striking beauty and gentle eyes; Maria with the mischievous laugh and wild expressions; Tanya with her simple elegance and a look that instantly tells me I'll always be hers.

"Today calls for a celebration," I say.

"What are we celebrating?" Maria asks, her eyes wide with excitement. My Masha loves a party.

"We're celebrating life and family," I say with a smile and touch her cheek gently. "And we're celebrating Anna's seventeenth birthday, a worthy moment indeed." Anna blushes and ducks her head.

I look around at their flushed faces, and I speak slowly and deliberately. "I'm sorry, my darlings," I begin. "I'm sorry for abandoning you these last months."

Tanya reaches for my hand and pulls it into her lap. "What matters," she says, her voice soothing and calm like a sleepy brook, "is that you're back now." I smile, pulling her hand to my lips.

"So, how about that celebration?" I ask.

"How do we celebrate, Papa?" Anna asks, standing up and smoothing her wrinkled skirt. "We have no food to prepare."

"Nonsense," I reply with a wave of my hand. "Tanya, what do we have to eat today?"

Tanya grins and stands up next to Anna. "I have four potatoes, half a head of cabbage, one onion and a loaf of bread. And, of course, salt."

"Very well," I say. "We'll have borscht."

"Papa," Maria answers, "it's not borscht if it's just potatoes, onion, and cabbage. There's no meat and no beets." I laugh at the look of horror on her face.

"Dochka," I say with a grin. "It's borscht if we believe it to be borscht."

Slowly Maria smiles back. She nods her head. "Fine," she says with a giggle. "We'll have borscht."

Tanya and Anna head for the kitchen to prepare the feast, while Masha and I go to the sitting room to prepare the table. We always sit together in this larger room when we celebrate. I pull the small table away from the wall and wipe the thin layer of dust from the surface. The dark wood is scratched, but otherwise still looks beautiful and rich. It's a solid table that I built for Tanya just after we moved to Kiev when I got my first construction job. I put it together with scraps and spent hours carefully cutting and carving away at the wood until it was perfect.

Squatting low, I reach under the table and run my hand over the inscription on the bottom, which reads, *To my Tanya. We will fill each corner with love. 1921.*

I crawl under the table and lie on my back, staring at the letters scratched into the wood. To the right of the inscription I carved the night before I presented my new wife with her gift is the name *Sergei Ivanovich, July 28, 1923.* Beneath his name reads *Anna Ivanovna, March 2, 1925,* and just below that, *Maria Ivanovna, May 14, 1927.*

"We filled the table," I whisper, running my hand over each name. My fingers linger on Sergei's name, the child who made me a father, whose voice still rings in my head.

Maria climbs under the table and lies down next to me, her shoulder pressed tight against mine. "I used to love lying under here when I was little," she says with a smile. "I feel like our family starts right here at this table."

Turning my head, I study my youngest child's profile—the way her nose curls in softly at the bridge and her long, dark eyelashes sweep like a feather up and down over her eyes. I grab her hand, my fingers interlacing with hers.

"This is exactly where we begin, *dorogaya*," I say.

Maria turns and smiles at me, and my heart skips a beat. I didn't realize how much she had grown. "I love you," I murmur. Maria leans over, throwing her arm across my chest in a fierce hug.

"I love you, too. Thanks for coming back, Papa," she whispers in my ear.

We lie like that for some time, as the smell of onions and potatoes fills our small flat. I run my fingers through my daughter's long, wiry hair and remember it all. The shrieks of laughter when the children were little and I chased them in circles around the room; the pad of small feet as they stepped up to our bed each morning and climbed in close; the sound of Sergei's voice when it dipped below the timbre of a child and into that of a man.

These are the moments I cherish: the moments that will keep me living and breathing and fighting. My family. All that I have in this terrifying world. They're my breath and the light that will outshine the horrors of the shadows.

"*Ahem.*"

I look up in surprise to see Anna and Tanya knelt down, bemused smiles on both their faces. "The feast is prepared," Tanya says with a smile.

I nudge Maria, who has fallen asleep, and she pushes herself up groggily, her hair matted to her cheek. "Time to eat?" she asks, and we all laugh. Maria and I crawl out from under the table and help Tanya and Anna bring the food in from the kitchen. As we pull our chairs up to the table, we all look at the empty spot where Sergei sat, always entertaining us with his vivid stories and wild antics.

"Wait, please," I murmur. I push back abruptly and grab the fifth chair, pulling it into his spot. I place my hand on the table for a brief moment as if to feel him near, then I walk around the table and sit back down in my place. The girls watch closely, waiting to see if I slip away from them again.

"I'm hungry," I say, picking up my spoon. "Are we going to eat this fine meal or simply look at it?"

With a laugh, we all dig in to the weak soup and stale bread. No meal has ever been grander.

The week following our celebration meal is filled with much laughter and chatter. As though making up for lost time, the girls talk incessantly, sharing their fears and their own haunted memories. It's my turn to listen, and I do, offering each one of them ample time to surrender her own heartache. They share their hearts, but mine remains vaulted shut. I cannot share the horrors I saw at Babi Yar. I cannot tell them what happened to Polina, that I saw her take a breath and that I failed to protect her.

If I couldn't protect her, will I be able to protect them?

It's Tuesday again, and we're all going together to the market. Tanya has a bag full of salt to sell, and the girls need to get out and breathe in the crisp air. I sense their frustration at being cooped up inside the flat. I haven't let them go back to school this year. It just isn't safe.

I step out of the bathroom to find them all dressed and ready, each in her best outfit and with hair pinned neatly in place.

"You all look lovely," I say with a smile. I pull on my warm boots and my tall, thick hat and coat. Though we approach the middle of March, the air is still cold, and last night new snow blanketed the ice-packed ground. Winter hangs on as long as possible this year, and I find myself longing for the respite of spring.

"Let's go, my beautiful girls," I say, opening the door for them. As Tanya walks past me, I grab her hand and stop her. Leaning forward, my lips brush hers gently as I pull the heavy sack of salt from her hands.

"You are breathtaking," I whisper. Tanya looks up at me, her eyes dancing with passion. For a moment, we're frozen in a time that can never last long enough.

"Mama, Papa, come on!" Maria calls from below, and Tanya smiles wide. Stepping out into the dim hallway, I pull the door closed behind me with a heavy thud. Tanya and I walk down the stairs, our hands clasped tightly together. As we pass Josef and Klara's door, my heart thumps wildly. Tanya sees my pause and squeezes my hand.

We take our time walking to the market, relishing the quiet morning. Others are on the streets, but not many. Most people keep their heads down and move quickly, not wanting to be exposed for longer than necessary. Maria and Anna walk in front of us, Maria's arm tucked tight in her sister's. Their heads press together, and they laugh from time to time.

Today is a good day.

We step into the small *magazin* and Tanya pulls away, taking the salt with her. She knows whom to speak with to get the right price for her work. The girls and I take a few minutes to walk around the room, looking at the many bare shelves. There's a short line of people standing silently, ration cards in hand, waiting to receive whatever they can to fill hollow stomachs. Three people stand behind the counter, the guardians of the precious commodity of food.

As we wait for Tanya to finish, the door opens and four Nazis walk in. Instinctively I push the girls behind me, my entire body stiffening. I haven't been in close proximity to a Nazi since that night in the trees, and I feel every emotion rush back.

The men hold their guns in front of them and stand very tall. The oldest of the four clears his throat, then speaks in heavily accented Russian.

"All boys and girls age fourteen to seventeen will come with us now for deportation to Germany," he says, his words clipped and cold. My heart sinks. My hands quake. I feel Maria grip my shoulder as a small whimper escapes her throat.

The older Nazi looks at me and moves my way. I don't make a move, waiting until he's just a few feet in front of me.

"*Nyet,*" I say evenly. He stops and cocks his head to the side.

"Excuse me?" he says.

"I said no."

The man throws his head back and laughs out loud, then abruptly stops and flips his gun up, training it at my temple. I reach my hands back and clasp the hands of my daughters, but otherwise do not respond.

"The two girls standing behind you will come with me and report for duty in Germany, or I will shoot you and everyone else inside this building." His Russian is flawed and broken. I hate the way he taints my language.

"They will *not* go with you," I reply through clenched teeth, and I feel the terror closing in on me.

"I'm going to count to three," he says softly, his finger resting on the trigger. "I'll count in your language so that you understand."

I grip tight to the hands behind my back, wishing to turn back time and stay home. Why did I bring them out of the house? I feel the horror of my failure once again press upon me.

"*Odin,*" the Nazi says, his eyes narrow and dark. No one in the store dares move as the other three Germans have all raised their guns as well. "*Dva,*" he whispers as a slight smile curls his thin lips upward.

"Wait!" I jump as Anna tears herself away from my grasp and steps in front of me. She shakes wildly, her hands raised in surrender. "I'll go," she cries. "Please, don't shoot. I will go with you."

The Nazi grins, then thrusts his chin forward. "Bring the other girl with you," he purrs, and I feel Maria's hand pull from my own. She steps out from behind me and grabs her sister's hand. "I'll go. Please leave our papa alone," she says, her voice quavering. She sounds both terrified and brave all at once.

The Nazi lowers his gun, motioning to the men behind to do the same. "Good girls," he says. "It's for the better, old man," he says to me with a haughty grin. "They will enjoy living in the beautiful land of Germany." He turns to a boy standing behind one of the counters, two fresh loaves of bread in his hands. "You, too, *Untermensch*," he sneers. "You come with us."

The woman standing next to him lets out a wail and falls to the ground, her head sinking into her hands. The boy wipes his hands slowly and kneels down next to her. "Shh . . . Mama, I'll be back," he murmurs. Then he kisses her cheek and pulls off his white apron, laying it over her shoulders. "I love you," he says. He stands up, eyes shining bright, and walks to us.

"Good, that was easy," the Nazi says. "Is there anyone else here?" he asks, looking around. When he sees no one, he turns back to the three teenagers trembling before him. "Come," he says. "*Schnell.*"

"Wait!" I cry, and he stops.

"What is it?" he sighs, clearly impatient and ready to move on.

"Can we say good-bye?" I ask, my voice breaking.

"You have one minute," the Nazi replies, looking bored and uninterested.

Tanya rushes over from the corner where she has been standing, her hand pressed over her mouth in horror. It's our worst nightmare and greatest fear. We will lose them all.

Maria and Anna bury their faces in my chest, and Tanya throws her arms around us all.

"Papa. Papa," Maria sobs, her hands grasping at me. Anna reaches up and places her hands on my cheeks, her eyes bright with fear and sorrow.

"Don't leave again, Papa," she says, so fiercely I feel the heat of her words pierce my heart. "Do not leave Mama alone when we're gone, do you understand? Do you, Papa?" Her voice is desperate.

I nod and grab her shoulders. Leaning forward I press my lips hard to her wet cheek. "I promise, *Dochka*," I whisper. "I won't leave. I'll be right here when you get back." Anna nods and turns to her mother, melting into her arms. I pull Maria up off the ground into my arms as I did when she was small, and she wraps her legs around my waist, her arms clinging to me like a child who's seen a ghost.

"You have to be strong, Masha," I whisper in her ear as my heart tears. "You cannot let them break you. I need you to come back to me, my darling. I need you . . ."

"Papa. Papa." Maria says my name over and over, her voice dripping with grief.

"Alright, enough!" the German yells. I slowly set Maria down and pull her face back to look into her eyes.

"You can do this," I cry, my voice desperate. "You're stronger than I am—I know it. You'll survive this, and you will come home. I'll be here, Masha. I will be here."

My daughter nods and turns to her mother, who pulls her in tight and weeps bitterly. "I love you," she cries. The German grabs Maria's arm and yanks her from Tanya's grasp.

"I said enough," he barks. He turns to leave, pushing Maria and Anna in front of him. He nods toward the boy, who steps up next to Anna, and the three teenagers are pushed out the door, all four Germans walking in a pen around them. I pull Tanya to my side, and we watch as the door slowly swings shut, the last remnants of our life flitting away like a leaf in the wind.

MARIA IVANOVNA
March 3, 1942

Anna grabs my hand and holds tight as we march down the street with the four Nazis. The boy from the market walks quietly next to us, chin held high.

"We'll be okay," Anna speaks, her voice a whisper. She says it to me, but mostly I think she says it to Papa: a gentle message carried on the wings of the wind, a prayer that he'll believe and will not retreat again.

"Where are we going?" I whisper to Anna.

"You go to Germany," the Nazi to my left barks. I don't look at him. I'm too afraid to see his face, to know who he could be.

We walk until my feet ache and the buildings that house my entire life fade behind us. I look up ahead to see a large group of people standing in the center of a courtyard. We have walked far from the store, far away from Mama and Papa, far from home.

As we approach the group, I realize they're more youth like myself, all rounded up like cattle and brought together for . . . for what? Why are we here?

We gather, and the Germans surround us, creating a barrier to keep us penned in. The group consists of mostly girls. Of the roughly thirty students standing in the frigid air, only four of them are boys. Many of the girls weep. Others, like Anna and I, stand in shock.

After fifteen minutes of waiting, the tall German who pulled me from my mother's arms in the market climbs on a low wall in front of us.

"Listen to me, all of you," he yells. "We will march together to the train station where trains wait to take you to beautiful Germany. If you stay close and follow orders, this will be quick and easy. If you try to run, we'll shoot you. Do you all understand?"

No one responds. We simply look at the man who has just changed the course of our lives in stunned silence. This is real. We're leaving. Was it really only this morning that I felt happy?

We turn and begin to walk slowly toward the train station. Despite the chill in the air, my palms sweat. Feeling panic well up in my chest, I gulp in quick breaths, the cold air burning my lungs. I've never been on a train before. I've never left Kiev except to visit our dacha just outside the city limits. I want to go home. I just want to go home.

Anna grabs my hand and holds it tight, but it doesn't quell the trembling. In front of us, one of the soldiers jabs his gun in the side of the boy from the market. The Nazis shout as we walk, their guttural speech harsh and cutting. Finally I see the train station in the distance, and I feel my throat close. This is it.

We move to the large brown building and are pushed into a long line. Others are already here, a row of weeping and shaking young people. We are fear, lined up for all to see. As we're herded into a solitary line, someone catches my eye, and I squint to make sure I'm seeing her correctly. She's close to the front, standing completely still, her shoulders slumped. I see only the side of her face, but then she turns and looks back. I gasp.

"Polina," I cry. Anna snaps around to look at me.

"What did you say?" she hisses, and I point to the girl.

"It's Polina," I breathe, and Anna gasps. Polina's eyes are sunken deep in her head, and a noticeable scar cuts across her forehead. She's thin and looks dreadfully sick, but I know it's her. I raise my hand slightly to wave, but she quickly turns and looks forward again.

"It's her, isn't it, Anna?" I ask, but Anna doesn't respond. She's watching a Nazi soldier march toward us. I grab her hand and squeeze tight. The Nazi stops in front of the boy from the market.

"You come with me," the soldier commands. The boy glances at us and gives a gentle nod. We watch as he's swiftly escorted away.

"I wonder where they'll take him," Anna murmurs.

I don't want to know the answer to this question.

The line moves forward slowly toward the front, where two tall, pugnacious German women stand, their backs stiff. As each girl steps forward, one of the women snatches her passport and identification papers, and the other grabs her by the wrists. I watch as the big-boned German purses her lips, studying each girl's hands closely. The women then converse quietly and assign the waiting girl to a train.

On and on it goes until I see that Polina is next in line. The first German reaches out her hand for Polina's identification papers. Polina shakes her head and I see the woman look down disapprovingly over her jutted nose and hairy upper lip.

We all have identification papers that are to be carried on our person at all times. They give our names, our birth dates, our nationality, and race. I know why we're to have them—so the Jews can be quickly identified and weeded out. In this case, I think it's good that Polina doesn't have her papers. Her looks are so altered that she no longer carries the appearance of a Jewish girl, and so I think she may be spared such a fate.

The other German woman grabs Polina's thin wrists and turns them slowly. She speaks quietly to her partner, and the two laugh. It's a terrible sound, like the cackle that Papa used to make when he told us the fabled tale of Baba Yaga. Grabbing Polina's shoulders, the German woman gives her a shove toward a waiting train. Polina stumbles and falls to her knees, then slowly pushes herself up and joins the others who trudge toward this unknown fate.

"Anna," I whisper, "what if we're separated?"

Anna looks up, for the first time noticing what's happening at the front of the line. She looks at me in horror, her eyes wide and bright.

"Listen to me," I say, turning to face her straight on. The line moves forward, and we step in unison. We're getting close, our fates to be determined in just a few minutes. "If we do, you have to survive," I whisper. "We both have to come home alive, Anna. We have to."

Anna looks at me and nods, struggling to comprehend. I grab her shoulders and pull her in close. "I love you," I say. Anna grips at me, desperate.

"I love you, Masha," she whispers back. We stare hard, memorizing the moment. The line moves forward. Step.

Then it's my turn. I turn to face the German women and hand over my identification papers. The woman on the right grabs my hands and pulls them up roughly. She runs her coarse thumb over my palms then turns them over and studies the back. My hands are strong and rough. I have never had the delicate hands of a young lady.

Handing back my papers, the German jabs her stumpy thumb to her right, pointing at the line directly behind her. It's the same train that Polina will board. I'm momentarily relieved. Stepping in line, I turn and watch them look Anna over closely. My sister, the beauty with the delicate features, stands tall and poised. The fear that entangled her earlier is waning, and I see her strength beginning to shine through.

Then my heart stops. They send her to the other train.

Anna looks at me, and our eyes lock. *I love you*, I mouth, and she says it back. In that final moment, I feel my soul sever and tear in a way that feels like I've swallowed fire. The heat boils out, and my eyes burn with hot tears. Anna holds up one hand to her lips and kisses her fingers gently. I do the same, and we reach out to the gap between us.

The final good-bye.

My line inches forward as my vision blurs. I can't see her anymore. Anna is lost in the sea of heartache that surrounds us, her silky hair no longer visible to my trembling eyes. I have never felt a more solitary feeling than this moment. German soldiers mill about the room, their caps pulled low over stoic features. Some jeer and mock us openly. Others simply march, their eyes trained forward, poised and ready to issue justice on us, their charges. We're *Untermensch*.

I have heard the word so many times since the Nazis first infiltrated our home. It's ugly, and it tastes bitter on my tongue. I know what it means, but I can't understand or fathom how anyone truly believes such a thing. Subhuman? I'm made of flesh and bone just as each of these men in uniform. How can my worth as a person possibly be determined by something as small as geography?

For the first time, I find myself face-to-face with the evil that lies in man. I didn't think we could possibly be capable of such cruelties. I knew they were happening. I saw how they changed my family, my life. But I didn't want to believe it. Are we as people inherently good or evil? I thought I knew, but today . . .

My hands shake violently, and I quickly tuck them under my arms, a bitter chill running down my spine. Lifting my eyes, I watch as Polina is lifted into the waiting car of the train. She disappears into the dark, and I wonder what's beyond the door.

"Davai! Bistreye!" I jump when he pushes the butt of his gun into my side. It's cold and sharp and feels like a knife. I stumble forward to catch up to the line that has moved forward significantly. It's almost my turn to board. There are few left behind me. Soon we'll depart. I cannot believe how this day has changed.

I reach the car doors and stare up into frightened eyes. The car is full, all of them crammed together, shoulders pressed tight. I don't see how I'll possibly fit and I look up bewildered for a moment before he prods me again.

"Davai!" he repeats. I reach up and two of the girls grab my hands and pull hard. They hoist me into the car, propelling me through the crowd into the packed-tight center. There is little room to move, and it's already very hot. It takes a moment for my eyes to adjust to the dim surroundings, but when they finally do, I realize that we're to be transported exactly like cattle.

One small window stands high above us, bars covering it—our cell on wheels. The train car smells thick of manure and grass. Most of the girls are quiet, though some still cry softly. No one is hysterical, and for that I'm grateful. It's all I can do to keep from breaking down myself, so I take in deep breaths and force myself to open my hands and let them hang slack at my sides.

I crane my head, looking for a glimpse of Polina, and I quickly find her pressed against the hard, wooden wall of the train car. In the dim light, her face looks white, her stringy hair hanging heavily over ghost eyes.

I slowly begin to push my way through the crowd. We're all young—a car full of youth who just had all the promise of a future pulled away in a single, solitary blow. We are the future, stolen from the past.

I push and move until I've finally made my way to the wall where

Polina stands. She looks at me, and it takes a moment for her eyes to focus and register. I've seen that look before. It's the same way Papa looked at me for months after returning from Babi Yar.

"Polina," I whisper. To speak out loud would be too much. She's like a small fawn, frightened and caught, stuck in a trap without promise of release. My whisper, like the rustling of a leaf in a quiet forest, stirs her soul, and she jumps.

"Masha," she whispers back so softly I can hardly hear the words.

"Polina, I—" Stopping short, I realize I don't know what to say. I fall silent and study her closely. The scar on her head is thick and gnarled, the result of a deep wound that didn't properly heal. What happened?

"How is your papa?" she asks, and my throat tightens.

"Changed," I say, a small choke tugging the word back inside.

Polina nods, and her eyes drift to my shoulder, fixed in a place that's far away. "We're all changed," she breathes, and in a moment of clarity, I reach forward and grab her hand. It's small, icy. I pull it up and press my lips hard against the back, her bones sharp and thin.

"I'm here, Polina," I say, my voice hoarse with emotion. "Papa told me to survive, and I'm going to. We'll do it together. We'll go back together when this is all over."

Polina sighs and lifts her eyes to mine again. "I don't want to go back, Masha," she murmurs. "I want to die."

The words float from her lips and fill the small cabin where they linger above us all, a solitary wish for all the pain and fear to end.

LUDA MICHAELEVNA
March 5, 1942

Stepping outside, I take a moment to collect myself. I smooth my coat over the undeniable bulge in my abdomen. In two short months, we'll welcome the heat of summer, and I will meet my child. I feel a flutter of excitement and anxiety course through me, leaving my fingertips tingling with anticipation.

Looking up, I notice Baba Mysa staring at me from the small kitchen window. I have angered her these last few months with my insistence on taking afternoon walks alone. "You're being foolish," she mutters every day as I pull on my boots and coat. I hate her displeasure with me, but the alternative is unimaginable.

Abandoning my afternoons with Hans is something I cannot do, and so each day I give Baba Mysa a hug and thank her for honoring my desires. She has seen the difference the time alone has made in me. I'm happier than I've ever been, and for the first time smiles come quicker and easier than tears. Baba Mysa only lets me go because she believes the fresh air has been good for me.

She doesn't know.

Nobody knows that every day at two o'clock I round the corner and spend the next hour talking and laughing with the man I have fallen in love with—a German.

I lift my hand in a slight wave and give Baba Mysa a smile. She shakes her head and backs away from the window. Sighing, I turn and make my way down the sidewalk. Stepping up to the alley, I feel my pulse quicken. I will see my love in just a moment. I look around to make sure no one watches as I slip into the shadows and walk to where Hans always waits.

"Hans?" I say quietly. He steps forward into a band of light, his mouth split in a wide grin. My heart skips a beat, and I rush forward into his arms. I live for this moment every day when I will feel him close to me.

"Hello, my beautiful girl," he whispers in my ear, and he leans in to kiss my forehead. Pulling away, I look up in his eyes, so clear and blue, full of honesty and truth and goodness. He pushes me back and places his hands on my stomach.

"How are you feeling today?" he asks.

"Happy," I say with a smile. And I am. I'm happy.

"Good," he says. He pulls my hands up and kisses each one. "I'm happy, too."

I grin, and we walk to the nearby crates to sit down. Hans holds my hand tight and pulls it up to his chest. "I live for two o'clock. Did you know that?" he says with a laugh.

I lean into him with a giddy laugh. "So do I," I whisper.

For several moments, we're silent, both relishing the nearness and tenderness of the moment. Hans finally kisses the top of my head. "I brought you something," he says.

Reaching into the bag at his feet, Hans pulls out a fat, red apple. I laugh with delight and clap my hands. "Where did you find this?" I ask, taking it from his hand. Just yesterday, when he asked what my favorite food was, I told him that I longed to taste an apple. I haven't seen any in the market for weeks, and I've craved the juicy sweetness of my favorite fruit.

"I took it from the kitchen at the barracks," he said with a smile. "Go on . . . eat it!"

I take a giant bite of the apple and close my eyes, the flavor overtaking me. I open my eyes to find Hans watching me with a strange look of amusement and infatuation.

"What?" I ask, swiping the back of my hand over my mouth.

Hans doesn't respond for a moment as he studies. I sit quietly, looking back at him with curiosity and a bit of insecurity. What does he see?

Perhaps I shouldn't have eaten the apple in front of him. I lower my eyes to my lap, suddenly embarrassed by my behavior.

"I love you," Hans says. My eyes snap up.

"What?"

"I love you," he repeats, and I know he means it. He leans forward, his face so close, and says it again, this time in German. *"Ich liebe dich,"* he whispers, and he completes the distance, brushing his lips across mine. When he pulls back, he takes the apple from my hand and brings it to his mouth, taking one large bite.

I'm stunned silent, until I see the mischievous twinkle in his eye. I grin and snatch the apple back from him.

"I love you, too," I say, and suddenly I am laughing hysterically. Hans leans forward and stops my noisy laughter with another kiss. "Say it in German," he says. I comply. *"Ich liebe dich,"* I say quietly.

Every time we meet, Hans teaches me to communicate in his native tongue so that I can better understand what's going on around me. He is my sweet, dear protector.

I sit back again and look at him, his lopsided grin filling me with such joy that I'm momentarily lost. I don't hear her footsteps until it's too late.

"Luda!"

I gasp and drop my apple. It rolls and stops at her feet. Hans and I jump up, me smoothing out my skirt and him leaning back into the shadows.

"Baba Mysa!" I cry. Her face is full of pain and fear. I've hurt her deeply—the only woman who has ever shown me unconditional love. My chin trembles, and I feel the familiar lump form.

"Stop," she says holding up her hand. "I don't want to see your tears, so do not let them fall in my presence."

I swallow hard and blink twice. "I'm sorry, Baba," I say quietly. "I didn't want to lie to you. I didn't know how I could possibly tell you."

"How you could possibly tell me that you are meeting a German man in the shadows?" she asks. Her eyes dart to Hans, who hasn't moved. I reach out to him and take his hand in mine. He takes a halting step forward into the light. I want her to see him, to see his kind eyes and gentle features—to see the good in him so unlike his countrymen.

"Yes, Baba. I didn't know how to tell you that I've fallen in love with a good man. A German man."

"After what they have done to you?" Baba Mysa hisses, her eyes falling on my stomach. I wince and feel Hans shrink back. He doesn't want to make things hard for me.

"Baba, he's not like the men that hurt me. He's a German, but he's not a Nazi." I look up at Hans, whose face has softened. He looks down at me with a small smile.

"He's dressed like a Nazi," Baba Mysa replies. Then she sighs and shakes her head. "I knew I should never have let you go out of the house alone, Luda. It was too dangerous. I have failed you."

Dropping Hans's hand, I rush to Baba Mysa and hug her fiercely. She doesn't move as I squeeze her. "Please, Baba," I beg. "Please understand I didn't do this to hurt you. You've been so good to me, and I love you so dearly. Please forgive me for lying to you. Please, Baba."

Despite my efforts to stop the tears, they now fall freely. Baba Mysa still stands motionless, and after a moment I pull away from her. "I'm sorry," I mumble.

Hans steps to my side and puts his arm around my shoulders protectively. "Luda has spoken of you very much, Baba Mysa," he says gently in his richly accented Russian. "She's told me of the love you've shown her and how she didn't know if she would be alive if it wasn't for you."

Baba Mysa looks up at Hans, her eyes narrowed and lips pursed together. "I don't want to cause any friction between Luda and the family that's taken her in and given her so much to live for," Hans continues. "I love her. I want nothing more than to see her happy and to hear her laugh. I don't want to destroy any piece of goodness in her life. I'm sorry if I've done that."

Baba Mysa looks hard at Hans, then at me. I lean back in the crook of Hans's arm as I wait for her to speak.

Sighing, Baba Mysa shakes her head. "This isn't safe, Luda," she says. "It's not safe for either of you." She shifts her eyes to Hans. "How will you make this work in the long term?" she asks him. "You cannot marry her, or live with her—you would both be in terrible trouble for such an act. You cannot build a relationship on one hour a day in a dark alley. How do you expect this to last?"

Hans and I shift nervously. We've never discussed the details. I had thought briefly of the impossibility of our situation but had never wanted to dwell on it. I just wanted to live in the love that had finally given me some light.

"I could take her away," Hans says softly. I look up in surprise.

"What?" I breathe.

"We could escape, you and I," he says. "We could go to America and build a life there."

"But . . . what about Baba Mysa and Katya and Alexei and Oleg?" I ask.

Hans shakes his head. "I don't know, Luda," he says with sadness, and I realize that he, too, has ignored the impossibility of our situation in order to live in a moment of bliss.

Baba Mysa steps forward and grabs my hand. "Come, Luda," she says, her voice sad and tired. "We'll go home. I won't speak of this to anyone else." She shifts her gaze to Hans. "I believe that you love her," she says with a little more gentleness, "and I see goodness in your eyes, but this . . . relationship cannot work. There is no future in it." Baba Mysa looks from Hans to me. "You need to end it."

Pulling my hand from hers I shake my head. "No, Baba." I look into her eyes, searching, longing for her to see the depth of love that I feel and the only happiness I know. "I can't end it."

Hans steps forward and places his hands on my shoulders, turning me toward him. His brow is furrowed, and a deep crease has settled in the space between his eyes, like a chasm of grief that threatens to open up.

"Perhaps we should just slow down, take a break and figure things out," he says, and I hear it in his voice. He's torn, filled with a depth of pain that I know too well.

"No, Hans," I whisper, my voice quaking. "I can't take a break. I can't walk away. I can't be without you. I can't—"

Hans stops my protest by pulling me into a tight embrace. I press my cheek against his chest and let the tears fall freely, my heart tearing in two. His hands circle the back of my head as he pulls away, pressing his forehead to mine and looking at me closely. His heart is tearing, too.

"I'm not leaving," he whispers. "I'll be here every day at two o'clock, waiting and trying to find a way to make this work. I won't go anywhere without you."

"I love you," I cry.

Hans kisses the end of my nose, then steps back. He nods at Baba Mysa, who has watched with a stony expression. I reach up and run my hand down Hans's face and smile, then step back and turn around. Baba Mysa tucks her arm inside my elbow, and together we trudge out of the dark alley. We step out into the bright street, the afternoon sun offering a stark contrast to the dark pain that settles on my chest.

Turning the corner toward our flat, Baba Mysa stops and turns to me. "I am disappointed and hurt, Luda," she says. I nod.

"I'm sorry."

Baba Mysa grabs my chin and turns my face down to hers. "Look in my eyes, child," she commands. "He's a German, and though he may be a good man, he is still the enemy. You cannot fall in love with the enemy."

I'm silent as we turn and make our way to the entrance of the building. As the door squeaks open and Baba Mysa begins the slow journey up the stairs, I wait for the door to slam shut behind me. In the echoing boom, I whisper my reply.

"It's too late."

MARIA IVANOVNA
March 6, 1942

It's been three days since I last saw my family. Three days of horror, of fear, of fatigue and heartache and panic. Sitting now on my bunk in the barracks, I try to wrap my mind around all that has happened and how quickly my life has changed.

For three full days, we rocked slowly along the tracks, all of us stuffed tight into the train car and wrapped in heat and terror. We were a car full of teenage girls ripped from the ones we loved. The tears fell freely, and emotions ran hot. By the afternoon of our second day on the train, girls were screaming and wailing. Panic set in, and several girls beat on the sides of the train until their fists were raw and bloody.

Others tried to shut out the wailing. Polina and I wrapped our arms around one another and slid to the floor, each a lifeline to the other. After a while, fatigue set in, and most of the screaming faded into pitiful wails.

If the sounds of our enclosure didn't send me over the edge, the smells threatened to. We all forfeited every bit of dignity as time went forward. With no other options, girls defecated publicly and vomited repeatedly from stress and heartache. Even I had to finally give in to the demands of nature, and with the deepest of sorrow in my eyes I released the pressure on the floor right where I sat.

Never have I felt such a sense of shame.

Polina did all she could to allow me some sense of dignity. She didn't mention it and gently turned her eyes away from me when I could resist no more. And she did not complain when together we had to sit in the mess.

By the third day, everyone had made a human pile on the floor. In an unspoken agreement, we all allowed the smaller girls to lie on top of the larger ones, making a long patchwork of grief and fatigue.

It was this day that I thought we would die. I envisioned the Nazis pulling open the door to find us all rotting in our own stench, and somehow I took comfort in this vision.

But it was not to be so.

Instead, we pulled into a station, and the door opened. The light that streamed into the cabin assaulted my eyes and left me blind. We were all so weak by this point that the Germans charged with herding us out the door had to physically lift and set us on our feet. Polina and I did not let go of one another's hands. We clung tight as they set us upright and both of us, stiff legged and squinting, followed the line of females into the unknown.

We were soiled, dirty, and smelled of human feces and vomit. We didn't look like young girls but old women. What a difference three days made.

Four girls didn't make it. I watched as their lifeless bodies were pulled from the train car and tossed onto a waiting truck with such indifference that I wondered if our captors were, indeed, even human. How can one witness death with no expression at all?

I still do not understand it.

We walked in a straight line, stumbling and falling every few seconds. My tongue was swollen and tight, my longing for water so strong that the second time I stumbled to my knees and fell I couldn't stop myself from leaning forward and licking the dirty grime from the ground. Polina pulled me to my feet, her head shaking violently.

"You can't do that," she whispered.

On we trudged, Polina's arms firmly around me. Despite her frail nature, Polina was surprisingly strong.

"How are you so calm?" I whispered as she guided me along the path.

"I've been doing this for a while," she answered. "You learn to do what they say. It's the only way to stay alive."

"Is that how you survived?" I asked.

Polina nodded her head. "They took me from the woods where your father and I tried to escape. They beat me and threw me into the ditch, assuming I was dead. I just let them assume. I crawled out days later when the shooting finally waned. I made my way out of the woods to a small village where an older woman took me in. She gave me food and clothes . . . then gave me back to the Germans." Polina's voice trailed off.

"She . . . she gave you back?" I asked, horrified. "Why?"

Polina shrugged. "Everyone is afraid these days, Masha," she replied. "Yours is the only family I've met who thinks of others above themselves."

I let this sink in as we walked along silently. The road next to us changed, the streets disappearing as we headed down a thinly worn path toward . . . nothing. We were in the German countryside, the early spring air cool, but not cold. The flowers in the field burst with spring color, their buds small but open. Birds chirped happily in the distance. The entire countryside screamed against the reality of our situation, of where we were and to whom we belonged.

If I closed my eyes, I could imagine that I walked down the path to the dacha, Sergei by my side, headed for the peace that only summer could bring. Mama would be in the garden, tending to the potatoes and dill. Papa would be whistling softly as he headed to the lake to fish. Anna would be rummaging in the kitchen, preparing the fresh bread for our dinner. Sergei and I would leap through the high grasses, laughing and chasing one another with the reckless abandon of youth without cares.

But I couldn't close my eyes. If I had closed my eyes, I would have fallen, and weakness is not an option in the place where I now exist. So that day, in the warm German sunshine, I kept my eyes open wide, I pushed out the memories of Sergei and the dacha, and I clung to Polina, a forsaken Jewess without hope for tomorrow.

We both knew she didn't have long.

"You have no identification papers," I whispered, desperate for her and she nodded.

"Why'd they let you on the train?"

"They'll make a sport of me," she answered. I marveled at her strength.

She didn't sound afraid, but then she also knew death to be a welcome experience in this life we were being forced to live.

We rounded a corner and immediately noticed the long, barbed fence that stretched before us. It was high, and the sharp spikes gave the beautiful landscape a dark and ominous feel.

"We're almost home," Polina whispered to me, and I felt such a measure of fear overtake me that I dug my nails into her arm. We walked another four hundred meters to the entrance where a tall, crudely built structure welcomed us in. We walked under the sign, the German letters painted in crooked fashion: *Jedem das Seine.*

"'Everyone gets what he deserves.'" Polina whispered the translation of this sign, and I blinked back hot tears. The cruelty of it all was too much.

When we first arrived at the camp earlier today, we walked to a long, narrow building where our identification papers were taken from us. When Polina could not produce papers, the Germans murmured softly to one another and made notes on their boards. We were sent to the bathhouse, where they stripped us naked and sprayed us with such force that I thought the skin would fall from my body. As I faced the stream of frigid water, I opened my mouth wide and sucked down as much of it as I could before being ordered to turn. Water was the only redemption of my day. We were issued drab clothing, thin and scratchy with a large patch over the left breast that read OST.

Ostarbeiter. That is my new label. No longer *Untermensch,* I am now an "eastern worker" who has a purpose: to serve the German. To work on their behalf. A slave laborer. I am OST.

Our heads were shaven, and we were each given a dry, crusty roll and a small tin cup of warm, brown water. It did nothing to satiate the deep hunger I felt, but it was enough to get me through the evening. We got another piece of bread before bed and were sent to the barracks, where a long line of hard benches hung from the wall. A bit of straw covers each bench. One by one, we wearily climbed into the bunks where I now lie, wide awake, staring at the ceiling as I try to comprehend my new reality.

FREDERICK HERRMANN
April 6, 1942

I was ten years old the first time my father took us all to Berlin. It was 1934, and the sights and sounds of the bustling city as we exited our train at Berlin's Lehrter Bahnhof left me wide-eyed and awed. We rushed directly from the train to the Nazi-provided car as Father urged us to waste no time. He had a big party to attend that night, and he planned to take us with him. The SS officer appointed as our transport stood rigidly next to the black car, and I felt his dark eyes fall on me in disdain as I slid into the back seat and shrunk in intimidation.

That trip to Berlin was the first time that I felt truly awed by my father's status. He was so important that, as we exited the car, hotel staff hurried to us, picking up bags and rushing to our room in a fashion worthy only of someone important.

We stood in our expansive room on the top floor of the Hotel Esplanade and looked out over the beautiful city bustling below us. Talia and I pressed our noses to the cool glass and pointed out the cars and people walking below.

"The cars look like small toys," I cooed just before my father stepped up behind us.

"Stand up children," he snapped. Talia and I stood and faced our father, my heart beating like a drum.

"Good. Now, who can tell me what we worked on earlier this week?"

Because I was always so frightened of my father, it seemed to take me a long time to register any question he asked. Panic left me mute so Talia picked up the slack, thrusting her hand in the air.

"Talia?"

"We learned to remain quiet and calm and to not speak unless asked a direct question," she said with a smile, her bright red hair cascading over slender shoulders. Father smiled and ran his hand down her cheek.

"Very good, my darling," he said. "Now, Frederick," he said turning to me. "How are you to greet any official that walks your way?"

My heart raced as I searched for the words to answer my father. I couldn't find them, so I merely thrust my arm straight up in the air. Father sighed and shook his head.

"Yes, Frederick," he said with a heaping portion of annoyance, "but what do you say when you greet them?"

My hand, still high above my head, shook as I searched for the greeting that I knew but couldn't seem to voice. Why did I always feel so incompetent in his presence?

Talia snapped her heels together and threw her arm up next to me. *"Heil Hitler!"* she said, tossing me a sideways glance.

"Heil Hitler!" I repeated after her, and Father nodded.

"Very good, Talia," he said, looking away from me in obvious disgust. "Now go prepare yourselves for dinner."

Lying back on my bunk in the barracks, I think of that visit to Berlin. The memory dances through my mind in moving pictures, every emotion joined together in one fluid movement. It would be the first of several trips my father took us on. We went to parties in the grand city attended by the finest in the Nazi Party. We strolled the beautiful walkways of the Tiergarten in the spring, when the blooms sent brilliant petals of color dancing to the ground as though it were a parade. Father would walk stoically alongside Rudolph Diels, chief of the Gestapo, talking through the early afternoons. In the evenings, he spent his time in the company of Goring, Goebbels, and when time permitted, with the Great Führer himself.

I was not always privy to the meetings with the men in power, but on the occasions that Father would allow me to tag along, I stood tall and proud among them. I wish I could relive those days when the message and the mission seemed so well defined and solid. It all seemed perfectly right at the start of this war, when my boots were fresh against the soil and the actions were still ideas.

Turning on my side, I look at the other men in the room with me. I know what we've all been taught. I believe the message of my country with all of my heart. We're the superior race, and as such, it's our duty to overtake the world and cleanse it, bringing it into the submission for which it was originally designed. I am Germany's son. We are all her sons.

Sliding off my bunk, I head to the bathroom, where I splash a little cold water on my face. There's a single, cracked mirror hanging on the wall for us to use when shaving. I look in it and see what everyone else sees—a skinny boy with thin lips and a dotted complexion. My eyes are red and bloodshot from lack of sleep, and I seem to have developed a permanent grimace. Sighing, I push myself up a little straighter and hold my shoulders back tight as my father taught me to do.

What would my father see if he looked at me now? Who speaks to him of me? I think of the men in the other room, and I wonder which of them was sent to be father's spy.

I walk out of the bathroom and gather my belongings. Dressing quietly, I slip out onto the street just as the morning sun begins to rise above the horizon. I don't have to report to duty until eight o'clock, so I decide to take a quick walk to the nearby park that rises up high above the city. When I reach the top of the worn trail, I slow down my pace and look out over the valley where the Dnieper River cuts a slow path.

It's now the month of May, but the early morning air remains cold, and my breath forms large puffs of steam each time I breathe out. The weather could very well be the downfall of our country's quest. In Munich we have rough winters, but it's nothing compared to this kind of cold. Our thin, regulation overcoats made the long winter months difficult and burdensome. Even now, I wrap my arms tight around my shoulders and look up at the sky, gray and foreboding. I turn the corner at the top of the trail. That's when I see him. We lock eyes and freeze.

It's him—the man from Babi Yar. He *is* alive. I knew he didn't die that day, and a surge of anger overcomes me. I reach for my gun, pulling it quickly from the back of my pants. I point it at him, hands shaking.

He looks at my trembling hands, and his head cocks to the side. His face is drawn and sad, full of remorse. We stare at one another for a long, still moment. Finally I speak.

"Stop right there," I say, my Russian chopped and grammatically poor. "Come with me to headquarters to face punishment for breaking curfew."

The man shakes his head before answering. "*Nyet*. I will not do that," he says. His voice is not defiant or angry. He says this as though he's merely declining an afternoon walk with a friend.

"You know who I am, don't you?" I ask, taking a step forward. My knees knock.

"Yes," he replies. "You're the boy who couldn't kill me at Babi Yar."

I feel the blood rush to my head as a surge of anger overtakes me. Taking another step forward, I clench my teeth. "I can kill you today," I growl, and the man smiles.

"You won't," he says. "You're scared, you're cold, and I know these woods much better than you do. I'll run, and I will get away. Which will be more humiliating: for me to outrun you, or for you to simply let me go?"

I think about his words for a moment, letting them slowly sink in. It takes a few seconds for it to all translate in my mind, and by the time I'm ready to answer, he has turned and begun to make his way slowly down the hill. That's when I realize he's right. I lower my gun and watch as my captive walks in freedom from me once again.

It's then that I realize once and for all: I will always be a disappointment to my father.

MARIA IVANOVNA
June 4, 1942

The pleasant German spring has given way to the heat of summer. Not that the heat could bother me, as I spend all day inside an armament camp, assembling the weapons that the Nazis are using to fight my family.

The armament facility is a one-hour walk from the camp where we sleep. We wake each morning long before the sun rises and accept our ration of dry bread and muddy water before trudging through the dark, German soil to the factory. By the time we return to the barracks, it's dark again.

Nobody tries to run. At least no one has tried to since the first week when Karina tried to tear into the darkness in hopes of escaping.

The Nazis dragged her lifeless body back and hung it just outside the gates for all of us to see each morning as we left and evening when we arrived back. They only took her corpse down when the skin began to rot off the bones.

Polina is still with me, but she grows weaker each day. Because she is Jewish, she's treated more harshly. She's not given the morning rations, so I share my bread with her. She tries to insist that I keep it for myself, but I cannot get her words out of my head: *"Yours is the only family who thinks of others above themselves."*

At the factory, we work with chemicals that are mixed and poured into metal shells, all of which are shipped to the Nazi front line and used to kill the very men who are fighting to free us. Polina must do the same work that the rest of us do, but she's given nothing to protect her from the elements. She's not permitted to wear safety goggles, or gloves, or a mask to keep from breathing in the harsh chemicals. And as we trudge home in the dark, she clings to me, her skin and hair covered in the thick, yellow dust—residue of the chemicals with which we work.

My world has become my nightmare of yellow.

A deep, rattling cough has settled in Polina's chest, and I see her movements slowing down steadily. She's sick, and there's nothing I can do to stop it. Nothing but offer her half a piece of stale bread and a hand to hold on to in the darkness.

It's been nearly a year since the war began—since everything changed. I have nothing left of my former life but the memories that haunt my dreams—the echoes of laughter and sorrow that drown in a swirl of black and yellow each night. I worry about Sergei and wonder where he is and what he's doing. Is he alive? Is he well?

I've convinced myself that Anna is safe and refuse to consider the possibility that she might not be. I've heard from the other girls that when they examined our hands at the train station, they were looking for strong hands that could perform hard labor. If the hands looked too soft and the girls too dainty, they were sent to another part of Germany to work as housekeepers or nannies.

I pray this is where Anna is, because then I know she must be safe. In a house full of children with only the chores of cooking and cleaning, Anna will be in her element, and it gives me hope for her survival.

I cannot think of Mama and Papa without sorrow burning inside. How frightened they must be with all of us gone and no hope of knowing where we are. It's the thought of them that gives me the most heartache.

It's dark tonight, and we're finally heading back. We work sixteen hours a day, and the labor is exhausting. We stand the whole time, sometimes lifting heavy containers. My fingers are raw and rough from the long days of moving metal and turning and screwing on the caps that will seal the fate of one of my countrymen.

Polina wheezes steadily next to me, her chest giving off a deep rattle. So sick.

"You shouldn't work tomorrow," I say, my voice thick with fatigue.

"If I don't work, they'll kill me," she responds.

"I thought that's what you wanted," I answer quietly. I immediately regret my words. Polina labors forward a moment in silence.

"Yes," she says finally. "It's what I want, but . . ." She grows quiet, and I wait as a coughing fit racks her body. Stopping to lean forward, I hear her coughing up fluids and spitting bitterly in the grass at our feet. I cannot see her in the dark, but I can guess that she spits out blood and my heart goes cold.

Taking a breath and straightening, Polina pulls hard on my arm. "Help me back," she whispers. I hear the sound of the German boots coming up swiftly behind us.

"Walk quickly!" he snaps, jabbing me in the side. Polina and I stumble to catch up to the moving line.

"I don't want to die at their hands," Polina whispers, her voice tight and constricted. "I don't want them to have the satisfaction of being there in my last moments. I want to die on my own." I'm baffled by both her resignation and her strength. Tears prick my eyes, hot and bitter as we step across the threshold of the camp, our home in sorrow.

"I just need to lie down," Polina says. Most of the girls make their way to the bathhouse where they'll wash off the grime of today's work, but I turn with Polina, and we slowly walk back to our barracks. I pull her through the door and set her down gently before heading to the lamp and striking a match to light the wick inside. The single burning lamp gives off an orange glow, which dimly flicks at each barren wall with a sorrowful shadow. I pick Polina up under the arms and drag her to the small pallet on the floor that's left for the sickest girls who are unable to climb into the bunks along the wall.

She's so light, her body nothing but skin stretched taut over bones.

Laying her head in my lap, I run my fingers over her shaved head gently. Polina looks up at me, her eyes hollow and gaunt. I can already see the life fading in the black. The thick scar on her forehead juts out in a gruesome line. Her breathing is now shallow and very thin.

"Thank you," she breathes, her chest rising slightly, then sinking deeply. I can see the bones protruding from beneath her dark brown dress.

"Shh . . ." I whisper back. "It's okay, Polya."

She shakes her head, signaling to me her desire to speak more. She wants to share, and I must listen.

"Your family . . . has been . . . so good," she whispers, each word a gasp. "You have all . . . shown me that there's . . . still good . . . in the world."

The tears spill freely, dripping hard down my cheeks and off my chin. I run my hands up and down her hollow cheeks, silent sobs heaving up and out of my own thin body.

"Please . . . keep . . . living," Polina gasps, and the black of her eyes starts to thicken. "Don't let . . . them . . . win . . ." The final word escapes as a gasp, and the black spreads completely, leaving her expression vacant, glassy, and still. The quiet of the moment is so profound I cannot breathe. I place my hands over her eyes and push the lids slowly down.

"I promise," I whisper, and I mean it.

I will live.

LUDA MICHAELEVNA
June 15, 1942

I think of him every day. I long to see him and have schemed a hundred different ways to get out of the flat to go meet him, but Baba Mysa will have none of it. She watches me every moment, refusing to let me out of her sight. To keep me occupied during the daytime hours, she has decided to teach me to knit.

"You must know how to make clothes for your baby," she mumbles every time she sees me looking wistfully out the window. So hour after hour, we purl yarn into tiny hats and shoes, blankets and shirts. And all the while I think of him.

Alexei and Katya watch us curiously. They know something happened, but true to her word, Baba Mysa has not spoken of what she saw in the ally. No one ever questions Baba Mysa, so for now my secret is safe.

But they want to know. I can feel their questions in the stares, and at night I can hear Katya open and close her mouth in an attempt to ask but never with the courage to actually produce words.

By far, though, it is Oleg who leaves me feeling desperate and alone. He sits in the corner, brooding. Somehow he seems to sense that I have given my heart away, and the jealous anger that swims in his eyes makes me uncomfortable. I avoid him at all costs and try to make sure I'm never alone in a room with him.

Baba Mysa looks up from the tenth pair of booties she has made and stares at me for a long moment. I don't return her stare, but instead will my fingers to move the yarn in the right pattern. I'm clumsy and poor at this task of making clothing, and it adds to my frustration. I drop my hands to my lap and stare out the window once more.

"You'll have the baby soon," Baba Mysa says quietly, and I nod. I've felt the pressure begin to build in my abdomen at night, and I sense that the time is nearing when I will finally hold my child in my arms. The thought terrifies me.

"It is very painful," Baba Mysa says with a small sigh, and I turn to face her.

"What's it like?" I ask. My eyes fill with tears of fear, and I pull my arm around my swollen stomach.

Baba Mysa returns my gaze steadily. There is tenderness in her eyes. I know that she cares for me deeply. "It is a wonderful, beautiful hurt," she says gently. "You must remember one thing when you're deep in the most painful moments."

I sit perfectly still and wait, my heart beating wildly at the thought of it all. "What?" I ask.

"When the baby is born and in your arms, the pain stops. It's over. So remember that when you're in the middle. Remember that you just have to get to the end for the pain to stop."

I nod slowly and wait for more, but Baba Mysa offers no more advice. "Is . . . is that all?" I ask. I was hoping for more detail on what to expect.

"That's all you need to know," Baba Mysa answers. "If you know too much, you'll get scared." Her fingers work quickly around the knitting needles, moving them back and forth and up and down in perfect rhythm. I sigh and set aside my project.

"I'm going to go lie down for a bit," I murmur.

I move slowly to the bedroom, the muscles in my back straining against the weight of my middle. Leaning back against the narrow couch, I finally fall into the hard cushions. Sleeping has proved nearly impossible on the thin couch these last few weeks, but the idea of lying on the floor and trying to get back up is almost laughable. I spend many nights pacing the floor and thinking of him.

Looking out the window, I lose myself in the moments that we had together—the feel of his arms around me, the bass of his laugh, and the tender touch of his hand against my cheek. I'm so lost in my mind that I don't even hear Oleg slip quietly into the room. I jump when he clears his throat.

"Oleg!" I exclaim. I try to stand up, but he motions me to stop.

"Stay, Luda," he says, his voice sharp. I sit still and again place my hands instinctively on my stomach.

"I have something to say to you," Oleg says evenly. I nod my head once.

"I have loved you from the moment you fell through our front door so many months ago," he begins. His voice is laced with pain, and I feel a dreadful sense of shame at the hurt I've caused him.

"I've longed to protect you from the pain that has followed you and wanted nothing more than to give you the love I felt you deserved." He pauses and looks out the window for a moment, his eyes shining and bright.

"Oleg, I—" He holds up his hand and cuts me off.

"Wait, Luda," he says. "I'm not finished." Oleg walks to the couch and sits beside me. He reaches forward and grabs my hand and pulls it into his.

"I know that you've fallen in love with someone else," he says, and my heart skips a beat. "I don't know who it is or how you could have possibly met him, but I saw the look on your face when you came back from your afternoon walks, and I knew you were meeting someone. Am I right?" Oleg looks deep into my eyes and searches for the answer that he knows is already there. I nod slowly.

"Yes, you're right," I whisper.

Oleg sighs and drops my hand. "Why have you stopped meeting him?" he mumbles.

"Baba Mysa told me not to see him again. She thinks it's too dangerous," I answer. My voice is laced with sadness.

Oleg looks up at me in surprise. "Who could be so dangerous that Baba Mysa feels it necessary to cut off all contact?" he asks.

I remain silent. I cannot tell Oleg that I love a German. In my heart, I know that it will destroy him. He watches me closely as my hands move up and down over the baby. I keep my eyes forward, away from his prying stare.

"Will there ever be any room in your heart for me, Luda?" Oleg asks, and I turn to look at him. His long, handsome face is full of sorrow. He doesn't have the same manly look as Hans, but his boyish looks give away his vulnerability and goodness.

"Oleg, I do love you," I say. "But I don't love you the way that you love me, and I'm not sure I ever will."

Oleg sighs and nods. The anger has dissolved, and in its place I have left him broken and embarrassed.

"I'm sorry," I whisper.

"I'm sorry, too, Luda," Oleg says sadly. "I won't bring this up anymore." Oleg stands and glances back down at me. Our eyes meet, and I'm nearly melted by the look of tenderness that he gives me. He reaches down and runs his hand across my cheek.

"You're worthy of love from a good man, Luda," he murmurs. "I hope that he is good." Grabbing his hand, I press it to my lips gently.

"You're worthy of the love of a woman who is willing to give it back," I say, and he gives the faintest hint of a smile. Dropping his hand, Oleg walks slowly out of the room and closes the door. I close my eyes and lean back on the couch again.

I wake up hours later, and the light from the window has faded to a dusky gray. I open my eyes slowly and blink several times, trying to discern how much time has passed since I lay down. The pain hits me with a sudden force, and I lean forward with a gasp, gripping my stomach. It's tight and hard, and I pant as the pain rolls over me and the pressure in my middle pins me to the couch. I realize that I'm sitting in a small puddle of water and move to stand up when another wave of pain hits.

"Baba!" I call out through clenched teeth. Baba Mysa rushes into the room, her eyes wide. Alexei and Katya follow closely after her.

Leaning down, Baba Mysa grabs my hand. "It's okay, *dorogaya*," she purrs. "It's alright. The baby is coming."

I nod and close my eyes tight, rocking back and forth slowly as the worst of the pain subsides. Suddenly the room feels vast and hollow. I hear Baba Mysa talking, and it's as though she is far away, despite the fact that she's standing right next to me.

"Alexei, I want you to gather the blankets and pillows together and put them on the floor, then leave the room, please," she says to Alexei, who immediately moves in obedience. "And you need to tell Oleg to go find the doctor. I can deliver this baby, but if there are any complications, I want a doctor nearby and ready." Alexei nods. I think of his wife, of Katya's mother, lying on a pallet waiting for a doctor who wouldn't make it in time, and I'm suddenly frightened.

"Katya," Baba Mysa says, turning to my friend who looks terrified and ready to flee. "I need you to go to the kitchen. In the cabinet above the stove there's a small tin tub. Take that down and boil some water and fill the tub halfway. Then bring it to me along with a small bowl of cool water." Baba Mysa looks at Katya and waits for her to move, but she seems frozen.

"Katya!" Baba Mysa barks. Katya jumps. "Did you hear me?" Katya nods and runs from the room. I sit very still, willing the pain away. Alexei brings in the last of the pillows and helps Baba Mysa arrange them on the floor. I sit up to move, and my abdomen tightens again. I feel the twist in my back, like a knife turning. Pain courses down through my legs. I let out a small yelp and lean forward.

"Go, Alexei," I hear Baba Mysa whisper and she rushes to me. "Don't hold your breath, Luda," she says firmly. "You must breathe. We'll do it together." Taking a long, slow, deep breath in, Baba Mysa forces my chin up to look in her eyes. I slow my breathing to match hers, and in a moment the pain ebbs, and I'm offered a brief reprieve.

"This hurts," I moan as Baba Mysa helps me to the floor. She doesn't respond, but instead lays me flat and positions the pillows to give me more comfort. I hear the door open and look up to see Katya tiptoe into the room.

"Here's the water, Baba," she whispers, setting down a small bowl. She runs to the door where she's laid down the tin tub, which steams from the boiling water inside it. Baba Mysa nods. "Thank you, Katyusha," she says. Katya turns to leave, but Baba Mysa stops her.

"I'll need your help," she says. "And so will Luda. I'd like you to stay." Katya's eyes widen, and she looks from Baba Mysa to me in fear.

"I—" she begins, and I cut her off.

"Please, Katya," I beg. I reach for her hand. "I'm so scared."

Katya looks at me, then takes a step forward and grabs my hand, sinking to the floor by my head.

"Good girl," Baba Mysa says. She hands Katya a small pile of torn rags. "Dip these in cool water and lay them over Luda's forehead and neck," she says, and Katya complies. I barely have time to relish the coolness on my forehead when another wave of pain rips through me. I let out a cry as my whole body responds, writhing and moving with the pressure that threatens to overcome. Finally I lie back, gasping.

"How long will this last, Baba?" I ask. Baba Mysa moves to my feet and spreads my legs gently. I feel my face get hot as she checks to see the progress the baby and I are making. She looks up with a small smile.

"You're one of the lucky ones," she says. "You won't have to do this long. This baby is coming fast."

I nod just as my body contracts again. Grabbing Katya's hand, I squeeze hard as a long, low growl escapes my throat. It is a primal, guttural moan of pain that cannot be controlled or stopped. When the pain moves past, my throat feels raw and dry.

"Can I have some water?" I ask. Baba Mysa nods at Katya and she dips a rag in the cool water, then squeezes it on my tongue.

"Katya," Baba Mysa says, "go see if Oleg has returned yet with the doctor. I want to make sure everything is okay here before I allow Luda to begin pushing." Katya nods and pushes up.

"Please don't be long," I cry. Katya's presence is soothing and comforting to me, and I find myself a little more frightened when she steps away. Katya looks down at me with a tender smile.

"I'll be right back," she says.

Turning to Baba Mysa, I see her watching me, searching my face. "You're going to be an excellent mother, Luda," she says with a smile. I want to smile back at her, but the pain rolls in again, and I give myself to it.

For the next several hours I move in and out of pain, which comes with greater intensity as the moments drag on. Oleg doesn't return with the doctor, and as the daylight fades into the black of night, I can sense everyone's concern over his absence.

"He should have come back by now," Katya whispers to Baba Mysa, who works furiously with brow furrowed each time I cry out in pain. Finally, when I feel like I can go no further, I let out a scream as the pressure mounts with such force I think I'll split in two.

"This is it, Luda," Baba Mysa cries. "I see the baby's head. It's time to push."

"I can't," I cry. I'm exhausted. My back feels like it's been tied in a thousand knots, and my head is pounding. Katya leans over me and looks in my eyes.

"Luda, your baby is coming!" she says, her eyes bright with excitement. "I know you can do this. You are the strongest person I know. You can do it!"

I nod, and she helps me sit up a little. Clenching my teeth, I let out a scream and push as hard as I can. I feel my face going red, and the world starts to fade to black. Just before it fades completely, I feel the split and a release. Collapsing back to the floor, the room spins slightly as Katya lays a cool rag on my forehead. It's very quiet.

Too quiet.

"What's wrong?" I ask. "Where's the baby?"

I sit up and see Baba Mysa working feverishly around the baby's head, mumbling something about the doctor and Oleg. "Come baby," she croons. She pulls back a cord from the baby's neck and I see blue and hear silence.

"Please don't die," I whisper over and over. "Please don't die, baby. I need you."

Baba Mysa gently massages the baby's chest, and the silence is broken by a tiny squawk. I watch Baba Mysa let out a sigh of relief. She crosses herself, offering up a prayer of thanks and blows a kiss at the baby before holding it up to me.

"Luda," she says gently. "Meet your son."

My eyes fill with tears as I take in his tiny face, his features swollen and closed tight. His fists are balled and his mouth is open, emitting a strong cry. I reach for him, and Baba Mysa lays him in my arms.

"You fit," I whisper to my boy, my tears falling fast and hard. "You fit here. This is where you belong." I look up at Katya, who's also crying. "This is my son," I say. My whole body is shaking, and I suddenly realize I'm desperately cold.

"Katya," Baba Mysa says as she works to clean me up. I hear the snip of scissors, and suddenly my son is free of my body. He's free to walk this world on his own, free to grow into a man. I pull him in tight and feel a longing to protect unlike any I've ever known.

"Katya, dip the rags in the warm water and roll them up in the sacks, please," Baba Mysa says. Katya and Baba Mysa work quickly, placing warm bags under my feet and arms. They cover me with blankets and gradually the trembling slows. Still my baby lies on my chest. He roots and cries.

"Let him eat, Luda," Baba Mysa whispers, and she gently pulls my shirt down. Immediately my son latches on and I look up at her in surprise. She smiles and nods. "It's okay," she says. "You'll learn, and you will be fine."

Looking down at my son against my breast I feel the tears fill the corners of my eyes once more. "You're mine, little one," I whisper. I trace the line of his hair and his tiny ear. "You're mine."

I wake up hours later to the squeaks and squirms of my hungry child. I pick him up gingerly and push myself to a sitting position. Baba Mysa must have bathed and wrapped him up while I slept. He smells clean and his light blond hair sticks up in soft tufts on his head. Holding him up, I marvel at the perfection of his features. There's a familiarity that I see in him. I feel as though I've always known him—like somehow he's always been right here with me.

I settle into nursing him, the process a little more painful this time. Leaning back against the wall, I think of Hans once again. I wish he could see my son.

My son.

"I should give you a name," I whisper, rubbing my hand slowly across his tiny back. I run through a list of names, saying each one aloud until I find one that fits.

"*Aleksandr*," I say gently and smile. That is his name. "My little Sasha," I croon, letting the tender nickname roll off my tongue.

I don't want this child to have any part of my own father's name, and because he doesn't have a Ukrainian father, I decide to give him Alexei's surname. A knock at the door startles me. I grab a nearby blanket and throw it over my chest and shoulders, embarrassed to be caught in such a vulnerable position.

"Come in," I call, and Sasha jumps in my arms. Baba Mysa pushes the door open slightly and peeks her head in. Her eyes are tired, her face drawn and long. "May we all come in?" she asks.

I pull Sasha from me and cover myself quickly, then nod my head yes. Startled from his comfort, he lets out a small cry of protest, then quickly falls asleep in my arms, his mouth still moving in rhythm to his suckling.

Alexei, Katya, and Baba Mysa all file in. Alexei hands me a small bouquet of flowers, leaning down to kiss me gently on the forehead.

"I'm so proud of you," he says, his eyes swimming with tears. I've never seen this sort of emotion from Alexei before.

"Thank you," I say shyly. "This is my son." Everyone sits on the floor and crowds in close to stare at his tiny perfection.

"This is Aleksandr Alexeiovich," I say with a smile. "Sasha."

Alexei looks at me with wide eyes. "Aleksandr Alexeiovich, huh?" he says, and he reaches out for his namesake. I gingerly place Sasha into Alexei's arms and notice that Katya's face has darkened. I reach for her hand and give it a reassuring squeeze. She looks back at me, and I nod gently. I know it hurts her to see her papa so enamored with my child. She sighs and squeezes back at my hand.

"Where's Oleg?" I ask. They all fall silent. I glance out the window. It's bright outside. The sun rose some time ago. Oleg has been gone a long time.

"Alexei, where is he?" I ask again. Alexei shakes his head, tears gathering again in his eyes.

"He never returned last night, Luda," Baba Mysa answers softly. I look wide-eyed at the three of them, chins trembling, shoulders quaking. Then I sit up straight, wincing.

"Baba, you have to find Hans," I say, the words tumbling out in a rush. Baba Mysa looks up at me sharply and shakes her head. Alexei looks back and forth between the two of us.

"Who is Hans?" he asks.

I take a deep breath and close my eyes. "Hans is the man I fell in love with," I answer. I open my eyes to see Alexei and Katya looking at me, their faces frozen and registering confusion. Baba Mysa shakes her head slowly.

"Luda, you don't need to do this," she says.

"Yes I do, Baba," I say. "Oleg is missing because of me. Hans might be able to find out what happened to him."

"Yes, but at what cost?" Baba Mysa asks, her eyes boring into me.

"At what *gain*, Baba?" I cry out in exasperation. Baba Mysa shakes her head again and slumps down, defeated.

I look back to Alexei, still cradling my son gently and Katya who has dropped my hand. This could be the final nail in our friendship, but I know I must tell them now.

"Hans is the German soldier I met the night you and I lured them to the flat and stole their guns," I tell Katya. "He's a good man, gentle and kind. He doesn't agree with what his country is doing."

"How did you fall in love with him, Luda?" Alexei asks. His voice registers shock and pain, and perhaps a hint of betrayal.

I quickly relay the story of how Hans and I met the first time and how we met so many times afterward until Baba Mysa caught us.

"You knew about this?" Alexei says, turning to his mother. She raises her chin up and nods yes, looking her son evenly in the eye.

"Alexei, he is *good*. I promise he's good," I say, and I look slowly at all three of them. Katya turns away from me, disgusted. "He'll help us find Oleg if you will just go to him and ask!"

I turn to Baba Mysa. "He'll be in the alley today at two o'clock. He told me that he would go there every day and wait for me to return. You have to go to him, Baba. You have to try."

Baba Mysa sighs and shakes her head. "Luda," she croons, "that was weeks ago. He'll have given up hope at this point." I shake my head firmly.

"No. He'll be there. I know he will." Turning to Alexei, I reach for my son and pull him back into my arms. "Alexei, I'm sorry that I deceived you and that I hid this from you. I'm sorry that I fell in love with a German, but I'm not sorry that I fell in love with Hans. I know he can help us. We have to try."

I stare intently at Alexei, and he nods slowly. "Alright," he says. I hear the fatigue and worry in his voice. Turning to Baba Mysa, he grabs her hand. "Mama, you and I will go at two o'clock to find this Hans. You can show me where he'll be waiting for Luda. And you can also explain to me how you knew about this for so long without sharing it."

Baba Mysa sighs and nods her head. "Come into the kitchen, you two," she says to Katya and Alexei. "We'll talk there." Turning to me, she gives a slight nod. She's unhappy that I forced her hand; I see it. "Luda, I'll bring you some chai and bread soon," she says.

"Thank you, Baba," I whisper.

I watch as the three of them retreat, a solid unit of grief, frustration, and despair. When the door closes, Sasha and I are alone.

"I think it's going to be just you and me, *Sinok*," I whisper. *Son*. The word is still foreign, and yet the evidence lies in my arms. I have a son.

IVAN KYRILOVICH
June 19, 1942

Tanya and I have fallen into a quiet routine. Our days are spent working and cleaning and preparing for the desired return of our children, which we cling to with all the hope of those who cling to life when death seems imminent. I go with Tanya to the salt piles twice a week now to gather the salt. The piles are dwindling as many others have discovered them, and the salt isn't pure. It's dirty and grimy, and we spend hours each day sifting through it in our flat, picking out the dirt by hand.

When Tanya isn't working at the library or dealing with the salt, she sews new clothes for the girls. She made a blanket for Sergei that sits folded in the corner neatly, waiting for his return with great expectation. We haven't heard from him in months. The last letter we received was so heavily censored we couldn't really make out much of anything that he wrote.

But it meant he was alive. That note, along with the two others we've received over the months, lies on top of a small chest of drawers. I pull it out and unfold it every night, willing myself to feel his hands on the paper.

During the daytime hours, I spend much of the time staring out the window. The shadows of hell still follow me, and I feel the constant potential of slipping back into the abyss. But I cannot forget Anna's words the day the Germans took her from my arms.

Don't leave again.

Tanya walks through the room, her peppered hair pulled in a loose bun. She catches my eyes and pauses a moment. She knows I'm fighting the dark. Our gazes search one another deeply. The light that still flickers inside her grieving eyes is the only thing that keeps the darkness at bay. I need her like I need the air I breathe.

"Would you like any chai?" Tanya asks, her voice a haunting melody.

"Will you sit and drink with me?" I ask.

"Of course," she replies.

"Please," I say with a smile. "I would love to have chai with you, *lyubimaya*." She is *my love*.

Tanya turns and hurries to the kitchen while I look back out the window at the passing clouds. Though I haven't ventured out today, I can sense the warmth in the air. The day is still and bright, so full of promise. The beauty of the outdoors is in such contrast to what happens in the world that it leaves me dizzy.

How can life be anything but gray again?

I think of the German boy often—the boy who altered me forever by forcing me into the line at Babi Yar. I want to hate him and have tried to for some time, but there's something about the way he looked at me when we met in the woods that haunts me. He was conflicted and scared.

I place his youthful face next to my Sergei's and realize that they're not so different. They're boys learning what it means to lead and take charge in life. They're young men who have simply been programmed differently.

Do I fault the boy for the evil that was obviously nurtured in him by a culture that doesn't see the value of human life? Do I hate the boy who's doing what he was told to do because he believes it with all his heart?

I saw the conflict in his eyes that morning. I felt his doubt. I cannot hate him, as much as I would like to. I pity him, and I pity my own boy who's making equally difficult decisions—my own boy who's pulling the trigger and ending life. One ends life out of hatred, the other out of self-defense. Both boys forever will have scars for their decisions.

Tanya walks in carrying a tray with two tin cups, both steaming with hot chai, and two slices of bread. She sets the tray down on the table and arranges the cups in front of each of us, then she sits and pulls her chair close to mine.

Tanya looks out the window at the fluffy white clouds. "Beautiful day," she murmurs.

"I was just thinking the same thing," I say.

Tanya looks at me, her thin, dry hands wrapped around her cup. "What else were you thinking?" she asks.

I haven't told her anything about the days following Babi Yar. I haven't spoken of the young Nazi, or Polina, or the inner torment I feel for not protecting her from those animals. I haven't told her my fears for Sergei and my regret for the choices he must make every day. I haven't shared myself with my wife in a long, long time.

Leaning forward, I take the cup from her hands and set it on the table then wrap my own hands around hers.

"I was thinking about Babi Yar," I say softly. Tanya pulls in a deep breath. She nods and waits. I take my time, gathering my thoughts and filtering them in a way that is coherent.

For the next hour, I share with Tanya the stories of darkness. I tell her about cradling the child inside the ditch and about the hollowness in Polina's eyes as we stumbled naked through the forest. I tell her of the cold that penetrated to the very core and left me desiring death and release. I describe the moment that I heard the butt of the German gun make contact with Polina's head and the sound of her whispering my name as they dragged her away.

I don't speak of the guilt, but I know she can sense it, and her hands grip mine tighter, sweaty palms communicating a solitary promise to never leave. Tanya doesn't speak, but she listens, her eyes wet.

Finally, I tell her about the boy who started it all—the Nazi soldier who committed evil acts but whom I cannot hate.

"I saw him again," I say quietly. "Just a few weeks ago, in the woods. I came to the place high up above the Dnieper and he was there."

Tanya's eyes narrow, and she leans back in her chair, dropping her hands in her lap. Her expression has changed from sorrow to anger, but she still doesn't speak. She waits, her eyes moving from my face to the clouds.

"He was confused," I tell her, searching her face for some clue as to how she's feeling. "I could see the fear and the doubt in his eyes. I could sense his reluctance, and I realized that he's not so different from Sergei."

Tanya's eyes flick to my face. "He is *nothing* like my Sergei," she snaps, her words laced with fire and protection. "My Sergei is good. He chose *good*. He is *protecting* life, not ending it."

I reach forward for her hands, but she pulls away. A small sob escapes her. I drop my hands to the table and look hard into her watery eyes.

"My darling, our Sergei is doing *both*. He's protecting *and* ending life. He will never be the same for it."

Tanya drops her face into her hands, bitter sobs racking her thin shoulders.

"I'm sorry, *dorogaya*," I whisper. "I'm so sorry. I shouldn't have told you these things."

Pushing up, Tanya glares at me. "No. You shouldn't have told me these things," she spits. I fall back in my chair, stunned by the heat of her words. "I don't want to hear of your pity for that monster, and I'll never get the image of you leaving Polina out of my mind. You've abandoned all of us during this war, haven't you?"

She pushes back from the table, the sound of her chair scraping against the floor sending a chill down my spine. I watch as she storms out of the room and leaves me alone with my failures.

FREDERICK HERRMANN
June 21, 1942

"Herrmann, stand!" I leap to my feet and stand at attention as Sturm-bannführer Hitzig marches swiftly into the barracks. The men around me look up curiously, wondering why I'm being summoned this late in the evening.

"You have a visitor," Hitzig snaps. "Dress in uniform and meet me outside in ten minutes."

I raise my arm straight above my head and click my heels in salute. Hitzig turns on his heel and marches back out of the room. He came in just a few months ago, replacing Paul Blobel who's being further utilized to coordinate steady and drastic attacks against the Jews after news of his grand success at Babi Yar spread throughout the upper ranks. Hitzig is a sniveling, whiny man, and I loathe his leadership, though I would never share these feelings with anyone else.

I look around at my comrades, all of whom have their eyebrows raised. I grab my things and dress in a hurry. Turning, I run into Nikolaus.

"What's going on, Frederick?" he whispers.

I shrug. "I don't know, Nikolaus," I snap. "You heard the same information I did. I have a visitor."

"Who could possibly be coming to visit you this late at night?" Nikolaus asks. Sighing, I brush past him and rush for the door. I hear the men buzzing behind me. Their voices trail after me every time I leave a room. They're against me—I can sense it.

Stepping outside, the warm summer air is a refreshing break from the stale smell of the barracks. The general stands against the building, inhaling deeply from his freshly rolled cigarette.

"Well done, Herrmann," he says with a wink. I nod. "Shall we go?" I fall into step behind him, making sure to match his steps while still allowing him to remain ahead of me. Our arms swing back and forth in rhythm.

"You're quiet," Hitzig says.

"I don't know what I'm supposed to say," I answer.

"Aren't you curious as to who is here to see you?" he asks.

"Of course," I reply with surprise. "But I didn't feel it was my place to ask questions."

Hitzig chuckles and nods. "You've been trained well, Herrmann," he says. "Not that I'm surprised."

So Hitzig knows who my father is. We walk up to the building that once served as a cinema for the local people of Kiev. It's now the German command center where major military operations are organized and put into action.

Stepping inside, I need a minute to get used to the swaying feeling that accompanies the dim orange lighting. As I focus, I see him in the corner, and my heart turns cold with fear. Strolling up to me, he stops short just a few feet away, his chin held high. He looks down at me over a sharp nose. He's dressed in a sharply pressed black suit and holds a top hat under his arm with an air of regality. He thrusts his arm up. *"Heil Hitler!"* he cries.

I return the salute. *"Heil Hitler,"* I reply, my voice cracking. I drop my arm, shame and embarrassment immediately enveloping me.

"Hello, Frederick," he says. His voice is not warm, nor is it cold. It's . . . indifferent.

"Hello, Father," I squeak, and I see the disappointment flick across his face. "What are you doing here?" I ask.

"I've come to check the status of our position in this country. When we finally overtake Kiev for good, the Great Führer has asked that I manage the architectural rebuilding of the area into a German hub."

I nod my head, not sure of what else to say. We stand in awkward silence for several minutes, both sizing one another up. I finally speak again.

"How is Mother?" I ask. My mother's face floods my mind as I remember the worried look that seemed to perpetually cloud her features. For so long I saw my mother as simple, misled, somehow beneath and not worthy of my father or me. But in recent months I've found myself longing for the comfort of her presence, a feeling that only adds to the growing sense that I am weak and unfit for my father's approval.

"Your mother's fine," Father says. "She sends her love."

This is followed by another awkward pause. Thus far, my father has not attempted to touch me. No hug or shaking of the hand. Just an awkward and cold salute. I feel his eyes boring into me, sizing up and determining just how deeply my disappointment to him will run.

"Let's walk, Son," he says. Father sweeps past me, and I stand still for a moment, gathering every ounce of my courage to follow him. I catch Hitzig's eye and see the amusement twinkling behind the surface. He sees my fear and finds it amusing.

He now knows just how weak I am.

I spin on my heel and march out the door behind Father, trying hard to make my shoes click the floor with some authority. Instead, the rhythm of my gait gives away my lack of confidence, and the hollow echoes reveal my fear.

Father and I step out into the street. It's dark and silent. Because of the imposed curfew, very few people are walking around. Every once in a while we see a wayward solider swaying and stumbling back to the barracks after too much fun at a local nightclub, but other than that, the streets are hollow and still.

"Which way should we walk, Frederick?" Father asks, and I look up in surprise. He has rarely before asked my opinion, and I feel a thin line of sweat break out on my upper lip. Is this some sort of test? Am I expected to take him somewhere important, to guess where it is he wants to walk?

With my heart beating wildly, I point to the right, deciding to walk Father to the center of town. Kreshadik Street is Kiev's main hub, where once upon a time I imagine quite a bit of hustle took place. It's not nearly as grand or opulent as the streets of Berlin, of course, but there's something about Kreshadik that brings me some comfort, despite the rubbled streets and buildings. It's the exchange of life that happens on a busy city street that gives it an air of importance, and my Father is one to only appreciate importance.

We're silent as we stroll, and I wait for him to speak. I know better than to be the first to initiate conversation. A few minutes later, my father finally breaks the silence.

"I got a letter from Blobel last week, Frederick," Father says, and my blood runs cold. So this is why he came. Father is here to follow up on a letter from his colleague. I nod and wait.

"He had quite a lot to say about you," Father continues, reaching into his pocket and pulling out a small, silver flask. He unscrews the top and takes a quick drink, the rich bourbon scent floating into the street like a ghost.

I look up at the stars above us, the black sky dotted with white holes, and I try to think what on earth Blobel could have possibly said that caused my father to make such a drastic trip. I know that my father has not come to give me praise, and as I stare at the sky, I long to escape.

"Are you curious as to what he had to say, Son?" Father asks, his face twisted into a sneer. I swallow hard and nod my head, giving the proper response, if not the courageous one.

Father reaches into his pocket again, this time pulling out a letter. He stops walking and turns to me, opening the letter quickly. Using the moon's light, Father begins to read. The first few lines are simple formalities. It's the second paragraph that causes me to quake:

> "Your boy is fine, Tomas, though I must say his lack of leadership and courage have surprised me. He follows every order, yet takes little initiative to move on his own. It is as though he's afraid, but what he fears I don't understand. While I never had a single problem with him, and he accomplished every task I, or any of his superiors, gave him, I felt for some reason a little disappointed each time I looked at him. I couldn't help but feel as though he were a waste of great, Aryan blood."

Father stops reading and folds the letter slowly while I stand before him shocked and exposed. I take in slow, deep breaths and stand stiff at attention. Father tucks the letter back into his coat and runs his hand down his face and over his smooth-shaven chin.

"So what do you have to say for yourself?" Father asks. His voice is cold and icy. I open my mouth to speak, but find that I can hardly draw in a breath, much less form words. In a sudden move, Father's hand snaps up and clamps down on the back of my neck. He squeezes so hard that it feels as though my bones will break, and he pulls my face to his so that our noses are nearly touching. I can see the fire of anger blazing in his eyes, and the bourbon on his breath stings and chokes.

"You have shamed us, Frederick," he hisses, spitting the words out like a bitter poison. "Your cowardice has been noticed and observed by one of the great leaders of this army, and you have left me humiliated and ashamed."

I pull back against his hand, trying to release myself from the hatred and anger, but he squeezes harder. I feel my eyes growing hot and wet, and my Father, seeing the tears glisten, releases and shoves me backward. I stumble, catching myself just before falling. Swiping my hand across my eyes, I pull myself up straight and take in several deep breaths as my Father claps his hands together, wiping away the grime of shame.

Turning slowly, Father reaches up and straightens his hat. He begins to walk slowly back in the direction that we came. I stand still, wondering briefly if I should just run.

"Come now, Son," he commands, his voice sharp, dripping with disdain. I turn and fall into step just behind him. We walk in silence back to the command center. Stopping just outside the door, Father turns to me.

"You are a great disappointment," he says. "Even more so than your sister." I don't respond. I look him in the eye and see that it's true. I have let him down deeply.

"I have a meeting scheduled with Hitzig tomorrow," Father continues. "He and I will determine what your next step should be in this war and how we can best utilize a cowardly soldier with the best grooming our great nation has to offer."

With each word my Father speaks, I find myself shrinking further and deeper into the pavement. Father steps close to me, and I flinch. "I'll give you one more chance, Frederick," he says, his voice low and measured.

"You have one more chance to prove you're worthy of my approval and worthy to bear my name. If you let me down again . . ." Father stops and sighs, stepping back and looking out into the street.

"You are no son of Germany."

Turning quickly, Father pushes the door open and enters the command building, where I imagine he will quickly subdue the room with his power and confidence. He doesn't invite me to join him, and I understand my dismissal. I'm to go back and earn his approval.

I watch the door swing shut and jump when it slams. Numb and humiliated, I turn and slowly begin making my way back to my bunk.

MARIA IVANOVNA
June 22, 1942

This morning, as I drag myself from my wooden pallet, I hear the whispers again. The girls around me, new *Ostarbeiter* who joined us a week ago, speak softly of a place called Auschwitz and another called Bremen.

Alyona Semenova stands up beside me. She came to the camp three weeks ago and has become a dear friend. She links arms and leans in close.

"It's better that we're here," she whispers. I nod. The stories I hear of these camps give weight to her claim. It's been one year since the bombs first fell on my city and four months since the Germans marched me away from my family. It feels like a lifetime.

We're all sick, though I assume it will only get worse when the winter settles in. We've been told that we're not prisoners but workers. I don't understand how this could be when we're not paid for the work that we do and are kept inside a barbed fence. For twelve hours a day, I move heavy machinery back and forth, handle harsh chemicals, and trudge through the yellow dust of the factory in a trance. The only things that keep me moving are my friendship with Alyona and the thought of seeing my family again.

Sometimes, though, the shadows close in, and I let them swallow me up. There's a pole at the front of the camp with a noose hanging over it— trying to escape this place holds a penalty of death. Though no one has been strung up since the girl who tried to run early on, I feel my palms sweat and tremble each time we trudge past that spot.

I pull my dress over my head and sigh as it hangs loosely on my gaunt frame. My shoulders jut out at an odd angle, and I can't seem to keep the worn material from sliding around throughout the day.

"Here, let me help," Alyona says, stepping up behind me. She pulls the material up in two sections around the back of my neck and ties it in a knot. I look down and smooth it out, making sure the faded patch is still fully shown.

OST. I am still *Ostarbeiter*. I am a slave.

"So . . . another day?" Alyona says. I nod with half a smile. I'm weak with hunger, as the rations have been sparse these last few weeks. Apparently, we haven't been working hard enough in the factory.

"I'm hungry," I mumble, and she puts her arm around me.

"So am I," she says sadly. Together we trudge out into the early morning air. It's dusky, the summertime hours giving us more of a glimpse of our surroundings. Beyond the barbed wire and grotesque wooden fences, the German countryside is beautiful. It's mountainous and green and lush with the glory of nature.

In the gray haze, I pull in a deep breath and feel the pang of hunger momentarily wane. If only the fresh air could sustain me.

We push to the mess hall for our morning allotment of stale bread. Sometimes we're also allowed a cup of hot water. Today, though, when we walk in, the table is empty and those who have arrived before us stand slumped and defeated.

"What's going on?" I ask someone, a frail mouse of a girl named Svetlana. She shrugs her shoulders, her eyes brimming with tears.

"There's no food today," she says, and her chin quivers. I see the desperation, and I understand. The prospect of working all day without some sustenance is too much to consider. I put my arm around Svetlana and kiss the top of her head. Her hair is thin and patchy.

"Shh . . ." I whisper as she cries quietly. Svetlana's shoulders tremble.

"I can't make it," she whispers. I look desperately at Alyona, and her eyes meet mine with the same mournful doubt. Taking a deep breath, I push Svetlana back and wipe the tears off her cheeks.

"Well," I say, willing my voice to sound relaxed and upbeat. "Let's make a game of today, then." Svetlana breathes in ragged breaths as she stares back at me.

"A game?" she asks.

I nod and glance at Alyona, who looks equally curious.

"Today is a contest," I say. "We'll see who can fill the most artillery shells by the end of the day."

Svetlana shrugs her shoulders. "You can't have a contest without a prize," she mumbles.

I put my hands on my hips and look at her sternly. "Well, I know that," I say impatiently. "Of course there will be a prize." Svetlana eyes me warily, and I force a grin.

"The prize will be a grand feast tonight in the barracks," I say with a mischievous wink.

"How can you possibly promise such a prize!" Svetlana cries. I shush her, looking around to make sure we haven't been overheard. The other girls arrive, and all notice the empty tables. I see their curious stares and wave them all over, whispering the details of our contest.

"You can't get us any food," they cry, and I shake my head.

"I can get you food," I say. "It will be grand and beautiful and glorious, but I'll only give it to the girl who believes me and fills the most artillery shells today."

I see the group speaking softly. Several shrug, and nod their heads. I smile a genuine smile this time. "This will be great!" I say with excitement.

A whistle blows from the front gate, and we rush out of the empty room. The Germans watch us closely as we line up. With a great deal of glee, I notice their obvious disappointment. We're excited to get to work, despite being deprived of food. I can see that this reaction was unexpected, and I delight in the Germans' agitation. Standing close behind me, Alyona whispers quietly in my ear.

"I hope you've got something planned for tonight," she breathes. I nod. I do have a plan. I just hope it works.

Working without any food at all is every bit as difficult and painful as I thought that it would be. At midday, the gnawing pangs inside my stomach twist and pull. I wipe my brow, adjusting the small paper mask that covers my nose and mouth. I glance at Sveta and furrow my brow in concern. The whites around her eyes have turned a pale gray, and sweat mats her hair. I watch her sway on her feet, every once in a while grabbing the table to steady herself.

"Svetochka?" I ask. She glances at me, her eyes slow to adjust. "You okay?"

Shaking her head, Sveta sways again. I steady her and lean in close. She whispers something, her voice lost in the factory noise.

"What?" I ask.

"I feel strange," she whispers. "I feel so heavy."

Sveta's eyes flutter, then she slumps. I catch her just before she hits the floor. Someone behind me shouts, and two German soldiers march swiftly to us. They kneel beside Sveta, one of them moving her head from side to side.

"She needs food," I say. The German closest to me looks up, and I shrink back, not from the anger or evil or hatred that I see in his eyes, but because of the concern.

He nods his head and speaks to me in broken Russian. "Yes. I know she needs food," he says. His comrade looks up, and I watch curiously as they communicate a nonverbal message. The German who spoke to me puts his arms under Sveta's body and gently scoops her up.

"I'll take care of her," he says. His eyes dart around the room. He clicks his heels and tosses me a stern look. "Now get back to work," he orders sharply. I push up to my feet in defiance as he turns to leave, Sveta's listless body hanging from his arms. The German glances back over his shoulder and gives me the slightest wink before walking swiftly out of the room.

I turn back to my table, my hands shaking. Pulling out a box of empty artillery shells, I quickly begin going through the motions of filling them, all the while trying to dissect what just happened. Alyona, who has been working at another table, steps up beside me and helps me fill the shells with the chemical powder.

"What happened?" she asks quietly. She doesn't look at me, and her hands don't miss a beat. I take her cue and continue to work while explaining what just occurred.

"I really think he's going to try to help Sveta," I murmur.

Alyona doesn't answer but continues to pour and push, twist and turn, pack and tighten. Together we empty the box, and reach under the table for another.

"Are you still planning on serving this imaginary dinner tonight?" she asks.

"Of course!" I exclaim. "Are you keeping track of how many shells you fill?" Despite my confusion and hunger, I can't help but smile. I hear the grin in Alyona's voice as she answers.

"I'm on number 463," she says. I can't resist the urge to shoot her a sideways glance and raise my eyebrow.

"I'm on 467," I challenge. Alyona's hands begin to fly through the motions as she scoops shell after shell onto the table in front of her. Together we work under the fire of competition until at last the final bell rings at the end of the day. We step back and my eyes widen at the mound of artillery shells stacked before and around us.

"How many did you fill?" I ask.

"I'm at 852," Alyona replies. She rubs her hands together, soothing the tight muscles and aching fingers. "You?"

I sigh and put my arm around her shoulders. "I owe you a dinner," I say with a weary smile.

We trudge back to the barracks as the evening sun sinks lower behind the German mountaintops. I wrap my arms over my chest and press down hard on the hollow spot beneath my ribs. If I push hard enough, the pains wane and the hunger feels less persistent.

We're moving slowly tonight. It has been a long, weary day. I think of Sveta and of the kindness in the eyes of the German who carried her out. The idea that someone might care gives me hope. Right now, the need for hope is the only thing stronger than the need for food.

We enter the barbed gates and move as quickly as our famished bodies will allow to the washbasin and then on to the mess hall. The tables are set up and Helga, the woman responsible for serving our food, stands behind the serving table, a pot in front of her and ladle in her hand. She's a short, plump woman with long, dark hair that she keeps pulled back in a tight bun. Her face is drawn and weary, but her eyes are kind. Though she looks aged, I suspect Helga to be quite young. She is one of very few German women who work in our camp, and I find her presence somewhat comforting.

Alyona leans forward to whisper softly. "I hope my promised dinner involves more than what Helga offers." I turn to look at her out of the corner of my eye. She smiles and winks. She knows I don't have real food to offer. Of course I could not offer real food. But I offered hope, and I will at least make her dinner a special event.

"Just wait until we get back to the barracks," I reply.

The line moves slowly forward. When I reach the table, I grab a small tin cup and hold it out for Helga. She keeps her eyes down as she drops in a ladle full of food. I hesitate for a moment, hoping for more.

With a sigh, I pull my arm back and look down at the mushy substance in my cup. I believe it's rice, but I can't tell. I bite my lip as I step to the side. Just before I leave, Helga raises her eyes to mine. They're filled with the waters of remorse.

She lowers her eyes again and spoons a clump into Alyona's cup. Together Alyona and I make our way to a table and sit down to look at the food before us. I'm so hungry that I cannot wait long before using my fingers to scoop it out. As I raise the food to my lips, I feel something move down my hand and over my wrist. Yelping, I jerk my hand back, the food in it slipping onto the table. Horrified, I look closely at the runny, white rice.

"There are bugs in this food," I say to Alyona. Her eyes widen.

"Maggots," she says. I look up at the other girls, most of whom shovel the food into their mouths without paying attention to what they're eating.

"What do we do?" I ask.

Alyona shrugs. She scoops up a bit of the rice and quickly puts it in her mouth and swallows. "We eat," she says with a grimace.

I look over at Helga. She meets my gaze, and I feel a moment of deep frustration. She knew she was feeding us infested food. I look away and quickly eat the rest of the food in my bowl.

Thirty minutes later, we're all gathered inside the barracks, and I stand in the center of the room. My stomach churns, heavy and sick.

"You all worked so hard today," I say. I look around the room at the hollow eyes, the sunken cheeks.

"Alyona filled 852 artillery shells, more than anyone else." I offer a grand gesture in Alyona's direction. The girls all clap, a few even offering up small smiles. Alyona stands and waves her hand dramatically.

"Thank you," she says with a curtsy. "Oh thank you so much. You are all too kind."

A few of the girls giggle. Even I feel the natural motion of an unforced smile taking over. It feels good. Alyona turns to me, and I notice a thin line of sweat over her upper lip. Her skin has a greenish pallor, and in the candlelight I notice the desperate flecks of illness dancing in her eyes.

Swallowing hard, she forces a smile. "So what do I win?" she asks. A sharp pang grips at my insides, and I fold over. A few of the girls gasp as I force myself to stand back up.

"I'm fine." I wave them off. Alyona sinks to her knees, looking up at me with a glistening brow.

I grab a pile of hay and set it in front of her. My stomach rolls and cramps as I arrange the straw. I begin to speak, forcing the words to come out calm. "Here is your grand dinner," I say. "Borscht with extra sour cream, of course."

Alyona nods. "Of course," she whispers.

"And warm, dark bread hot out of the oven. With butter. And a steaming glass of chai."

I sink to my knees in front of Alyona, the stabbing pains in my stomach pulling all strength from my legs. I look around and notice that most of the girls are folded over, hands clutched to stomachs.

I look back at Alyona with wide eyes. "What's happening?" I ask.

"I think we're finding out what happens when you eat maggots," she whispers and with a wretch, she folds over and vomits.

Within minutes we're all violently ill, rushing in a mass outside where we fall to our knees and release onto the dusty earth. We cry as we wretch and heave over and over. I crouch on my hands and knees, the pain in my stomach twisting like a knife and burning like fire in my chest and throat. I have thrown up all I ate earlier, but I continue to heave and gag, the acidic bile of my stomach expelling from my wracked body.

Alyona collapses next to me, shaking. "Masha," she cries, big tears spilling down her cheeks. "It hurts. It hurts. Oh God, it hurts, Masha."

I grab her hand and lie down beside her, listening as the other girls continue to vomit and cry out in pain. Footsteps on the ground rouse me, and I lift my head to see the Nazi guards rushing toward us.

"Get up!" they yell. They grab us under the arms and pull us roughly to our feet. It's pitch black outside except for the light of the moon. We all stand, still clutching our stomachs and crying in desperate pain.

"Quiet!" the tall German yells. He raises his gun in the air, pulling the trigger and sending a shot to pierce the sky. I look up expecting to see the blood of the moon.

"Back to your barracks!" he shouts. The others herd us forward, but the pains are so sharp we cannot stand straight. Many fall back to their knees. Including Alyona.

"Get up!" One of the soldiers grabs Alyona, who has fallen at his feet, pulling her up straight. She lets out a scream of pain and in projectile fashion vomits on his coat. I catch a glimpse of it in the moonlight and realize she has thrown up blood.

The German runs his hand over his soiled suit and lets out a growl of rage. He raises the butt of his gun high over his head and before I can think, I step between him and Alyona. I feel the pain of the blow for only a moment. Then the relief of unconsciousness swallows me.

LUDA MICHAELEVNA
June 23, 1942

I pick up my squirming child before the grunts turn to wails, and I nestle back on the couch with him, looking down at his perfect, round face in the moonlight that streams through the window.

His eyes are closed, and his face contorts as he tries to get comfortable. I wrap the small blanket around him and put my pinkie in his mouth in an effort to stave off his hunger for a little while longer. He grabs hold and sucks furiously, and despite my fatigue I can't help but smile.

"Shh . . ." I whisper, and the rhythm of his moving mouth begins to lull him slowly to sleep. I study his features, as I've done every day in the last week since his birth. His cheeks are full and soft and surround a perfect red mouth. His eyebrows are tiny and white, framing his small features. His fuzzy hair is also a white blond, and I can't help but take notice of his strong German features.

Neither can Katya.

"He looks like a German baby," I heard her hiss yesterday morning outside my door. She thought I was asleep.

Baba Mysa sighed in reply to her granddaughter's observation. "He *is* a German baby, Katya," she said.

In the eight days since Sasha's birth, my connection with Katya has severed once again, this time worse than before. As if the shock and horror of my carrying a German child wasn't terrible enough, it seems my confession of love for a German man was just short of blasphemous.

Seeing Sasha each and every day only reminds her of the reality I have chosen for myself.

Looking down at him, I take in everything, and I concede that it's true. He is a German baby. But he's also mine, and it's not so hard for me to forget the awful nature of his conception and imagine, for just a moment, that he belongs to Hans.

I pull my son closer to my body as I look up at the moonlit, starry sky outside the window, and I think of *him*. I smile knowing that he'll be back again soon. I have seen him every day this week, and it hasn't been a secret. Hans is working hard to find out what happened to Oleg. I feel my heart sink when I think of my friend.

Alexei paces the floors of the flat much of the day as he waits for Hans to return with some news. He is lost in the thoughts and fears of a father whose world has just been shattered. Baba Mysa has urged him to go out into the streets. "Go walk, Alexei," she begs each morning. "The fresh air will clear your head, and you'll think better." But Alexei stubbornly refuses.

Hans has worked tirelessly to find out if anyone knows what happened to the teenage boy who disappeared in the night. Every day, he comes to the flat early in the morning, before the streets bustle with activity and the suspicious gazes of neighbors question the frequent visits of a Nazi to our flat. Yesterday was the first time he had any real news to share, though the information was sparse. All we know is that Oleg was taken prisoner for being on the streets past curfew, and that he was sent to a POW camp outside the city. Hans left today to see if he could gather more information. I look out the window and lose myself in all that has transpired in just a few short days.

A few hours later, after the night sky fades into the dusky gray of morning, I stand up and dress quietly, my infant son finally sleeping soundly on my bed, his tiny backside raised in the air as he nestles in a tight ball. Patting him gently, and securing the blanket around him, I step out of the room and head to the kitchen. I've just poured my chai when I hear the knock at the door.

"*Kto tam?*" I ask quietly, my mouth pressed to the seal of the door.

"It is I. Hans."

I pull the door open, and he quickly slips in. I shut the door and secure the lock, then turn to face him. He looks at me with desperate eyes.

"I must talk to everyone immediately," he says with urgency. I nod and rush past him. He grabs my hand and quickly pulls me back, brushing the hair off my forehead and kissing me gently between the eyes.

"Hello," he says. I offer a shy smile, then rush to inform the others of his arrival. Katya sits in the corner, a book in her hands, but she doesn't read. She simply looks out the window in a haze of sadness.

"Hans is here," I tell the family. We move to the kitchen where Hans stands stiffly next to the window. We gather close, but no one sits. Some news is better received standing.

"Oleg is alive," Hans says. Baba Mysa lets out a cry.

"*Bozhe Moi!*" she yelps, raising her hands to the ceiling. *My God.*

The blood drains from Alexei's face, and he stares at Hans with a stony expression. "You saw him?" Alexei asks.

"I spoke to him," Hans says. Katya's hands cover her mouth, her eyes brimming with tears, and I look at the man I love with deeper admiration than ever before.

"Where is he?" Alexei asks. Hans sighs, pinching the bridge of his nose.

"He's being held prisoner and used for slave labor just outside the city," Hans says. "Getting him out won't be easy."

Alexei grabs a chair and lowers himself down. "What kind of labor?"

Hans grabs the back of the chair in front of him and leans on it, then stands up again. He's nervous and fidgety. His eyes dart back and forth to each one of us. I take a step toward him and grab his hand.

"What is it?" I ask. Hans looks hard at me, and I nod, squeezing his hand in reassurance. He nods back, then shifts his gaze to Alexei again.

"Oleg and the other prisoners are being forced to construct a secret hideout for Adolf Hitler. It's a place where wartime operations will be discussed and where Hitler will vacation and hide."

"What?" Baba Mysa gasps. She sinks down into a chair next to her son. Katya shrinks back against the wall.

"Hitler is constructing a hideout in Vinnitsya?" Alexei asks, his eyes wide with shock, anger, and fear.

Hans nods. "This is top-secret information among the ranks," he says. He and I sit across from Alexei and Baba Mysa. "They call the hiding place *Vervolfy*." Werewolf.

"When will it be completed?" Alexei asks.

"Very soon, I imagine," Hans replies. "The prisoners are now digging underground tunnels that will allow Hitler the freedom to wander from one building to another without exposing himself outdoors. I'm told he's planning his first stay in the month of July."

"That's just a couple of weeks away!" I exclaim, and Hans nods soberly.

"There isn't much time," he says.

"How is Oleg?" Baba Mysa asks. Her voice is tired and her eyes drawn.

Hans looks at her closely. "He's tired," he answers. "And I believe he's sick. All of the prisoners are sick."

Everyone sits quietly for a moment as we digest this news. Finally, I speak. "What are we going to do?" I ask.

Hans looks at me, and then turns to the rest of the group. "I'm going to get him out." He glances at Alexei. "But I'll need your help, Alexei Yurevich. If we don't move quickly, Oleg will be killed."

Alexei leans forward, pressing his elbows against the table and looking hard at Hans. "They'll kill all the prisoners when construction is complete, won't they?" he asks. Hans nods slowly.

"Will you be safe?" I ask.

"Stupid girl!"

We all jump at Katya's outburst. She shoves herself away from the wall and lunges toward me. Alexei manages to catch her just before her fist hits my face. "You're worried about this . . . this . . . *German* while my brother is being forced to build a hideout for the devil? I hate you! *I hate you!*"

Alexei drags his daughter from the room as she writhes and squirms in his arms. The tears fall hot against my cheeks, and Hans wraps his arm around my shoulders protectively. In the background, I hear my son begin to wail.

"I'll get the baby," Baba Mysa says, standing up slowly. She looks at Hans closely. "Forgive my granddaughter's emotions. Thank you for your help."

Hans nods, and Baba Mysa moves quickly to retrieve Sasha.

"I'm sorry, Hans," I cry. "I'm so sorry."

"Shh . . ." Hans whispers. "It's okay. I understand why Katya doesn't trust me. But I don't like her anger at you."

"I'm so afraid," I weep. I bury my face in his chest, his strong arms engulfing me in a tight embrace.

Hans lets me cry for a moment before pushing me back. He wipes the tears from my cheeks gently and offers a small smile. "I'm afraid, too," he says. "Which is why I have to do what I'm going to do."

The sound of his voice stops me cold, and I look up at him. His eyes burn bright and his jaw is set firm. "What are you going to do?" I ask.

"I'm going to free Oleg," he answers. "And then I'm going to kill Adolf Hitler."

IVAN KYRILOVICH
June 28, 1942

Bolting upright, I grasp my chest and take in long, gasping breaths. It wasn't real. It can't be real. Lying back down, I glance out the window and take note of the early morning sunlight pouring into the room, as the nightmare vision of my son, bloodied and broken, rolls through my mind. It felt so real, so tangible. I can't breathe.

In the stillness, my mind wanders again to the children. Where are they? I think of Anna and her quiet, sensitive nature that so similarly mirrors her mother. Is she being treated with gentleness in return? I fear that too much cruelty will break her and leave her unable to function—unable to live.

And what of my Maria? I feel her name wash over my lips, "Masha," my wild, impulsive girl with a strong sense of justice. Is she well? Is she working or is she fighting? I think of my own willingness to disregard safety and go after Joseph, Klara, and Polina, and realize with great heaviness that if Maria's impulsivity kills her, it will be entirely my fault. The child is too much like me.

Then I think of my Sergei, the visions in my dream leaving me sick with fear and worry. Where is my boy?

Tanya wakes and pushes herself up. She stretches, then turns to face me, her face drawn, eyes hollow. "Good morning," I say quietly. She stares, but doesn't acknowledge my words. A strange silence has settled over us this last month. Like a vapor, Tanya moves in and out of the room. It's as though the grief has finally become too heavy. I'm losing her.

Tanya pushes herself up and moves silently through the motions of dressing. I long to reach out to her, to hold her close, but the chasm between us feels too great.

"I'm going to work," she mumbles. "I'll be home for dinner."

I open my mouth to speak, but I'm not fast enough. She moves from the room before I can form a response. A moment later, I hear the front door open, then shut with a dull click.

I flit through the house for most of the day. I consider heading out, but the energy it would take leaves me overwhelmed. Most of my time is spent staring out the window, reliving the past. The memories always begin so joyful, but they end in mourning. By three o'clock, I'm utterly exhausted. I lie down on the bed and immediately fall into a deep sleep.

When I wake it's dark. I bolt up in panic. "Tanya?" I call, my eyes shifting left to right. There are no lights, no sounds. It's deafening. "Tanya!" I fall back to the bed, my head spinning. I'm disoriented and confused.

I don't know the time, and my mind races with all the things that could have happened. *"Tanya!"* I yell. The sound of crying pierces the room. I push up on my elbows and will myself to keep steady.

"Where are you?" I ask. A light flickers on in the corner. Tanya sits at the table, her hands shaking. She clutches a piece of paper in her right hand, and her face is puffy and swollen.

"What is it?" I ask, my heart sinking low. I fall back onto the hard pillow and stare at the ceiling, which sways back and forth like the Dnieper River on a windy day.

"It's Anna," Tanya says. I sit up again as something in her voice captures me. It isn't devastation, but rather the sound of elation. "It's a letter from Anna!" she cries. She throws her head back and laughs. "Anna's alive, Ivanchik. She's alive." She laughs again as the tears fall. For the first time in weeks I hear my wife laugh, and the sound is magical.

"Alive?" I ask. "Read it to me, darling, please!"

Tanya lays the letter on the table, smooths it out, and begins to read:

"Dear Mama and Papa,

"I received permission from the lady of the house to write to you. I live in northern Germany, far out in the country. We're away from the fighting, and I am well. I work as a cook for a Nazi general's family. I've never met the general, but I know his wife and daughter well, and they are good people. They have treated me well, and I'm grateful for their protection. The hours are long, and the work is hard, but I've found much satisfaction here.

"There are many young Ukrainians working on this farm. There's a boy here from Kiev. His name is Boris, and he's seventeen. He works hard in the fields. It's back-breaking work. He reminds me so much of Sergei. He's gentle and kind and has a wonderful sense of humor. I've found that I love him very much, and we're talking of marriage. I hope you'll love him as I do. We look forward to the day we will return to our home and be reunited with our families.

"And how is Sergei? Do you have any news from him? And what of Masha? I think about her every day. We were separated at the train station so I don't know where she is now, and that frightens me. I hope that she's behaving and keeping quiet. The Germans are strict and hard, but if you follow their rules, they can be very kind and helpful.

"I love you, Mama and Papa. I hope that you're well and that this letter brings some joy and relief. I was so happy when the mistress of the house agreed to mail it for me. I think of you every day. I will survive this war, and so must you. Just think of it—we'll all come out the other side of these years with our lives and our spirits still intact!

"I must go now. How I long to hug you close. Rest tonight, dear Mama and Papa, knowing that I'm well. There's hope in knowing.

"With all my love,

"Anna"

Tears stream down my cheeks and pool on the pillow behind my ears. Tanya's voice breaks, and she rushes to me, the letter still clutched tight in her fist. Lying down on the bed next to me, her body heaves with racking sobs. I turn on my side and wrap my arms around her.

"She's alive, Tanya," I whisper. I stroke her gray-brown hair. "She's alive, and we're alive, and we must believe that Masha and Sergei are alive."

Tanya nods and pulls in long, ragged breaths. She pushes up on her elbow and looks at me. Her eyes are swollen, her face splotchy and red. She has never been more beautiful.

"She's alive and she's in love," Tanya says and both of us laugh. "Our Anna in love." Tanya shakes her head. I reach up and run my hand down her cheeks, wiping away the tears.

We stare at one another for a long time, letting the overwhelming confliction of emotions sweep back and forth. Tanya breaks the spell with another smile. She wipes her eyes, then reaches up and places her hand gently on my cheek. "I've missed you," she whispers.

"I love you, Tanya," I answer. Tanya smiles, and her eyes crinkle at the corners.

"I love you, you stupid, crazy man," she says and she leans forward and kisses me deeply. Just like that, we're young again, lovers caught in the embrace of hope and future. We spend the night wrapped in passion, and in the morning, I sit up slowly. The room stays steady.

The world has settled.

MARIA IVANOVNA
June 29, 1942

With a soft moan, I try to lift my head, but something weighs me down. I feel heavy, like I've been stuffed and laid out beneath a mass of stones. With great effort, I manage to pry my eyes open and focus on my surroundings.

Panic threatens to rise. Just before it fully settles, a light splits the room, and my eyes shut involuntarily. From behind lids squeezed tight, I feel the light pierce, then fade. I push my eyes open again. It's not so bright now. The dim bulb overhead sways back and forth, casting golden glows from one side to the next, like spirits dancing above me.

Her shadow darkens the swaying bulb, and my eyes open a little wider. Focusing, I finally make out her concerned eyes and pinched expression. Her hair stands in wild tufts, the light glowing through the strands and illuminating her head in a sort of wild fire.

I form my lips around the word and force the air forward. It comes out as a whisper only, my throat dry and scratched.

"Helga."

"Shh," she says. She lays a cold cloth on my forehead, and I feel immediate relief from the heaviness. I look around. I'm in a small, stone room. I'm covered in heavy blankets, which explains the weight on my body. Helga lifts my head and pours cool liquid into my mouth. I gurgle and choke before swallowing hard.

"Dankeschön," I rasp. She smiles and nods her head.

"Where am I?"

Helga looks at me quizzically and shakes her head. She doesn't understand. I fall silent as my eyes continue to dart from left to right, trying to make sense of where I am and how I arrived here.

The last thing I remember is the sound of the German boots marching toward us. We were sick. I hear the screams. I see Alyona's desperate eyes.

"Alyona!" I gasp. "Where's my friend?" I ask. She looks at me, and I see it in her eyes. I see the sadness and regret. I force my mind to slow down and pull out the limited German that I've picked up since arriving at the camp.

"Is Alyona dead?" I ask. It's the only question I can think to ask in the tongue of my enemy. Helga's eyes fog, then fill with tears. She nods her head, very slightly. She understood my question, and I understand her answer.

My friend is gone.

I feel the tears on my cheeks and turn my head away from Helga so she doesn't see them fall. The cool cloth slips away, and the air blows across my bare forehead. Helga sighs and shuffles out, leaving me alone in my sorrow.

Sometime later, I hear the door open again. I keep my face turned away, not interested in trying to communicate with Helga anymore. As I've lain alone in the glowing room, my anger and hatred for her has built. She served the maggot-filled bowls of rice that nearly killed us all. She is the one who made the choice to let us eat that food, and as a result, Alyona is dead.

The side of my bed sinks with the weight of someone sitting next to me. I jump as the sound of a man clearing his throat breaks my obstinacy. Turning my head, I see the man who took Sveta away that day in the factory. His face is soft, his eyes gentle. He looks back at me for a moment before speaking.

"My name is Ewald," he says in thickly accented Russian. "I'm so sorry for what happened." I narrow my eyes and remain silent. Ewald takes a deep breath and turns his face toward the door where Helga stands silently, wringing her hands. I look back at Ewald.

"My friend is dead," I say. My voice cracks with emotion, but I push it back. "My friend is dead because *she* fed us infested food." I toss a glare at Helga.

Ewald nods. "I'm sorry about your friend," he says softly. "Helga is terribly sorry, too. She served your food out of duty, not malice."

Before I can stop myself, I rear up and spit hard at his face. Ewald jumps up from the bed and wipes his cheek. Taking a deep breath, he looks up at the ceiling before looking back down at me.

"Helga is going to take care of you until the fever breaks and you're stronger," he says. His voice isn't cold, but it isn't as gentle as when he first spoke, and I feel some satisfaction in knowing that I ruffled him. "When you're well," he continues, "you'll be transferred to a new service assignment."

"So I'm still a slave?" I ask. My voice is thick and hot and comes out stronger this time. I'm angry at his orders—at his attempt to justify the actions that killed Alyona. Ewald looks at me sharply.

"I am not so hateful as some of my comrades," he says in a low voice, "but I'm not without some belief or conviction of my own, either. Your service to our country is necessary and important. I will not bring harm to you for it, but if I were you, I would be careful not to bring harm to yourself."

Ewald spins on his heel and marches to the door. I watch as he stops next to Helga and smooths her wild hair back. He leans forward and kisses her nose gently, then whispers something in her ear. She ducks her head and swipes a hand over her eyes. Both of them look back at me once before leaving together, closing the door firmly behind them.

The next few days pass in a hazy blur. The fever leaves me listless and achy, and my head pounds with such ferocity that I'm sure it will split in two. Helga flits in and out of the room anxiously. I sense her desire to make amends, to purge herself of the guilt that haunts and torments. I, however, cannot give her the pleasure of forgiveness.

The longer I lie pinned beneath the blankets, the more anger and hate fill my being. I'm entirely buried in these feelings, and I cannot even bear to look Helga in the eye. My brokenness will not accept her remorse or her regret.

I feel it when the fever finally breaks. My body is wet with sweat. In an instant, the fog lifts, and I feel the fever flee. I'm weak and worn, but no longer heavy. The relief is welcome.

Helga walks in about an hour later with a bowl of broth and another bowl of cool water for my forehead. She sees me sitting up, and her eyes widen. Rushing to my side, she places her hand on my forehead. I turn my eyes downward so they don't meet hers.

Helga sits by me on the bed silently for a few minutes. I can smell the broth in the bowl that she's set next to me, and my mouth waters. For the first time in days, I feel a genuine hunger. I wait for Helga to retreat—to back away, but she doesn't move.

"Forgive me," she says quietly. These are the same words she whispered the night she served us the contaminated food. Despite my resolve not to acknowledge her, my eyes fly up to her face, and I feel the hot daggers of hatred pool in bitter tears.

"I can't," I hiss. "You knew you were feeding us that food. You knew!" Breaking down in sobs, I put my hands over my face.

"I'm sorry," she cries. "Forgive me. Forgive me." She rocks back and forth, and I watch through blurred eyes as she pleads, the hatred easing with each fallen tear. This is her penance.

Helga pushes to her feet slowly after several minutes. Murmuring something in German, she turns and walks out the door. I don't stop her, nor do I confirm forgiveness. I feel her disappointment as the door closes behind her.

LUDA MICHAELEVNA
July 7, 1942

It's here. In two days they plan to rescue Oleg—in two days the three men I love most in this world may not survive. The fear of what may come has wrecked me entirely.

Sasha has been my only balm. When I'm not nursing him, I hold him in my arms, the warmth of his tiny frame a soothing comfort to the tumult that overwhelms my soul. He spends a little more time alert these days, and I'm entirely captivated by him. His eyes are bright and inquisitive, and his mouth in constant movement. It seems as though he wants to speak, and I wish that he could. I long for someone to tell me it's all going to be okay. I want to know what will happen next.

Soon Hans will free Oleg. I know that he'll succeed, because I don't believe him capable of failure. When I compare Hans to my father, I'm left dizzy from the differences. My father, the coward, cannot even begin to measure up. The only thing he ever succeeded at was making me feel useless.

Last night, I sat on the floor outside the small kitchen and listened to the men whisper their plans, their hushed voices laced with intent and fear. With Sasha tight against my chest, I close my eyes and will myself to remember every plan, every movement, every step laid out.

Alexei somehow managed to convince two men from his partisan group to come and help. When they walked in earlier and saw Hans sitting in the flat, I watched their eyes glaze over. It is a testimony to the level of trust that people have in Alexei that they were willing to formulate plans with a German soldier.

What they plan seems impossible. I've run through each step a thousand times, and I don't see how they can pull this together without one, or all, of them dying. They have diversions planned for each step—plans to draw Nazi guards away from the compound and keep them occupied long enough for Hans to seek out the prisoners, find Oleg, and get him out into the dark of the woods.

My mind is swimming with the details when a soft knock on the bedroom door startles me. Assuming it to be Alexei, I feel my heart sink. I'm still afraid to speak with him, too scared to face the betrayal that clouds his eyes. Standing up, I hold Sasha tight against my chest like a shield of protection. The door opens, and I gasp in happy surprise to find Hans standing in the doorway.

"May I come in?" he asks. He steps in and closes the door quietly behind him. Walking to me, he stops close and looks down at Sasha who's now alert and content to gaze about the room. My baby is still so small and delicate, but his eyes are big and bright. Hans smiles and puts his hand on top of Sasha's head.

"Sometimes I imagine that he's mine," Hans says quietly. I look up at him and search his face, willing myself to memorize each line around his eyes, every mark and contour that gives him an air of confidence and goodness.

"I'm scared," I whisper, and he nods.

"I know."

Hans leans forward, swallowing Sasha and me in his arms. I stand still in his embrace for several minutes.

"*Ich lieben dich,*" he says quietly.

"I love you, too," I whisper, and the tears catch in my throat. Pushing me back, Hans wipes my eyes with his thumbs then kisses my forehead tenderly. He leans forward and kisses Sasha, and I listen closely as he whispers something to my son in his native German.

"What did you say?" I ask as Hans straightens up. I adjust Sasha, laying him over my shoulder, my hand cradling his bottom gently. His tiny face burrows in the crook of my neck.

"I whispered a prayer of strength and safety over him," Hans says. "It's the same prayer my father used to whisper over me when I was young and he left town. It always made me feel important and brave."

"You've never mentioned your father before," I say. "What was he like?"

Hans searches my face and pushes a strand of hair off my forehead. "My father was a good man. Though misguided in his beliefs, his intentions were noble. I respected him greatly."

"Is he still alive?" I ask.

Hans shakes his head. "He died three years ago."

"I'm sorry."

Hans gives a sad smile. "I'm sorry, too."

There are more things I want to ask Hans. I realize in this moment that I know very little about him. Does he have siblings? Is his mother alive? Who is this man who has taken all of my trust and all of my heart into his hands? I open my mouth to ask the questions when the door bursts open. Katya stands in the doorway, her pretty face pinched and clouded with anger.

"I need to change," she says. Her voice is dull, devoid of any feeling. Hans nods and kisses me on the cheek. My eyes fill with tears again as he takes a step back.

"Please be careful," I beg.

"I will," he promises. "You stay inside and keep safe." Turning on his heel, Hans strides past Katya. He pauses very briefly beside her and nods his head, but she refuses to look at him. In a heartbeat, he disappears out of the room. Seconds later, I hear the front door of the flat close, and I'm left with nothing but hope and the weight of my child to keep me warm.

Katya flits quickly through the room, pulling on her skirt and boots and lacing them quickly. She runs her fingers through her long blond hair, pulling it back away from her face and tying it into a low knot at the base of her neck.

"Where are you going?" I ask. My voice is cool and gathered, though inside I feel as though a storm is passing through.

Katya sighs. "I'm going to help Papa prepare for the mission," she says impatiently.

"You aren't taking part, are you?" I ask, surprised.

"I said I'm helping prepare," Katya snaps. She straightens and faces me, her eyes icy and narrowed. "Papa won't let me participate in any more real missions since you decided to go and fall in love with a German. He says it's too dangerous for our young female minds." I feel the heat of her words and step back as though I've been slapped.

"I'm sorry I've made things difficult for you, Katya," I murmur. Katya spins and stomps to the door, yanking it open. She stops and turns her head just slightly back toward me.

"I'm sorry you came to stay here at all," she says. She steps out of the room and slams the door behind her. Sasha jumps in my arms and begins to cry. Feeling numb, I walk to the couch and sit down, pulling him to my breast. As he soothes and drinks, I close my eyes, and fight against the sorrow.

The day drags on slowly and without mercy. Baba Mysa tries to occupy my mind with tasks, and it wears on my patience. I drop the small bit of yarn that fumbles between my fingers and look up at her in frustration. She's still trying hard to give me the tools I need to make Sasha's clothing, but I fear I'm an unruly student.

"I'm sorry, Baba," I mutter. "I just can't think about this today."

Baba rocks slowly and rhythmically back and forth in her rocking chair, her hands moving in perfect rhythm. The yarn begins to take shape, a perfect hat for Sasha's tiny head.

"I want to tell you a story, Luda," she says. Her voice is soft and warm. I sigh as I melt back into my chair, nodding my head in concession.

"I was born a long time ago, deep in the heart of Ukraine. My father was a farmer, and my mother was his strong and doting wife. I grew up among the rows of wheat and vegetables that my father grew."

Setting her work in her lap, Baba Mysa leans back and a serene look overcomes her face.

"I can still smell the scent of the cherry trees that surrounded our small country house. I feel the cool air of fall and remember every bit of peace as I walked along behind my father through the rows of potatoes. Everything about that time was simple and sweet."

She pauses, and I look at her impatiently. I enjoy hearing a bit about her childhood, but I don't understand what she's trying to communicate.

"When I was ten years old, my father took me into the fields to harvest the potatoes. For hours, we pulled plants from the ground and filled baskets, which we lined up in a long row at the edge of our field. My parents would clean the potatoes later in the day and sell most of them in the local market. At least, that's what they did every year before this one."

Baba Mysa's voice trails off, and I study her face. Her eyes are bright and clear as she stares hard at the wall, the memory playing out before her on an invisible stage.

"On this day, as father and I neared the last row, he told me a joke. I don't remember what the joke was, but I wish I did, because those were the last words he ever spoke to me."

My eyes focus in tight as I absorb the shock of her story. Her eyes remain still on the wall, wide and pained.

"As I laughed at his silly words, a man on a large horse rode quickly up to us. He shouted something about danger coming and told us to run. My father told him to take me, and the man scooped me up and fled with me. My last vision of my father is the sight of him standing in the fields, covered in dirt, his arm up in a solitary wave good-bye. I never saw him again."

It's quiet for some time as I process Baba Mysa's story. She wipes her eyes several times, and I don't speak in order to give her time and space. After a few moments, I finally work up the courage to say something.

"I'm so sorry, Baba," I say quietly. "I'm so sorry you had to go through that terrible ordeal. But . . ." I pause, unsure of how to proceed without sounding harsh. "I'm just not sure I understand what that story has to do with me," I say, and then I cringe. The words sound so selfish coming out of my mouth, and I immediately regret them.

Baba Mysa turns her head and studies me closely. She nods in approval at my acknowledgment of, and reaction to, the selfishness in my statement and she waits a beat before responding.

"It has nothing to do with you, child," she says firmly. "But you can learn from it." I nod and wait for her to continue, figuring it's best to remain quiet at this point.

Baba Mysa sighs, and her fingers begin moving in and out of the yarn on her lap once again. "Life is full of heartache and hardship," she says. "Very rarely will life make sense, and it will almost never seem fair. But if you remember that pain and heartache aren't unique to only you, that you're not the only one mired in circumstances that seem too great to bear, you'll do much better in life." She stops and turns to look closely at me.

"You're not the only one hurting right now, and you're not the only one afraid. More importantly, if this plan goes poorly, you will *not* be the only one affected. Please do not assume that you will be, and remember that when this is all over, for you, life will go on."

I sit back in my chair and look down at my hands. I nod slowly as my eyes well up with tears. In the bedroom, Sasha begins to wail, his little voice strong and urgent. Baba smiles gently and sets down her knitting. "I'll get the baby," she says. "I could use a little snuggle time right now."

Left alone, I reflect on her words and what she obviously meant to communicate to me. I listen to her sing softly to Sasha and hear the creak of the boards as she slowly walks him back and forth in the next room, and I smile. For the first time, I realize how wonderfully blessed my life has become.

I have a son and a family and love. Why didn't I see it before? Why did I feel so lost in the dark when so much of my life is full of light?

Baba Mysa walks into the room. "I think he wants to eat," she says, and she lays him in my arms. Looking up at her, I offer a smile.

"Thank you, Baba," I say, and our eyes meet. She looks deep, and I nod slightly. She places her hand gently on my cheek, and I lean into it.

"My darling," she says, and I see the tears dance in the corners of her eyes. "Don't ever forget that you're safe and *you are loved.*"

I lean back in my chair as Baba Mysa slips away to make tea. For the first time, I feel the tension in my shoulders relax, and a confidence in the future gives light to the darkness.

"You have to survive, Hans," I whisper in the quiet room, and I send my quiet prayer up and out into the void with the hope that it reaches his heart and brings the protection that I long for him to have.

MARIA IVANOVNA
July 8, 1942

Stepping off the train, I pull my sack of clothes tight against my chest and try to quell the nausea in my stomach.

"Come quickly," Ewald says. I fall into step behind him, my head bent low. Staring at the back of his freshly buffed boots, I try to make myself invisible. As we walk, I attempt to process all that has happened in the last twenty-four hours.

Was it only a day ago that I lay in a bed tucked deep inside a German barrack, longing to be released and to know what would happen next? How it all changed so quickly.

Yesterday as I lay against the hard pillow, Helga burst into the room, her frizzy hair a little wilder than usual. Gesturing vehemently, she looked scared and harried and frantic. She pulled my arms, lifting my shoulders from the bed as I fought in protest.

Helga babbled over and over in German as she pulled me to my feet, then held me steady while the room spun. I hadn't stood up since the illness hit, and in that moment, my head lolled, and I wasn't sure if I could remain upright.

"What are you doing?" I protested, as she tried to pull off my thin gown. She grabbed my clothes, which hung on the wall in front of the bed, and shook them at me. I pulled them on quickly, not because I understood what she wanted from me, but because her urgency compelled me to move.

Minutes later, Ewald strode into the room and closed the door behind him. Helga stepped back and leaned against the wall, wringing her hands.

"Good, you're ready," he said to me. "We need to go now. Our commanding officer is on his way, and he's not a kind man. We have to get you out of here fast. Stay close to me and move quickly."

Ewald yanked open the door, then turned to Helga, who looked like a wild animal caught in a trap. He gently issued a command in German, and she nodded her head. My last vision of Helga was of her stripping the bedding off the bed, removing any trace of my existence.

The memory will forever remain with me of moving through the shadows from one room to the next until we emerged out a back door. My first vision after weeks of lying in a dark, damp room was of a black car with the Nazi emblem outlined on the door. Ewald grabbed my hand and propelled me forward, opening the door and shoving me into the car in one swift movement. He threw a blanket over me and hissed, "Cover yourself."

Moments later, as I lay trembling beneath a scratchy burlap blanket, we bounced and rumbled away from the prison camp that had been my hell. Ewald spoke over the engine, and I listened without movement.

"We're going to be stopped in a minute," he said quietly. "I'll do my best to keep them from searching the car, but if they should insist and you're found, I must pretend I don't know how you got here. Remain still and quiet. Here we are."

The car rolled to a stop, and I heard Ewald speaking to two men outside. The voices grew louder, and Ewald shouted something with such anger that I felt my blood run cold. A moment later the car began to move again. It took most of the remainder of the car ride to calm myself.

We arrived at the train station, and Ewald got me quickly aboard and into a room without drawing any attention to either of us. We spent a long night on the train, Ewald staring at me in measured silence. He didn't tell me where we were headed, and I didn't ask. Some things are better left unknown.

We departed the train early, and I now follow him quickly, trying to keep up with his long stride. Lost in thought, I don't notice that Ewald stops walking, and I run hard into his back. I mumble an apology. "Forgive me," I say. Ewald sighs.

"Look up here," he says, and I look up, meeting his gaze. "You can't look like a scared, lost little mouse or people will get suspicious. You're here to work as a farmhand. That's your *job*. You're not a prisoner, so don't act like one."

"Forgive me, but I *am* a prisoner," I respond, and immediately regret my words. Mama always told me I talk too much.

Ewald steps back and studies me closely then nods his head. "Well, you're not a criminal, anyway," he concedes, then turns and we begin walking again.

I don't know if I should trust Ewald or fear him. As I study the back of his head, his dark blond hair cropped close and peeking out from under his officer's cap, I find myself in awe of him. It's the first time I have ever studied a Nazi so closely, and I can't draw my eyes away.

"Come," Ewald commands, and I jump. He points to another black car emblazoned with the Nazi sign that symbolizes my inferiority.

"Where did you say we're going?" I ask timidly after he slides into the front seat and starts up the engine. Ewald sighs the same way my mother used to sigh when I asked what she felt to be nonsensical questions.

"We're going to my sister's home in the country. You're going to work as a farmhand for her. The work will be hard, but you'll be treated well. My sister is kind and fair, but she expects hard work and will punish those who don't meet her expectations. Are you prepared to work hard?" He raises his eyebrows.

"Of course," I answer. Ewald nods and turns back around.

"Very well," he says and we slowly pull into traffic. "If anyone stops us, don't make a sound and do not look at them. I'll handle it."

I nod and look out the window as the beautiful countryside of Germany looms before us. Ewald and I are silent for some time before he speaks again.

"You need to learn German," he says quietly.

"Why?" I ask. Ewald takes a deep breath and glances at me in the mirror that hangs in front of him.

"You're in real Germany now," he says. "And you'll probably be here quite some time. You should learn the language so you can function."

I sit silently, mulling over his suggestion.

"Do you know any German at all?" Ewald asks, and I nod my head.

"A little," I answer in German, and I see his eyes crinkle at the corners in a smile. "I picked some up from the guards at the camp," I continue in German. I know my grammar is poor, and I've used the wrong tenses, but I think he understands me.

"Good," he says. "Learn quickly. You'll need it."

I sit back and close my eyes. We exit onto a wide, open highway, and the bustle of the city is fading behind us. I don't want to talk anymore, and I don't want to practice German. I don't want to learn German at all.

I want to go home.

I wake up to the sound of the car hitting gravel. The small rocks pop and buzz all around, and I bolt upright, my heart beating wildly. Ewald turns to look at me with a wide grin. "You missed the most beautiful part of the drive," he says with a smile, and I look out the window. Mountains surround us, and a deep green countryside greets me.

"*Schön,*" I murmur. "Beautiful." Ewald smiles softly.

"This is my home," he says, and I take note of how his voice has changed. It's softer and gentler. He has one hand on the steering wheel, and the other leans out the window, his palm held open as if he's trying to catch the German air.

"This is what we're fighting for," he says quietly. He says it in Russian, so I know he means for me to hear and understand. I look back out the window and sigh.

"I miss my home," I whisper, and Ewald looks back at me with eyebrows raised.

"Smooth your hair," he says. I run my hand over my head self-consciously. My hair hangs ragged and wavy over my shoulders. I haven't seen a mirror in many weeks and have no idea how I must look to Ewald. Despite my lack of excitement to work for his sister, I want to look presentable. Ewald looks back and gives a quick wink.

"Better," he says. I blush.

Moments later, Ewald turns into a gated drive, and I smell the strong odor of cattle. I look out the front windshield at the large white house sprawled at the end of the drive, and my stomach flips. We make our way up to the house and slow to a stop. Ewald hops out of the car.

"Come with me," he commands. I push open the door and stumble out. My head gets light, and I lean forward for a moment, then will myself to stand tall and stay upright.

"Ewald!" I stand to see a young woman running down the front steps. She jumps into her brother's arms with a small shriek, and he laughs and catches her, spinning her around.

"Helena," he says and he kisses the top of her head affectionately. They look at each other happily, and my heart aches as I think of Sergei. My eyes fill with tears, and for a brief moment, I forget where I am.

"Maria!" I jump and focus back on Ewald and Helena. I quickly swipe my hand across my eyes and give a brief nod.

Helena narrows her eyes and studies me. She murmurs something to Ewald, and he chuckles. I push my shoulders back and force myself to stand taller. After a moment of study, she nods her head. Pointing at my sack, she urges me to follow. She grabs Ewald's arm and begins speaking quickly. I strain to understand, but cannot pick up even the subject of which they speak.

Once inside, Ewald grabs my elbow. "Come with me," he says, and he guides me away from a watching Helena. We climb a steep staircase, and just as we reach the top, I hear an infant wail. My eyes widen, and I look at Ewald.

"My sister had a baby two months ago," he says. "Her husband died three weeks before the baby was born. He died in the Soviet Union." Ewald looks at me, and I take a deep breath. "She feels the sting of her husband's death, especially with the baby around," he says. "But she's a fair-minded girl, and she knows that you can't be to blame. She'll treat you well."

"Are there other farmhands here?" I ask. Outside of the baby's cry, I haven't seen or heard another living soul. Ewald nods.

"A few who come help for periods of time during the day. Our parents ran this farm. Helena and I grew up here, and we have a faithful group of people who help keep the house and the business running."

"What happened to your parents?" I ask.

Ewald stops and turns to me. "They were killed in a car accident four years ago," he says. "No more questions."

We start walking again as Ewald leads me to the far end of the house and opens a door that leads to yet another staircase. He motions me forward, as I clutch my bag and tentatively climb the stairs. We reach the top, and I look around the small attic room. It's dark and musty, and the ceiling hangs so low that I duck to move around. In the corner sits a narrow bed, a chair, and a small table with a lantern on it.

"This is your room," Ewald says. I move to the bed and sit down. A lump forms again, and I take long, deep breaths to stave off the fear. Ewald senses my rising panic and grabs the chair. He sets it in front of me and sits down.

"It's okay," he says with a gentle smile. "This is a good thing that has happened to you. You'll be safe here, and you'll have food. The work will be hard, but not as hard as the factory."

I nod and blink hard against the tears. "Yes, I see that," I answer. I clear my throat against the quavering. I get the sense that Ewald wants my appreciation, but I can't help but question his motives.

Ewald looks at me intently, and I suddenly feel a little uncomfortable. "Why *did* you do this?" I ask. Ewald takes a breath. He leans forward and puts his elbows on his knees.

"How old are you, Maria?" he asks.

"I'm fifteen," I answer. Ewald nods.

"I did this for you because you're young and you deserve a chance to live."

I narrow my eyes, the lump in my throat dissolving. I feel a building confidence with Ewald, but I don't trust him. I'm confused by the way he treats me.

"Alyona deserved a chance to live, too," I say. "So did my friend Polina. I held her in my arms when she died inside the barracks that you help run. They deserved to live as much as me. So why am I here, and why do their bones lie buried in a hole in the ground?"

Ewald pushes up and runs his hands up and down his legs. I've made him uncomfortable. He opens his mouth to speak, and I wait. His kiss happens so fast I don't have time to react. His lips press hard against mine as I sit paralyzed and terrified. Ewald's hands grasp the back of my head, pulling me in close. I squeeze my eyes tight and pull back.

Ewald leans back. "I'm sorry," he says after an awkward pause. "I shouldn't have done that." He pushes up from the chair, bumping his head on the low-lying rafter.

"I'll go now," he says, and I see his cheeks turn a deep crimson. I sit stunned and silent on the bed, my stomach tied in knots.

"I've never met my nephew," Ewald says. "I'll stay a few days with Helena and the baby to make sure all is settled, then I'll leave. I will go back to the factory . . . back to Helga." He flushes again as a look of shame washes over his face. Then he turns and ducks out of the room.

He closes the door behind him, and I'm left in the room, my head spinning, my heart thumping, and my world dark and mad. I wipe my mouth with trembling hands.

I've never felt more alone.

LUDA MICHAELEVNA
July 9, 1942

I feel this night will never end. I'm not even sure I want it to. Morning will bring the truth. Light will burn out hope, and I'll be left with reality. Will that reality include my Hans?

The men set out hours ago to rescue Oleg. Alexei was nervous when he left. I watched from around the corner as Baba Mysa and Katya hugged him good-bye. My heart constricted and pulled as I watched this family—my family—cling to one another. I felt the depth of their fear, and the realization that I was the one who caused all this heartache left me physically pained.

Just before leaving, Alexei turned and caught my eye. In two long strides, he was in front of me. He pulled me into his arms tight, and I buried my head in his chest.

"I'm sorry, Alexei," I whispered.

"Shh," he answered, and he kissed the top of my head. Pulling me back, he wiped my face and gave me a smile. "We'll be back soon, *doro-gaya*," he said. Moments later, he was gone, and we were left alone with our fears and heartaches, each of us battling an individual grief.

That was four hours ago. Baba Mysa brings tea and sets it before me. "You should try to get some sleep," she murmurs, and I nod.

Katya sits on the other side of the room, her hands folded tightly on her lap. Her eyes drift from the window to Baba Mysa's face, but never to mine. Sasha stirs, and I rock him gently. As he sleeps, his brow furrows before he breaks out in a happy, slumber-induced grin. I smile despite my fear.

Baba Mysa leans over and looks closely at Sasha. She, too, breaks out in a grin. "There's nothing more calming than an infant," she says as she reaches up and gently strokes his soft, tufted, blond hair. She glances over at Katya. "You should come watch him sleep, Katyusha," she says. Katya shifts in her seat and shakes her head one time, her lips pursed together. Baba Mysa sighs.

"Katya," she begins, leaning forward to stare hard at her granddaughter. "I understand you're hurt. You feel betrayed by your friend. You feel as though we've welcomed the enemy into our midst, and you're heartbroken over Oleg, am I right?" Katya nods, her eyes filling with tears.

"Okay, so you're hurt and angry," Baba Mysa continues. "So what? We're all hurt and angry." She gestures toward me. "Luda has a father who doesn't care about her, who left her to be attacked and abused. I lost my father as a child and never again had the privilege to grow up in a home where there was laughter or love. You're hurt and sad, you say? Well so am I." Baba Mysa thumps her chest. Katya can no longer contain her tears. They fall freely onto her porcelain cheeks.

Baba Mysa stands up and walks to her granddaughter, wrapping her shoulders in a tight hug. "There's so much to be hurt and angry about, *dorogaya*," she whispers as Katya leans into her, sobs racking her shoulders. "But there are things to love, too. Like that tiny, beautiful, innocent baby over there."

Katya looks up and wipes her eyes. She takes a deep, halting breath before pushing herself up and walking to me. Sitting down on the couch, she looks over at Sasha. His mouth looks like a delicate pink bow, and his small hands are tucked beneath his chin.

Katya reaches over and lays her hand gently on his head. He stirs briefly, then settles again. "Do you want to hold him?" I ask. Katya doesn't look at me as she nods her head. I slowly pass my sleeping son to her.

"He's warm," she whispers, and she looks at me for the first time. Our eyes lock, and in a single look I say everything I've wanted to say. *I'm sorry. I need you. I love you. Forgive me.* Katya nods, and just like that, the spell of anger is broken. We're together.

Baba Mysa stands in the corner, smiling at both of us. "Okay," she says and lightly taps her hands together. "We must celebrate this moment right here. I have honey and a few chocolates hidden away in the cabinet. We'll have chai and remember the good thing that happened this day."

I look at Baba Mysa and find myself offering a genuine smile, because she's right. This is a good moment.

The chai and sweets are exactly what we need to get us through the night. They're a necessary distraction, along with Sasha's nighttime needs, to keep me from drowning in fear. In the very early hours of the morning, we all begin to drift in and out of sleep. For me this is fitful and frightening, filled with the images of my imagination. Waking up is the only thing that chases away the demons, so I fight hard to keep my eyes open.

Just as the morning light begins to push its way over the horizon, we hear a click at the door. All three of us stand and rush to the front room. The door opens with a loud creak, and in walks Alexei with Oleg tucked firmly under his arm.

Katya yelps and rushes forward to help Alexei with her brother while Baba Mysa murmurs thanks to God. I push the door closed, and together we move into the room where we lay Oleg on the floor. He trembles and shakes as we lay blankets over him. I stand up and back against the wall, a mountain of fear pushing against me.

I thought he'd come back with them. I thought I would see him right away.

Katya notices the look on my face and turns to her father. "Papa," she says quietly. "Where is Hans?"

Alexei looks at her, then turns his head to catch my eye. His face is drawn and laced with fatigue. He licks his cracked lips before speaking. "Hans didn't come out of the woods with us. I . . . I don't know what happened, Luda," Alexei says.

Oleg moans, and Baba Mysa grabs his hand. "Katya," she says firmly. "Go put the kettle on the burner and prepare the mugs. We need to get these boys warmed up and fed." Katya nods and pushes to her feet. I take a step toward Oleg and study him closely. He's very thin and dirty. His cheeks have sunken into his face, and his shoulders protrude from beneath his shirt. He looks old.

Oleg opens his mouth and moves his lips, trying to form a word.

"Shh, don't speak my darling boy," Baba Mysa whispers in his ear, but he shakes his head and clears his throat. Alexei moves in and leans over Oleg.

"What is it, *Sinok*?" he asks.

"He saved me," Oleg croaks. Katya walks in and stops to listen to her brother's sick, tired voice. "He came in and pulled me out of my bunk. I thought he was another one of them coming to beat me, but he put his hand over my mouth and pulled me outside. He told me to walk toward the forest and to not make a sound." Oleg's shoulders shake as Baba Mysa rubs his arms gently.

"I thought he was taking me to the trees to kill me, but just as we reached the edge of the camp, another soldier came around the corner and stopped us. They argued, and I couldn't understand what they were saying, but finally the man who woke me was waved on. We got to the woods, and he told me to run in a straight line. He said he couldn't come because he'd been seen and they'd be looking for him. He told me to run and not stop so I did. I ran until Father stopped me." Oleg leans to the side and falls into a deep, chesty coughing fit. I wince as he heaves and chokes. Alexei rubs his son's back.

"I heard a gunshot," Oleg gasps. I slide to the floor, my hand clutching my chest, willing myself to take a breath. Everyone is still for a long time before Baba Mysa breaks the silence.

"How are the other men who helped?" she asks.

Alexei gives a short nod. "They're safe," he says, and I hear the relief in his voice.

Sitting down, I turn to Alexei. "Did they kill Hans?" I ask. Alexei looks at me, his eyes full of sorrow.

"I don't know," he says. "Hans is smart and very capable. If he can save himself, I believe that he will."

"Who was the man who saved me?" Oleg croaks from the floor. We all freeze. How do I explain our relationship with Hans to Oleg right now?

The kettle in the other room whistles. "I'll get it," I murmur, pushing to my feet. I'm eager to escape this moment. Katya moves in to sit down in my place. She grabs her brother's hand, holding it tight between hers.

"You're going to be okay, Oleg," she whispers. She leans over to kiss his forehead.

I rush to the kitchen and stand over the steaming kettle, willing the tears to stay away. My throat burns as grief and rage push down. Just as I open my mouth to scream, I hear a knock at the door. My hands drop, and I step cautiously into the hall. Baba Mysa and Katya stand behind Alexei, who motions me back out of sight. I listen from the kitchen.

"Kto tam?" he asks quietly.

A deep voice replies, and before I can stop, my feet have launched me into the foyer where Alexei yanks open the door. I fall into Hans's arms with a cry.

I look up at Hans. "I thought they killed you. I didn't think I'd see you again." My throat closes as he pulls me into him. He smells like the outdoors, a mixture of dirt, smoke, and the fresh morning air. Alexei claps him on the back and motions him into the kitchen.

"How did you get away? How did you explain Oleg's disappearance?" I ask as we all settle down. Baba Mysa rushes back to the kitchen to prepare the chai and to stir up a healing drink for Oleg to sip.

"I told them I'd been sent to monitor the situation at the camp, given Hitler's impending visit, and I caught Oleg eating stolen food in the bunkhouse," Hans said, his mouth set in a grim line. "I acted like I took Oleg into the forest to shoot him."

"That's why Oleg heard a gunshot," I whisper. Hans brushes the hair from my forehead.

"Yes," he says. "I shot my gun in case anyone was listening."

Alexei leans forward and rests his elbows on his knees. "But you don't have a body to prove it," he says. Hans nods.

"I had to find one," he says quietly. "They've killed a lot of men out there these last few weeks. There are piles of bodies waiting to be buried or burned just beyond the line of trees. I found the body that was the least decomposed and told them it was Oleg. By luck, I managed to pull it off."

I lean into Hans's shoulder and grab his hand. "I'm so glad you're okay," I whisper. In the room behind us, Sasha lets out his high-pitched wail. He's hungry.

"Let me get him," Alexei says as I begin to rise. He rushes to the room and emerges a moment later cradling Sasha gently in his arms. He coos and smiles at my squirming boy, and I'm overwhelmed.

I look at the faces surrounding me, and despite all that we've been through, I feel a deep sense of comfort and belonging. Alexei lays Sasha in my arms, then Hans leans in and wraps his arm around both of us.

Baba Mysa walks back in with a tray full of steaming mugs, and we all sit together in a circle. We're somber, but content. Though the world feels as though it's spinning out of control and Oleg coughs repeatedly in the other room, I relish the peace of this moment. Looking down at Sasha, I smile and lean forward, pressing my lips very lightly against his ear.

"We're going to be okay," I whisper. His eyes are big as he studies me, his little hands and feet kicking up and down. He stares, and in that moment, his face lights up in a wide-awake grin.

I look up, hoping someone else saw the glimmer of joy in my boy's face. Instead I lock eyes with Oleg, standing in the doorway, and my heart sinks. Shock and horror have replaced fatigue, and I feel all of his pain in one momentary gaze.

FREDERICK HERRMANN
August 1, 1942

It was the laugh that made me look up. She rounded the corner, her arm tucked tight into a friend's, and they both froze at the sight of me sitting on the bench. Though she quickly shifted her eyes to the ground, I could not keep mine from staring, studying her face. How was it possible for her to sound so much like the laughter of my past?

She bore no physical resemblance to Talia. Her hair was a light brown, where my sister's had always been a deep red. And of course, this girl was a Soviet. Talia had been a proud German. *Had been.*

I looked closely as she and her friend turned, quickly making their way back down the path away from me. I wanted to see if there could possibly be any other resemblance of Talia inside this Soviet girl. But it was only the laugh, the way it seemed to be tangled up in the back of her throat and then fought its way out into the open in raucous delight. That was the way Talia sounded when she wanted to withhold her humor, but simply couldn't resist the delight. Turning away from the Soviet girl, I lean forward and rest my elbows on my knees.

For an hour I've sat still on this bench, head bent low. I'm trying to chase the images away—all of them. The gas van filled with bodies covered in vomit and excrement. The spirited redheaded girl with her death eyes glazed over. Children screaming and the smell of burning flesh.

It's all inside me, and the noise from the sounds and smells all work together to keep me dizzy and wrapped in darkness. But now I've heard her laugh, and all at once I fall back into the memory of our last trip to Berlin together as a family of four. It was the last time I heard Talia laugh like that, the open delight of youth that so defined her younger years. I close my eyes and fall back into the memory as effortlessly as if it had occurred yesterday.

Father, Mother, Talia, and I walked along the streets amidst the bustle of the bright city lights. Mother had her arm tucked into Father's. Even then, I knew that they shared no love or even conviction of purpose. It seemed Mother was as compelled as Father to project an image that demanded respect, though why I never quite understood. Mother had always been a source of genuine comfort for me, but it was only in public that Father allowed her near to him.

Talia and I walked a few paces behind, always quiet, reserved, and obedient. Those were the expectations—at least the expectations placed upon me. As father's beloved child, Talia had the freedom to enjoy life a little more than I did. On this particular day as we walked along the sidewalk, a bird relieved itself just above me, the slimy, white mess hitting my shoulder. Though she tried to suppress her amusement, she couldn't contain it, and the laughter bubbled out of her, filling the air around us with effortless delight. Father spun around at the sound, and Talia quickly covered her mouth with her hand. Seeing the mess on my shoulder, Father rolled his eyes and handed me his handkerchief.

"For goodness's sake, Frederick, clean yourself up," he demanded. "You can't go in to dinner looking like that."

Minutes later, after Talia helped me wipe my arm clean, we walked into the restaurant and stood in awe. We were surrounded by SS officers, each one tall and powerful. Father knew them all and held such a high position in the community that he was treated like royalty at every gathering.

Of course Herr Hitler was there, too. I felt his eyes studying me the second we walked in. He watched me closely then, and I suspect he watches me now.

Father guided us to a table in the far corner of the room where four men were seated at a long table with their wives. Talia and I were the only children in attendance. Sensing their eyes on me, I stood straighter, clasping my shaking hands behind my back.

I was directed to sit next to a thin, drawn woman whose jet-black hair was pulled into a tight bun at the back of her head. She sat across from her husband, Eugen Steimle, a thin man with round wire-frame glasses and a straight mouth that pressed together to form a somber line across his face. I knew he was young, much younger than my father, but the air with which he moved and spoke gave a sense of dour gloom. I instantly did not like him.

The conversation that evening was as dull as it had ever been at one of Father's dinners. The men spoke of nothing but Germany and "the mighty quest" that they claimed was their calling. They whispered their reverence for Hitler and formulated all the plans for how Germany would soon become a pure and holy nation. Steimle spoke little, but when he did, everyone stopped to listen.

He was a brilliant man, a teacher at the university, fluent in three languages, and an SS officer. Early in the dinner, father made us all aware that Steimle had been the leading socialistic activist of the Verbingdung Normannia, a student corporation created to promote the socialistic values that would comprise a strong Germany.

I observed that night the obvious admiration that Father had for Steimle. I had no doubt that I'd been positioned next to that man for a reason. Steimle was everything that my father hoped I would become—smart, strong, proud . . . German.

Everything about that dinner was predictable: the men leading the discussion until Father asked Steimle what his opinion was on how to best encourage and lead the young people of our nation. Steimle pushed his glasses up high on his nose and leaned forward, his hands grasped tight in his lap.

"I believe that the youth of our nation need to be given firm truths about the direction of our society and what must be done to help us save our people from insidious danger and weakness," he said in his quiet, joyless voice.

And then Talia, my confidante, my friend, my sister, broke the reverie.

"Forgive me, sir, but what danger are you referring to?" Talia's voice came out strong and confident, and I saw Father's shoulders stiffen, his hand gripping tightly around his glass of bourbon. Mother turned, wide eyed, and stared at Talia.

Could she not see what she was risking? Why couldn't she do as Mother and keep her mouth closed?

Steimle looked at her closely, then offered a thin smile. "A good question from one of the very youth to which I was referring," he said. Talia nodded politely.

"We're headed to the establishment of a holy and pure race, something you've no doubt heard mentioned before by your wise and knowing father," Steimle began, his hands gesturing exaggeratedly at Father. "As difficult as it may sound, we must be willing to do all that it takes to bring Europe to a place of purity and to establish our great Germany as the head of this unconquerable race. Do you understand?"

Talia sat quietly for a moment, her eyes narrow and defiant. Just as she opened her mouth to speak, Father interrupted. "Of course she understands," he said, his eyes forced into a smile. "She's my daughter." Lifting his glass toward Talia, Father shot her a look that everyone at the table could interpret.

Don't speak again.

Talia slumped down into her seat and closed her mouth. That was the end of the conversation and the last that Steimle spoke that evening. But as I watched my sister's expression harden and her jaw lock tight, I knew it wouldn't be the last time that Talia shared her thoughts. That was the night that I knew I would one day have to turn my back on my sister.

It was just two years later when she left forever.

Opening my eyes, I pull myself from the memory of that evening and look around the quiet park high above the Dnieper River. I never heard Talia laugh like that again. The thought hits me, and I suck in a deep breath as I try to swallow the emotion. The sound of the Soviet girl's laughter has awakened in me a longing that I thought I'd suppressed. It's a longing that I cannot voice—even the thought of it sets me trembling in fear at what Father would think of such weakness. This one thought reverberates through my soul until I blink back tears in frustration and shame.

I miss my sister.

MARIA IVANOVNA
November 10, 1942

It has been months since Ewald brought me to this farm and left me with his sister, months since he kissed me in the attic, and in that time I've found that he saved me from one hardship and dropped me right into another.

The mistress of the house is neither kind nor gentle as Ewald described her. She's harsh and cruel, and I believe she's entirely bent on breaking me. My only saving grace has been the particular brand of stubbornness that makes up all of my being.

Every morning at precisely eight o'clock, Helena expects me to be in the drawing room of the house where we work on my German speaking skills. I don't know why she's so desperate to see me learn the language, except that I think she wants to prove to her brother what a fine teacher she is upon his return.

The problem is that Helena also expects me to have accomplished all of my morning chores before we begin our German lesson. I must be up early enough to make the breakfast rolls, milk the cow, feed the horses, clean the bathrooms, sweep the kitchen, and change and dress the baby.

I rise each morning at four o'clock, before the sun has even begun the process of rising. By the time eight o'clock rolls around, I'm utterly spent. Helena desires nothing less than perfection, so I will myself to concentrate, to soak in her instruction and speak in a tongue that is entirely foreign to me.

When I miss a question, or forget even the smallest of grammatical rules, I get a slap with the ruler across my wrist. If I sigh or reveal any kind of belligerence, I get a slap with the ruler on the back of the neck.

Yesterday I fell asleep. I didn't mean to, but she droned on with such monotony that my eyes grew heavy. I woke up to the violent, stinging slap of a ruler across my cheek. Reaching up, I run my hand gently over the bruise that runs from the corner of my mouth to my ear. I sigh as I look out at the black sky.

Standing up, I pull on all of the clothes I own. I tie my second pair of socks together to form a scarf, which I wrap tight around my ears. The air has turned cold, and though my room is hardly warm, I dread walking outside to the stables and barns. I creep down the staircase, all the way to the kitchen, where the buckets stand waiting for today's milk. I'll milk the cow this morning, and this afternoon I'll milk the goats that graze in the nearby field. This is a loathsome task, as they're mean and wicked creatures.

I tuck my hands into my sleeves and pick up the bucket, then open the door and suck in a deep breath as a wave of frigid air hits me. I trudge through the field to the barn, where the cow stands steady in the far back corner. Yesterday Helena ordered me to add more hay to the cow's stall. "We don't want her to get too cold now, do we?" she asked. I nodded, but inside I screamed.

The cow's pen is warmer and more comfortable than my attic bedroom.

I pull a stool up to the side of the cow and set the bucket down, then begin the steady, rhythmic tug, drawing the warm milk from her. She glances at me from the corner of her eye, at first seemingly insulted, but she soon relaxes, grateful as I release the pressure in her middle.

While my hands work in rhythm, I recite today's verbs and vocabulary words. I practice sentence structure and try to remember the dialogue Helena asked me to memorize. I get lost about eight lines in, and I mentally prepare myself for a few slaps across the hand today.

Lost in my own responsibilities, I don't hear the door to the barn slide open. I don't know he's there until I feel him step up behind me. I whirl around with a gasp, and the cow stomps her feet at the interruption.

"Oh!" I cry in surprise, and he smiles apologetically. I don't stand up, but merely look up at him awkwardly.

"Hello," he says with a slight bow.

"What are you doing here?" I ask. "It's the middle of the night!"

Ewald chuckles. "I had a few weeks leave, and Helena is my only family. I wanted to see her so I made my way up here. It's a surprise—she doesn't know I'm coming."

I finally push myself to my feet and nod, tucking my crazy hair behind my ear. I feel my palms shake, and I'm suddenly uncomfortable and nervous. Ewald steps forward into the glowing light of the kerosene lamp and studies me closely. I shift my eyes away from him and try to turn my head so he doesn't see my cheek, but he grabs my chin and turns my face toward him.

"What happened here?" he asks. I don't look at his face, but I hear the surprise and concern in his voice. I think for a brief moment before answering.

"I slipped coming down the stairs from the attic," I say softly. "I fell into the corner of the door."

Ewald takes in a breath then pulls my face up so that I'm forced to look at him. I forgot how handsome he is, and I force myself to breathe slowly. His eyes glow in the lamplight, his face warm and golden. His blond hair shines on top of his head. I blush as my eyes meet his, and he drops his hand.

"How is Helga?" I ask, and this time Ewald blushes.

"I suppose she's fine. She left shortly after you to go back home to her family. I haven't heard from her since."

"I'm sorry," I say politely, but I find myself curious at his treatment of me. Ewald sees me studying him and pulls himself up straight.

"I take it Helena has been working hard with you on your German," he says, and I nod. He gestures his hand and speaks, this time in his native tongue. "So talk to me. Show me what you know."

I stand mute for a brief moment, then I blurt out today's dialogue. Once again, at around line eight I stumble over the words and stop abruptly as Ewald laughs out loud.

"Why are you laughing?" I ask. Ewald shakes his head.

"Ask me that question again in German," he says, his eyes twinkling, and I sigh impatiently.

"Why are you laughing?" I ask again, this time in German, and Ewald doubles over, clutching his sides.

I spin around on my heel and grab the bucket of milk. "I'm trying," I bark, and I stomp past him. Ewald grabs my arm and stops me.

"I'm sorry," he says, his eyes still crinkled with laughter. "But you looked so terrified as you recited a monologue about chickens and goats, and when you asked me why I was laughing, you mixed up your tenses and it came out all wrong and—" He stops at my hurt look and takes a breath.

"I'm sorry. I shouldn't laugh. I just thought you'd be better at this by now."

I shrug my shoulders. "I'm not good at languages," I say. "I started learning French when I was seven, and I still can't speak a full sentence."

"That's because you're not learning correctly. You can't learn a language by memorizing poems about farm animals or reciting verb tenses. You need to speak it. You need to have conversation and listen to the rise and fall of the words." Ewald switches from Russian to German, his voice low and melodic.

"You need to hear the sounds as a native speaks and pay close attention to how they all fit together to form sentences. And then you just need to try." He looks at me and raises his eyebrows.

"What do I say?" I ask him in German, and he smiles.

"Tell me what you're going to do today. And tell me why you're up milking the cow at four o'clock in the morning."

With full understanding of the need to protect myself from Helena, I think quickly. "I like the quiet in the barn," I say, and I wince as I hear the grammatical inconsistencies. Ewald shakes his head.

"It's okay," he says. "Keep going."

"I get up early so I can be better prepared for the day, and so I can bake the kittens in time for breakfast."

Ewald bursts into laughter again, and I growl and stomp my foot.

"What!" I demand.

"I didn't realize you enjoyed eating small cats so much," he says with a smirk, and I blush yet again.

"It's hard!" I exclaim, by default falling back into the language that is native to my tongue. "I understand almost everything that's said to me, but I can't speak back."

Ewald nods. "I'll speak to Helena about that," he says, and I feel a knot settle in my stomach. I am most certain there will be repercussions when Helena is left alone with me again.

Ewald and I walk quickly out of the barn. He turns toward the house, but I don't follow. "I'll see you at breakfast," I say, turning toward the stable. "I need to feed the horses."

Ewald jogs up to me and falls in step. "I might as well help you out," he says. "I'm not going to be able to sleep right now anyway, and I don't want to wake anyone inside. Do you mind the company?"

I shrug my shoulders and try to brush off the nagging feeling that Ewald is pursuing me. I set the milk bucket outside the stable door, then Ewald and I go in together and feed the horses, shovel the hay, and clean out the stalls.

"This was my job growing up," Ewald tells me as we work. He speaks only in German now, and I make it a point to listen closely to the words as he speaks them. "I hated doing it back then, but now . . ." He stops and looks around. "Now I would give anything to have this responsibility over the other tasks I'm given on a daily basis."

My mind drifts to Alyona and Polina and all the other girls from the barracks at the camp, and I stop. Ewald is a part of that life. He's a part of that darkness. He senses my discomfort and sighs. Stepping back, he looks around the stables.

"It looks nice in here," he says. "You do good work."

"Danke," I murmur.

Early signs of morning are beginning to paint the sky, and I rush out of the stables toward the kitchen. "I must go and prepare the morning meal," I say. Ewald nods.

"I'll see you later today," he says as I turn and quickly make my way into the kitchen where I trip, sliding across the floor, milk sloshing over the side of the bucket. Confusion, anger, and fatigue roll over me in a giant wave, and I take deep breaths, willing myself to calm down. Pushing myself up, I move to the big black stove and fill it with wood, then strike a match and set the fuel blazing.

I feel the fire begin to burn and crackle, and I take in a deep breath. *When will this war end?*

At precisely eight o'clock, I walk into the drawing room with my head high. I've brushed the flour from my face and smoothed my hair as best I can. Helena likes a tidy appearance. I stop just inside the door as Ewald turns and faces me. He stands by the fireplace, his back straight and shoulders squared. He's not in uniform, and it's the first time I've seen him in everyday clothing. He looks younger, more boyish. I cannot prevent the blush from lighting my cheeks.

Helena sits rigid on the couch, her face pinched and eyes darting from Ewald to me. I give a quick curtsy toward her. *"Guten Morgen,"* I murmur, and she nods her head. I rush to the hard, wooden chair that stands in the middle of the room and sit down, crossing my ankles and placing my hands gently in my lap.

Helena stands up and clears her throat. "I understand you and Ewald had a little chat this morning," she says, her words crisp and sharp. I nod. Helena glances at her brother, who gives her a soft smile. She sighs and turns back to me.

"Ewald believes we should focus less on the technicalities of the language and simply begin speaking and conversing, so today that is what we will do."

I nod again. *"Juwhal,"* I answer. *Okay.*

Helena nods and sits back down on the couch. "Good," she says. "Now, tell me, Maria, how are you doing this morning?"

I search my brain for the correct response, willing the words to form on my tongue. "I am well, today. Thank you." My reply is safe, formal, and boring. Helena seems less than pleased, but I can feel Ewald's pleasure from where he stands, and it warms me. He steps toward Helena and leans forward, kissing her gently on the cheek.

"Thank you for helping her," he whispers. He stands back up. "Well then," he says, looking back and forth between both of us. "I'm going to go find that nephew of mine and spend a bit of time getting to know him. Then I think I'll go for a walk if it's not too cold. You two enjoy your lesson." Ewald winks at me and my cheeks grow hot again. In just a few long strides, he's out the door, and I'm left alone with Helena.

I look at her and the color immediately drains from my face. Her face is icy, her eyes narrow and angry. She stands up, walks briskly toward me, and leans down, her face inches from mine.

"I don't know what you're up to with my brother, but it stops today—right now," she hisses. My brain races to translate what she's said, and form a proper response.

"No, I—" but she won't let me continue.

"Ewald will be here for three weeks," she says, her teeth bared, stretching her thin lips into an angry line. "When he leaves, I will make your life hell. So I suggest you watch yourself around here. Stay away from him, and don't you dare speak of me to him again."

I nod my head and grit my teeth hard. Helena stands up and runs her hand over her hair gently. It's piled up high on her head today, giving her a much more mature and regal look. She's a pretty girl when she isn't glaring and seething with anger. I continue to blink hard as she walks back toward the couch.

"Now, tell me again," Helena says. "How are you doing today?"

I take in a deep breath and shudder. "I am doing just fine," I answer.

I manage to avoid speaking to him for one week. When he enters the room, I leave. I feign headaches whenever he pursues me and spend as much time as I can locked in my tiny, cold attic room.

On his seventh day, Ewald finally catches me on my early morning rounds.

"Why are you avoiding me?" he asks. The stable is dark, and the horses snort and paw at the ground at the interruption. I turn to face him. He stands in the shadows so I back up, giving him space to step into the lamplight.

"I—I'm not avoiding you," I say softly, and he raises his eyebrows.

"You just spoke to me in German," he says with a smile, then chuckles as I gasp in surprise.

"I did, didn't I?" I respond, and despite my discomfort in his presence, I laugh. "I wasn't even thinking!"

Ewald smiles and nods. "That's the point," he says, and he crosses his arms over his chest. "So tell me again. Why are you avoiding me?"

I open my mouth to speak, then close it again. I sigh as I grip the shovel in my hands and lean on it. "I think it makes Helena uncomfortable when we speak," I say. Ewald throws his head back and laughs.

"You're worried about what my sister thinks?" he says. "Helena may not like us speaking, but she's perfectly harmless. She'll get over it with time."

I look down at my hands and can still feel the sting of the ruler. "I don't think so," I mutter and turn to finish shoveling out the stable. Ewald steps up behind me and grabs the shovel. He turns me around slowly, and I feel my heart begin to race.

"I like talking with you," he says, his eyes searching my face. He's so close. I take in long, slow breaths.

"I—I like talking with you, too," I whisper, and Ewald leans in to me. I push him away just before our lips meet.

"But I can't do this," I say, this time in Russian. I need to communicate to him all that's in my head. "*We* can't do this. It isn't right, and your sister is not harmless. She would be furious if she knew you were here with me." I step back away from him, and he tips his head to the side curiously.

"I don't really care what my sister thinks," Ewald says. "But I do care about you. I can't stop thinking about you. I came back here to see you, not Helena."

"You shouldn't have done that," I reply.

Ewald sighs and runs his hand through his hair. "I know it doesn't make sense," he says. "But there's something about you that fascinates me. You're strong and vulnerable all at once. You say exactly what's on your mind, though it always seems to surprise you when you do so. There's something in me that wants to protect you. You're just . . . magnetic," he smiles.

It's my turn to laugh, and I do so heartily. Ewald furrows his brow. "What's so funny?" he asks.

"No one has ever found me magnetic," I answer. "My sister, Anna, is the one everyone's drawn to. She's beautiful and sweet and proper and smart. I have never been the object of anyone's attention."

Ewald drops the shovel and steps toward me quickly. In one brisk movement, his mouth meets mine, and we're locked together. At first I push and resist, but he draws me in tighter, and I finally give in. For several minutes I stay wrapped in his arms before finally pulling away.

Ewald looks at me, his eyes swimming with affection. I look down and try to clear my head. I have never kissed a boy before, never even desired to do so, and now there is this man here—a German man—and I'm confused and frightened by the conflicting emotions that course through my brain.

"I'm sorry," I murmur. "But I just . . . I can't do this with you. It isn't right. You're German. I'm Ukrainian. Our countries are at war with one another."

"When is your birthday, Maria?" Ewald asks and I stop, looking up at him.

"I'll be sixteen on May 14," I answer. "How old are you?"

"I'm twenty-three," he says, and he takes another step toward me. I step backward, my back against the stable wall. "You're young, and I'm guessing you've never been in love before?"

I nod. "Yes, that's true," I reply. "And I am not in love right now," I say. Ewald sighs and runs his hand through his hair.

"I don't think I'm in love with you, either, Maria," he says gently. "But I am fascinated by you."

"I may be young," I say with a wry smile, "but I'm wise enough to know that fascination with someone is not a firm base for love. Our worlds are too different, Ewald."

Ewald smiles and reaches out, laying his hand gently on my cheek. I grow warm at his touch, and I lean into his hand.

"Can I kiss you one more time?" he asks. I don't respond, but the look in my eyes gives him the freedom to lean in once more. His kiss is gentle and warm. He pulls back and searches my eyes. "Maybe I can meet you here in the mornings when Helena and the world are still asleep, and we can just . . . be together. I won't tell her that I'm seeing you."

I sigh and bite my lip as I look up at his handsome face. *"Juwhal,"* I answer softly in German, and he laughs.

"Now," I say as we step away from one another. "If you're going to be here, you have to help me clean this place up." Ewald grins.

"It's a deal," he says with a wink, and together we finish the morning chores.

For the next ten days, Ewald meets me in the barn in the darkness of night. We talk and laugh, and in that time my German improves rapidly. I no longer have to think about verb tenses or stop to translate every word in my head. I simply speak, and I feel his pride at my improvement.

While I enjoy our time together, I also cannot escape the nagging feeling that this is very, very wrong. Ewald's stares are sometimes tender and inviting. His intensity leaves me feeling warm and protected. But other times, I catch him watching me with an almost animal hunger, which makes me uncomfortable.

Tomorrow is his last day here with us, and as I rise early, I feel the knot inside my stomach settle heavily. Spending this time with him these last weeks was foolish. I'm aware that the physical nature of our relationship is crazy, but somewhere in this time that we've been together, I've grown to depend on his fascination with me. I also feel safer around Helena when Ewald is nearby.

I creep down the stairs to the kitchen, grab the milk bucket, and head out to the barn. The wind is biting, and my teeth chatter mercilessly. I slide open the barn door and grab the lamp, lighting it quickly. The barn is cold, but the walls keep the wind out, which makes it bearable. I sit down on my little stool and begin milking the cow, all the while listening for Ewald's boots on the hay.

The door finally slides open, and he steps inside with a grin. "Sorry I'm late," he says sheepishly. "I couldn't quite wake up this morning."

I laugh. "Well, I'm already finished milking. Want to come with me to the stable?"

"Of course I do," Ewald says. He steps close and kisses me on the cheek. "I won't have many more opportunities to do that," he says, brushing my hair away from my face. I feel my cheeks grow warm, and I step away quickly.

"We should get moving," I say, pushing past him.

We speak very little as we shovel the stable, brush the horses, and fill the troughs. Finally, Ewald pulls me away from the work and engulfs me in a tight hug. "I'm sorry," he whispers, kissing the top of my head.

"For what?" I ask.

"For leaving you behind. I'm sorry for forcing you into an impossible relationship. I'm sorry for a lot of things." He pushes me back and looks deep into my eyes. "But I'm not sorry for falling in love with you."

I look back at him in surprise. "How are you in love with me?" I ask. "You hardly know me!"

Ewald smiles. "I know enough," he says. I lean into his embrace, my head tight against his chest. I know that I don't love this man, but there's something comforting in his affection for me, though I still suspect his feelings are more physical than they are emotional. I close my eyes and immediately my mother's face appears before me. Her eyes swim with disapproval.

"We should head inside," I murmur, pushing away and blinking hard against the vision. Ewald nods. He picks up the milk bucket, and together we trudge out into the blustery wind.

"It's going to snow soon," Ewald says. "I can smell it."

We make our way toward the house. Just before we get to the door, Ewald grabs my hand and pulls me to him. He kisses me passionately, and I return the emotion, pushing away every notion of foolishness that chases me. I don't know what love is, and I don't know how I feel about Ewald, but I do wish that this morning didn't have to end. Right or wrong, I cannot ignore the impulse of this one moment. Ewald pulls back and hands me the bucket.

"Have a good day, beautiful girl," he whispers, and he enters the house. I stand frozen, allowing him the chance to escape to his room. I don't know why I look up at the window above, but when I do, I see her staring at me. She holds a candle just below her chin, and it casts shadows across her face that send a shiver down my spine.

Helena glares at me for a second before floating away from the window, leaving me to stand in icy fear.

FREDERICK HERRMANN
January 20, 1943

"Herrmann!"

Leaping to my feet, I stand tall at attention next to my bunk. The other men in the room scramble up as well, all of us rigid as Sturmbannführer Hitzig strides across the room, his tiny eyes wild above his sharp nose. Tall and thin, Hitzig's gangly frame makes him appear more comical than imposing and has quietly earned him the nickname "Giraffe" by some of the other men.

I raise my arm in salute. *"Heil Hitler!"* I say, my voice neither too loud nor too soft.

Hitzig stops in front of me, his hat tucked securely beneath his arm. He looks down at me, his mouth pinched in a tight line.

"Get dressed, Herrmann," he says. His voice is strained as though he swallowed a desperate concoction of anger and fear. "You're needed at the command center."

I nod, and with a click of my heels, I turn and pull my clothes off the rack by my bunk, unable to hide my trembling fingers. In less than three minutes I'm dressed, and I walk sharply behind Hitzig out of the building. I hear the rest of the men murmur as I leave the room.

The air is crisp and bitter cold. This is my second winter in Kiev, and I find it more wretched than the last. I tug my thin coat up under my jaw and clench it to keep my teeth from chattering. The walk isn't far, thankfully, and in a few minutes we're out of the chill of the January air.

It's been seven months since Father visited and read me the letter from Blobel. In those seven months, I've done all that has been asked of me. I fought when asked to fight—killed when asked to kill. I called operations, organized paperwork, ran errands, and answered every challenge placed before me.

I spoke to no one of my experience with the Ukrainian man on the hill. Though sometimes I hear Father's voice in my head commanding me to find the man and finish what I started at Babi Yar, I can't bring myself to comply. It's a terrible lapse in German character, but the only way I can see atonement is to purge myself of all doubt.

I must pull the trigger. I've availed myself of all emotion, zealously accomplishing my work as a true and moral Nazi soldier. My passion for domination has turned my comrades against me. They look at me as I pass. I hear them whisper when I leave the room. They're plotting against me. I know it. They see my weakness and plan to exploit it. My only recourse is to keep pulling the trigger.

Keep killing.

This will win Father's approval.

This will make Germany great. It will make me great.

It's only the darkness that betrays my resolve. At night, when I close my eyes, the nightmares taunt me, and every time I wake, I find myself longing for my mother and sister. I ache for the comfort of mother's arms around me—arms that I spent most of my life pushing away. And I replay the sound of Talia's laugh over and over, like the call of a muse. What a weak creature I am, indeed.

Though I've had no communication with Father since his visit, I know he hears of me. Standartenführer Paul Blobel has returned, his mission now to destroy all evidence of the killings at Babi Yar. We begin burning and burying the bodies this week. But there's more to Blobel's return. I know it. He's been sent back to check on me. And now I am being summoned to his presence.

Things are happening in this war. I feel the charge in the air as commanders and officers bark out frantic orders. I've heard murmurs that our forces are losing their grip on key cities, and without doubt the leaders of our nation are placing great emphasis on the need to fully secure Kiev.

"Come inside, please," Hitzig says, gesturing toward an open door. I step into the cold, drafty room and take in the sights. The walls are bare, gray cement, and a maze of cracks lines them from floor to ceiling, the veined markings of consistent shelling—war rained down. A small table stands in the center of the room with two chairs pushed in tight on either side. The rusted metal lamp in the corner casts an orange glow that runs downward along the gritty floor and shoots across the room. I walk to the table and turn to look at Hitzig, who stands erect at the doorway.

"Forgive me, sir, but is something wrong?" I ask. The building is eerily quiet, and I suddenly feel ill at ease.

Hitzig takes a deep breath, then lets it out in a low, raspy sigh. "He'll be here to talk with you soon." He turns on his heel and marches out of the room. I listen to the hollow sounds of his shoes clacking against the floor. A door opens, then closes, and the building is again silent.

I pull out a chair and sit down, then immediately stand. Pacing the room, I run through the events of the last few days, trying to decipher what I could have done wrong. It's been a relatively quiet week. The New Year celebrations were quieter this year, less raucous than the last. Our influence on this area is waning, and our hold on the Soviet Union is less sure than it was a year ago. The Red Army managed to open a corridor to Leningrad last week. Just the thought of it leaves me ill. Leningrad—the city my father always dreamed of inhabiting—may slip through our grasp. I close my eyes and remember the way Father would wax poetic about all that Germany could do when we finally had the land of the Soviets in our grasp. Losing Leningrad would be a blow to his mission.

I freeze at the sound of boots marching down the hallway, two sets, both headed in my direction. I force my shoulders back and clench my hands to keep them from trembling. The knob turns, the door swings open, and he steps into the room as I blink in surprise. Father's brow is furrowed, his back rigid. His hair has grayed, and his shoulders are thin and gaunt. He looks old and sick. I'm shocked at the sight of him.

Paul Blobel steps in behind him, the familiar glint shining in his eyes. I knew it. I knew he'd been sent here to watch me. I stand unmoving at the sight of the two men I fear most.

Father's shoes clip across the hollow floor, and in three long strides he is before me, staring hard through narrow, sunken eyes. "Well, don't just stand there, boy," he barks. "Salute your father and this officer properly."

My stomach flips. I throw my arm up in a stiff salute. *"Heil Hitler!"* I cry out. Father and Blobel return the salute. Father gestures toward the chairs in a command to sit, and I quickly comply, willing my heartbeat to slow and my breathing to regulate.

"Well, Frederick," Father begins, still standing over me, his back straight and stiff, his eyes devoid of emotion. He places his hat on the table, and grasps his hands behind his back. "Hitzig tells me you've done everything he's asked of you. He even says you have gone over and above the commands given you. He says you've been a model soldier."

I return my father's gaze and wait for the expected reprimand. Instead, Father nods his head, but I don't sense any approval in his eyes. His gaze is steady, and the solemn nature of his stare accentuates the deep wrinkles that furrow his face, leaving him so very old.

"I trust you've enjoyed being reacquainted with my old friend here," Father says, waving his arm toward Blobel, who grins at me fiendishly. I feel a hatred bubbling in my chest for this snake of a man, and I refuse to offer him more than a glance. Blobel gives a short laugh and bows slightly.

"I'll leave you two alone to talk," he says with a hiss. He spins on his heel and leaves the room, and I turn slowly to my aged father.

Grabbing hold of the chair, Father slides it out and sits down across from me. He folds his hands, places them on top of the table, and stares hard at me.

"Your mother is dead, Frederick," he says. It takes a moment to register his words. I blink and let them bounce around inside my head before they finally take hold and sink down into my soul.

"I . . . What? When?" My head spins. Father doesn't move, but instead watches me fight against my emotions with a look of shame and disgust.

"Calm down, boy," he spits. I close my eyes, and the image of my mother's face immediately fills the dark place—her eyes always so sad, so unsure, so filled with a longing to protect. I spent my entire life pushing her away, and now I long for her more than anyone in the world. I open my eyes and look back at Father, and I immediately resent his callous attitude.

"It's really better this way," Father says, his eyes narrowing. "She was sick for some time, and the pain grew intense. It was cancer."

"Why didn't you write and tell me? Why didn't anyone tell me to go home and see her?" I ask. My voice wavers.

"Oh please, Frederick. Don't act like such a child. You had a job to do. There was no sense in distracting you from that. Your coming home wouldn't have changed your mother's fate any more than it would have had I returned home before she passed. My leadership was needed in Berlin, so of course I had to remain there. The difference between you and me is that you needed to stay just so we could keep your head in the game."

Father wasn't there when she died, either. Mother died alone. At once, the colors around me ignite, and I slam my hand against the table.

"What the hell does that mean?" I shout, looking my father straight in the eye for the first time in my life. I don't waver from his gaze as my chest heaves up and down. Father returns my stare, and very quickly I regret my outburst. I'm conflicted, afraid and angry, each emotion pushing over me like a tidal wave.

"Forgive me," I mumble. My words sound slurred, my voice foreign. I lower my eyes again, but I can still feel his hot, angry stare.

Father places his hands against the table, and he slowly rises to his feet. He's bent forward at the waist, his face lit with fury. "You have the nerve to lose your temper with me, and then you take it a step further and ask for forgiveness?" he hisses. "You're both disrespectful *and* weak."

I blink hard as Father pants in anger before me. After a moment, he lowers himself back into his seat. He's tired. I can see it in his movements.

We sit silently for several long minutes before I speak again. "Does Talia know?" I ask. "Have you found her?"

At the mention of his beloved daughter's name, Father's face drops. His eyes are drawn, and the sadness puts out the heat of his anger.

"Your sister is no longer a part of our lives," he replies. "She has disappointed me even more than you. I'm a scorned man by both of my children."

And just like that, the air leaves my lungs, and I slump. For the first time, I accept the thing that I think I've always known deep inside.

I will never please my father.

I gulp in a few deep breaths, willing the oxygen to bring back my vision. Pushing my shoulders straight, I look once again into the eyes of the old man before me. He's broken and ruined: alone without a wife to speak of his invisible virtues, and with two children who have let him down. And in an instant I realize I *hate* him.

"Is that all you came here to tell me?" I ask icily. Father looks at me with dark, cloudy eyes.

"I came here to tell you that you're a disappointment," he says. I stand up abruptly, pushing the chair back with such force that it clatters to the floor.

"All I have ever done, Father," I say through clenched teeth, "is try to please you. It has always been my desire to bring honor to your name. Always." Tears prick at the corners of my eyes, and my whole body quakes. Again I see my mother's face, and my vision clears, Father is finally coming fully into focus before me. He's weak. The man I have longed to emulate is a coward, and I am just like him. There is no longer a future for either one of us.

I take a deep breath before speaking again. For the first time in months I feel my head clearing, the fog slowly burning away the lies as the truth ignites before me. "I see now there's nothing I could ever have done to make you happy," I say.

Father stands and grabs his hat. He puts it on his head and draws in a long, deep breath. "Well, then," he says, his voice weary, "I believe we've both said all that needs to be said." He looks at me, and I see nothing but scorn and shame. "You're a failure," he says softly.

"And you're a coward," I answer back. Father looks shocked, but I leave no opportunity for him to respond. I spin on my heel and march out of the room, leaving him with nothing but the shame of his own failings.

Slamming open the door leading into the street, I welcome the bitter cold that rushes over me like a flood. Turning to the left, I march up the sidewalk, the hill sharp and steep. My feet skid and slip, and I fall to my knees with a thud, pain shooting through my leg like a knife. I push back to my feet and continue forward, wincing with each limped step. My shoulders shake, a mixture of anger, grief, and cold.

I reach the top of the hill and stop next to a blackened building, the effects of this war leaving stains everywhere. I turn to look back down at headquarters. It's mostly dark inside, but I can still see the faint orange glow of lights. I assume my father is still there. I wish him dead.

Then it hits me, and a sob escapes before I can hold it back. My mother is gone—my meek, quiet mother whom I always saw as weak. I understand her more, and regret and remorse send me into waves of grief. Like me, she was always bent to Father's will. She didn't agree with him, but she couldn't rock the boat. To do so would have cost her everything because it would have meant forfeiting her children to his grasp. She tried to protect us from him. I think of the night she tucked me in as a small boy and whispered her secret to me.

"Don't grow up to be like him."

Her words pierce, and I know now that she wasn't weak. My mother was strong. She was strong enough not to be swayed into believing Father. Talia had this same strength. But nothing could save them from Father, and nothing will save me, either. I am finished.

"I'm just like him," I whisper into the void. "I *am* weak." The night sky sweeps up my despair and flings it into the cavern of space between the present and eternity. I've spent my entire life with one goal, one purpose: to win father's approval. *My life is wasted.*

I lean against the wall and drop my head back with a crack. I rest against the rough surface and take notice of the frigid air against my body, so cold it burns.

"Tomorrow," I whisper, pushing away from the wall and picking a sorrowful path of purpose down the hill toward the barracks.

"Frederick."

The whisper haunts, but I cannot see the source of the voice. I peer into the darkness, squinting my eyes for some glimpse.

"Come to us, Frederick. Come and see what your greatness has accomplished. Come, Frederick. Come."

I take a step toward the whisper. My heart beats quickly, and my palms sweat. I squeeze my hands into fists in an attempt to steady myself. A faint light appears in the distance. I quicken my steps toward it. Ghosts can't stand in the light.

"Come closer, Frederick. Come and see."

The words are breathy, almost a hiss. I run now toward the growing light, longing to break free of the darkness.

"Frederick."

I come to a halt as the light overwhelms me. I shield my eyes with my hands, trying to see who it is that whispers my name.

"Frederick."

The whisper is right next to me, cool lips pressed against my ear. I whirl to the right, and open my mouth in a silent scream. It's her: the red-headed waitress from the nightclub. Her eyes are completely black, her skin pale. A thin trickle of blood drips down her upper lip. Her head lolls to the side as she fixes her death stare on me.

"See what you have done, Frederick," she whispers. I follow her pointed hand to the mound of bodies, each of their faces familiar to me. They are my dead. The pile writhes and squirms together like worms fighting and pushing their way to the surface, and in the center, a space opens up for something that wishes to escape.

I want to look away, but my eyes are frozen on the image before me. As the bodies part, two figures emerge. They turn slowly to stare at me, their eyes deep and sunken into blue-streaked cheeks. It is Mother and Talia.

Their mouths move slowly, thin lips calling my name in short, staccato gasps. I try to scream but can't, so I throw myself to the side.

I wretch myself from my bottom bunk and thrash on the floor for a moment, the weight of the nightmare leaving me disoriented and confused. After a short moment, I realize where I am and quickly pull myself back into bed.

I squeeze my eyes shut in an attempt to block out the visions of my dream, but as soon as I do so, I see them all—every person I've killed since the war began. I see the woman with the fur coat and the husband and wife clinging to one another at Babi Yar. I see the sobbing, pleading mother as she grasps her infant. I hear the cries of the farmer's wife as I force him to his knees. I feel the spray of blood warm against my cheeks when I pull the trigger.

And as each person dies again right before my eyes, I hear his voice, the man from the woods. The only one I ever let live.

"You are not a killer," he whispers over and over. His voice overcomes the awful whispers of my dead. His terrible loop of lies.

I am a killer, I think as I force my eyes open and stare at the bed above me. I am the most evil of killers because I killed without conviction. I killed to please. I killed not for sport or with purpose but for approval.

I killed in vain.

Swinging my legs over the side of the bed, I push myself up, my joints stiff and tight from a night of tension. I fell asleep in my uniform, and it's wrinkled and disheveled. I don't bother to change. I slide my hat down low over my forehead and carry my shoes out of the room before putting them on. I desire no attention, no questioning eyes. I know they're all curious as to what happened last night.

Let them wonder.

Stepping out into the early morning sunshine, I squint and allow a moment for my eyes to adjust. The light is intense and stabs like a dagger. The air still bites, but the sunlight takes away the sting. When my eyes have finally grown accustomed to the brightness, I turn and walk back toward headquarters.

Stepping inside, I look around the still, quiet room. A young soldier sits in the corner, a steaming mug of Soviet chai sitting before him. He looks at me with eyebrows raised.

"I need to speak with Blobel," I say, my voice gruff and clipped. "Is he here?"

The soldier nods and juts his chin toward a closed door at the end of the hall. I walk quickly to the door and give two short, staccato raps.

"Enter!" Blobel barks. I push the door open. He stands at his desk, a box sitting before him. He looks at me in surprise, his eyebrows high on his narrow forehead.

"Herrmann," he says as he turns to face me. "I trust you had an . . . *interesting* discussion with your father last night." As he speaks, his long neck stretches forward so that he stares up at me. His gaze is both amused and sarcastic.

I resist the urge to cringe and answer with only a slight nod. Blobel narrows his eyes, studying me closely before shifting his round eyes from my face and leaning back against his desk.

"So what are you doing here, Herrmann?" Blobel asks.

"I need permission to take one of the cars, sir," I answer. I look steadily at him as I make my request, and Blobel pushes himself up, trying to lengthen his stance to match my own. I don't break my stare, my eyes piercing his in defiance.

"And why do you need to take a car, Herrmann?" he asks.

"I need to run an errand . . . for my father," I answer. I'm not asking, and as our eyes remain locked I defy Blobel to deny my request. I have never made such a bold and assuming demand, but I no longer care about the rules that Father so tirelessly drilled into my head. Blobel laughs, a mirthless, ugly sound that sends chills down my spine.

"Well then," he says, eyeing me closely. "Who am I to deny the son of the great Tomas Herrmann?"

This time I cannot hide my disdain. I *am* the son of Tomas Herrmann, a man scorned and shamed by his entire family—a man impossible to please. Yes, I am his son, and I'm shamed for it. I think of Talia's bold words that final day with Father, and at once I understand her anger, and in my understanding, I feel connected to her once again after so many years.

Blobel waves his hand at me. "Take any car you want, Herrmann," he says, his voice trembling with laughter. "Just report back to me when you've finished your . . . errands." A wicked smile cuts across his face, and I spin on my heels to escape the heat of his stare.

Rushing to the front room, I hold my hand out to the soldier on guard. "I need keys to one of the cars," I demand, my voice sharp. He glances toward Blobel's door, then back at me. Shrugging his shoulders, he reaches into his desk drawer and pulls out a set of keys. I grab them and race out the back door, quickly find my car, and slide into the front seat. The leather is icy, and my teeth chatter involuntarily. I start the engine, giving it a brief moment to warm up before kicking it into gear and pulling out.

I know where I'll go.

Twenty-five minutes later, I allow the car to roll to a stop. I stare out the window at the vast expanse of land. This is the place where it all began, where my spiral into shame and death took root. And this is the place where it will end.

I push open the door and step outside. Immediately, I sense the oppression of this place. I feel the heat of hell, a heat I helped ignite. I walk slowly through the fence toward the clearing. Articles of clothing still lie in small piles, and I stop briefly to look at them. Reaching down, I pick up a small brown teddy bear, a child's companion until death parted them.

I study the bear closely, noting his button eyes and the worn patch on his arm where he was obviously dragged. I close my eyes and try to chase the images away, but they're there, waiting for me. The smell of death is strong in this place, and the haunting cries of women and children chase my thoughts.

I open my eyes and drop the bear. My hands feel as though they've been burned, and perhaps they have. I walk past the second gate and step over the threshold that looks down over Babi Yar. The sight brings a wave of nausea that I cannot fight as I lean forward with a violent wretch. The bile and acid from inside my empty stomach come out with such force that I feel my throat go instantly raw.

I cannot look away, though the pain of the sight cuts me deeply. More have been killed in the sixteen months since we began our cleansing here in Babi Yar. The tangle of bodies is deep, and high, and long. The cold temperatures have preserved most of them in such an unblemished state that I must fight the urge to shout out to them.

Get up! my heart screams, but I know it's no use. They're dead, and it is I who killed them. There are so many bodies piled up that it looks like a woven braid of knees and elbows, all locked together and topped with mouths open wide in pain and horror. Thousands and thousands lie here, naked and exposed, and I cannot remember why.

Why have we done this? What use was it to us, to me? What sort of darkness sees such suffering and looks the other way?

I think of the men in my group, the men of Einsatzgruppen C, and I'm stunned at the images that fill my mind. The men are laughing, smoking, playing as they kill. This was sport to them. Shooting these men and women was as common an act as shooting a deer in the woods.

"But why *shouldn't* we have done this," I say out loud, my mouth and throat still burning. I must remember what brought me here, because the sight before me is too horrible to have been created in vain. "They said this land was ours to make holy," I whisper, repeating the words I've heard over and over all my life. "We're to build a nation pure and set apart."

Looking up, I stare at the blue sky through the trees, searching for confirmation from the heavens that what I accomplished here had true weight. I try to see the faces of the ones who once held such deep respect in my heart. I search for the conviction that makes this all worthwhile, makes it right. But I see no justification for my actions. I see only the face of my father, and I feel at once that I have been terribly tricked.

"I am a fool," I whisper. I take a step forward, and my foot slips, tossing me down the steep, slippery embankment. I land hard on top of the pile of frozen bodies. The stillness is nearly suffocating. There are no sounds to be heard outside of the beating of my heart. Their mouths are open, but they are silent. I sit up and turn around to see whom I landed on.

She's young—three, maybe four. Her hair is dark and curly, her lips blue. Her eyes are open and vacant. She doesn't look sad or scared. Instead she seems peaceful, perhaps even calm. The only evidence of her horror lies in the large, gaping hole that splits her forehead. This is the place where all the world was cut off from her. Was she the owner of the bear?

I stand up and look down the ravine, the bodies piled high as far as I can see. I look back at the girl and feel the weight of my guilt upon me like an ever-tightening vice. I look up the embankment and realize I'm trapped. I will never climb out of this ditch.

I pull my gun from my jacket and turn it over in my hands. I try to remember the pride I felt the day I was handed a Nazi-issued Luger, but there's no pride to be seen, no honor to be found. I pull away my thick gloves so that I can feel the metal cold in my hands. I turn it over again, then release the lock, listening to the click echo through the cavern. Cocking the gun slowly, I imagine the bullet slipping into the chamber. I hear no sound as I raise it up with shaking hands.

I gaze out over the sea of bodies one last time, then down at the tiny girl. I long for her forgiveness—hers and all the others. But I know I shall not have it. There will be no peace for me. Heaving in a deep, ragged breath, I scream from the very pit of my soul, the tears flowing freely and hot.

"Heil Hitler!" The scream is guttural and primal, but the sound of my own voice no longer shocks me. I'm already dead.

I always thought I'd grow up to be a great man. I had to look no further than my father to see what greatness looked like. The face of a great man was framed by the accomplishments he attained in front of all who watched. I look slowly around at the hollow eyes. They're all watching me, and I feel their stares settle upon my soul. They see now what took so long for me to see myself.

I am not a great man.

I press the gun hard against my temple and squeeze the trigger.

IVAN KYRILOVICH

February 24, 1943

I remember well the night we got notice of my older brother's death. It was during the time of the Great War, when all of Russia and Ukraine were in upheaval. My brother, Pavel, had been gone a little over a year, and my father had grown belligerent and impossible in the months after his departure. Mother and I learned to move around him, to stay just out of his reach.

Father spent most of his mornings in the fields, ordering me to work harder and faster. I lived for the moment that he left for lunch, when he'd go into the village and sit with the other bitter men of his generation, and together they drank and discussed all the ways that Ukraine could and would be better.

Those were the men who gave voice to the Bolshevik Revolution. They were the men who felt certain that Ukraine would be a better nation when the Czar finally fell and a common Soviet power could be established. Ukraine's greatness was spoken in the melody of drunken old villagers. I despised them.

Mother handled the grief of Pavel's departure much differently. Her suffering was silent and completely alone. Each morning, she cried softly as she gathered the eggs from the hen house, her sobs soft and mournful. By the time she had breakfast prepared, however, her tears were dried, her face soft and serene.

Mama was strong, but my father weak. His only escape came in the men of the village and the bottle of vodka that he brought home every afternoon.

The day the letter arrived telling us that Pavel's life ended on a cold hill in northern Austria, my father had ironically not taken a drink. The night before he had been so drunk that he tripped and fell into the fire where Mama boiled water. His hands were so badly burned that he couldn't move and, therefore, he couldn't drink.

The letter arrived just as Mama placed a loaf of bread and steaming bowls of broth on the table. The knock at the door was sharp and rapid, and Mama froze. I looked from her face to Father's, both glowing in the orange light of the fire and revealing a fear so deep that neither could move. I pushed back my chair and ran to the door, swinging it open to find our neighbor, Olya Valerevna, standing at the door.

"This came today just before the post closed," she said quietly. I remember the rasp in her voice and the way it left me with chills running down my spine.

I took the tightly folded paper and thanked her before shutting the door and turning to face my parents. Mother already had tears running down her cheeks, and Father's eyes were dark.

I opened the paper slowly and read the words with a shaky voice:

"WE REGRET TO INFORM YOU THAT PAVEL KYRILOVICH PETRO-CHENKO WAS KILLED IN ACTION ON OCTOBER 2, 1916, AT HIS POST IN AUSTRIA-HUNGARY. WE THANK HIM FOR HIS SERVICE TO OUR GREAT NATION."

I laid the paper on the table in front of Father, his burnt hands limp and black in his lap. He stared at it a long time.

"It shouldn't have been him," Father murmured, his shoulders slumped forward in despair. With a wail, Mama swept her hand across the table, scattering the dishes with a crash and sending Father scrambling to his feet as he growled and screeched in a rage.

And I stood motionless in the corner. The older brother whom I could never live up to was gone forever, and I felt . . . nothing. No sadness, no remorse, no grief.

The months after the notice of Pavel's death were spent trying to defend myself against Father's endless attacks. If he wasn't mumbling about how he wished I'd been the one to die instead, then he talked endlessly about his high hopes for the Bolshevik Revolution.

"We will be a great nation," he slurred every day. "We'll be great when the Bolsheviks get the stupid cowards out of power."

In March 1917, two significant things happened. The first was the fulfillment of my father's predications. The Bolsheviks forced the emperor to abdicate, and the revolution became a success with the fall of the Romanovs and the ascension of Vladimir Lenin into power. Father came dancing home the day the news came to our village. "Don't you see, you stupid boy?" he cried. "We can now establish a strong Ukrainian Republic. We will be Soviets! This is the start of our country becoming a dynamic power." Father was victorious that day, and it was the closest to happy I had ever seen him. I hated him for it.

The second thing of significance to happen in March 1917 was the day I met Tanya. She had just moved to town to live with her grandparents after both her parents were killed in the revolution. She was sad and shy and innocently beautiful. I knew the first time I saw her that she would be mine forever.

That was a long time ago in a life that feels oddly disconnected from the one I live now. I try to remember the boy I once was from time to time. I try to connect myself to him, but I can't. It seems as though I have lived two lives, each with enough heartache to stand on its own.

Tanya sits at the table, her chair turned toward the small window located high on the wall. The sky outside is blue and bright, and every once in a while, a bird glides by. Her hair is loose, hanging down over the back of the chair. In the two years since the war began, her hair has gone from brown to almost completely silver. It's long and full and hangs in soft waves, framing her petite features.

I can't see her face, but I feel her peace. I move into the room and place my hands gently on her shoulders, leaning forward to kiss her softly on the head.

"*Dobrei utra*, my darling," I murmur. *Good morning.* She turns her face up to mine, eyes smiling. I lean over and kiss the tip of her nose, then turn and shuffle to the chair across the table. She has placed a mug of chai there for me, and I wrap my hands around it, breathing in deep the aroma of comfort.

"How are you?" I ask before taking a sip. Tanya looks at me, then turns her face back up to the window. Her eyes search the sky as though she's looking for an answer to a question I don't know.

"Ivan," she says, her face still turned upward. "What do you know of God?"

I take another sip of tea as I ingest the question. "I don't know much," I answer. "I don't even know if I believe there is a God. Why do you ask, darling?"

Tanya shrugs her shoulders. "We've never discussed it," she says. "I guess I've never thought about it much myself, but lately I wonder . . ."

Her voice trails off, and I see the tears gathering in the corners of her eyes. I set my mug down and reach across the table to grab her hand.

"What is it, Tanyushka?" I ask.

Tanya shakes her head and blinks hard. She takes a deep breath, composing herself before continuing.

"I wonder if perhaps I've missed something all these years in not considering that there might be a God."

I wait, not wanting to rush her and completely unsure of how I should respond. I've long since made my peace with the idea that there is no God.

"When the children were growing up, I told them about the saints," Tanya continues. "I taught them to pray to the saints because that's what my mother did for me. I wanted them to have something they could believe in that existed outside of themselves. But I never mentioned God to them." She turns and looks at me, her eyes filled with questions. "Did I deprive them in some way by not giving them a better understanding of God? Would that hope have given them more to cling to in these dark days?" I open my mouth to answer, but she continues on. She doesn't want answers right now.

"Maria asked me once about God," Tanya says. She pulls her hand out of mine and grabs her mug. "She came home from school and asked me why we didn't pray to God and . . . Ivan, I didn't have an answer for her. I just told her that if she wanted to pray to God, she could, and she wanted to know how to pray. Oh my. Remember how many questions she asked?"

Tanya chuckles, and I join her. Maria was a delightfully curious child. Her incessant talking exhausted us then, but now, with all the silence and stillness, I find myself longing for her chatter. Tanya and I both let our laughter fade as the memories overwhelm.

"Tanya," I finally say. "Truthfully, my darling, I know very little about God, and I've never been interested in knowing. My mother was a strong believer in the spirit life, and before the revolution I remember her frequently attending a local church. I think I even went with her once or twice when I was very young.

"But my father wanted nothing to do with it, and Mother was never one for fighting him on the subject. I remember the icons that she had under her bed. She pulled them out every once in a while and prayed before them, but I didn't understand why. I guess . . ." I sit back in my chair, pinching the bridge of my nose. Tanya turns toward me with a look of concern.

"What is it?" she asks.

"I guess I have a bit of my father in me, after all," I say with a sigh. "I've always tried so hard *not* to be like him, but in this way I fear I'm much like him."

Tanya smiles gently. "I think it's okay to question and doubt, darling. There's certainly enough evidence for you to hold to a belief that there's no such thing as God."

"What evidence do you mean?" I ask.

"Well," Tanya replies, "what kind of God allows men like Hitler and Stalin to tear innocent children from their mother's arms?" Tanya stops cold and puts her hands over her face. I push back my chair and rush to her, pulling her into my arms.

Her shoulders shake as she gasps for breath.

"Shh . . ." I whisper, stroking her silver hair.

"I'm so, so scared, Ivan," Tanya whispers. "I'm so scared they'll never come back, and I'm scared that if there is a God, He won't hear me." Tanya's whole body shakes under the strain of her grief.

"My darling," I whisper. "Perhaps it's time you and I both begin to search out the possibility of there being a God." I push her back and pull her hands away from her face, which is red and spotted with grief. "Maybe it's time we made peace with God . . . or made peace with no God. And in that peace, perhaps we'll find hope again."

Tanya nods slowly, taking deep, halting breaths as she tries to regain her composure. She looks at me and speaks with a quaking voice. "I don't even know where to begin," she says.

"I don't either," I say. "How does someone learn about God?"

"I think there is a man quietly operating a church close to town," Tanya says. "I've heard of him while working the salt flats. Maybe we could take a walk?"

An hour later, Tanya and I make our way out onto the sunlit streets of Kiev. Turning down Shamrila Street, we pause a moment to take in the sight.

"Spring is here," Tanya murmurs, and I breathe in deeply. The air is crisp, but the sun warm. Blades of green peek from the frozen dirt, and I grab Tanya's hand. We're both desperate to push out the dead of winter.

Others are out today, mingling and enjoying the beautiful weather. The ever-present soldiers mar my serenity, but outside of seeing an occasional Nazi, I'm pleasantly relaxed. If I allow myself for one moment to forget the pain of the last two years, I feel as though life is almost as it once was.

An hour later, we arrive at a small building, blackened by the effects of smoke and bombs. I look up at it and squint.

"How do you know this is it?" I ask.

"I don't," she replies. "We'll have to step inside to find out." We push the door open and step into a dark, damp room. Two tables sit at the other end, each with numerous candles lit beneath a painted icon. The old, wooden paintings give me chills as we walk forward. This is the part of religion that feels so foreign and frightening.

I study the first icon. It's a picture of a young woman, her face long, drawn, and sad. She holds in her lap a child. Both mother and child look upward, giving them the expression of piety, and perhaps fear. Their lips are parted, and the baby reaches up with one chubby arm. Each of them has a golden halo above their heads.

Tanya stares at the icon next to me with her head cocked slightly to the side. "It's the Christ child," she whispers. I nod. I've heard the stories of the Christ born to a virgin—a young girl named Maria.

Tanya moves on to the next icon. It's small, and we both lean in to look at it. A man with long, sad eyes holds tight to a cross, his face pious and drawn. Two angels hover over him, and a faded crown rests on his head.

"I don't understand where these came from," I whisper. "I thought all religious relics were destroyed."

Tanya shakes her head. "No. Many were preserved and hidden." She looks back at the picture with a sigh. "I just wish I understood it all," she says. "Why does he look like that? And why is he wearing a crown?"

I spin when I hear the footsteps, and Tanya and I both freeze as he steps from the shadows. He's hunched over inside a long robe, and he moves slowly forward, leaning hard against the staff in his right hand.

"I'm sorry," I say, my voice echoing against the bare walls. "We were just curious."

The man nods his head and smiles. "This is the place to be curious," he says. "Can I help you?"

I open my mouth to speak, and suddenly feel ridiculous. I don't know where to begin or what to ask. I close my mouth and look at Tanya, who gives me a soft, patient smile.

"We're curious about . . . God," she says. I clear my throat. It all feels very awkward. How on earth do I articulate my questions before a stranger? My knowledge of the spiritual realm is simplistic, uneducated, and riddled with disbelief. I don't even know what to call the man standing before me.

I squirm under his deep gaze. His face is kind, the wrinkles around his eyes betraying a love for laughter and joy. His mouth is small and parted as though he wants to speak but has not yet been given permission. As our eyes meet, I sense that he knows and understands all of my questions. He has accepted them silently so that I won't have to give them voice.

"These are difficult times, yes?" the man says, looking from me to Tanya and back again. We both nod. "Tell me how the times are difficult for you," he says, leaning against his staff.

"I . . . would you like to go someplace and sit down?" I ask him, noticing his frailty, but he waves me off.

"Why?" he asks, his eyes twinkling. "Because I am an old man? I will be no less old in a chair, I can assure you."

Tanya smiles, and I nod, then clear my throat again. "Well," I begin. "All three of our children have been taken. Our son fights somewhere in the West. We believe he is in the Galicia region, but we're not certain. We haven't received a letter in many months." I feel my chest constrict, and I stop to take in a long, slow breath. Tanya grabs my hand.

"Our daughters were both taken last year. They were taken right off the street, right from my hands." My voice cracks. I shake my head. Tanya continues.

"They're in Germany." Like mine, Tanya's voice trails off, and she searches the old man's face. I feel her questions. She wants reassurances. She wants to hear that this God we know nothing about has something planned—something that will give her hope. She wants to know that the saints are on our side.

The old man sighs, the light from his eyes dimming. He nods, first at Tanya, then at me. "Yes," he says softly. "These are terrible times indeed." He turns to face the first table and gestures toward the icon of the mother and child.

"There's much room for doubt in these days and plenty of reason for question," he says. "But belief that there is a higher purpose and acknowledging the beauty of truth will carry you far through this tragedy."

I feel my heart sink. This is exactly the thing I feared in seeking out God. There are no answers, and if hope can only be placed in some mystical reason beyond my understanding, then what reason could there be for my heartache?

"Forgive me," I say, turning to the old man. "I don't know that I believe in—"

The old man holds up his hand, and I immediately quiet. He turns to me, and the right side of his face, rippled with scars, is illuminated by the candles. It gives him an almost angelic look, and I at once feel equally horrified and mystified.

"I watched many of my dearest friends die before my eyes," he begins. "When the revolution turned against the Church, I saw the fires light. I heard their screams, and I listened to their guttural cries as their throats were slit."

I put my arm protectively around Tanya as she moves closer to me.

"I saw these things, yet I did not stop believing," he says. He turns back to the icon. "I prayed to the Holy Mother and to the Christ child. I prayed to the saints and recited the lines of faith that I grew to love so dearly. I saw tragedy, but I did not stop believing. Even when they sent me to Siberia." He turns back to me. Tanya's shoulders tremble as she presses against my side.

"I spent fifteen years in the harsh winters of northern Siberia. I was beaten and abused and forced to work from the darkness of morning to the darkness of night. The conditions were unbearable, yet I bore them because I didn't stop believing."

"But why?" I ask. "Why do you believe? It all seems so pointless."

The old man smiles and nods his head. "You would be surprised, my friend, at the power in believing in something outside of yourself. When you acknowledge that the pain of this world is unbearable, you're able to finally surrender to the One who alone is worthy of carrying the weight."

He reaches out and grabs my hand, pulling it to his heart. "I believe because it's true," he whispers.

"How do you know it's true?" I reply. I don't pull my hand away because there's comfort in the warmth of his beating chest.

"Look at us here," he gestures to the hollow room. "We are openly discussing God in a place that not so long ago killed many of my friends for similar conversations. God cannot be suppressed under the evil of man. The world is harsh and cruel and full of pain. But God is real. The Holy Spirit and Mary and the saints—they're real. To believe is to trust, and when you trust, your life has meaning and purpose outside of the mere endurance of hardship."

He takes my hand and slowly lowers it back to my side. Tanya looks up at me, then back at the old man.

"Would you teach us?" she asks. "Would you teach us how to believe?"

He smiles and looks at me with eyebrows raised. He's waiting for me to agree, and I hesitate. I feel Tanya's eyes on my face, imploring me to agree, and I nod my head. I won't deny my wife the opportunity to hope.

The old man gestures toward the floor, and Tanya and I both kneel before the table. I stare at the icon above the candles, the dancing flames blurring the picture, making it seem less sinister and more comforting. The old man chants a prayer over us. His words come out almost as a song, and I try to understand it all.

I finally give up and let the prayer fall onto my head, soothing like the balm of a warm summer day.

MARIA IVANOVNA
April 11, 1943

I'm lonely.

My days are slow and isolated as I move through each passing moment in a fog. There's little light, and hope has long since faded away. Hope died the day Ewald left town and Helena beat me so severely I didn't think I would walk again.

I close my eyes and try to block out the horror of that morning when she dragged me out of bed and into the barn. She tied my hands to the door and horsewhipped me. I can still hear the sound of the whip as it moved through the air and landed with a crack on my shoulders, back, and legs.

Since that day, Helena and I have moved through the house in measured silence. She doesn't speak to me, and I do everything in my power not to cross paths with her.

My only reprieve comes on Sunday mornings when Helena takes the baby into town, and I'm left alone. Now that the weather has warmed and spring pushes into the German countryside, I make use of the gift of Sunday morning.

Today, I walk a little farther than before until I find a small lake nestled in a sprawling green meadow. I sit down, and for the first time in a week, I release the air that feels trapped in my lungs.

Turning my face toward the sun, I breathe in deeply. Life isn't quite so scary in the daylight. At night, the dreams chase me, and I find myself wrapped in terror. The loneliness doesn't subside in the daylight, but I feel less entangled.

I don't hear her footsteps.

"Hello," she says quietly.

I scramble to my feet. Standing behind me is a young girl, perhaps my age or a little younger. Her long blond hair is combed and tied neatly in a bright blue ribbon. Her dress is made of fine fabric, and her shoes glint in the morning sun. She smiles at me as I step back.

"I'm sorry," I mumble, turning to walk away.

"Wait!" she calls. I stop, turning back to face her.

"Why are you sorry?" she asks. Her eyes are concerned, and her face wrinkles in confusion. I search for the right words in German to answer her.

"I didn't know I was intruding on your land," I say, my face flushed.

She smiles and waves her hand at me. "Oh don't be silly," she says with a laugh. "This isn't my land. I just like to come here and sit. Kind of like you. It's peaceful here." She turns and looks out over the lake. In the distance, the mountains loom large and dark against the brilliant blue backdrop of the sky.

"Yes, it is," I murmur.

"What's your name?" she asks, taking a step toward me. I step back and narrow my eyes.

"Maria," I answer.

"I'm Greta," she replies. She reaches out her hand toward me. Warily I place my hand in hers, and she gives it a firm shake. I drop my hand back to my side and stare at her awkwardly.

"So . . . where are you from?" she asks.

"Kiev," I answer. "Soviet Union."

She takes in a deep breath and looks at me more intently. I shrink back. "Oh, don't be uncomfortable," she says, her words tumbling out. "It's just I've never actually seen a Soviet before. My father talks about your people a lot, but I didn't know . . ." Her voice trails off.

"Didn't know what?" I ask.

"I didn't know you would look so much like us," she answers.

It's quiet for a moment before I finally speak up. "Well, I should be going," I say, and she nods.

"Can you meet me here again sometime?" she asks. I look up in surprise. Her face is eager, her eyebrows raised in hopeful expectation.

"Why?" I ask.

Her face falls, and she shrugs her shoulders. "Well," she says with a small sigh. "I'm terribly lonely. My sister died a year and a half ago, and my parents are still so wrapped up in her passing. I'm alone all day every day." She looks at me with wide, round eyes. "I just want a friend," she says.

I hesitate a moment, unsure of whether I can trust this strange girl standing before me. Her willingness to share something so personal right away frightens me, but her face is so hopeful and expectant that I finally give in and nod.

"I have free time every Sunday morning," I say softly. "I'll meet you back here next week."

Greta grins, revealing a perfect set of white teeth. I can't decide if I like her or if she annoys me, but as I take in her obvious joy at the prospect of friendship, I find it impossible not to offer a small smile in return.

"Until next week," I say with a nod, and she bounces up and down, clapping her hands in front of her chin.

"Yes. See you then!" she says with a laugh.

I head off down the path back toward the prison that houses my sorrow. For the first time in many months, I find myself smiling almost involuntarily, though truthfully I can't decide if I really intend to come back and meet this girl. I'm conflicted, a sense of both dread and hope swirling inside of me like a funnel.

One week later, I make my way back to the lake. I vacillated back and forth every day over whether I should and finally came to the conclusion that I had the power for the first time in over a year to make a decision for myself. I choose companionship.

Greta is already at the lake when I arrive. Once again, she's dressed superbly, her hair loose and long down her back. She sits at the edge of the water tearing the petals off a flower, and tossing the torn pieces into the still water.

"*Guten Morgen,*" I say, my voice soft and shy. I jump when she lets out a squeal of delight. She jumps to her feet and hugs me hard.

"Oh you came!" she says happily. "I was so afraid you wouldn't."

I chuckle as Greta claps her hands. "Oh I made you laugh. That is wonderful," she says. "You're very pretty when you laugh."

I shake my head in disbelief at this girl's peculiar cheerfulness as I turn to look out over the lake. The water is still, and the surface glints in the morning sun, making it look like a thousand crystals dancing in the light.

"So, Maria," Greta says, nudging me with her shoulder. "Tell me about yourself. If we're going to be friends, then I simply *must* know all there is to know about you."

I look at her, then look away again, trying to decide how much I really need to share. How much of my life can a girl this happy really understand?

"And don't worry if you don't know how to say everything in German. I'll help you out if you make any mistakes."

I smile and nod my head. "I'm fifteen years old," I begin, and Greta immediately interrupts me.

"Oh that's wonderful! I'm fifteen years old, too! When's your birthday?"

"May 14," I reply. Greta squeals again.

"Oh that's so soon—only a month away!" she cries. "You must let me spoil you on your birthday, Maria. You just must."

I laugh again, and shake my head in amusement.

"Okay, tell me more," Greta says shaking my arm.

"Well, I have an older brother and sister," I continue. My voice gets soft. "I haven't seen them in a long time."

"Where are they?" Greta asks.

"My brother, Sergei, is fighting for the Red Army. I don't know where he is. He left almost two years ago."

"And your sister?"

"Anna is here in Germany, I think," I answer. "We were both forced to leave Kiev on the same day. She was put on a different train, though, so I really don't know where she landed." I blush at my obvious poor choice of vocabulary, and Greta shakes her head.

"I understand what you mean," she says. Her face is solemn as she looks at me closely. "I'm sorry for what my countrymen have done to you and your family," she says.

I look at her and feel the tears begin to well up in my eyes. *"Dankeshön,"* I answer, and before I can stop myself, the tears begin to fall freely. Greta pulls me into her arms.

"Shh . . . it's okay," she says, running her hand down my head. "It's alright."

After a moment, I quit crying and sit up. "I'm sorry," I mumble. Greta smiles gently as she shakes her head.

"Don't be sorry. Friends are supposed to comfort one another, aren't they?"

I smile and give a slight nod. "You're a very positive person," I say. Greta shrugs her shoulders.

"I guess. I don't know." She smiles at me. "So where do you live now?" she asks.

"I live back that way." I jut my head in the direction of Helena's home. "I live with a woman named Helena Daucher. I work for her."

Greta nods her head. "Is this Helena Daucher good to you?" she asks. I fall silent, my eyes shifting out over the glassy lake. I don't know how to answer, but my silence seems to be enough for Greta.

"It's okay. You don't have to answer me," she says with a wave of her hand, and I smile gratefully. I look up at the sun and realize it's time for me to head back.

"I should be going," I say. "Helena will be home soon, and she likes her lunch to be prepared when she returns."

Greta's smile fades as a look of disappointment crosses her face. "Oh. Alright," she says.

"But I'll be back next week," I say with a smile. "And I want to hear all about you when I return." Greta grins again. She leans in to give me an excited hug.

"It's so good to have a friend," she says as we embrace. She has no idea how much I agree with her.

We meet every Sunday, and I find myself looking forward to those meetings with greater intensity every day. I've never had a friendship that felt quite as unique and so much like a kinship as the relationship I share with Greta. Each week it seems we find more that we have in common with one another.

I roll to my side and look out the window at the morning sun. Another blessing of my Sundays is the rest I receive after the milking and breakfast. Helena takes the morning to prepare herself and the baby for their morning excursion, so I go back to my room and lie down until she leaves. If it weren't for Sundays, I don't know if I'd make it through this confinement.

I stand up and stretch, my muscles sore and tight from another restless night's sleep. Peeking out the window once more, I watch Helena climb into the car, setting her small son on her lap before pulling away from the house. She's dressed in a lovely blue dress that hangs to just below her knees. Her blond hair is piled high on her head. She looks regal and elegant.

As she leaves, I drink in the gorgeous day. It's May 16. My birthday was two days ago. I quickly put on my own tattered dress and pull a comb through my hair. I lace up my shoes and rush down the stairs and out of the house in less than ten minutes. I run all the way to the lake, eager to share the morning with the friend who has become like a sister.

When I step out of the trees, I see Greta standing at the place where the water meets the sand. Her gorgeous blond hair is twisted in three long braids, which have been wound and woven together to form a fascinating knot at the base of her neck. She stands tall, her back to me, and I again pull my hand self-consciously over my own straggly mane.

When she hears my footsteps, Greta turns and greets me with a wide, happy grin. "Happy birthday!" she shrieks, jumping up and down and clapping her hands. I laugh as she races to me, throwing her arms over my shoulders.

"You're sixteen now," she squeals. "That's a grown woman. Oh, I just can't wait to turn sixteen." I grin at her gushing, and she grabs my arm, propelling me forward. "Come," she says, smiling so broadly that I fear her face will split in two. "I have a surprise for you."

I follow her around the high grasses to a clearing just before land falls into the crystal clear water. There she has prepared a beautiful spread of food, which sits on a light pink quilt in the sand. Fruit, pastries, breads and jams are all laid out, and my mouth immediately begins to water. In the center of the blanket is a large box tied tight with a red bow.

"Let's open your gift first!" Greta says with a hop. She grabs my hand and drags me toward the blanket. I'm stunned by this gesture of kindness, and I blink hard against the tears that pool in my eyes. Greta leans down, grabs the box, and thrusts it toward me.

"Here," she says. "Open it!"

I pull the box to me and sink down onto the blanket. Tugging on the ribbon, I let it fall by my knees as I pull the lid off. I gasp as I peer into the box. Inside is a beautiful dress made of the finest material. It's bright blue and trimmed in lace. I pull it out and hold it up. It is the finest piece of clothing I have ever seen.

"Do you like it?" Greta asks, her eyes dancing. I nod my head slowly. "I know you won't have much occasion to wear it right now," she says. "But I wanted you to have it for the day you're given the freedom to leave. I want you to have the finest dress to wear when you arrive home."

I swallow hard as I run my hand over the soft fabric. "Can I try it on right now?" I ask and Greta smiles wide.

"Of course!" she says with a happy giggle. I quickly slip off my tired, dirty dress and pull on the gifted item. It feels soft and light and sweet against my skin. I spin around once as Greta squeals with glee and gushes over me in such girly fashion that I find myself laughing hysterically. We sit down to eat, and I lean back in the warm grass as Greta tells story after story of her younger years when she and her sister would dance through life in a frolic of simple happiness.

Lost in her stories, I suddenly notice how high the sun hangs in the sky.

"It's late!" I cry, jumping to my feet and pulling the dress off. I quickly change and delicately fold the dress up, placing it back in the box. Turning to Greta, I hold out the box. "This is the finest gift I have ever received," I say. "Would you please hold it for me for now? I fear what Helena would do if she found it."

Greta takes the box and nods with a concerned look. "Are you going to be okay, Maria?" she asks. "Do you need me to come back with you?"

"No, thank you, Greta. I must go back alone, but I have to go quickly."

I lean forward and give her a quick kiss on the cheek. "You are the dearest friend I've ever had," I say. "Thank you for giving me the grandest sixteenth birthday." Greta smiles, her face flushed.

"Go," she says. "You're late!"

I nod and spin on my heel, running as fast as my legs will carry me through the forest. In less than fifteen minutes, I burst onto the dirt road just a few meters from the house. I see Helena's car sitting in the front, and my heart sinks. I slow down and wipe the sweat from my brow, taking in deep breaths to calm myself.

I reach the house and walk quietly up the front steps, easing the door open. Stepping into the foyer, I hear Helena upstairs in the nursery singing to her baby. For all her faults, I must admit Helena is a wonderful mother.

I tiptoe to the kitchen and pull on my apron, then quickly set to making lunch. As I chop up vegetables for the salad, I hum quietly, a smile spread across my face. I don't hear her walk into the room, and I cry out when her boot makes contact with my backside.

Whirling around, I grasp the knife tight in my hand as I steady my breathing. Helena's eyes are wide and fierce.

"Where were you today?" she asks. I don't reply. "Where were you!" she screams.

"I went for a walk," I sputter. Helena laughs ruthlessly.

"Were you out there whoring yourself out to another man?" she asks, her words dripping over my soul like venom.

"I—no! No. Of course not!" I say in shock.

"Is Ewald here now? Is he back? Are you meeting him in secret, you little tramp?"

"I don't know what you're talking about!" I reply, my voice raising to a shout. "I went for a walk. I sat beside a lake. That's all!"

Helena leans back on her heels and narrows her eyes. "My brother sent a letter," she growls, her voice angry and low. "He should be here any minute now. What a coincidence that you were out alone somewhere on the very day he is to arrive."

My hands begin to shake and the knife slips, falling to the floor with a clang. Helena wipes her hands on her skirt and stares at me steadily. "I'm watching you, girl," she hisses.

My blood runs cold as she leans forward and picks up the knife. She holds it out to me, her hand steady and unmoving. I reach for it, my own hands quaking. Her eyes flash with hatred, her anger moving through the air like the smoke of a blaze. I pull the knife from her grasp, and she turns to leave the room.

"Watch yourself," she says icily just before walking out.

I stand in stunned silence, my heart constricted and lungs heaving. I must leave. I cannot see Ewald again. I have to escape before he arrives.

I put the knife down and pull off my apron. Wiping my hands on a nearby towel, I quickly make my way to the back door. Grabbing the milk bucket, I step out into the bright afternoon sun. I walk toward the barn, swinging the bucket by my side. I step inside the barn and wait a moment for my eyes to adjust to the dim light.

Rushing to the bales of hay in the back, I dig through them and grab the bag that I hid away months ago, after Helena whipped me. I knew I'd need to leave eventually, and I'm prepared now to make a hasty exit. I push open the back door of the barn then make a mad dash toward the cover of the trees. It won't be long before Helena notices I'm missing.

I run until it feels as though my lungs will burst. When I reach the lake, I drop to my knees and drink deeply from the cool water. Sitting up, I try to remember which direction Greta points when speaking of her home. She points toward the mountains. I grab my shoulder bag and take off running again, heading in a straight line toward the horizon of mountains.

Moments later, I come to the crest of a hill, and look down in the valley below to see a beautiful white house nestled in the trees. This must be Greta's home. It is just as she described it.

The house is pristine, the entire perimeter surrounded by vibrant flowers of every color imaginable. The rolling meadows that provide the backdrop are bright green, and I feel as though I've stepped into a painting. I pause to slow my breathing when I see her round the corner. I rush down the hill toward my friend. Greta hears my sobs and turns toward me. She races forward to meet me, grabbing my shoulders.

"What's the matter, Maria?" she asks, her face laced with concern.

"I think Helena is going to kill me," I gasp. "I have to get away. Please, Greta. Please help me."

Greta nods and pulls me by the elbow toward the house. "Come inside," she commands, her voice laced with authority. Greta closes the doors behind us, and turns to face me. "I've been thinking," she begins as she moves from window to window throughout the house, pulling the panes down and drawing the curtains until we stand in cool darkness.

"I think I know of a way to keep you safe, but it's going to require that you go away. Right now."

"Go away where?" I ask. I draw in long, deep breaths, willing myself to stay calm.

"My father has a friend, Gerhard Mueller," Greta begins. "He and his wife, Lisolette, used to live close by, but they moved a year ago. It was a difficult time." Greta pauses, wringing her hands as the memory moves past. She shakes her head and presses on. "I know that Herr Mueller would take you in without any questions. He and his wife are good people."

"But . . . where do they live?" I ask.

"I can lead you to the train station and get you on a train to their town. It's a three-hour train ride from here. They own and operate a shop. You could work there as an employee. No one would ever have to know where you were from." Greta stops, her eyes filling with tears.

"Oh my friend," she says, rushing forward. She pulls me into a tight hug. "I don't want you to go, but I think this is the only way. You can't stay here, because if Nazis find my family . . ."

I pull back as Greta's voice fades. Her eyes are downcast, her chin trembling. "What will happen if they come here, Greta?" I ask.

Greta sighs. "My mother is Jewish, Masha, and my father is Christian," she says softly. "I'm half Jewish. If the Nazis find us, they'll kill us all."

My hands go icy cold as I step back. "I've put you in danger," I whisper. Greta shakes her head.

"No, you haven't," she replies. "You are a gift to me from God. I just know that it's Him who brought us together. You've helped me through my loneliness, and now it's my turn to help you. If there was any way for us to keep you here, I know that we would. But my mother would be terrified, and my mother is not a strong person."

I nod, puzzled by her curious talk of God, then reach down to grab my bag, pulling it up slowly. "We should go then," I say. "Before they return. What do I say to Herr Mueller when I arrive?"

"Tell him that Henry, Lizbet, and Greta sent you. Tell him we said he could give you a job and a place to live. I know he'll accept you."

Greta grabs my hand and squeezes it tight. "I wish things didn't have to change," she says, choking on her words. I squeeze her hand back.

"I'll be okay," I answer. She nods. Then her eyes light. "Oh my!" she cries. "Wait here!" She races up the stairs, and I listen to the sound of her shoes pounding across the hollow wooden floors. Minutes later she returns with the dress she gave me for my birthday.

"Quick, put this on!" she commands. "We'll fix your hair, and get you cleaned up. You can't attract any attention as you travel."

Minutes later, Greta and I leave the house and run around back where an old, beat-up truck stands on the gravel driveway. Greta leaps into the driver side as I slide into the passenger side. She puts a key in the ignition and the truck shakes and sputters to life.

"Do you know how to drive this?" I ask.

"Papa taught me," Greta replies with a small smile. "Mother hated that he took me driving. She thought it was improper for a young girl, but Papa felt I should know." She tosses me a sly glance out of the corner of her eye. "It's a bit of an adventure, isn't it?" she asks.

I sit back and close my eyes. I would be happy if life were less adventurous.

LUDA MICHAELEVNA
June 18, 1943

I bolt upright in bed, my heart beating wildly. What did I hear? I glance down at the pallet on the floor where Sasha sleeps, his chubby legs hanging off the blanket and resting on the hard wood. I reach down and readjust him so that he's fully on the bed.

He's nearly one and a true delight. His hair is thick and blond, hanging over his ears in tight ringlets that I cannot bear to cut. His cheeks are round and pink, and his arms and legs unfold in a series of rolls. I run my hand over his soft head and offer up yet another whispered plea for his safety.

I jump at the sound of a rap on the door. That's what I heard that stirred me from sleep. The knock is sharp and urgent. I jump out of bed and pull my robe on over my long nightgown. Katya sits up on her bed.

"What is it?" she hisses.

"Someone's at the door," I whisper back. She jumps up. We tiptoe out of the room as quickly as we can and step into the hallway. Baba Mysa is there with her hand clutching tight at the top of her nightgown. Oleg stands beside her, his thin face shadowed in the soft darkness of nighttime.

Since returning from his captivity, Oleg has remained quiet and contemplative. When he discovered my relationship with Hans, he withdrew from me almost completely. I fear that the trauma of losing my love to a German man has been much greater on his soul than the trauma of being held captive.

Alexei stands at the door and presses his ear tight against it. *"Kto tam?"* he says, mouth held close against the hard wood.

"It is I—Hans," comes the reply. I rush forward toward the door as Alexei pulls it open.

"Hans!" I cry. Hans puts his finger to his lips and gestures for Alexei to close the door. His eyes are wild, and his hands shake with a fearful tremble.

"I cannot stay long," he whispers. "Can we go into the other room?" he asks Alexei. We all follow the two men into the sitting room.

"Please," Hans says to Baba Mysa as she reaches for the lamp. "Leave the lights off. We must be quiet."

"Hans, you're scaring me," I whisper. "What's the matter?"

Hans sighs and runs his hand through his hair. "I don't know where to begin," he says. I hear the pain in his voice despite his whispers. It leaves me chilled.

"Just tell us what's going on," Alexei says. He's gentle, but firm. None of us have the patience to drag this conversation out.

Hans nods. "Shortly before we freed Oleg several months ago, I began working closely with a comrade and one of our leaders to assassinate Hitler."

I gasp, and Baba Mysa puts her arm around my shoulders, pulling me into her.

"We had a plan set to kill him shortly after he left Vervolfy in early March. The hope was to carry out this plan before they killed all of the prisoners, but we were too late." Hans looks at Oleg who returns the gaze evenly. "When Hitler left camp, the idea was to smuggle a bomb onto his plane that would detonate about thirty minutes after takeoff, but something went wrong and the bomb malfunctioned. Our plan failed."

Alexei nods his head. "Given that Hitler is still very much alive, I think we all understand that it failed. But what's happened since then?"

"My comrades and I have continued to develop ideas and think of ways we can take Hitler out of his position of power. He's destroying Germany. We must stop him."

"He's doing more than simply destroying *your* beloved country," Oleg spits out in anger, and Alexei turns with a sharp look.

"Oleg," he hisses, "now is not the time, Son." Oleg crosses his arms in defiance, his gaze still hot and angry.

"Why are you here tonight, Hans?" Alexei asks.

"I've raised suspicion, and I'm being watched very, very closely. I didn't realize they suspected my treason until this evening when one of the men I worked with on the assassination plot was summoned to our local head-quarters and told he was being sent back to Berlin to face trial. I imagine it will only be a matter of time before the same happens to me."

Hans looks at me closely, his eyes welling up with tears. "If they question my comrade, as I suspect they will, then I fear that puts you, my darling, in grave danger. He knew about my relationship with you." Hans steps forward and grabs my hands, squeezing them tightly. "It's only a matter of time before they come for you, Luda."

"What do we do?" I ask him, ignoring Baba's indignant huff behind me.

Hans sighs and looks down at me. "We need to get you out of the country."

The room explodes in a barrage of shocked gasps and frantic whispers. Katya cries while Oleg unloads his anger at Hans. Baba Mysa pulls me back to her again and whispers frantic words of prayer and fear as she runs her hands through my hair. Only Alexei and I remain silent, our eyes locked on one another. He raises his eyebrows, and I give a slight nod.

Alexei holds up his hand, and everyone falls silent.

"But what does sending Luda away do for the rest of us? If the Nazis come looking for her, they'll find us, which leads me to believe that we're all in grave danger."

Hans nods. "You're right. This is why I want the rest of you to go to the safe house for a time. Take only the few things that you absolutely need, but leave everything else behind. If they come to your flat, it must not look as though you've moved out."

"But Hans, I don't understand." My eyes shift from his face to the others. Everyone looks at me gravely, their eyes sad and frightened. Even Oleg's face is erased of all anger and is left full of pity.

"What, my darling?" Hans asks, turning to face me.

"Why can't I just go to the safe house with them? Why can't we all hide there together?"

"Because, Luda," Hans says gently, pushing my hair away from my face and tucking it behind my ear. "You're too easy to find. Your name, your description, your baby. They will know it all soon. And if they capture you, they'll torture you as a means of getting to me. I cannot bear that."

My blood runs cold, and my hands shake as I back away from him. "Why did you do this?" I ask, my words barely audible. Hans furrows his brow and looks at me quizzically.

"I don't understand, *dorogaya*," he says. He takes a step toward me, but I hold up my hand in protest.

"Why did you take this risk? Why did you try to kill that man?"

Hans sighs, his shoulders slumping forward. "I told you before we freed Oleg that I was going to do this," he replies. Baba Mysa gasps in surprise.

"Luda!" she says. "Why did you not say something to us?"

"I didn't think he would really do such a foolish thing," I reply without looking at her. My eyes remain firm and fixed on Hans's face. The room remains still for a long time before Alexei breaks the silence.

"Hans, we need to discuss this more," Alexei says. Hans whirls around to face him.

"There's nothing to discuss," he hisses. "Don't you understand? They'll kill Sasha without even blinking an eye. And then they'll slowly and painfully torture Luda. There is no alternative but to get her out."

"But how are we to do that?" Alexei asks, his voice soft and calm. "And where is she to go when she leaves?"

Hans looks at me with remorse. "Get her to the border, just outside of Lvov. I'll have a contact there waiting for her and the baby. He'll get her to Germany safely, where my sister will be waiting to retrieve her."

"But is it really safer for Luda and Sasha to travel to Germany alone? It seems to me that puts her in more danger," Alexei says. I hear the strain in his words as he fights for composure.

"Believe me, Alexei, I've considered all the options. This plan has the lowest risk. But I will need the help of your partisan friends to get her safely to Lvov. And it needs to happen quickly. My contact will be waiting for her on Thursday."

"But that's in three days!" Katya cries, and she rushes to me. "Oh Luda, please don't go," she begs. "Please. I don't want to lose you, Luda. Please." I look at Hans. His eyes are wide and full of frustration, shame, and despair.

"Come back tomorrow night," I say softly, wrapping my arm around Katya. "I'll tell you my plans then."

Hans nods and takes a step toward me, but I shake my head. He sighs and turns to Alexei and Baba Mysa, who now cling to one another.

"I'm sorry," he says, his voice cracking. "I never wanted to bring more difficulty to you. All I've ever hoped to do is help."

Alexei nods but Baba Mysa simply purses her lips and looks away. Hans moves toward the door with a slight nod of his head, and in a quick moment, he's gone.

We all stand silently in the room for a long while before Alexei finally speaks up. "We should go to bed," he says. "We have a long day tomorrow."

Katya and I trudge to the room that we share with my son. She clutches my hand as we make our way toward our beds. Just before I lie down, she turns to me. It's so dark in the room that I can barely make out her silhouette.

"Luda," she breathes. "I just want you to know how sorry I am for all the time I spent being angry and jealous. You're my sister. I love you." She drops my hand and walks quickly to her bed on the floor. I listen to her cry for a long time before we both finally doze off.

Sasha wakes early, and I let him crawl on me for a long time before dragging my weary body from the bed. I carry him into the kitchen where Baba Mysa has laid out a spread of bread and cheese for all of us to eat. I sit down with Sasha on my lap, and tear a piece of bread into small pieces, which he immediately shoves into his hungry, waiting mouth.

Alexei walks in and pours himself a steaming mug of hot chai. "Would you like some?" he asks. I nod yes.

He hands me my mug and sits down next to me. Leaning forward, he places his elbows on the table and makes kissy noises at Sasha, who giggles in delight, drool dripping off his chubby chin. Alexei grabs Sasha's hand and runs his thumb across the back of it. I watch, and my eyes fill with tears.

"I think I need to go," I say. Alexei is silent. Tears gather in his eyes as he continues to rub Sasha's soft hand.

I hand Sasha another bite of bread. Reaching over, I grab Alexei's hand and squeeze it firmly. "I love you, Alexei," I say, my voice cracking. Alexei pulls me to him, his hand warm and firm on the back of my head. Sasha squirms between us.

"You don't have to go, Luda," he says softly. "You can stay here. We'll figure out how to hide you."

Taking in a deep breath, I tip my head back and look up at his face—this man who has become a father to me in every way possible. He looks into my eyes, and with that one glance I know he understands. I won't have to defend my decision to him.

"I think I do need to go, Alexei," I say quietly. "I need to go for the safety of my son and for the safety of you and Baba Mysa, and Oleg and Katya. You're my family. I can't put you in danger by staying near."

Alexei narrows his eyes. "It's more than that, though, isn't it?" he asks.

I nod. "Yes. I need to go and live with Hans's family. I need to establish my home there so that he can come home to me. He's my family, too, Alexei. Despite all that's happened and the foolish choice he made, I still love him. I need to go so that someday, if we're lucky enough to make it out of this wretched time alive, we can build our own family."

"And if something happens to Hans?" Alexei asks.

"Then I'll hope and pray to be reunited with you all again when the time comes," I reply, a fresh set of tears pricking my eyes.

Alexei smiles and leans forward to kiss my forehead. "My darling, we will pray that prayer no matter what happens. You are as much a daughter to me as my other two children. Sending you away like this is not my preference, but I'll do everything in my power to see that you get to where you need to go safely. Just know that you will carry with you a piece of my heart when you leave."

"I love you, Alexei," I whisper again.

"I love you, my brave little daughter," Alexei whispers.

By the end of the evening, most of the plans are set. Alexei spends the afternoon meeting with the men in his partisan group, all of whom are connected with contacts across the country. Alexei's friend, Valeri, joins Baba Mysa in glaring and mumbling under his breath as they solidify each step of the journey.

"It's too dangerous," Valeri says repeatedly, and every time he does, Baba Mysa throws her hands up and mutters something under her breath about no one ever listening to her.

"You're better than the best in these types of operations, my friend," Alexei replies after Valeri's latest outburst. "If anyone can help us pull this off and get Luda safely to the border, it's you."

Valeri crosses his arms in a huff and nods his head reluctantly while I sit in the corner, a knot in my stomach. Katya sits next to me, her hand grasping mine. Baba Mysa spends the day cuddling and cooing at Sasha, and my heart tears each time I watch her with him. I'm smart enough to know that Sasha and I will probably never see her again, and I'm overwhelmed with a sense of dread and guilt for the pain my leaving will cause.

Oleg paces the room all day. He's frightened and angry. At one point our eyes meet, and I remember his longing to love me. I think of his offer to take care of me and the baby and wish briefly that I could have returned his love. How much simpler this all would be if only . . . but no.

When the sun begins to dip below the horizon, Valeri stands and stretches. "I must go," he says. He turns to look at me with dark eyes. "You need to sleep and make sure the child sleeps. I'll be here at daybreak, as soon as I can safely walk along the streets. I will come for you, and we'll leave before the rest of the town stirs. Be ready and have only what you can carry with you."

I nod. "Thank you," I whisper. Valeri grunts in return. He and Alexei kiss cheeks quickly, and in a moment he is off. I'm left alone with my grieving family. They all look at me, sorrow etched deep in their faces. Baba Mysa holds a now sleeping Sasha tightly, rocking him back and forth against her chest.

I walk to where she's seated and crouch in front of her. "You're the only babushka I have ever known," I whisper. "You fought for me and loved me, and it's because of you that I survived the darkest and most terrible days of my life. I'm so sorry to cause you such pain and sorrow." My voice catches, and I take a halting breath. Baba looks at me, her eyes swimming but soft.

"My Luda," she says, her voice quiet and gentle. "You are a joy, and I could not be more proud of you. Thank you for letting me love you, and thank you for giving me the gift of time with this baby boy. I will miss you both forever."

I lay my head in Baba Mysa's lap and weep until I'm exhausted. We all cry now, even Oleg, who sits in the corner with his back to us. I see his shoulders quake, and I cannot bear the weight of this sorrow.

Finally, Alexei stands. "Valeri's right. Luda, you need to get some sleep. Hans will be by sometime tonight, and you'll leave early. You must be alert if you're to make it through the next few days."

I nod and stand up, the room spinning. Baba Mysa stands up slowly and hands me my sleeping child. "Take care, my Sashinka," she whispers in his ear, and she lays a soft, tender kiss on his cheek. She turns and walks to the kitchen where we all hear her sink heavily into a chair and sob bitterly. I turn and walk into the bedroom with Katya close behind me.

"You don't have to go, Luda," she says, her voice pleading. "Please. Please stay with us."

"I can't, Katya. I wish I could, but I know that I cannot. This is the only way we all stay safe."

"But what if something happens to you?" Katya asks, her voice rising. "What if you're caught or hurt?"

"Katya, I think if I stay here, we'll all be caught and hurt." I look at Sasha. "I can't risk that."

Katya is silent. She looks down at the floor, totally dejected and lost. I lay Sasha down on his pad of blankets, and I turn to Katya, pulling her into my arms.

"If it wasn't for you, I think I would already be dead," I say as she cries on my shoulder. "You rescued me and brought me into your home and shared your family with me. You rescued both of us," I say, gesturing to my sleeping child.

"I love you, Luda," Katya says, and I squeeze her tight.

"I love you," I whisper.

After a few minutes, Katya pushes back and brushes the tears from her eyes. She looks at me and gives me a small, mischievous grin. "You've changed, you know." I tilt my head to the side with a crooked smile.

"What do you mean?"

"When you first came to us, you were so shy and quiet and scared. You were like this little mouse. You were afraid of men, afraid of your own shadow. And now look at you. You're a mother, you had a wild secret love affair with a German, and you're about to escape the country all by yourself." Katya grins wider. "You're amazing," she says, and despite the weight of this evening, I let out a laugh.

"Amazing or crazy," I say as I turn to lie down in my bed.

"You can be both," Katya says, lying down. "Amazing and crazy has made you strong."

In minutes, we're both sound asleep.

Hans comes in the dark of night, as promised. His short, insistent raps at the door come at four o'clock, and I quickly pull myself up. When I walk into the room, I see him and Alexei talking in whispers. I stand and wait in silence, not wanting to interrupt them. Hans looks up and locks eyes with me, and Alexei stops talking. He places his hand on Hans's arm and leads him into the kitchen, motioning me to follow.

"You two need to talk," Alexei whispers. "Take a few moments to say your good-byes." He walks out, and I turn to face Hans.

"My darling," he begins. I rush into his arms. "I am so sorry," he whispers, his face buried in my hair. "I'm so sorry I've put you in this terrible mess. I was a fool. I should have thought about how my actions would affect you. Forgive me, please."

I tilt my face up to his. "Shh," I whisper, kissing him. His hands tangle in my long, loose hair as we drink in one another. He kisses the tip of my nose gently, and I wrap my arms around his waist.

He finally pulls away and looks at me with tenderness. "Alexei told me the plan. He told me Valeri will move you through the country today and tomorrow. My contact will be at the train station in Lvov tomorrow night. He'll get you from Poland to Germany."

"How?" I ask.

"The hope is to get you safely across the German border by train, but should it seem too dangerous, my contact will lead you by foot and car across the border. My sister, Sophia, will meet you in Germany, and she'll take you to a safe house in the German countryside."

"I don't have identification papers for Sasha," I say, and Hans nods.

"I know. They're creating some for you. They'll take care of all of that before you cross into Poland."

"But what if we're stopped before we get into Poland and they ask for our papers?" I ask. I suddenly feel very sick.

"We can only hope that doesn't happen. But Alexei and his men are working on their stories so that they'll hopefully be able to talk their way out of any danger."

"How did you set all of these plans without being caught?" I ask. I lean forward on the table as the room spins.

"I'm taking every precaution necessary to ensure that you're well cared for and that you make it into my sister's care safely."

"Will your sister like me?" I ask. Hans smiles and pulls me up, turning me slowly and kissing me again.

"My sister will *love* you. She's worked hard throughout the war to protect those who need protecting. She's brave and smart, and she'll keep you safe. We just have to get you through Poland." A hard look passes across Hans's face, clouding his handsome features.

"What's wrong with Poland?" I ask.

"Death is in Poland," he whispers.

My hands grow cold, and I lean into Hans's chest, his heart beating loud and strong against my ear. "I'm scared, Hans," I whisper.

"So am I, darling. But we must remember that this is our best chance to be together—just the two of us forever."

"What will you do?" I ask.

Hans tightens his grasp around my waist as he speaks. "I'll try to stay off their radar. I'll give them no reason to suspect that I could have anything to do with the plot to kill Hitler. I will survive."

His last words are a whisper, a vapor of hope that floats through the room, thin and veiled in doubt.

For several minutes, we hold tight in our embrace. I only pull away when I hear Alexei clear his throat. "It is five thirty," Alexei says quietly. "Hans you must leave. Luda needs to get ready to go. Valeri will be here shortly."

I look up at Hans, my eyes wide and frantic. "I love you," I whisper.

"I love you, too. And I'll do everything I can to come back to you. We'll be together, my love. I know that we will."

With a final kiss, Hans pulls away and rushes out the door. As he passes Alexei, he pauses. The two men grasp hands.

"Thank you, my friend," Hans says with a respectful nod. Alexei returns the gesture and looks at him evenly.

"We'll get her there safely," he says. "But it's time you laid low. Don't do anything more foolish. You need to survive so that you can take care of Luda and Sasha."

Hans nods, and with a final glance, he disappears out the door. I look at Alexei and take a deep breath. "It's time," I say, and Alexei nods. I hurry to the next room where Oleg, Katya, and Baba Mysa stand huddled together. I embrace Katya first, silently holding her tight. There are no words left to say.

Turning to Baba Mysa, I fall into her waiting arms. "You be careful, my Luda. And make sure you eat. It will do you no good to get skinny and sick."

I smile and kiss her cheek. "I love you, Baba," I say softly as I stroke her thin, wiry gray hair. "Thank you for everything," I whisper. She covers her mouth to deny the sobs. Alexei puts his arm around his mother and pulls her to him.

Turning to Oleg, I look up at his dark, blank stare. "Oleg," I say as I grab his hand. It's cold and clammy. "I'm so sorry for the pain that I caused you."

Oleg looks back at me. Slowly he leans down and gives me a kiss on the cheek. "Stay safe, Luda," he says. His voice is hollow and sad.

I rush to the bedroom and gently lift Sasha up off the bed. He's sleeping soundly, his hair sweaty and matted against his head. I grab the small bag with a few of our things in it and put it over my shoulder. When I walk out, Baba Mysa hands me a small sack of bread and a few bananas.

"You'll need to feed him often to keep him quiet," she says. Tears streak her cheeks, but her voice is calm and measured, a testimony of her strength. She tucks the food in the bag on my shoulder, and we all turn at the soft rap of the door. Alexei opens the door slowly as Valeri steps in.

"Ready?" he asks. I nod my head, blinking hard. Never before have I felt such a sickening sorrow.

"Let's go." Valeri turns and marches out the door. I step into the hallway, stopping in front of Alexei. He leans forward and kisses Sasha gently on the head, then kisses my forehead. "Stay safe, my darling girl," he whispers. "I hold hope that someday we'll meet again."

I nod, unable to speak over the lump in my throat, then step into the dark hall and hurry down the stairs. I don't hear the door shut behind me. Alexei watches and listens until my last steps leave the building.

Valeri and I walk briskly through the early morning fog. He leads me down alleys and quiet streets. Thankfully and mercifully Sasha remains asleep on my chest, though I know it won't be long until he wakes, and he will be hungry. My arms burn from the weight of carrying him, but I don't speak. I simply follow my guide.

We cross a small bridge over the Dnestr River and just on the other side, a car waits. Valeri slides inside and jerks his thumb toward the back door. I pull it open and duck in quickly. When I lean over to pull the door shut, Sasha wakes up with a start and immediately begins crying.

"Quiet him down," Valeri orders. I pull my son into me and bounce him up and down. Still he wails, so I put my finger in his mouth and he sucks furiously, but this only lasts for a moment.

"He's hungry," I say. Valeri nods.

"Feed him," he orders.

I flush, then quickly untuck my shirt and pull it up. Sasha finds my breast while I do my best to remain covered as we bounce over pitted roads.

"I've never been in a car before," I say quietly. Valeri doesn't respond. Looking out the window, I watch as the countryside moves quickly past. Buildings have already given way to sprawling fields, and I realize that I'm the farthest away from home that I have ever been.

"You'll come to know car travel very well today," Valeri finally says.

I lean back and close my eyes. With Sasha warm against my skin and the methodical rocking of the car, I am suddenly very, very tired.

The morning drags on, and I find myself bored and almost disappointed. I expected this day to be much more dangerous and exciting, but for the better part of two hours we've traveled the road in quiet, almost completely alone except for a rare car or two.

Around lunchtime, as my stomach begins to growl, Valeri slows the car. "We're coming to our first meeting point," he says. "This is where you and I part ways. Keep the child quiet and do not make eye contact with anyone, understand?"

I nod and sit up. Sasha kicks and gurgles on my lap, but is otherwise calm and happy. Valeri pulls off the main road and turns onto a narrow, gravel drive that leads deep into the trees. As the summer sun disappears behind the towering oaks, I feel my heartbeat quicken. Sasha looks up and around, his eyes wide and curious. I stroke his head as we slow to a stop under a small grove. Valeri pushes open his door and turns to me.

"Stay here."

He steps out of the car and disappears in the trees. I take a few deep breaths to calm myself as Sasha squirms under my tightening grasp. A few minutes later, Valeri comes back with a young man following close on his heels. He pulls open the door and leans in, his large face peering over the back of the seat with intensity.

"This is my nephew, Kostya. He'll get you from here to Lvov. He has traveled on many partisan missions for us. He's wise and a quick thinker. Listen to his words very carefully and do everything he says without question, understand?"

I nod. "*Spaseeba*, Valeri Kyrilovich," I say softly. Valeri nods.

"Be careful, little one," he says before ducking out. Kostya slides into the front seat and starts the car. The two men speak softly. I strain to hear what they say, but cannot make it out. In less than a minute we have backed up out of the grove and are headed toward the open stretch of road.

"If we're stopped by the Germans or by any Soviets, you are my wife," Kostya says, turning to glance at me. "And the child is my baby. You don't need to speak to them unless asked a direct question. We were visiting your ailing grandmother, and we're now headed back to our home in the Galicia district."

I nod, but do not speak. Sasha lets out a squeal and flaps his chubby arms in the air. I hear Kostya sigh. "The child has to stay silent," he says crisply.

"I'll try," I reply. I cannot mask the frustration in my voice. I don't know how to keep a baby happy and silent in a car with little for him to touch or do. I set him on the seat next to me much to his delight. He rolls onto his knees and pushes up against my leg, his face turned up to me in rapturous delight. Despite my worry and heartache, I can't help but smile at his innocence. The light in his eyes gives me hope.

We drive for hours, stopping once just outside of Ternopil, where Kostya puts more gasoline in the car. He brings me a piece of bread while there, which helps ease my growling stomach. I've tried not to eat much of the food that Baba Mysa sent with me as I know that it's more important to keep Sasha satisfied. It's late now. As the sun dips below the horizon, I feel a knot develop in my stomach.

"We're just outside of Lvov," Kostya says softly as he maneuvers around yet another pit in the road. "We'll stop at my comrade's house to get the passport and papers for your son, then he'll get you to the train station where the contact will be waiting to escort you to Germany."

"Do you know who will take me across the border?" I ask. Kostya shakes his head.

"I don't ask for details," he replies. We pull off the road, and he winds down a long dirt drive toward the rolling hills of the Ukrainian countryside. It's beautiful here. The setting sun has left the sky streaked with brilliance, reds and yellows dancing across the horizon from one side to the other with painted precision. Sasha sleeps soundly in my lap now, his breathing slow and steady.

Kostya slows to a stop before a small, wooden house. He turns and looks at me, his dark black hair falling loosely over his forehead. "Come," he says. I pull Sasha up to my chest and push the door open. Very slowly I stand up, my legs and back stiff from the day spent in the car.

"Come quickly," Kostya says, his eyes darting left to right. "We're not in a safe area. We must not remain out in the open for long."

We rush to the door where Kostya raps several times in rhythmic suc-
cession. The door flies open and Kostya pushes me in, then steps in behind
me and pulls it shut.

"This her?" the man says, his eyes running up and down my small
frame. I shrink back a little as Kostya nods his head.

"*Da*. And that's the child. You have to hurry. She has to be at the train
station before it gets too dark. We can't risk her being questioned."

"Come here," the man says gruffly. I step forward.

"What is the child's birthday?" he asks.

"June 16, 1942."

"Good," the man nods. "And he was born in Vinnitsya, correct?" he
asks. I nod.

"Alright. Go and sit down while I finish these up. Kostya, give her a
bowl of borscht and a plate of bread. Would you like chai?" He looks up at
me, and I'm taken aback by the kindness in his eyes. It doesn't match the
harsh sound of his voice.

"Yes," I answer. "Thank you very much."

For half an hour, I sit quietly in the corner, sipping my chai and wishing
we could move on. Sasha will wake soon, and I would rather not have to
entertain him during the most dangerous and difficult leg of this journey.

Finally, the man stands and hands me a stack of papers. "Put these
with your own passport and papers," he says. "Don't lose them."

I nod and lean forward to retrieve my bag off the floor. Sasha lets out a
wail as he wakes, and the man looks around frantically. "Keep him quiet,"
he says, his brow furrowed and fearful.

"I'll try." I shove Sasha's papers into my bag and pull him up to my
shoulder, patting his back gently. He pushes against my legs and kicks
in frustration at having been woken so rudely. "May I please have a piece
of bread for him?" I ask. The man hands me the bread, and I place it in
Sasha's flailing fist. He immediately goes quiet as he sucks on the snack.

The man sighs and runs his hand through his hair. "The man who
will escort you to the train station will be here soon. You should know
that this man is a Red Army soldier, though he won't be dressed as one

tonight. He's not a simple partisan, like us. But he's still one of the good guys. He daily risks his life to help people like you escape. Listen and respect him."

A moment later I hear a rhythmic rap at the door. "That's Sergei," the man murmurs to Kostya. I stand up and pull my bag over my shoulder, adjusting Sasha on my hip. The door opens, and a man steps in the room. His face is young, his eyes soft and kind.

"Ready?" he asks. I nod in return. I follow him out the door, which closes behind me with a soft click. The sky is now dark, and the air has cooled down considerably. I wish Sasha had warmer clothes.

"We must move quickly," the man says. I slide into the back seat of his car, which is much nicer than the one that Valeri and Kostya transported me in. The seats are plush and made of smooth leather. The car is dark and sleek.

"My name is Sergei Ivanovich," the man says, sliding into the seat in front of me. I nod.

"I'm Luda. This is Sasha," I reply.

"Luda, we're going to the train station in Lvov. We'll probably be stopped somewhere along the way. I am going to tell them that you were visiting your grandmother in the countryside and were late on returning so I offered to give you a ride. When we get to the train station, I'll escort you to the platform of the train that will take you to Germany, and I'll leave you there. I cannot risk being captured by the German guards on duty there. Another contact will join you for the border crossing."

Sergei glances back at me, his eyes confident, yet kind. "The man escorting you out of the country is German, but do not fear him."

I nod. "What if we're stopped inside the train station or on the train?" I feel panic stirring inside as I think of all the ways this could go wrong.

Sergei shakes his head. "The story we've devised says that you have been commissioned by Sturmbannführer Brambott to escort his child to safety in Germany."

I look quizzically at Sergei and he shakes his head. "The less you know, the better. This story was concocted by our German counterparts, and they believe it will work, so it's all you need to accept."

For several moments we ride in silence as I mull over my next steps. I don't understand how I can possibly get from one point to another without being caught and interrogated. I don't understand why a Red Army soldier wearing plain clothes is currently driving me in a car. I clear my throat, and Sergei glances back. "Yes?" he asks.

"Forgive me for asking," I begin, "but how is it you're working with the partisan group? The partisans in Vinnitsya that I know hate Red Army soldiers almost as much as Nazi soldiers. Why do they trust you?"

Sergei is silent, and I immediately regret asking such a bold and personal question. "I'm sorry," I say quickly. "I shouldn't have asked."

"No, it's fine," Sergei replies. Sasha lets out a squeal, and I see Sergei's head duck in surprise. "It's a good question. The man who drew up the passport and papers for you is really the only one who trusts me. Late last year I saved his daughter when a group of my fellow soldiers tried to—" Sergei stops short, shaking his head. "Well, they were trying to hurt her," he says, and I wince. I know what he means. I have evidence of his implication in my arms.

"I'm not like many of my comrades," Sergei says. "I wanted to fight to protect my country from the enemy. I was naive when I joined. I didn't realize that the enemy could easily be dressed just like me."

"Where are you from?" I ask. I don't know what it is about this man, but I find myself longing to speak with him. Perhaps it's the knowledge that once I leave his presence, I'll be accompanied by a foreigner to a strange land, and I may never return to my own country again.

"I'm from Kiev," Sergei answers. "And you're from Vinnitsya?"

I nod.

"How old are you, Luda?" Sergei asks.

"Seventeen," I answer.

"I have two sisters," Sergei replies. "One is eighteen and the other just turned sixteen. You remind me very much of my youngest sister."

"What's her name?" I ask.

"Her name is Maria," he answers. "She's brave and spunky and full of life."

I blush, knowing that he must think similar things of me. "Do you ever hear from her?" I ask.

Sergei shakes his head. "No. I haven't heard from my family since I left for the war two years ago. I send letters when I can, but I don't know if they've received them. I have no idea . . ." His voice trails off.

"I'm sorry," I murmur.

I feel the car slowing, and I look out the window to see what's going on. We're still some distance from the city. Peering out the front glass, I see a man standing in the middle of the road, his hand held up.

"Luda, sit back into your seat and hold the child close." Sergei says, his voice strained. I quickly sink into the plush leather and pull Sasha into my chest.

"What is it?" I ask.

"These are Red Army soldiers," Sergei says. "Don't say anything to them unless they speak to you first. Just go along with my story. Try to look confused."

That won't be hard, I think.

Sergei slows the car and rolls down the window. *"Dobrei vyechr,"* he says.

"Evening," the man replies. He leans down and peers into the car, looking back at me with narrow eyes. *"Kto eta?"* he asks, jerking his chin toward me.

Sergei turns and looks at me, then looks back at the man. "I found her wandering on the streets outside the city. She said she was lost."

The man juts his chin out toward Sergei. "Who are you?" he asks. Sergei reaches into his back pocket and hands the soldier his identification papers. The man studies them for a moment, then looks over the seat at me.

"What's your name?" he asks sharply.

"Ludmilla Michaelevna," I answer, almost in a whisper.

"I need your identification papers," he says, reaching his hand over the seat. I rifle through my bag, my hand firmly wrapped around Sasha. I pull out both sets of papers and hand them to the man who holds them under a small flashlight and studies them closely.

"You're from Vinnitsya?" he asks, and I nod. "What are you doing here?"

My eyes dart to Sergei who doesn't move. He shows no emotion and gives no signal for how I should answer.

"Uh . . . I needed to get away," I answer. "My father is abusive. I had to leave him. I was afraid he would kill me or the baby." It isn't really a lie, and I hold my breath as he looks from me to the baby and back to the papers.

"Why would you come here?" the man asks. "You know we're at war, don't you, stupid girl?"

I suck in a deep breath. My hands are sweating, and I feel nauseous from the pressure of his stares. I nod. "I do know," I answer. "My grandmother lives in the city. I hoped I would find her here."

The man throws his head back and laughs. "How did you get this far?" he asks. "And with a child?" I feel my cheeks heat up at his mockery.

"I found rides," I answer with a little more confidence.

The man laughs again and hands my papers back to me. "Take her to town and drop her off near the center, then leave," he says to Sergei. "She's no threat. She's just stupid. Don't put yourself in danger just to save her from her own idiocy."

Sergei nods and starts the car again. The man waves us past, and as we slowly roll by, I see him laughing and shaking his head. I swallow hard over the frustration of being mocked as I stuff our papers back inside my sack.

"Sorry about that," Sergei says quietly.

"You could have been more helpful," I mutter.

Sergei shakes his head. "No, I couldn't," he says. "If they found out what I was really doing, we'd both be killed."

"But they're our soldiers. They're on our side, right?" I ask.

Sergei sighs. "I used to think so, but now I'm not sure. The leadership of the Red Army is tricky, especially in this region. There are many who are fighting the good fight. But there are others who've made it their mission to fight against our own countrymen. The brutality with which they fight one another is—" Sergei stops short and glances back.

"Well, it's hard to explain," he murmurs.

"I don't understand," I say quietly, leaning forward. "Why would we fight our own men?"

Sergei pauses for a moment, his eyes narrowing. "There's a group of people here who think of themselves as partisans, but they aren't like the partisans you likely encountered in your town. These men are more than underground fighters—they're a guerrilla army that's sprung up in this region. They're nationalists—angry men who believe in fighting for the independence of Ukraine. They're prideful and ugly." Sergei's words are laced with frustration and bitterness.

"What's wrong with being a nationalist?" I ask.

Sergei glances up and over his shoulder, his eyes wide. "You must never ask that question around here," he hisses. "These men are not nationalists in the protective sense of the word. They're brutal in their quest for Ukrainian independence. They're fighting against the Germans, yes. But they're also fighting against the Red Army, against the Soviets."

"But aren't you fighting against the Red Army by helping the partisans?" I ask.

"Well, perhaps technically, but I'm doing so in a way that promotes peace rather than making the war more terrible. The men and women that I help aren't part of this guerrilla army. They're simply partisans who want to see our country survive—they're not hoping to usurp all power and build their own nationalist movement by force."

I nod. "I see."

"We're close to the train station," Sergei says after a moment of awkward silence. I look out the window to see buildings slowly rolling by. Some are crumbled and war torn, but others remain intact, tall against the backdrop of a dark night.

Moments later, Sergei parks the car in front of a dark building, and we quickly get out. "This is it," he says. "Stay close to me, keep your eyes down, and move quickly."

We walk into the building and through the lit halls. Sasha sleeps on my shoulder, and I'm grateful for his fatigue, though the weight of the child in my arms leaves me panting.

I don't look up to see how many others are in the building with us, or to meet the inquiring eyes of strangers. I stay a step behind Sergei, matching two steps to every one of his clipped steps.

In less than ten minutes, we're on the platform. Sergei's eyes shift around nervously.

"I must leave you now, Luda. I can't stay here long." He looks over his shoulder. "The station is quiet tonight, but I can't risk confrontation with a Nazi." I look around, but don't see anyone on the silent platform.

"Wait here. Your next contact will be in shortly." Sergei smiles and bows his head slightly. "It's been an honor to bring you this far, Luda. Good luck. I wish you all the best in your new life."

"Thank you, Sergei Ivanovich," I whisper, my words choked. "You're a good man. Your family must be very proud. I hope you get to see them again soon."

He ducks his head again, then spins on his heel and walks out, leaving me alone on the cavernous platform.

I shift Sasha, who dozes on my shoulder, and I close my eyes for a brief moment. Fear and fatigue have left me nauseous. I open them back up at the sound of footsteps. A small German man in a gray army uniform stands before me.

"Who are you?" he asks. He speaks sharp German, and I'm momentarily stunned, unable to find the words to answer his question.

"I asked you a question, girl!" he barks. I open my mouth to speak, but am interrupted.

"She's with me," a man's voice speaks from behind. The uniformed man in front of me glances over my shoulder at the voice.

"Heil Hitler!" he says. The two men salute.

"Who is this, and why is she here?" the soldier asks.

"This is the woman transporting Sturmbannführer Brambott's child back to the homeland," the officer, my escort, says. The soldier nods, but his face bears the marks of a man confused.

"Who is Sturmbannführer Brambott?" he asks.

"He's the commanding officer in Chernivtsy," the man by my side replies, as if the soldier is a simpleton.

"Ah," the soldier says, nodding his head knowingly. "I've heard of the problems that some are having with fathering Soviet children. I'm surprised he would really want to send the child back to Germany. Seems too risky."

My escort shrugs his shoulders. "I agree," he says. "But I simply follow orders and my orders are to get this girl and his child safely into Germany."

The man nods. "Well then," he says, and nothing more. His eyes probe, and I lower mine to break the gaze. *"Heil Hitler!"* he says again. He spins on his heel and marches away, glancing back at me once with a quizzically amused look.

The officer steps in front of me and adjusts his hat on his head. "Are you Luda?" he asks, looking down at me. I nod.

"Well then," he says with a grim smile. "My adventure begins."

IVAN KYRILOVICH
August 29, 1943

I stand in front of the door and take in a long, deep breath. In the months since Tanya and I began visiting this hidden church, I've struggled with a sense of doubt, of fear and shame.

Today I visit alone. I need to speak with Father Konstantin by myself, to pose my deepest questions. Now that I've arrived, however, I can't seem to take the step inside, so I stand here, staring at the cracked, wooden doorway.

I jump when the door swings open. Father Konstantin emerges from the dark interior, his bent frame leaning heavily on the stick by his side. I lean forward in a slight bow. "Good morning, Father."

"Ivan Kyrilovich," he says with a smile. "I sensed I'd find you here."

I tilt my head to the side with a curious glance. "Did you?" I ask. He nods, his eyes sparkling bright.

"Please, come in," he says. I step past him into the dark, drafty building where the three tables stand lit by candles beneath the odd, yet comforting, icons. When Tanya and I come together, she immediately rushes to the tables and kneels. She has embraced the prayers of this old man and repeats them over and over.

I, on the other hand, cannot utter a word. I still don't know if I believe.

"Tell me, Ivan Kyrilovich," Father rasps, his words echoing through the hollow room. "What is it that holds your soul captive?"

I fold my arms up over my chest to stave off a sudden chill, and I look into the gentle eyes of this man who confounds me. Father Konstantin leaves no room for gradual development in a conversation but rather dives right into the heart, wasting no moment. Time is precious, after all.

"I—I don't think that my soul is held captive," I sputter.

Father Konstantin leans in, his eyes boring deep. "Ivan Kyrilovich," he whispers, "we're all held captive by something."

I shake my head. "I don't know what to think of all this, Father," I tell him. "I don't know if I can believe, if I can accept the idea of God. It just all seems so . . ." I stop, and my cheeks flush. I feel like a child standing exposed, entirely unsure of myself.

"It all seems so Western?" he asks. I nod and offer an apologetic smile.

"It's a terribly judgmental thought, is it not?"

Father Konstantin shuffles toward the tables as I follow. In the short time since we first met, I've observed the way he's slowed. He is sick.

We stop before the table that lights the icon of Mother Mary and her Christ child. "It's natural to be confused, Ivan Kyrilovich," Father says. "For many, many years, the message of the Church has been darkened and snuffed. I would not expect one who has never been taught the tenants of the faith to embrace it wholly and without question."

"My wife does," I answer, and he nods.

"Yes. Women tend to embrace more quickly. By nature their souls are more pliable to the spiritual realm, particularly when they have experienced the loss that your wife has experienced."

"But I worry about that, too, Father," I reply. "Do I allow my wife to follow a useless path based only on the emotions of these dark days? How do I protect her?"

Father Konstantin looks up at me in surprise. "You trust her," he says. "Though women tend to embrace God more quickly based on emotion, they're not so naive as to be completely fooled. Your wife's emotions allow her to embrace faith more readily and wholly. Your pragmatism and doubts will allow you to embrace it fully, but only if you allow yourself."

I turn to look at the icon, the pious face of the young girl igniting a host of conflicting thoughts and feelings. "My whole life has been lived upon the principles of practicality," I say quietly. "I've so carefully orchestrated my fate, because I was told by all of society that God and religion were dead and useless. I believed in the idea of Utopia, Father. I had faith that if I just carefully planned and worked, that my life would go according to the plan I laid out."

"And has it?" he asks. "Has your life gone according to plan?"

"No," I whisper, blinking hard.

Father Konstantin grabs my hand and leans forward until his eyes meet mine in the thin stream of candlelight.

"Ivan Kyrilovich," he says, his voice weak and tired. "Your questions are good. They're honest and real. Thank you for asking them. Unfortunately, my dear man, I cannot tell you what to believe. But I will encourage you with this: that which man has left you with is darkness. The belief that a utopian life can be created through hard work is false. Utopia is unattainable. Can it even be defined? What is utopia to you? Would it be the same for me? You don't have the power to create perfection. Vladimir Lenin didn't have the power to do that. Josef Stalin doesn't have the power to do that.

"Life is a series of trials, all strung together by moments of beauty. But when the string of joy and beauty breaks, what is left to hold life together if there is no God? *That's* the question you need to be asking."

Father Konstantin steps back and draws in a deep breath. "You're wrong if you think I don't have the same doubts as you, my friend," he says softly. He looks at me from the corner of his eye. "Even *I* have to work out my faith," he says.

I look at him for a moment, studying his lined face. Then I turn toward the table with an impatient sigh. "But what does it all mean, Father?" I point to the icon in frustration. "Who was the Christ child? Why is His birth significant? How do I believe if I don't understand?"

Father Konstantin takes a deep breath and leans more heavily on his staff. "Ivan Kyrilovich, let me tell you as concisely as I may what I believe to be absolute truth. It's this belief that helps me release the doubts and the fears, the captivity that wars inside my heart."

I put my hand under his elbow to steady him as the candle flickers in his tear-filled eyes. Then I wait, and I listen.

"I believe in one God. I believe He is the Maker of earth, and of all things in it. I believe in one Lord, Jesus Christ, and I believe Him to be the Son of God, begotten of the Father before all worlds, Light of Light, Very God of Very God, of one essence with the Father, by whom all things were made."

Father Konstantin gestures toward the icon and I shift my eyes to stare at the infant, the Christ child. I feel a sweeping of my soul as I stare into His eyes—the eyes of the Son of God.

"Ivan Kyrilovich, I believe that Jesus Christ came down from heaven for our salvation, to free our captive souls, and that He was born of the Holy Spirit and the Virgin Mary, and was made man." Father Konstantin begins to cry in earnest, his voice now coming out in a gasp as large tears roll down his cheeks.

"I believe Christ was crucified also for us under Pontius Pilate, and suffered and was buried, and the third day He rose again, and ascended into heaven. I believe that He now sits at the right hand of the Father, and He will come again with glory to judge the living and the dead."

Father Konstantin shifts his gaze to me, and I can see the yearning in his eyes. "Oh my dear boy," he whispers. "Soon I will see Him face-to-face. Soon the veil before my eyes will be no more, and the suffering will pass behind me. But before I go, I long to know that you understand, and that you, too, believe."

I lead Father Konstantin silently to the small room in the back of the church where he lives. He has grown more frail each time I've visited. As I help him sink onto the bed, I feel tears well up in the corners of my eyes.

"I understand it, Father," I whisper. He looks up at me hopefully. "I understand, but . . . I don't know yet if I believe."

Father Konstantin nods just before his eyes close. "Understanding is the biggest hurdle, my son." He drifts to sleep.

An hour later, I trudge up the stairs to our flat, each step weighted with the questions that plague me. Pushing open the door, I close it softly behind me as I breathe in deep the scent of fresh bread. After removing my shoes and pushing my feet into my worn *tapochki*, I trudge into the kitchen. Tanya sits at the table, her hands wrapped around a piece of paper. She looks up at me, and I see the tears.

Rushing to her, I fall to my knees at her feet. "What is it?" I ask. Before she even speaks, I know. I've seen that look before. It's the same look my mother wore the night we learned of my brother's death.

Tanya hands me the letter, her fingers trembling. I grab it and read slowly, trying to wrap my mind around the words on the page:

WE REGRET TO INFORM YOU THAT YOUR SON, SERGEI IVANOVICH PETROCHENKO, HAS DIED IN SERVICE TO HIS COUNTRY ON JUNE 25, 1943, IN THE GALICIA DISTRICT.

I read no further, but let the paper slip from my fingers. Tanya slides from her chair to the floor and wraps her arms around my shoulders as we both dissolve into the bitter, heart-wrenching tears that can only belong to those who have suffered the ultimate grief.

My son. My Sergei. I will, indeed, never see him again. I will never know his stories of the war. I won't feel the strength of his hug, or see him maneuver through life as a man. My memories of him will forever end the day I dropped him off at the office of the registrar to enlist as a soldier of the Red Army.

My son is dead, and the world is dark, and in the bitter hot moments of grief on the floor, I release my doubts. There is no longer anything holding me to this world; no semblance of control left in this wicked, wretched life. Now the only thoughts that float through my mind are the words of Father Konstantin: "Belief that there is a higher purpose and acknowledging the beauty of truth will carry you far through this tragedy."

I pull my devastated wife close. Utterly spent and destroyed, we stay there the rest of the afternoon until our eyes have gone dry, and we drag our numb bodies to the bed.

Without evil, how would we know good? In the darkness, with my wife whimpering by my side, I confess my belief. There must be more to this wretched life. There is hope in the words that Father Konstantin so faithfully prayed.

In the darkness I whisper it like a covering. "I believe in God the Father. I believe in His Son, Jesus Christ. I believe. I believe. *I believe . . .*"

MARIA IVANOVNA
September 24, 1943

I pull myself slowly from my bed and stumble to the window. Looking out over the German countryside, I inhale deeply. The mountains are closer here than they were when I lived with Helena, and every day I wonder what it must be like to stand atop the very highest peak and look down on the world below. Does it look as bleak from up there?

I turn and pull on my dress, then tie my apron around my back and put the kerchief in my hair. I've been living with Gerhard and Lisolette Mueller for four months. Just before I got on the train, Greta wrote down Herr Mueller's address, and she scribbled a quick note on a scrap piece of paper asking Lisolette to look after me. Herr Mueller accepted me without question when I approached his shop with the letter in hand. He read it slowly then peered at me through his round glasses.

"You speak German well?" he asked.

"Yes. I'm almost fluent," I answered, and he nodded his head in approval.

"The story we will tell is that you're the daughter of our dear friend, come to help us run the shop," he said, peering at me over the top of his wire-rimmed glasses. "Call us Gerhard and Lisolette." I nodded in agreement, and have been working with him ever since.

Every day, I open the shop and stand behind the counter. Gerhard sells everything imaginable from fabric to tools to food and animal feed. He's a kind man and well respected within the community. Because of this,

I've never been questioned or spoken to with anything less than respect. Though it's obvious from first glance that I'm not German, the people that come into the shop treat me as one of their own.

I walk downstairs to the shop and grab the wash pail and rag. Every morning before I open the doors, I wipe down the shelves and sweep the floors. Lisolette always leaves a plate of bread and cheese out for me to eat, and a small pitcher of milk in the icebox by the front door. Though they pay me very little in wages, they allow me to stay in the apartment above the shop for free, and they feed me two meals a day without ever asking for payment. I'm daily grateful for their kindness.

After cleaning the shop and eating my breakfast, I check the clock by the door. At exactly 9:00, I push open the doors and let the crisp September air flow through the building. Another winter is coming, but this time I fear it much less. I have almost come to accept my life here. At least in this small town I'm far away from the war and from the constant fear of death.

It's a slow morning, as Fridays tend to be. Most people came yesterday and stocked up on their weekend rations. The only visitors who stop by on Friday mornings are older women looking for a few missing ingredients to that night's dinner.

I sit down on the stool behind the counter and lean forward, resting my chin in my hand. Looking down at my ragged and chipped fingernails I think about all that's happened since I left home. At the sound of footsteps, I stand up straight and brush my hand over my skirt.

"Hello, sir, may I help—" I stop in shock as I look up and come face-to-face with Ewald. My heart beats wildly, and I glance at the open door, hoping at once that no one and everyone walks in.

"Hello," he says. My cheeks flush at the sound of his voice.

"Hello," I whisper.

"You're a difficult girl to track down." I hear the hurt and anger in his voice, and open my mouth to reply, but no words come, so I close it again and wait.

"Why, Maria?" he asks. He leans over the counter and grabs my hands. "Why did you leave like that?"

I pull my hands away and tuck them into the pockets of my apron. "I had to leave, Ewald. I couldn't see you again, and I couldn't stay with your sister any longer."

Ewald stands up and narrows his eyes. "What's wrong with my sister?" he asks, his voice full of accusation. "She gave you a place to stay and food to eat. She saved you from that pit at the armament camp."

"No, Ewald. *You* saved me. *You* gave me a place to stay. Helena hated me, and she hated that you liked me."

Ewald sighs and pinches the bridge of his nose. "Just because it upset her a little didn't give you the right to sneak away in the middle of the night."

There's no sense arguing with him; he will never believe me. "I couldn't see you again, Ewald," I say with a sigh. "You just don't understand."

Ewald rushes around the back of the counter and before I can stop him, he sweeps me into his arms, his lips pressed hard against mine. I push on his chest, but cannot pull away from him, and finally I quit resisting.

After a few moments, I manage to push him back. Wiping my mouth with the back of my hand, I give him a small shove. "Please. Go to the other side of the counter. I cannot be caught with you here," I whisper.

"Can I see you tonight?" Ewald asks as he steps back to the other side of the counter. "Please?"

Everything in my soul screams against this idea, but I nod yes. "Tonight is the only time you can see me," I tell him. "Tomorrow you leave."

Ewald pushes away from the counter and walks slowly backward. "We'll see," he says. His voice is cool and clipped. I shiver.

The rest of the day moves by with an agonizing lack of speed. In late afternoon, Lisolette stops by carrying a tray of hot tea and pastries. "You look tired, dear," she says, setting the tray down in front of me.

"I am a bit," I reply. *"Danke."*

Lisolette pours the tea and sits on the stool next to me. "Maria," she begins. She looks intently at my face, and I feel my cheeks grow warm. "You're acting peculiar, my dear. Is something wrong? You can talk to me." She places her hand over mine. It's warm and soft.

My hands quiver as I try to decide how much to share. What do I tell her? She is kind and good, but she's also German, and I'm a Soviet. Lisolette senses my fear and sets her cup down. She reaches over and grabs both my hands.

"My dear, I know that you come from the Soviet Union. It's okay. You don't need to fear. I can see that you're a gentle and kind girl. I won't judge you for your upbringing."

A lump forms in my throat, and before I know it, I've told her everything. I've told her of my parents and of Sergei and Anna. I've told her of my father surviving Babi Yar and coming back from the dead. I've shared the day I was taken from the store and of the months I spent in the armament camp.

Then I tell her of my months with Helena and of Ewald. The words spill out of my mouth so quickly and with such force that I almost feel sick. I cannot tell the story quickly enough in German, and I make many mistakes. Lisolette doesn't seem to notice or mind.

Finally I run out of story. We're quiet, our tea cold in the delicate cups.

"That's quite a lot," she says after a moment.

"I'm sorry," I murmur. "Perhaps I've spoken too much." Lisolette shakes her head.

"No, my dear. I've long wanted to know about you, but my husband feared asking too many questions. He wanted to protect us should anyone come looking for you."

"Someone has come looking for me," I whisper. Her eyes grow wide. "Ewald came this morning. I don't know how he found me, but he's come and he wants to see me tonight."

Lisolette leans back and narrows her eyes. "And how do you feel about this?" she asks.

"I think it's dangerous," I answer, "but I would also like to see him." My eyes well up again, and I shake my head. "I'm very confused," I tell her. She pulls me into her arms, running her hand down my head the way my mother used to do when I needed comforting.

"See him tonight, child," Lisolette says. "Be cautious and careful, and tell him good-bye."

I nod. "But what if he won't accept good-bye?" I ask.

"Then Gerhard and I will escort him from the property." I hear the smile in her voice and it wraps me tight in a blanket of comfort. For the first time in nearly eighteen months, someone is protecting me.

Pushing me back, Lisolette wipes the tears from my eyes. "Tell him good-bye tonight, my dear, and tomorrow you and I and Gerhard will discuss the matter of getting you home to your family."

Two hours later, I stand nervously in front of the shop, my arms wrapped around my waist in an effort to stave off the cool night air. I hear him approach, and when he finally steps into the light, I see that he carries flowers with him.

"Hello," he says, offering me the large bouquet.

"Thank you," I murmur, and I gesture him inside. "I thought perhaps we could just stay here this evening," I say, stepping into the shop. It's drafty, but warmer than the street. "I live upstairs and I've made up a spread of food that we can eat."

Ewald smiles and nods. "I'm honored that you would agree to meet with me at all," he says, and he grabs my hand. "I've thought about you every day since we last met, Maria."

I look in his eyes and feel confusion and fear well up inside. I see in him a sense of possession. He feels entitled to me. This cannot be so. I drop his hand and walk toward the stairway at the back of the shop. We climb to my apartment, which overlooks the street below.

Ewald sits at the small round table by the window, and I set out the bread, cheese, and assortment of meat that Lisolette gave me earlier. I remember our conversation and her promise to get me home, and my heart skips a beat.

"What are you thinking right now?" Ewald asks. He watches me intently, trying to read my thoughts. I fear that he'll see inside my head.

"Nothing," I reply.

"Come now, Maria. Everybody is thinking something."

I set down our plates, and Ewald begins grabbing food from the tray, all the while his eyes are on mine. I don't know when or how to begin this conversation. How do I say good-bye to a man who thinks he loves me?

It seems too early in the evening to bring the topic up, so I simply offer a tentative smile.

"I'm thinking that this food looks lovely, and it's nice to have company for a change."

Ewald smiles. "Well, I couldn't agree with you more."

For the next hour, Ewald fills me in on the last six months of his life. He still works at the armament camp, but he's made it his mission to protect the girls who live there.

"You changed my perspective on all of this, Maria," he says. "You made me see that these girls are real people with real stories. Because of you, I've been able to see that they receive better treatment. We serve them good food, and I've issued strict orders against beating them. You have made life richer for many of your own people."

I'm quiet for a moment before responding. "Yes, but they're still slaves," I reply. "They've still been taken from their families and forbidden to return. I'm glad you're treating them well, Ewald, but it doesn't change the fact that your people have chosen to steal their innocence."

Ewald sits back and throws his napkin on the plate. His face clouds and his eyes grow dark. "Well, I still have to obey my own orders, Maria," he says. "I didn't make the decision to bring those girls here. The best I can do is make sure they're treated well while they're in my charge."

"And I'm glad you're doing that, Ewald," I say as gently as I can, though I feel my cheeks flush in indignation. "But in so doing you cannot continue to condone and justify the actions of your leaders. It's honorable that you're looking after their well-being, but don't pretend that it's okay to have the girls in a slave labor camp at all. It's a terrible thing."

Ewald sighs and runs his hand over his head. His hair is cut close in sharp lines around his face. He is so handsome, but I see how he has aged in the last few months. War is hard on everyone, even those in power.

"What do you want, Maria?" Ewald asks. "What could I possibly do to please you—to show you that I love you?"

"You could tell me good-bye," I whisper without even thinking. Ewald looks at me, stunned, and shakes his head.

"I don't want to do that," he says. "It took me a long time to track you down. I'm not going to let you go again."

"How *did* you find me?" I ask.

"I knocked on the door of every house within fifty kilometers of Helena's home. I finally came to the house of a young girl named Greta."

I suck in my breath. Could my friend really have betrayed my position like this? "Greta told you I was here?" I ask.

Ewald narrows his eyes. "Yes. She wanted to protect her mother. Her *Jewish* mother. She told me in return for not reporting them to the authorities."

I gasp and cover my mouth with my hand. "You threatened them," I whisper. Ewald stands up. He moves around the table to me and sinks to his knees.

"I was desperate to find you, Maria. I didn't even know that they were Jews. Greta's mother told me, stupid woman. She thought I had come for her. She didn't know who I was. So I simply played along and told her I was looking for a runaway house servant and in exchange for any information they could give, I would remain quiet. Greta told me about you immediately, but she didn't tell me where you were. She told me you had come, and then fled, and she didn't know where you'd gone. It took just a little bit of detective work for me to search out who Greta and her family might know that would be willing to harbor a runaway Soviet girl. This was the first place that made sense. I made a lucky guess."

I push him away with shaking hands and stand up, my chair clattering to the floor. "You need to go," I say. "Leave now, Ewald."

Ewald stands up and narrows his eyes. "I've done everything in my power, Maria, to take care of you. I've given and given, and you refuse to give in return."

He steps toward me as I back up. The look in his eyes is no longer kind. The patient façade has finally broken. He looks menacing and angry and . . . mean.

"Please, Ewald," I say, my voice louder than expected. "Please leave now. I cannot see you anymore."

In two strides, Ewald is upon me. He pushes me back against the wall, pinning me tight against the rough wood. "I will not leave until I've loved you the way I've wanted to love you for a long time now," he whispers. His voice comes out in a hiss, snakelike and cold. I squirm, but cannot get out from under his grasp.

"Please," I cry. "You're hurting me. Please don't do this."

Ewald presses his mouth against mine. It's not tender or gentle, but rough and painful. I turn my head to the side and let out a cry. "Ewald, no!" I yell. He presses his hand against my mouth.

"I'll tell you good-bye, but first . . ." he growls in my ear. His hand moves down my chin to my neck, then lowers to my chest. I sob as he gropes, the full weight of his body pressed against me.

It happens quickly. I collapse to the floor as Ewald is yanked backward and thrown across the room. Gerhard steps in front of me, a long, iron tire bar gripped tightly in his hand.

"Leave," he says. His voice is surprisingly calm. I pull my knees to my chest and wrap my arms around them, trying to stop the uncontrollable quaking of my body. Ewald stands up, brushing off his uniform jacket.

"This is a bad idea, friend," he says with a menacing sneer. "You shouldn't have gotten involved."

Gerhard rolls the tire bar around in his hand. He's a tall, broad man with thick hair and a full beard. He takes a step toward Ewald, swinging the bar slowly in front of him. "Let me tell you something, boy," he says. His words are slow and measured as he takes another step forward. "I know a thing or two about men like you. I know that you aren't used to hearing the word no, and that you expect to get what you want at all times. But tonight, you will not get what you want."

Ewald laughs and shakes his head. "Who cares," he says. "Like I need to have a little whore like her." He looks at me. *"Untermensch."*

Gerhard takes another step forward. "There's something else you should know," he says quietly. Ewald looks back at him, eyes dark. "You should know my brother is a commanding SS officer in Berlin. I will have no problem reporting back to him that you harbored and helped hide a Soviet slave."

Ewald laughs. "I'll simply tell him that his own brother is a lover of the Soviets," he spits. Gerhard cocks his head to the side with a curious stare.

"And who do you think he'll believe?" he asks. "His brother, or a foolish and stupid boy like yourself."

Ewald is quiet for a moment. He glances down at me, then looks back at Gerhard. With a frustrated growl, he grabs his coat and hat, and stomps down the stairs. We listen as he storms through the shop, sweeping items off the shelves. With each crash, I squeeze my eyes tighter. Finally, the front door opens and slams. Then all is silent.

I lower my head down onto my knees and rest it there. Gerhard kneels down beside me, his hand warm and tender on the back of my head.

"I'm sorry," I sob. "You've been so good to me. I'm sorry I brought you this trouble."

"Shh . . ." he whispers. "My wife told me everything today. Maria? Maria, look at me."

I look up into his gentle eyes. In the four months that I've lived here, I've never spoken directly to him, though I've often felt him watching me throughout the day.

"Lisolette and I had a daughter," Gerhard says softly. "She and Greta were the best of friends. Our daughter died four years ago of a terrible fever."

"I'm so sorry," I whisper.

"Having you here has healed a wound," Gerhard says gently. "But now it's time to get you home. It's time for you to ease your own mother's broken heart."

Lisolette appears in the doorway, her hair wild and eyes wide. "Well," she says, looking around at the mess. "From the looks of things both downstairs and up here, I'd say your good-bye was a success."

I smile, and she chuckles, rushing forward to pull me in her arms. "Oh my darling," she says. "We're going to do everything in our power to get you home. I don't know how, but we'll figure it out."

PART THREE

HOME

LUDA
June 21, 1944

Today marks a full year since Sasha and I escaped the Nazi-occupied Soviet Union and came to make a life in Germany. I still think of the journey here every day, of the fear and heartache that came with leaving my country behind. I miss Alexei, Baba Mysa, and Katya so much that sometimes my heart physically aches. I long to write to them but know that it would be too dangerous.

Crossing the border into Germany was easier than I had anticipated. The story that the partisans had developed for me was questioned only once at a checkpoint in Poland. It was the only time during the trip that I truly feared we wouldn't make it out alive.

As I waited for the Nazi soldiers to confirm the story of my transporting Sturmbannführer Brambott's baby to Germany, I prepared myself for the worst. I held Sasha tight and swallowed hard against the fear of what they might do to my child, a bastard German baby. If I think about it too long, I still feel the bile rise up in my throat. It's the single greatest fear I've ever felt, even beyond the day I was attacked.

But by some miracle, the soldiers came back and waved us on. When I asked the man acting as my guide what had happened, he shrugged, seemingly as surprised as I was.

"You just might be the luckiest woman alive, Luda," he said that night. I smile now as I think of the irony of his words.

Six days after leaving Vinnitsya, I met Hans's sister, Sophia. She is, perhaps, the kindest and gentlest person I have ever known. She met us at the train station in the middle of the night, and in less than three minutes, Sasha and I went from the train to the back seat of her car, hovering under the veil of darkness.

I didn't get to say good-bye to the man who took me from Lvov to Poland. I never even found out his name. The entire journey seems almost surreal and . . . miraculous.

Today, the tide of the war is shifting. Sophia fills me in on what's happening frequently.

"The Allies are fighting back," she told me last night. Her voice is always hushed, despite the fact that we live deep in the country, far from any happenings of war. But Sophia is involved in many of the partisan groups, and she hears news before most of her fellow countrymen.

"Germany has been defeated in Leningrad," she told me just after the new year. When she brought me this news, my heart skipped. Though I know and understand little of war strategy, I heard enough conversations between Alexei and his friends to know that Leningrad was crucial. Germany's defeat there was a big blow, and Sophia and I both knew it.

"The winters were too cold for our people," she told me. "We couldn't withstand the freezing temperatures. Your army was much better prepared for such weather." Sophia and I spoke of these things late last night as we huddled beneath a blanket. The small cottage that we live in is nestled at the base of the Bavarian Alps. Despite the warm summer days, at night the temperature dips, and we must cover up in thick blankets to stave off the cold.

"Our country has become foolish in this war," Sophia told me last night as we sipped our chai. "We've been defeated in Italy, and now we're losing the Soviet Union. Hitler's mission has outgrown his capabilities. It's only a matter of time before his regime is taken down."

"And then what?" I asked her.

"It's hard to say," Sophia answered. "It seems that all the world is fighting against one another."

I stand at the small kitchen counter this morning cutting bread into small slices, then dropping it into the boiling milk as I prepare Sasha's morning porridge. Sophia walks in, her light brown hair disheveled and hanging down over her shoulders.

Sophia is tall and broad and has a love for the latest fashions. She's older than Hans by eighteen months, but from the way she speaks of him, one might think she was his mother. She loves him dearly, but we don't talk of him often because the fear of the unknown is too stifling.

We haven't heard from Hans since I arrived.

"Guten Morgen," Sophia says, and she rushes over to Sasha, who raises his hand to her. She scoops him up and dances around the room with him in her arms. I smile and feel the tears prick my eyes at the way she loves my boy. I haven't yet told her that he's not Hans's son.

"Sophia," I ask as she places Sasha back in his chair, and turns to pour herself a cup of tea, "how did you and Hans come to be involved in the war the way that you are?"

Sophia looks up at me in surprise. "I assumed Hans told you about our parents," she says.

"Well, he mentioned a little, but not much. How is it that Hans is in the Nazi army, but isn't a Nazi? And how did you come to work with the partisans?"

Sophia sits down at the table and bites into a piece of bread. "Our father was a scholar," she begins. "He spent most nights sitting before the fire, reading to us from every book imaginable." She smiles. "I used to hate it, but now that I think back on those days, I realize how much he prepared us for such a time as this."

"How?" I ask. I sit down next to her and blow on the steaming bowl of porridge as Sasha bangs impatiently on the table.

"He opened our minds to the idea that there are many different ways to think. We weren't prone to adopt the narrow view of Hitler's regime because we were taught that all of life is a potential for learning and that mankind is more than the sum of one idea."

"But why did Hans join the Nazi army?" I ask.

"When our parents got sick and died, Hans was only nineteen. He needed purpose and direction, so I encouraged him to pursue the army. It would be much easier for a boy his age to join than to resist."

"He didn't agree with Nazi ideology, though, did he?" I ask. I scoop a heaping spoonful of porridge into Sasha's bowl, then hand him a spoon. Sophia and I both laugh as much of his first bite runs down his chin and onto his fat belly.

"No. Not completely. I don't think he knew what to believe, but again, our father taught us to think for ourselves. Hans was much too grounded intellectually to fully accept all that he was taught in the army."

We're silent for a while as I watch Sasha eat. After a few moments, Sophia puts her cup down and leans in close to me. "Luda," she begins, and my heart drops. I set down the spoon and turn to face her.

"Yes?"

"Sasha isn't Hans's son, is he," she says. It's a statement, not a question. I nod my head. Sophia sighs and leans back. She studies me carefully, then offers a thin smile. "He doesn't have to be for me to love him, you know," she says quietly. My eyes fill with tears.

For the next hour, I tell Sophia everything, from the day I was raped to the day I left Vinnitsya. As we speak, Sasha toddles around the room at our feet, chattering and laughing at everything and nothing. Sophia listens, her brows furrowed deep over her crystal blue eyes. When I finish, she pulls me into her arms and together we weep.

"Do you think Hans will return?" I ask. Sophia sighs.

"I don't know, Luda. But you and I are family now. You and Sasha will always have a place here and someday—Luda, someday this war will end. The world will be at peace again."

I don't know if I believe her, but as I push myself back and glance from her to Sasha, I realize that we're going to be okay. No matter what happens, we're all going to be okay.

Two days later, Sophia comes home later than usual. Her face is white as she walks through the door. I'm carrying Sasha, who I've just bathed, to the bedroom to put him to bed. "What's the matter?" I ask when I see the look of fear on her face. She shakes her head.

"Put Sasha down. I'll make some tea. You and I need to talk."

With trembling hands, I prepare my son for bed. I sit with him in the small wooden rocking chair by the window and rock slowly, tears streaming down my cheeks. I've waited daily for her to come in with some news of Hans. Today I fear the news will not be what I want to hear.

Sasha drifts off quickly, the result of a long day without napping. My boy has grown energetic and fierce these last few months. Being his mother is exhausting, but every night as I lay him down, I trace the contours of his perfect pink mouth, his round, full cheeks, and I think how grateful I am to have him. He's perfect and beautiful.

I'm eighteen now, though I feel much older. My birthday was last week, and Sophia and I celebrated quietly with Sasha. "Perhaps next year you can celebrate this day with Hans," she said as I blew out a candle on top of the small pound cake she bought in town.

Now, as I make my way down the stairs, I wonder if that dream has been crushed forever.

Sophia sits on the couch in the sitting room, her legs tucked up underneath her skirt. She looks up at me as I walk into the room. I stop and stare at her.

"Has something happened to Hans?" I ask.

Sophia's eyes fill with tears. "I don't know," she answers, and she covers her face with her hands, breaking down in mournful sobs. I rush to her side.

"What is it?" I ask. "What's happened?"

"There's been another assassination attempt on Hitler's life. It was unsuccessful again."

My heart grows cold, and the room begins to spin. "Was Hans involved?" I ask.

Sophia shrugs. "I don't know, Luda," she cries. She pulls back and wipes her face. "But I wouldn't be surprised if he had something to do with it."

"How did you hear this?" I ask.

"One of my sources told me today. From what they're hearing, no one knows who organized this plot, but they suspect Hitler will retaliate harshly." She breaks down in a fresh batch of tears. "They think he'll kill anyone even suspected of being part of the plot."

I hug Sophia close but for some reason, tears don't come to my eyes. I'm numb and cold, but do not cry. Something inside me remains peaceful.

"It's going to be okay," I whisper, and Sophia pushes back.

"I don't know if it is, Luda," she cries. "I really don't know if we'll ever find out what happened to Hans."

I think of Sasha, sleeping soundly in the room above us. I remember all the moments when life could have fallen apart but didn't, and for the first time I feel strong. For the first time, I realize that I can face anything that comes my way.

"Sophia, I'm not afraid." I look at her and despite the moment, I let out a laugh. "I'm not afraid," I say again. "We're going to make it through this—you, me, and Sasha."

Sophia sits back on the couch and wraps her arms around her waist. "I don't share your peace, Luda," she says softly. "But I'll trust your instinct."

I smile and grab her hand. We lean close to each other, each supporting the other's weight. I rest my head on her shoulder, she puts her head on top of mine, and together we remain, bonded to face whatever life may bring across our path.

IVAN
October 10, 1944

Kiev has been liberated from German occupation since late last year. Before they left, the Germans launched a massive campaign to cover up all evidence of the horrors that occurred at their hands. For days we could see smoke billowing in the air above Babi Yar as they burned the thousands of bodies that lay there.

My city, smoking and bloated with the stench of the dead, would not suffer occupation much longer. By the beginning of December, the Germans had retreated like dogs with their tails between their legs.

In the year since the Red Army took back the city, young men have marched onto our streets, and every day I stare at the face of each boy, hoping that maybe, by some miracle, Sergei will be among them.

I know he won't. I know that he's gone, but still I go each morning to Kreshadik Street to sit on a bench and watch the boys walk by. Their faces are hardened, the effects of war etched into their skin like the brand on a sheep. I listen to them speak, and the tone of their conversations is so different than it should be. They're still boys, all of them—boys who became old men in just a few years' time.

Today, one of them came to visit.

The knock startles Tanya and me from our quiet occupation. The only one who has visited us in months is Father Konstantin, but he died last week, adding more weight to the burden of the last four years.

I open the door, and he stares at me with hopeful eyes. The man wears a crisp Red Army uniform. He's very tall, with thick dark hair cut close to his head. He looks young, perhaps the same age as my Sergei.

"Hello," he says.

I pull the door open a little wider so Tanya can see past me. "Can we help you?"

"Are you Ivan Kyrilovich Petrochenko?" the boy asks. I nod in surprise. "Yes, I am."

"My name is Maxim Pavlovich Yakovlev," the boy says. "I was a friend and comrade of your son, Sergei."

My heart jumps. "Please come inside," I say, gesturing him forward.

When we're all settled around the table, Maxim looks from my face to Tanya's. "I know this must be a surprise," he says. I nod.

"Of course it is, but we're happy to have you."

Tanya leans forward on her elbows. "You knew our Sergei?" she asks, and Maxim nods.

"I knew him well," he says. "He was a good friend and a good soldier."

My head spins. "Can you tell us anything about his time in the war?" I ask.

"I can do better than that," Maxim answers. He reaches into the inside pocket of his coat and pulls out a small leather journal. "Sergei wrote inside this book several times a week. He told me that if anything ever happened to him, he wanted me to deliver it to you."

I take the journal and run my fingers over it. I close my eyes and envision my son writing inside these pages late at night while others slept. I feel his presence near.

Tanya gently takes the book from my hands and opens it up. Together we read the first page:

October 30, 1942
My dearest Mama and Papa,
    If you're reading this without me, then I apologize. I know your hearts ache, and I hate that it's on account of me.
    I'm writing these pages to remember. War has a way of

making you forget, and I don't want that to happen to me. I don't want to forget who you raised me to be.

These days are dark. I've seen and tasted and felt the horrible cold of death in a way that I never thought possible. Papa, remember the day you and I walked the streets of Kiev after the Germans first dropped their bombs? I was so scared that day—so scared of death. But now that I've seen it up close, I realize that death isn't so scary, after all.

It's the suffering I fear more. I hope you don't suffer, Mama. Don't suffer on my account. I've met a man here, a man who has become a dear friend. His name is Maxim. I hope you'll meet him someday, too. He has helped show me a different way.

I'm not scared of death anymore, Papa. I'm not scared at all. Thank you for teaching me to be brave. I couldn't do any of this if you hadn't prepared me to face life like a man.

I hope I make you proud.

I love you now and always.

Your son,

Sergei

Tanya and I cling to one another and cry. My shoulders shake as I digest the words of my son, so wise and insightful. He was years ahead of me when he wrote this message two years ago. The man he became humbles me. I look up at Maxim, who sits uncomfortably across from us.

"Thank you," I cry. Maxim nods.

"Sergei was the bravest man I've ever met," Maxim says softly. "He died fighting against the most wicked men this world has seen."

"The Nazis?" Tanya asks, wiping her nose with a soft handkerchief.

"No," Maxim replies, shaking his head. "He fought against a group of nationalists—Ukrainian rebels. Not partisans, but guerrilla warriors bent on destroying everyone—the Germans, the Soviets, anyone who threatens their independence. They're brutal and harsh, mean in every sense of the word."

"What happened?" I ask.

"Sergei made friends with a group of local partisans. Those were the good guys. He . . . helped them." Maxim stops and looks closely at Tanya and I as though judging our reaction to this news.

"Helped them?" I ask.

"He helped people escape the country. Sergei transported Jews and other locals who were wanted for various crimes across the border. He worked with the partisans to protect the people he felt were innocent victims of war."

I lean back in my seat and release a deep breath. Tanya grabs my hand and squeezes hard. "What happened to Sergei?" I ask.

"A large group of Jewish residents needed to leave the country. Sergei and a man named Kostya were working to find a way to transport them across the southern border, away from Poland. They had the residents hidden in an underground bunker outside the city. The night before Sergei died, he went to the bunker with Kostya to inform the Jews of the plan to get them out, away from the Soviets and the Nazis. But . . ." Maxim's voice fades for a moment. He clears his throat.

"The nationalists had already found them. Sergei came running back to the bunker and told us that there was a group we needed to take care of. I've never seen him so furious. Sergei was always calm. I admired that about him.

"We followed him back to the bunker where the nationalists had lined the Jews up and shot each of them one by one. But . . . there was a little one—a small girl who they threw through the air, laughing every time she hit the ground. The plan for dealing with these nationalist traitors was always to attack by surprise, but Sergei grew so angry that he stormed toward them . . ."

"We tried to back him up. He managed to shoot two of the men before the others got him."

Tanya lays her forehead on the table.

I cover my face with my hands, the vision of my son storming the gates of evil to protect an innocent.

"I'm sorry," Maxim says. "I said too much."

"No, my dear boy," I say, reaching out and grabbing his hand. "Thank you for sharing this. I was proud of my son before, but I'm more proud now. You've given us a gift."

Maxim nods his head and pulls his hand back. "Sergei didn't suffer," he says. "He died instantly, and he was a hero. We managed to finish off that particular group of fighters, but we lost two other men in our group that night."

"I'm so sorry for what you've suffered," I say. We're all quiet for a moment, ingesting the weight of the memories. Finally, I speak again. "Tell me, Maxim," I lean forward. "When Sergei died, was he lying in a field?"

Maxim looks at me uncomfortably, as if the details of that day are too painful to really conjure up. Tanya sits back up, her face spotted with tears, her eyes shifting first to my face, then to Maxim's. He nods his head. "He was."

I nod. Somehow I find comfort in knowing that the dream that haunted me for so long was really a gift. I was there the day my son entered into this world, and that vision, as horrific as it was, gave me the chance to be there when he left the world, too.

"Our group has been transferred to Kiev," Maxim says, breaking the silence. "I'm staying in the barracks just outside the city. I wondered if it would be okay for me to visit you occasionally. My parents died right after the war began. Sergei always spoke so highly of you and I . . . perhaps it's foolish of me."

Tanya stares at Maxim. Her eyes are red and swollen. "You come any time you want," she says. "You will always be welcome in my home. You can come every day if you'd like to."

Maxim nods politely. *"Spaseeba,"* he whispers.

"You gave me back my son," Tanya says, her voice wavering. "It's I who must thank you."

Maxim stands and reaches across the table to shake my hand. "I need to get back," he says.

"Thank you for coming," I say, as Tanya and I escort him into the foyer and give him his shoes. He laces them slowly, then stands up. He's a full head taller than me, and his broad shoulders give him an imposing air. Leaning forward, he wraps Tanya in a hug, his long arms swallowing her.

"Sergei loved you so much," he says as she breaks down again, wrapping her arms around him.

When she releases him, he straightens up and shakes my hand again.
"Come again, Maxim," I say.

"I will. I'll return very soon," he says with a shy smile. I open the door,
and Tanya and I watch as he trudges into the shadows, his large feet shuffling all the way down the stairs. Very slowly we step back into the flat. I'm
utterly spent, my eyes heavy with emotion and fatigue.

I turn to look at Tanya, and she looks as exhausted as I feel. "How are
you doing, my darling?" I ask, pulling her into my arms. She turns her
head and presses in close to my chest.

"For the first time in many years, I feel peace," she whispers.

So do I. I think of Father Konstantin, and all the words of wisdom he
spoke over me this last year. I think of his prayers for Tanya and me to
really know and experience God, and for the first time, I know peace. In
the still, dark moment of this frozen night, I embrace it. I think of our
life before the bombs, the river of our days flowing so calmly in a direction that I thought would last forever. In a flash, that river was turned,
unexpected and quick, dragging us along this unforeseen path. Like a
river from its course, life has swirled away from all I expected or planned.
Sluggish and slow, this river carves a new path. There are calmer waters
that wait.

MARIA
April 30, 1945

I sit up and look out the window, swallowing hard against the lump that always remains present in my throat. It's been nineteen months since Ewald came and Gerhard chased him away. Every day I've waited and expected him to come back, to drag me into the street and return the humiliation that I brought upon him.

It's been a long year and a half.

Despite their promise to help me get home, Gerhard and Lisolette have done very little planning. In the first few weeks after the incident with Ewald, I asked Lisolette about the matter, and each time she urged me to wait.

"We're working on it," she said. "But these things take time. You'll need to remain patient."

I finally quit asking. In the last month, I've felt nearly helpless with the energy of a caged bird.

My eighteenth birthday is approaching quickly. In just a few weeks, I'll officially be a grown woman. I've spent three years of my life in Germany, my days in Kiev seeming a lifetime ago. I try to remember the girl I was when I left—the impulsive girl with rough hands and wild hair.

I've grown taller, my hands smoother and somehow my hair has finally tamed itself. I'm scarred and emotionally beaten. The girl who left was swept away in the flood of war, but I think that girl is still somewhere inside. If only I could get back to find her.

A bright spot in the last nineteen months has been my regular corre-
spondence with Greta. Every week we write to one another. She apolo-
gizes in every letter for telling Ewald about me, and in every one of my
letters, I offer my forgiveness.

I stand up and pull my dress over my head. Today is another day,
headed into another summer, and still I dream of home. I'm pulling the
brush through my hair when I hear the door swing open and the pounding sound of someone running up the stairs.

"Maria! Maria!" Lisolette pushes open the door, which hits the wall
with force. I jump, dropping the hairbrush. "Gather your things, dear.
Only take what you can easily carry on your back. It's time to go."

I rush to my bed in the corner of the room and pull my box of belongings out from underneath. "What's happened?" I ask as I hastily shove
items into a small, brown sack, my hands trembling.

"We just heard it on the radio. This is sure to change everything. The
whole course of life will take a new path," Lisolette says. She paces back
and forth in the room, wringing her hands as she speaks.

I stand and turn to her. "What's happened, Lisolette?" She stops and
faces me.

"Adolf Hitler is dead."

The shock of her statement leaves me frozen. Hitler, the man behind
all this pain, has ceased to exist. I'm equally sickened and thrilled to hear
the news. Sickened by the fact that he escaped the fate of consequence so
easily, but thrilled that his torturous ideology has found an end.

"We don't know what this means for the war, my darling. It's been
suspected for some time that defeat is imminent. Berlin will soon fall, and
the Nazi Party will crumble. Now is the time to move. While the country
is in shock, we must transport you east. We cannot wait a moment longer."

I rush forward into Lisolette's waiting arms. "Oh my dear," she says,
stroking my head gently. "How I do love you as I did my own daughter.
Now I'll send you home to your mother so that her heart may be mended
as you've helped mend mine."

"Thank you," I whisper.

"Lisolette!" Gerhard stands at the bottom of the stairs. "You and the
girl must come now."

I turn to finish packing the few things I own. Carefully and gingerly, I pull out the dress that Greta gave me for my birthday two years ago. I roll it into a tight ball and push it quickly into my small sack. With a final glance around the room that's given me shelter and safety these last two years, I turn to Lisolette with tear-filled eyes.

"I'm ready," I whisper. Lisolette brushes the hair off my forehead.

"I'm glad for you, my dear," she says gently. "Now, we must hurry."

We rush downstairs to the car that waits outside the shop. I slide into the back seat while Gerhard and Lisolette take their places in the front, and we pull away. I turn to look back at the place that holds my sweetest months in Germany, and I blink against the tears.

"The first train that leaves will head through Czechoslovakia," Gerhard says. "I have a contact at the train yard who's going to help us get you into one of the storage cars. You must stay hidden from sight for as long as possible. We're hoping that with the shock of Hitler's death, the Nazis will be less vigilant about checking for stowaways, but if someone comes to check the car, you must be hidden well enough to evade them."

Lisolette turns to face me. "We've discussed this option of sending you by train for many months, but felt it was too dangerous with the many border crossings. But now is the best time, you understand?"

I nod.

"How will I know where to go?" I ask.

"Stay on this train until you get into the Soviet Union," Gerhard replies. "You'll cross through the southern tip of Poland first. That will be the most dangerous part of your journey. Once you get into the Soviet Union, you have to find the train that leads to Kiev. You should be safe from there. But Maria, listen to me." I lean forward.

"Don't tell anyone in your country that you've come from Germany. I've heard stories that the Red Army may classify laborers as traitors. Don't speak German in your own country and do not tell them where you've been for the last three years. If they ask why you want to go to Kiev, tell them you want to visit your sister. Do you understand?"

I nod, shocked at his words. Would my own countrymen really label me a traitor for my years of forced labor? I sit back and wonder at these words. The thought suddenly strikes me that I'm about to return home.

My stomach flips with fear and excitement. What will I find when I return? Will Mama and Papa be there? Anna and Sergei?

"Lisolette," I say, and she turns to face me. "Please write to Greta and tell her what's happened. Tell her that when it's safe, I'll try to write her again."

Lisolette nods. "I'll do it," she replies.

Five minutes later we pull up to the station. It's eerily quiet and still. A group stands crowded inside the main building. As I step out of the car I hear the radio playing, the words running in a loop repeating the news of Hitler's death.

We quickly walk past the mesmerized crowd and make our way to the far end of the platform. A man steps out from behind the building and motions us back. With no one nearby, we rush around the corner and follow him down the gravel walkway to the last car.

"Get in there, girl," he whispers, his voice gruff and thick. "Hide well and make sure you cannot be seen or found easily. Go on. Be quick. The train leaves in ten minutes."

I turn to Gerhard and give him a quick hug. "Thank you for everything," I tell him and he kisses both of my cheeks.

"Be safe, my girl," he whispers.

I glance at Lisolette who nods, her eyes sparkling with tears.

"I love you both," I say, then I hoist my bag into the train car and step into Gerhard's waiting hands. He boosts me up and I turn just before the man pulls the door closed, leaving me in the dark. There's a row of small windows at the top of the car, and I wait a few minutes for my eyes to adjust to the dim light that streams through them. The train car is filled with boxes and crates, most of them full of canned foods and cigarettes. I slowly make my way to the far back corner of the car and find a large, empty crate. Tossing my bag inside, I climb over the top and pull a board across the opening. In an instant, it is pitch black.

Hugging my knees to my chest, I remember the train ride that brought me to the country three years ago. The stench of vomit and feces and death still lingers inside that memory, as does Polina's face, which always seems brighter when the lights go out. I close my eyes and lean my head back, reminding myself to breathe. As it began, so it shall end.

Within moments, I feel the train give a jerk, my head banging against the side of the crate. I brace myself as we slowly lurch and pull from the station, and I feel the train begin to gain speed, moving faster and faster until we've left the place I've called home far behind.

For several hours, I sit crouched inside the crate. When my feet go numb and my back pulls in sharp pains, I push the top of the crate back and slowly pull myself to a stand. Looking through the windows, I can see the sky stretched across each narrow rectangle.

I take several long, deep breaths to quell the fear that wars inside when the train gives a lurch. I catch myself just before I topple out of the crate and quickly crouch back down, pulling the board back over my head. As we slow to a crawl and finally stop, I close my eyes and pray for silence.

I hear the men just before the train door slides open. They yell over the hissing and groaning of the engines. I can barely make out their words, but I hear enough to know what they're discussing. I imagine it's what all of Germany, and perhaps the world, is talking about.

"But don't you think they would give us a few more details?" one of them says as they hoist themselves into the train car.

"I hear that Goebbels will take his place. My grandfather told me today to expect him to follow the methods and ideology of the Führer without missing a beat."

"Well I hear that this will end the war. Without Hitler, we don't stand a chance against the Allies," the other man says. I hear boxes scraping and sliding across the floor.

"Which of these are going and which are staying?" one of the men asks.

"The first five boxes come off here. The middle section will be unloaded at the next stop. The final shipment goes to the Czechoslovakian border."

The men jump out of the car and pull five crates off the train, then slam the door shut again, all the while discussing the various facts they had heard throughout the course of the morning. It's finally quiet, and I stay huddled low. I now know how long I have before I must figure out a new strategy.

For what seems an eternity, the train is parked in the station. My knees and back scream in pain, but still I sit, quiet and unmoving. I finally doze off, only to be jolted awake almost instantly by the train's lurch.

This time I climb out of the crate and move around, my feet numb and burning. I move my hand along the back wall of the train car and realize that there's a door on this side as well. Locating the handle, I pull just slightly to see if it's locked. It moves easily and I stop before accidentally swinging the door open.

A plan begins to form in my mind. It's dangerous and ridiculous, and I can't begin to understand how I'll possibly survive, but I must. I must survive. I've come this far.

I will not die today.

It's several hours before the train slows again. I'm now famished, having packed no food or water for my journey.

"How could I have been so foolish?" I whisper several times as the hunger gnaws at my inside and leaves me fatigued and struggling to navigate the train's rocking. The sky has gone from blue to gray and is now a husky black. I see no trees or clouds, no stars or moon. I'm disoriented and utterly exhausted.

As the train slows, I rush to my crate and quickly fold into it. In less than ten minutes we've rolled to a stop. Once again, the door slides open. This time only one man climbs aboard. He whistles a low, quiet tune as he shuffles and moves boxes. I hear him grunt under the weight as he lowers them to the ground. Leaning my head against the side of my crate, I wait for the sound of the door closing.

I'm stunned when I feel my crate move. I brace my hands on either side of the box and bite my lip to keep from crying out as I slide across the floor. The wood covering me slips and falls to the ground and I look up in horror to meet the wide, surprised eyes of an old man.

His face is covered in dirt, the whites of his eyes illuminated by the twilight hour. There's enough light streaming in for me to see wisps of gray hair that peek out from under his sideways cap. His hands are covered in black filth, nails caked with soot.

I shake my head slightly, trying to form a word but he holds his hand out to me, and his head snaps up. He waits for a moment, then looks back at me and puts his finger to his lips. I nod. He disappears, and I remain frozen in my tomb. My eyes look up and out of the open train door. There's little moonlight this evening, and fear closes in on me with the darkening sky.

Moments later, he peers back over the side of the box and gives me a gentle wink as he lowers down a small handkerchief. With a grunt, he slides me back into the corner and pulls the wood back over the top of the crate.

In the darkness, I fumble to unfold the handkerchief. My fingers brush against something cold, and I close my fist over an apple. Underneath it is a thick slice of bread. I shove the bread into my mouth and chew slowly. My stomach growls impatiently until I swallow, nearly choking on the large bite.

The train lurches once again, and we're on our way. I bite into the apple, the juice spilling down my chin and dripping off my hands. With each bite, I feel strength return, and my head clears. As we pull forward on the rails to home, I think about the nature of this world. For all the evil, there is an awful lot of good. I'm thankful for the sweetness of the good.

We sputter down the rails through the night. Despite the unknown of my next stop, I sleep fairly well, lulled by the gentle rocking and melodic knocks. I dream of many things tonight. I see Sergei sitting by the summer dacha and Anna baking bread on an open stove in the trees. I see Greta walk from behind a cherry tree, and I hear Alyona laugh over and over. As I walk closer to the scene, all of them seem to slip further away until I'm left with darkness. It's then that I hear Polina's voice. It's a whisper that feels like a breeze over a glassy lake.

"Keep living. Don't let them win."

I snap up to a sitting position and look around wildly. As the reality of the moment pushes the dream away, I realize that the train is slowing. I must make my move now. I rush to the empty crate and reach inside for my sack. Pushing it on my back, I make my way to the back door and reach for the handle. With a sharp turn, I slide the door open then quickly duck to the side.

I peek around and look out. Day dawns. It's gray and misty outside, the very early morning covered in a foggy haze. I face a large, open field but can't see far due to the low-lying fog. I lean out and immediately notice the ladder within arm's reach. It's as though it was placed there for me.

Reaching over, I try to ignore the spinning wheels beneath my feet. I hoist myself onto the ladder and climb quickly to the top of the car, where I lie flat on my stomach between the slats. They are just high enough to hide me from anyone standing outside if I press tight enough against the metal roof.

The air is cold and wet, and my teeth begin chattering immediately. I hold on as the train slides and slips into the station. It's quiet, early. I remain still and wait.

When the door slides open below me, I hear the boy speak. He curses and leans out, his voice cutting through the air as though he were standing right next to me.

"Harald!" he calls. "That crazy old cat left the back door open again!"

I hear another curse as a man's boots stomp down the gravel path. They both climb in, and I can hear their muffled words below me.

"Someone needs to tell that idiot it's time to quit," the older man, Harald, says.

"Yeah. Time to die, fool!" the younger one says. They both laugh.

"Is everything here?" Harald asks.

It's quiet before the younger one answers. "Yes. Wait . . . Harald, look at this." I strain to listen through the metal roofing of the train car. Their voices drift out into the still air, and my heart sinks when I hear the next words.

"Where did this handkerchief come from? There's an apple core in here."

They're silent a moment before their words float up again, this time clearer. They're hanging out the back door.

"Stowaway?" the younger boy asks. I hold my breath as I wait for Harald's answer.

"Nah," he says finally. "It was probably just that crazy old owl. He really does need to quit working. He can't do anything right. All the same, we should probably inform the local police. They may want to search along the rails to see if they find anyone."

The two men take about ten minutes to unload the rest of the crates as I remain frozen on my stomach just above. I'm soaked, now, and faint from the cold and fear. Fighting against a sneeze, I pinch my nose so hard that my nails dig into the skin. Finally they get all the crates unloaded and placed on a cart to be picked up later in the day.

I don't move as the sun slowly rises. We're in the station most of the morning, and as the fog burns away, I grow increasingly fearful of being caught. After what seems an eternity, I hear shouts issued up and down the platform, and the train begins to hiss and cough. Moments later, we pull out again. I grip the slats of raised metal on either side. The train gathers speed quickly, and I decide it's safer to remain up top now that the car is empty of boxes.

For hours, I cling to the top of the train, my hands numb and my head pounding from tension, fatigue, and hunger. I have no idea that we've crossed the border into Czechoslovakia until we stop at the next station. There is chaos at this stop as people run around, shouting and yelling about the end of the war being near and the necessity to get home as quickly as possible. I hear some German at this station, but more Russian.

My heart skips as I recognize the tongue of my motherland for the first time in years. It's as though a part of my soul, which has long lay dormant, is reawakened. I prepare myself for a long night ahead, knowing it's at least another day-and-a-half journey into the Soviet Union.

It's cold this second night, and we stop frequently. It seems that the air is charged more and more with a tense energy at each stop we make. Though no one comes to the empty final car, I still hang on top, too afraid to take the risk of being caught. I know that I cannot trust anyone, even if they speak the language of my birth.

By the time the sun breaks the surface the next morning, I'm in tears. My fingers slip, and I doubt my ability to hold on much longer. As we roll to a stop, I keep my head pressed to the frigid metal, warmed only by the hot tears rolling down my cheeks.

My ears perk as I hear his voice calling across the dimly lit platform. The sun has not yet fully lit the morning sky. Has it really been two mornings since I left Germany? Or perhaps it's been three. I can no longer remember how long I've clung to the top of this train car.

"Chernivtsi to Kiev! Chernivtsi to Kiev!"

I raise my head just slightly, my neck burning from holding the same position for so long. The man calling across the station is small and round. He's a Soviet, his round face framed by a thick mane of dark brown hair.

I lay my head back down and feel my chest heave at the weight of his words. We're in Chernivtsi. We're half a day from my home.

"Gerhard was wrong," I whisper, raising my head again to watch the man stroll to the other end of the platform. "This train is going all the way to Kiev—it's taking me home."

Home. My throat is dry and raw, but I whisper the word over and over, each time feeling a little more strength and resolve return. I lift my head again and look up to see the man walking away. A young couple rush toward the train and jump into the door three cars up. The train shudders. Seeing no one else on the platform, I quickly slide up and over the rail, swinging my legs over the side.

My fingers slip and fumble, and my arms seem to have forgotten how to function as I sweep my legs from side to side looking for the ladder. The man has reached the end of the platform. He'll turn back this way at any moment and he will see me. I finally find the first step of the ladder, and I slide over the side, catching myself just before falling. I stumble down the ladder and reach for the train door. The handle is stuck. I push hard against it. The train jolts, and I nearly fall.

I grip the ladder and my chin and chest slam hard onto the side of the train. My feet swing just above the rails, the wheels of the train beginning a slow, groaning turn. I pull myself up, every muscle in my body screaming and aching. I reach for the handle of the door once more and push as hard as I can. It falls, unlatches, and the door slides open.

With a quick swing, I throw myself into the empty train car and wrestle with the door, finally pulling it closed just as the train begins to pick up speed.

It's warmer in the car, and I stay on my feet, pacing and stretching with nervous anticipation. I look down at my tattered, muddied dress, soaked and soiled by the days spent atop the train car. Pulling my bag off my back, I open it up and grab the dress Greta gave me. It's damp from so many hours in the elements, but it's clean. I change quickly, bunching up my dirty dress and stuffing it in my bag. I run my fingers through my tangled hair and sigh, realizing how dreadful I must look.

For hours I pace. I try to sit down, but cannot remain still. I'm scared and anxious, filled with anticipation. When the train slows, I'm surprised. I look out the small windows and realize the sky has grown dark again. Perhaps this is good. I can evade the stares easier in the dark.

In less than thirty minutes, the train moves almost at a crawl. With a grunt, I push the back door open and glance out at the station. I know this place. I've been here before. The platforms in Kiev are a bit more sophisticated, and the back door offers me less protection as it opens to another waiting dock for passengers.

Thankfully the platform is empty. Before the train even finishes rolling, I jump off and run as quickly as I can away from the lit areas. I jump off the platform and head into the trees, where I wait a few moments to catch my breath and make sure no one is following me before turning toward the outlying road.

When I emerge, I'm struck with an immediate sense of familiarity. It's been three years since I last saw home, but it smells just the same. The sense of remembrance is so strong I almost forget Germany altogether. For a brief moment, I allow myself to imagine that I never left—that I've been here all along.

It's a long way to the flat of my youth, but my heart beats so quickly that I run most of the way. I don't think about the possibility that Mama and Papa might not be waiting for me. I don't even consider the idea until I pull open the door of our building and stand at the bottom of the stairs. Looking up, I'm flooded with emotion. My chin trembles violently as I think of the hundreds of times I walked these stairs with my parents, with Anna and Sergei.

What will I find when I reach the top?

"Please be home," I whisper as I take the first step. My legs are heavy, and

fear mounts the higher I climb. But so does hope. I never really noticed how closely those two emotions were linked.

I finally reach our door and stop. I have no key. I don't know who I'll find when the door swings open. I raise my hand and knock once, twice, and a third time, then step back. My whole body shakes and trembles with violent expectation.

I hear the shuffling, and I think my heart may burst. I can't breathe. Slowly, the door opens, and he steps into the doorway. Behind him, a small woman with delicate features looks at me, her mouth open in a silent scream. I know them. They're older, but I know them.

"Papa? Mama?" My voice is small, timid. "I'm home."

EPILOGUE

MARIA
June 22, 1947

It's been two years.

Pushing myself up, I walk to the window and lean against the rim, the golden sun warm against my face. I close my eyes and turn my face up, hoping that today, like every other day, I'll feel a sense of peace in a world that no longer feels safe.

I open my eyes and watch the birds flit across the blue sky, and I try to remember the girl who once dreamed of flying like the birds. I lost her somewhere in the hills of Germany. I'm not sure she'll ever return.

Sergei is gone. Though I've been home for two years now, I still have to remind myself that he's never coming back. Some nights I just watch the door, waiting for him to open it and bound into the flat, but the hallway remains quiet, the door shut tight.

Sighing, I push away from the windowsill and wander to the other side of the room, falling back into the chair. Picking at the edge of my sleeve, I let my mind drift back to Germany, to the years of captivity that gave birth to unspoken dreams—unrealistic desires of the heart.

I imagined so many things about my return while I was in Germany, but I never expected it to be like this. In my dreams, Sergei was here joking and laughing, teasing me in that good-natured way that always made me feel loved and seen. Anna was always in the kitchen with Mama, the two of them bent over fresh bread, slicing cucumbers and tomatoes, and discussing the proper procedure to make the perfect borscht. When I dreamed of home, I saw Papa in the corner smoking his pipe and reading the paper, his face fresh and relaxed.

My dreams were of a life that didn't include war. I never really embraced the idea that Sergei might not come back. I had no idea that Anna would choose to remain in Germany. I thought life would flow seamlessly back to normal.

I was a fool.

I didn't once imagine that my own country might look down on me scornfully for my forced service of the enemy—that I would be a traitor for leaving. This alone has made it nearly impossible for me to find a job since my return, so I'm left with long, quiet days that offer far too much time to think—too much time to try to outrun the past.

Why didn't I consider that I would come home to find my parents forever altered? They speak freely of their pain, and passionately about their newfound faith, but they share very few details of the last two years. But then, there are many details I have left out as well.

I've never again spoken of Ewald. I don't mention his name, and every night before going to sleep I remind myself to forget the terrible error in judgment I made regarding his affections. When I think of him I feel intense shame, hoping that someday I may be able to erase him from my memory completely. When speaking of Germany, I talk only of Greta, and of the kindness shown to me by Gerhard and Lisolette.

I've told Mama and Papa about Polina, and I shared the precious memory of my friend Alyona. I thought Papa would retreat back into the darkness and holes of his past when I mentioned my interactions with Polina, but he only nodded slowly, and a peace washed through his dull gray eyes.

"It's good that she died with you, my dear," he said softly. Knowing the end of the story gave my father the missing piece of a puzzle that still produced dark dreams. I'm glad I told him.

I tried to hide the scars on my back so I wouldn't have to speak of Helena at all, but Mama walked in on me changing not long after I returned home and demanded the story. I edited the details and left out Ewald. I simply told her the woman I worked for after the armament camp was cruel and beat me. Mama cried for days after that, desperate to turn back the clock and protect me.

I want to turn back the clock so I can make one more memory with my brother.

My Sergei will not return, but in his absence we have the gift of his words. The journal that Maxim gave us has become a lifeline to the past, and we all draw in Sergei's words like cool air on a hot day.

Papa sits in the corner each night, his hands wrapped tightly around Sergei's journal. The smoke from his pipe wafts through the flat, and he rocks to a melody of life and loss. There's a sense of peace that has washed over Papa that I long for. He isn't shattered, though the twinkle in his eye is softer than it used to be. He speaks to me daily of his God, and I'm beginning to sway under his faith, to accept that maybe these things he tells me about God could be true. His words constantly remind me of Greta, and the ease with which she also spoke of God. The longing for this peace makes me curious to understand.

Sergei wrote to each one of us in his book, the words scrawled across the page in a way that indicates how fast his hand worked to keep up with his thoughts.

His letters to me still produce tears, though they no longer leave an aching sadness. Reaching down, I pull the worn book out of the basket that sits by my chair. I run my fingertips over the cover, trying desperately to feel Sergei's hand in return. I flip open the cover and turn the pages to my favorite letter:

Masha Pasha,

Do you remember that summer when you and I sat by the lake at the dacha? Do you remember what you told me you wanted to be when you grew up? You said you wanted to be an acrobat. I wanted to laugh when you said that, Masha. Just the night before, you tripped walking from one end of the room to the other. You, with the clumsy feet and wild energy, wanted to be an acrobat in the circus.

But I didn't laugh because you were so sincere. I heard the hope in your voice. Thank you, Masha, for sharing that secret with me. You probably don't even remember that conversation, but I do. I remember it because that was the day you taught me what it means to love someone so much that you want the impossible for them. I knew then, as I know now, that you probably wouldn't be an acrobat in the circus. But I believe more than anything, my darling sister, that you're going to do great things because you aren't afraid to try anything. You deserve to reach the highest mountain, Masha. Oh how I hope this war doesn't steal your tenacity for life. Don't let it, Masha. Don't let these dark days change the essence of who you are.

My Masha, you must know that you deserve love, and I hope you find it. Every time I walk into a battle I think of you, and I remember why I'm fighting. I'm fighting so you can live and dream and do anything you want to do.

Although I do hope, Mashinka, that you learn to walk in a straight line before you audition for the circus.

I love you, my dear and precious sister. I wish for nothing more in this life than to know that you're well and happy. I hope to tell you these things in person someday, but if I can't, and you must instead read this letter, hear my heart. You're my inspiration. Live life, Masha. Live it fully and wholly and without an ounce of fear.

With love,

Your (very handsome and wickedly clever) brother, Sergei

I've read that letter so many times I know it by heart, yet still I continue to read it again, always fluctuating between tears and laughter. Today is no different.

I look up when I hear the key in the door. The door swings open, and I rush forward to help Mama with the bags of food in her hands.

"Thank you, darling," she says as she kicks the door closed behind her.

"How was work today, Mama?" I ask. Mama got a job at the local supermarket, and in exchange for her work she receives a small salary and a few bags of groceries every week. This is good, as Papa has been unable to find work since the war ended.

"It was good," Mama answers. "I went by the post office on the way home. We got another letter from Anna. Papa will be here in a minute. I saw him on my way home. He and Maxim were talking around the corner."

My heart skips a beat when Mama mentions Maxim's name. I feel her look up at me with a twinkle in her eye. My cheeks flush, and I turn and move to the kitchen, depositing the grocery sacks on the table.

Mama walks in behind me and sets her sacks beside mine. Together we pull the items out and put them away.

"You seem a little flushed, dear. Is everything alright?" Mama's voice is casual, but I hear the meaning behind her question. I just don't know how to respond.

"*Da,*" I reply. "Just fine."

Mama raises her eyebrows, then shrugs her shoulders. "I'll make some chai so we can all sit together and read Anna's letter," Mama says. I stand mute, unsure of what to do or say. Finally, I turn and make my way back to the front room to wait.

Anna is still in Germany. I miss her. Each time a letter arrives, I feel my heart constrict with a longing for life the way it once was, when we were together and whole. Anna is now married to Boris, a Ukrainian man who was sent to the same farm in Germany and who worked as a farmhand throughout the war, sparing him the worst of Germany's wrath. Because tensions are so high between our countries, and due to the mistrust of all who were forced to work in Germany during the war, Anna and Boris chose to stay in Germany. She writes as frequently as she can, and each letter gives Mama and Papa such a boost of good cheer that I find myself wishing she could write every day.

The lock on the door turns, and Papa pushes it open. He shuffles inside, closing the door behind him. He turns and sees me waiting.

"There's my Mashinka," he says with a smile. I stand on my toes and give him a soft kiss on the cheek.

"Hi, Papa." He kisses the top of my head and puts his arm around me. Together we walk into the sitting room. Mama is there setting out the chai and a loaf of bread.

"Tanyushka," Papa says, and Mama rushes into his arms. He kisses her forehead gently. "How was work today?" he asks.

Mama pulls back and waves her hand in the air. "Oh, work is work," she mumbles. She reaches into her front pocket and pulls out the small envelope. "We got a new letter from Anna," she says with a wide smile.

Papa grins when he hears of the letter. He holds out his hand, and Mama places the paper into his palm.

Papa sits down as he slowly opens the letter and begins to read:

"My dear family,

"I hope this letter finds you well. I will open my letter with the best of news. Mama and Papa, you are grandparents! Boris and I had a son on April 10. His name is Sergei Borislavich. He's beautiful and wonderful, and how I hope you will meet him. Our German host family says they believe someday we'll be able to travel back and forth between our countries safely, perhaps sooner than many of us realize. But until that time, know that I speak of you daily to my darling Seryosha.

"Boris still works as a farmhand for the German family who we've worked for since we were brought here. Though I still sense their suspicion of us due to our heritage, they're kind and good, and they pay us fairly for our work. I have gone back to work as a kitchen hand just this last month, and Seryosha joins me each day as I work. He's really a delightful little boy. He looks a lot like you, Papa!

"Boris talks daily of his desire to meet you. He's said that the first chance we get to come visit, we will do so. I'm so thankful to have married a man like him, Papa. He's such a good worker, and he loves Seryosha and me desperately.

"Please write back. I received your last letter. It took four months to arrive, but I got it, and I was so happy to hear from all of you. And Masha, please write me separately and tell me all about you.

"I miss you all and love you desperately. With all my love from Germany!

"Anna"

"Oh Ivan, we have a grandson!" Mama claps her hands, tears of joy streaming down her cheeks. Papa sits back in his chair with a small smile.

"She named him Sergei," he whispers. I try to think of something to say, but when I open my mouth I simply let out a hearty laugh. Mama and Papa look at me in surprise.

"What is it, Masha?" Papa asks. His eyes shine bright, and I snicker again.

"I just can't believe Anna has a baby, and she named him Sergei!" I laugh. "It's wonderful and . . . I don't know why it's funny," I say with a snort. Mama smiles, brushing a strand of hair from my cheek.

"It's funny because it's happy," she says. "This is something to be happy about, and laughter is a good thing."

Papa opens his mouth to speak when we're interrupted by a knock at the door. "Ah, speaking of happy, that's probably Maxim," Papa says. "Masha, go let him in, please." I stand up slowly, unnerved by the twinkle in my father's eye and the mischievous grin that flashes across his face. He looks at Mama, who busies herself with the teacups.

Walking quickly to the door, I pull it open to face Max. He's dressed in a crisp shirt and clean pants, but dirt still clings to his hands, caked beneath his fingernails—the residue of a long day's work.

"Hi, Masha," Max says lightly, and I blush. I look up at him with a shy smile.

"Hi. Please come in," I say softly.

Max follows me into the sitting room and quickly walks over to Papa, who stands up to shake his hand. Max leans forward, kisses Mama on the cheek, and sits down in the chair next to her. Mama grabs his hand, giving it a tight squeeze.

In the two years since I've been home, Max has visited with us at least five evenings a week. He regales us with war tales of Sergei, and despite the fact that we have heard every story more than once, Max continues to retell each experience because he knows that we just can't get enough.

Max has become a balm to my own shattered soul. In recent months I've realized more and more that my love for Max goes beyond that of friendship. Just thinking of it leaves my cheeks flushed.

"Masha, are you alright?" Mama asks.

"What?" I jump, startled from my thoughts.

"Your face is quite red," Mama points out. I look at Papa and see the smile again, and I feel the heat grow on my cheeks.

"I'm fine. I'll go make some more chai," I mumble, grabbing the tray of empty mugs and hustling from the room. I settle the teakettle over the small flame on the stove, then turn around to find another mug and stop short at the sight of Max standing in the doorway. He watches me with a soft, gentle look in his eyes.

"Is everything okay, Masha?" he asks. Every time he says my name, my knees shake, and I have to swallow hard. I don't trust my emotions—they betrayed me before, so how am I to know if what I feel is genuine or misguided?

"Fine," I say, but my voice comes out a whisper. My heart thumps, and I feel entirely swept up in this powerful emotion.

Max takes a step forward. I look up at him, feeling quite small next to his tall, broad frame. He clears his throat, and I notice that he, too, appears nervous and unsure.

"Masha," he begins. My heart flutters at the way my name rolls off his tongue. "I—" Max stops and chuckles, shaking his head.

"What is it?" I ask.

"If Sergei were here, he would probably hit me for what I'm about to do."

My heart jumps as I gaze steadily at his handsome face. His eyes are dark and kind, his mouth turned up slightly in a mixed look of nervousness and amusement. He runs his hand through his thick, black hair, and I notice that his fingers tremble slightly.

"What are you about to do?" I ask, my voice quaking.

Max takes a breath and steps closer to me. He reaches down and grabs my hands in his, pulling them up to his chest. I can hardly breathe.

"Sergei loved you so much, Masha," Max whispers, and my eyes fill with tears. "He talked about you every single day, and he longed for nothing more than to know you would be protected and happy and free to live your life."

A single tear escapes my eye and rolls down my face. Max lets go of my hand and reaches forward, brushing his thumb across my cheek.

"I'm in love with you, Masha," Max says. "I want to be the one to protect you and love you and make you happy."

I take a deep breath and search his face. "Why?" I ask. "Are you just doing this because you think it's what Sergei would want, or are your feelings genuine?"

A brief look of disappointment flashes across Max's face. He tips his head to the side with a quizzical look, like that of a puppy dog hoping to receive approval. "Masha, I have loved you for over a year now, but I knew you weren't ready for this. I could see your conflict, and I knew you needed time to mourn and grieve the life you lost." I take a step closer, now almost fully leaning into his broad chest.

"So why are you telling me this now?" I ask. "What makes you think I'm ready?"

Max pulls me all the way in, and I lay my head against his chest. My whole body grows warm as he kisses the top of my head gently. He wraps his arms around me tight, and I slowly release the fears and doubts, abandoning them to this love that suddenly feels real and right and good.

"Your father told me you're ready. He's given me his blessing."

I push back and look up at him in surprise. "Papa told you that?"

Max smiles and nods. "He told me he thinks you're ready to love and be loved. Is he right?" Max's eyes search mine, and for a brief moment, the fears try to resurface. Ewald's face flashes through my mind as the shame of my poor judgment constricts.

But Max pulls me back. I blink and the image of Ewald melts away. All that's left is Max and love. I nod my head.

"He's right," I whisper. "Max I . . . I love you, too."

Max smiles and leans forward. He puts his forehead against mine and looks at me gently. "I'll make you happy, Masha," he says, and I smile.

"I'm happy right now," I answer. "I'm happy for the first time in a long, long time." I fall back into Max's embrace, and together we stand united until the teakettle begins to sing. As I gather the mugs and sugar and load it all onto a tray to take into the sitting room, I look over at the man who's brought color into the world again, and I smile.

This moment is the end and the beginning all rolled into one. "This is Sergei's wish come to life," I whisper. Max smiles.

"Dreams can still come true, *dorogaya*," he says with a wink. He picks up the tray, and together we walk into the sitting room. Max crosses the room and sets the tray in front of Mama and Papa, who both look back and forth between us with eyebrows raised and questioning eyes. I throw my head back and laugh, and Papa jumps out of his chair, clapping his hands.

He grabs Max by the shoulders and reaches out his hand to me. I walk forward into my father's waiting embrace, and Mama stands up to join our united circle. Together, we are finally complete.

LUDA
July 10, 1947

Leaning forward, I whisper my prayers over his soft, clean head. Brushing the strands of sandy hair off his forehead, I cover him with my wishes and all my hopes for his future.

"Mama," he says, and I sit up, surprised.

"Sasha," I whisper with a smile. "I thought you were sleeping. Were you tricking me?" I tickle him under the chin, and he giggles.

"I'm never sleeping when you come in here at night," he says with a mischievous grin. I throw my head back and laugh. My son, now five, is so full of spunk and life that I can hardly stand to be away from him. He breathes life and laughter into a room, and I'm unendingly grateful for the gift I've been given in him.

"Mama, why do you talk funny when you come in my room at night?" Sasha asks. His eyes are wide, framing his soft, round face all dotted with freckles.

"What do you mean?" I ask.

"You don't talk real," Sasha says. "You talk funny."

I smile and lean over him. "I'm speaking a different language," I tell him. "I am praying for you in the language of my father."

I speak only German to Sasha. I don't want him to stand out in this adopted country of ours for any reason, so I haven't spoken directly to him in Russian since we first arrived so many years ago. I save my native tongue for the stolen whispers uttered in the night. Whispers and prayers that I thought were a sacred secret.

"Who is your father?" Sasha asks. I sit up a little straighter and study him closely. He's still so young and innocent. I don't know how much to tell him and how to help him understand.

"My father's name is Alexei," I answer, and I swallow over my lie, over the secret that I cannot bear to utter. I will never speak of that other man to my son.

"Where is he?" Sasha asks.

"He lives in the Soviet Union," I answer. "In a town called Vinnitsya."

Sasha rolls to his side and yawns, then turns to look up at me. "Mama?" he asks.

"Yes, sweet boy?"

"Who is *my* father?"

I suck in a sharp breath and run my hand over his cheek again. His eyes are drooping, and I know he needs only a simple answer. "Your father is a good, good man who's protecting us all from harm."

Sasha smiles and closes his eyes. In less than a minute, his breathing evens out, and I lean forward to kiss his soft cheek. Swallowing over the lump in my throat, I stand up and tiptoe out of the room, making my way downstairs.

Sophia sits on the couch, her hands wrapped around a steaming mug of tea. She looks up at me with a smile. "Is he sleeping?" she asks. Then she stops and turns to look at me more closely. "What's the matter? Your face is white!"

I walk to the couch and collapse beside her, burying my face in my hands. "He asked," I murmur. Sophia doesn't speak. She simply waits. I turn to look at her. "Sophia, he wanted to know who his father was," I say. I hear the conflict in my own voice.

"What did you tell him?" she asks quietly.

"I told him his father was a good man," I answer, and Sophia nods.

"But you aren't satisfied with this answer, are you?" she asks.

I shake my head. "I don't want to lie to him, but how could I ever tell him the truth, Sophia? How could I ever tell him that I don't know who his father is—that he was conceived in the worst and most horrific way possible?"

Sophia sets her mug down and grabs my hand. "Luda, you don't have to tell him any of that," she says. "Especially not now. He's too young to comprehend that sort of . . . evil."

"I know, but do I ever tell him the truth?" I ask, my voice quaking. Sophia drops my hands and sits back on the couch.

"I don't know," she answers.

I lean back on the couch and close my eyes. It's been four years since I arrived in Germany, and we've heard nothing at all from Hans, yet somehow I still believe in my heart that he's alive. Sophia is less convinced.

"Have you heard any news?" I ask. It's the same question I ask every night. Usually Sophia has nothing new to report, but tonight she hesitates. I open my eyes wide to look at her.

"Have you heard something, Sophia?" I ask.

Sophia sighs. "I don't know if there's any truth to it, Luda," she begins, and I push myself up straight.

"Any truth to what?"

"I met today with some of the men in town who've continued to keep tabs on the fallout of the war. There are whispers of trials and hangings and consequences for the actions of many of Germany's leaders." Sophia picks up her cup again and sips her tea. I wait impatiently for her to continue.

"The Nazi Party, in theory, no longer exists," Sophia begins. "Of course, you and I both know that there are still plenty of people who cling to their ideology. I don't think those people will suddenly wake up to realize they were wrong."

"Sophia, please. What does this have to do with Hans?"

Sophia sighs. "Luda, the point is if Hans were still alive, he would have made it home a long time ago. The war has been over for so long. The fact that we have had zero communication from him is not a good sign."

"What did you hear, Sophia?" I cry, throwing my hands up in exasperation.

Sophia cuts her eyes at me, and I shrink back. "Sorry," I mumble.

She sighs, then continues. "One of the men said today that he believes there are many former soldiers who have been living quietly outside of Berlin and other western areas of the country until things die down a bit. There is a process of repatriation that needs to occur, and perhaps many are trying to lie low until they can more easily integrate back into society."

"Do you think Hans could be one of them?" I ask, my voice rising in pitch.

"Luda, please don't get your hopes up," Sophia says quietly.

"Hopes up?"

"My comrade, Wilhelm, told me he thought he saw Hans last week when he visited his brother in the countryside. He isn't totally sure, but he said this man looked very much like the picture I have."

My heart skips and my hands begin to shake. "It's him, Sophia," I whisper, and she shakes her head.

"We don't know that, Luda," she answers. Sophia and I have had many disagreements over whether or not Hans still lives. She's ready to move on. I'm not.

Sophia and I sit together in an awkward, quiet silence for a long time. I feel hope soar, and my consternation over the earlier discussion with Sasha fades away. All I can think of is my love and how desperately I long to see him again. I have almost forgotten the sound of his voice.

"I'm going to bed," Sophia says quietly. "I have to work tomorrow."

I nod and grab her hand as she stands up. "Don't give up hope just yet," I whisper. Sophia pulls her hand from mine with a sigh.

"It's too late, Luda," she answers. "Hope died for me a long time ago." She trudges out of the room, and I listen to her heavy steps on the staircase. Sophia works two jobs, something that's left her weary and emotional. In the mornings, she teaches at the local school. This fall, Sasha will begin school, and I could not be more thrilled that Sophia will be his teacher.

In the afternoons, after leaving the school yard, she makes her way into the city and helps with the cleanup. She is one of the Trümmerfrauen, the hardworking women of Germany who bend their backs to clean up the devastation of the Allies' bombs. She trudges home late at night, fatigued from her long days. I struggle to express how deeply I admire this woman who has become family. One of the greatest blessings of my life has been coming to live with Sophia. Despite our disagreements, she loves us dearly, and Sasha and I love her in return.

I walk to the kitchen to put away the teapot and notice a letter sitting on the counter. Picking it up, I let out a yelp of joy. It's from Katya. In the last year, she and I have written frequently as the mail service between our countries has picked up. Getting a letter from Katya is like receiving a piece of home.

I tear open the envelope and begin reading eagerly:

Dearest Luda,

I hope this letter finds you and Sasha well. How is your precious boy? He must be five years old now. I imagine he's quite joyful and lovely to be around, and I hold hope that someday I will know him again.

We're doing alright here. I have news, both good and bad. The good news first because it's always best to embrace goodness, yes?

Oleg got married last week. He married a lovely girl named Svetlana and they're very happy. For that, all of us are grateful.

Papa is working again at the town clerk's office. He doesn't enjoy the work, but he's glad to have something to do. He doesn't do well with idle time.

Now for the bad news: Baba Mysa is very sick. She's grown quite weak in the last few months, and she seems to get thinner every day. The doctor came yesterday and told us there is little that can be done. I fear there isn't much time left. She misses you, and she talks of Sasha every day. Could you find a way to send a photograph, Luda? And quickly? I don't know how much time we have left.

I'm well. I still attend classes at the university. I'm going to become a teacher. I haven't met a boy that I'd like to spend any regular time with yet, but I do have hope that I'll find love in the future. I often think about how Hans treated you and loved you, and I long for that kind of love from a man. Perhaps I will be as lucky as you someday.

Tell me, Luda. Has Hans returned to you yet?

I love you, my sister, and I miss you desperately. Write me back, please, and tell me all about yourself. And don't forget to send a photograph of Sasha for Baba Mysa.

Big kisses from me to you.

Katya

I slowly fold the letter back up and place it in the envelope. Trudging upstairs, I make it into my bedroom before I collapse on the bed. I knew I would likely never see Baba Mysa again, but the reality of it hits me, the grief tightening my chest and flooding my eyes.

I walk to the chest of drawers across from my bed. I pull out the few photographs I have, and dig until I find one of Sasha. It was taken just after Christmas. He has changed much since that time, but it will have to do for now.

I sit down and quickly scrawl out a letter to Katya, filling her in on our lives and begging her to give Baba Mysa extra hugs from us. I feel a pang of regret and sadness that I have not even spoken of Katya and Baba Mysa to my son. I've never been able to figure out how to frame the conversation in a way that he would understand.

I seal up the letter and crawl into bed, exhausted.

I wake up the next morning to the sounds of Sophia and Sasha chatting in the kitchen, and realize I've slept much too long. I throw on my dress, pull my hair back off my face, and rush downstairs.

"I'm sorry," I cry out, hurrying into the kitchen. Sasha sits at the table, a plate of eggs and fresh bread in front of him. Sophia smiles and shakes her head.

"That's okay. Sasha and I had a lovely date this morning, didn't we little man?" she says. Sasha grins wide, the eggs in his mouth spilling out onto his plate.

"Aunt Sophia let me gather the chicken eggs," he squeals, and we laugh—Sasha at our delight in him, and Sophia and I at his ever-constant need to yell when he gets excited.

"I need to leave," Sophia says with a smile. "What are your plans today?"

I reach out and ruffle the top of Sasha's head. "We're going to walk into town to mail a letter, and I'm going to talk to the owner of the grocery store about a job," I answer. Sophia raises her eyebrows.

"Luda," she says gently. "You know you don't have to work. We're doing alright."

I nod. "I know, but with Sasha starting school soon I'm going to need something to do," I answer. I lean forward, pulling her into a tight hug. She returns the gesture, and I feel the tension of the previous evening melt away in the embrace.

"Have a great day," I say.

"Danke," she replies. She leans forward and kisses Sasha on the cheek. "Good-bye, silly boy," she says, and he giggles.

"I love you, Aunt Sophia," he says. Sophia melts at his words and leans in for another long hug. Shaking my head, I wink at Sasha.

"You're good, Sashinka," I say with a laugh.

Sophia leaves, and I pull Sasha out of his chair and clean him up. "Can I play outside until it's time to leave?" he asks.

"Yes," I say with a nod, "but stay close to the house so I can find you when I'm ready." Sasha claps his hands and runs for the door in a bustle of little boy energy. I smile because I know he's headed into the beauty of his own imagination.

As I begin cleaning the kitchen and preparing the food that we'll eat for dinner, I think back on my life before Germany. It seems so long ago, almost as though those days didn't even belong to me.

I'm twenty-two now, but I feel much older. I think of Katya attending classes at the university and the world of possibilities that lie before her. It's a life I can only imagine, but one that could never be a reality for me. My life revolves around a little boy and the hope of a returned love. I understand what I'm missing, but I don't really care.

My imagination isn't nearly as developed as my son's, unfortunately. I can't imagine a life that looks any different than the one I have.

I'm lost in my thoughts when Sasha comes bursting into the house, shouting for me. I set the plates down and rush to the door.

"What is it, Son?" I ask as Sasha jumps up and down from one foot to the other.

"There's a man out there!" he cries.

"What? Who?" I ask. I push open the front door and stop cold, the wind sucked from my lungs. He is thin, a shadow really. But it's him. Hans.

"Luda."

Just my name. One whisper, and a thousand joys come flooding over me.

I yelp, jumping off the porch and into his arms. He spins me around, both of us laughing and crying. My arms squeeze tight around his neck, and he nearly crushes me in his grasp.

He sets me down, and I tip my head back to look up into his eyes. His face is streaked with tears as he pushes my hair back, both of us drinking in the sight of the other.

"Is it really you?" I whisper, and he smiles. He leans forward and kisses me, gently at first, then with a passion that takes over, the lost years pulling us tight. He pulls back and grins.

"It's me," he says.

"Where were you?" I ask. His face clouds over.

"I'll tell you everything later," he says. "I've been trying to get back to you the whole time."

I nod, and he kisses me again, picking me up off the ground and into his arms.

"Mama?"

Hans sets me down, and I turn to look at Sasha, who's standing on the front porch looking at us suspiciously. Hans looks at him, then looks down at me. "This is Sasha?" he asks. I nod. I reach my hand out to my son as he walks slowly to me. He places his tiny, dirt-covered hand in mine.

"Who is this?" he whispers, and I smile. Squatting down, I look deeply into his precious, innocent eyes. There's only one answer to give.

"Sashinka," I say softly, glancing up at Hans. "This is your father."

Hans looks at me in shock, then looks back at Sasha. He leans forward and places his hands on his knees so that he's eye level with my boy. Sasha looks back at him, his eyes scrunched in careful concentration.

"It's good to see you, my boy," Hans says, emotion choking his voice to a whisper. Sasha studies him for a moment before breaking into a grin.

"You wanna see our chickens?" Sasha squeals. "Aunt Sophia let me get the eggs out this morning!"

"Sophia!" I stand up quickly and look from Hans to Sasha. "We have to go into town to see her. Oh Hans, she's going to be so happy. We should leave now!"

Hans looks at Sasha and raises his eyebrows. "What do you say we go see Aunt Sophia, and when we come back, you can show me those chickens?" he asks.

"Alright," Sasha quips. "And you can also come see my room, and the new book that Mama got me, and my toy car that Aunt Sophia gave me for my birthday!" Sasha reaches up and grabs Hans by the hand. "I'm really glad you came home," he says, squinting up at Hans.

Hans squeezes his hand, then slips his other arm around my shoulders. He kisses me on the cheek and grins so wide, his face nearly splits.

"I'm glad to be home," he says. Together, we walk down the road, the three of us connected as one.

ACKNOWLEDGMENTS

This novel took flight on the rich soil of Ukraine where I sat in the presence of true bravery. It was in conversation with a woman named Maria that the longing to tell stories was birthed.

The characters in this book are composites of the hundreds of men and women I met while touring Ukraine. They don't tell one single person's story, but rather hundreds of stories combined. While the characters are fictional, the circumstances and horrors they faced were very real. I pray I did them justice in the retelling of it all.

There are so many others to thank—so many who believed in me and pushed me through the painful parts of writing so that this project would one day be complete.

Thank you to Bob Darden, who was the first person to make me truly believe that becoming a writer was an attainable goal. Your class changed everything for me, and I'm grateful that you set me on this particular trajectory.

To Dan and Sherry Bouchillon, who heard my big idea to write a book and wanted to be a part of it. Thank you for investing in my dreams all those years ago. Your gift made all of the research possible.

Thank you to Jeff Michelman for seeing something in a shy writer girl, and pushing me to get on the ball and finish.

To my dear Lakehouse ladies: Wendy, Bethany, Jenni, Angie, and Tammy. Our yearly creative retreats allowed me the freedom and space I needed to unearth these treasured characters. Thank you for believing in me, for encouraging me, for editing my work, and for celebrating with me when the contract came in. I love you all.

Thank you to Ruth Samsel from the William K. Jensen Literary Agency for your willingness to take my manuscript. You saw potential and you ran with it. You literally made my dream come true. I am so grateful.

And thank you to the team at Kregel Publications for taking the chance on an unknown girl with a really big story. Your chorus of voices worked together to sharpen and shine up this story so that it could most honestly be shared with the world. I'm thankful for, and humbled by, your confidence in this book.

A special thanks to Tatiana Mykhailenko, who urged her students to talk to their grandparents and gather stories of survival and then share those stories with me.

A big thank you to Victoria Marchenko, who gathered together the most fascinating group of Ukrainian war veterans I met in all my travels and who also showed me the remains of Hitler's underground bunker. It was a privilege to know her.

A very special thank you goes to Alexander Markov for his faithful translations and encouragement. And to Svetlana Tulupova, who became more than just my interpreter—she became a dear friend, and a sister across the sea. I am a better woman because of her friendship.

Finally, I need to offer up the largest thanks to my family. To my parents, Richard and Candy Martin, who taught me that life is an adventure and the world is worth exploring. Thank you for putting me on that plane to Ukraine so many years ago. You all believed in me first, and gave me the confidence to chase my dreams. I love you.

To my husband, Lee, who has cheered me on for sixteen years now. You're the reason I finished this book. You told me not to give up, and your belief made me feel like I could conquer the world. Thank you for being as excited about my dreams as I am. And my precious children: Sloan, Katya, Landon, and Annika. You all have been gracious with a mom who stays up too late, and gets up too early, who reheats a lot of meals, and is always behind on the laundry, all because the call to write tugs at me day and night. I am so proud to be your mom, and so thankful that I get to live out these dreams with you all by my side.

A portion of the proceeds from this book will go to World Hope Ukraine for the Hope House, a place dedicated to young women who have aged out of the orphanage and need someone to tell them they have value in this world. For more information on this transformative ministry visit http://worldhope.ca/projects/ukraine/hope-house-i-ii/.